me guessing until the very end, never sure who to trust or where the danger was hiding."

—Megan Miranda, *New York Times* bestselling author of *All the Missing Girls* and *The Last House Guest*

"Kate White's *The Fiancée* is exactly what we all need right now: a fast-paced, perfectly woven murder mystery, with a hearty dash of family drama. This one must not be missed!"

—Aimee Molloy, *New York Times* bestselling author of *The Perfect Mother* and *Goodnight Beautiful*

"Kate White's newest thriller *The Fiancée* is a perfect poolside or beach read, as this psychological thriller has everything a great summer read needs! Told in an almost locked-room style, as we are secluded at a wealthy family's sprawling estate, this mystery looks at what appears to be a picture-perfect family. . . . The constant threatening feeling in the air propels this psychological thriller to a truly surprising climax."

—*Nerd Daily*

"A twisty family drama."

—*Library Journal*

"A skillfully constructed page-turner. . . . Expert pacing, characters readers can love to hate, and an intelligent heroine make this a winner. White consistently entertains."

—*Publishers Weekly*

THE **SECOND** HUSBAND

ALSO BY KATE WHITE

FICTION

If Looks Could Kill

A Body to Die For

Till Death Do Us Part

Over Her Dead Body

Lethally Blond

Hush

The Sixes

Eyes on You

The Wrong Man

So Pretty It Hurts

The Secrets You Keep

Even If It Kills Her

Such a Perfect Wife

Have You Seen Me?

The Fiancée

NONFICTION

Why Good Girls Don't Get Ahead but Gutsy Girls Do

*I Shouldn't Be Telling You This: How to Ask for the Money,
Snag the Promotion, and Create the Career You Deserve*

The Gutsy Girl Handbook: Your Manifesto for Success

THE
SECOND
HUSBAND

a novel

KATE WHITE

HARPER

An Imprint of HarperCollins*Publishers*

THE SECOND HUSBAND. Copyright © 2022 by Kate White. All rights reserved. Printed in the United States of America. No part of this book may be used or reproduced in any manner whatsoever without written permission except in the case of brief quotations embodied in critical articles and reviews. For information, address HarperCollins Publishers, 195 Broadway, New York, NY 10007.

HarperCollins books may be purchased for educational, business, or sales promotional use. For information, please email the Special Markets Department at SPsales@harpercollins.com.

FIRST EDITION

Designed by Jamie Lynn Kerner

Library of Congress Cataloging-in-Publication Data has been applied for.

ISBN 978-0-06-294545-7 (pbk.)
ISBN 978-0-06-324619-5 (Library edition)

22 23 24 25 26 LSC 10 9 8 7 6 5 4 3 2 1

To Hunter and Hayley. Thank you not only for being my wonderful children but also for all the amazing support you've given my writing as my helpers, readers, and champions. It means the world to me.

THE **SECOND** HUSBAND

1

Then

THE SOUND WOKE HER, JARRING HER FROM AN EDGY
dream.

Had it come from outdoors, Emma wondered, staring
into the darkness—or from inside the house? Maybe the
noise had only happened in her dream.

But a few seconds later, as she lay alert in the twisted
sheets, it sounded again, shooting up the stairs and carrying
down the corridor outside her bedroom. It was the doorbell,
she realized. The vibrations clung to the air like those from
a tuning fork.

She rolled onto her side and squinted at the digital clock
on the bedside table.

1:47 a.m.

Her heart pitched forward. It was the middle of the night,
and someone was at her front door.

Could it be a prank? She pictured the teenagers who

sometimes congregated on the front lawn of a house down the street: sullen, private-school types, oozing with an urge to cause trouble.

After kicking off the duvet, she jabbed her arms into the sleeves of a terry cloth robe and grabbed her phone before hurrying barefoot to one of the small spare bedrooms at the front of the house.

At first glance through the window, the street below appeared deserted. And then she spotted the tail end of a dark car out front. The rest of it was blocked from view by the pitch of their roof.

No, not sullen teenagers then. Returning to the hall, she flicked on a light and descended the stairs with her heart in her throat, grasping the rail the whole way down.

In the front hall, she saw through one of the narrow windows on either side of the door that there were actually two cars parked in front of the house: the dark one—and a local police cruiser. Her stomach dropped. The police didn't show at your house at this hour because you'd been recorded running a red light earlier in the day.

She inched closer to the window and discovered three people standing on the wide stoop in the glow of the overhead light: a tall, burly man in a tan overcoat, a younger one in a police uniform, and a woman in a black puffer jacket.

The older man noticed her through the window. "Mrs. Rand?" he called out, cold air escaping from his mouth in ghostlike puffs.

Emma went to unlock the door and then, flustered, reminded herself of the intercom. She swiped the hair out of her eyes and pressed the button. "Yes?"

"I'm Detective Chuck Lennox, from the New York City Police Department. Can we please come in and speak with you?"

"What's this about?" she asked, barely able to hear herself over the whooshing in her ears.

"Ma'am, we'd prefer to explain inside."

"I—I need to see some ID."

"Of course. I'm going to put it up against the glass, all right?"

She returned to the window and read the identification card he'd pressed against the pane. The ID looked legit enough, with its bright blue and yellow lettering, not that she was any expert.

Emma deactivated the security alarm and tightened the belt on her robe, then ushered in the three strangers along with a blast of frigid March air.

As they stood in her hall, Lennox solemnly introduced Emma to the woman, Detective Martinez, a small brunette who couldn't be much older than thirty-five and was wearing the kind of comfort pumps the ads show women shooting basketballs in. Then he gave her the name of the patrol cop, which she didn't catch, though his uniform indicated he was from their town, Madison, New Jersey. Emma let herself fixate on the details because this way she didn't have to focus on the enormity of what must be coming next. Why else would they be here in the middle of the night?

"Please, what's going on?" she asked.

"You're Emma Rand?"

"My name's Emma Hawke, but Derrick Rand is my husband. What's the matter?"

Lennox's eyes flicked toward the living room, which was bright with light. She'd left two lamps burning when she went up to bed, the way she always did when she was going to be home alone overnight.

"It would be best if we could sit down," Lennox said. "Do you mind?"

"Uh, yeah, okay."

As they moved to the living room, Emma fished through the pocket of her robe, found an elastic, and unsteadily tied her hair into a ponytail. She and the two detectives took seats, while the patrolman remained standing by the entrance to the hall, like a bouncer at the front door of a nightclub.

"*Please*," Emma asked, nearly pleading this time. "What's happened?"

"I'm very sorry to tell you this, Ms. Hawke," Lennox said, "but it appears your husband was killed tonight in New York City."

His words seemed to hover in the air like a drone at eye level, vibrating slightly.

"Killed?" she finally said. "*How?*"

"He was shot twice in the torso. The location was a small alley on Greene Street in SoHo. Probably between nine thirty and ten thirty. It looks like it might have been an attempted robbery, but we don't know for certain yet."

She stared at Lennox, at the long, thin mouth that cut across the lower half of his face like a slit in a piece of cloth.

"It . . . it can't be him. Derrick's in the city tonight but at a conference. He's staying in Midtown."

"Unfortunately, we're fairly certain it was Mr. Rand. Can you please describe him for us?"

"Uh, about six feet tall, well built. Short brown hair . . . brown eyes."

Lennox nodded grimly. "Though the victim's wallet and phone were missing, we found a ticket in his pants pocket for a BMW parked in a nearby garage on Friday morning and registered in your husband's name. There was also a small leather case with business cards in the other pocket."

Reaching into his own pocket, Lennox withdrew a business card and leaned forward for Emma to take a look. It was Derrick's.

"Oh my god."

It was true then. Her thirty-seven-year-old husband was dead, was gone forever, was never going to come home from work, step into this room, and stretch his legs across the pale gray ottoman across from her. Ever again. She began to tremble, her arms and legs doing a crazy kind of twitch.

"Let's get you some water," Detective Martinez said gently. "Your kitchen is—?"

Emma flung an arm in the general direction. The detective was gone and back in less than a minute, and after offering Emma the glass, Martinez picked up a wool throw from the back of one of the armchairs and draped it around her shoulders.

It took both hands for Emma to grasp the glass, and she managed only a tiny sip from it before setting it down on the side table.

"Where is he now?" Emma asked, the shaking subsiding. "In—in the hospital? The ER?"

"He was declared dead at the scene, so he was taken directly to the city morgue," Lennox said. "On First Avenue and Twenty-Sixth Street."

Against her will, Emma saw it in her mind's eye—Derrick lying in one of those steel drawers they show on crime shows, his body zipped into a long black bag. His flesh already starting to decay.

She gulped. "Do I need to go there? To identify him?"

"Not tonight." Lennox unbuttoned his coat but didn't remove it. "That can be done in the morning when you might be feeling a bit stronger. But I do have a few questions for now. You mentioned your husband was at a conference. Can you tell us the nature of the conference and where it was being held?"

"It was an off-site management conference at the, um, Cole Hotel, for Alta, his employer. Like the card says, he's their head of financial planning."

"And where did you spend the evening?"

"Where? Uh, here at the house. Spouses and partners weren't invited."

"And you weren't alarmed when your husband didn't return home this evening?" There was nothing exactly challenging in his tone, but it seemed more deliberate than a moment before. She suddenly noticed that Martinez was jotting notes on a small pad.

"No—it's a weekend event, and it's not over until noon on Sunday. Well, today."

"And he decided to spend the nights in the city instead of coming back here? It's not that long of a drive."

"The sessions start early and there are dinners at night. . . . And he's part of management. He's—he was supposed to be present almost twenty-four seven. . . . Did anyone see anything? Anything at all?"

"We're still canvassing the area and hope to find out," Lennox said. "Can you tell us the last time you spoke to your husband?"

A sob caught in Emma's throat, and she pressed the back of her hand hard against her mouth.

"Tonight," she said after grabbing a breath. "Uh, last night, I mean. He called me around eight."

"Long conversation, short conversation?"

"Short. Just hello, how are you. He was grabbing a moment between courses at the dinner."

"And that was held where?"

"In a banquet room at the hotel. It was too big a group for a restaurant."

"Did Mr. Rand mention anything about heading downtown or needing his car for any reason?"

Emma shook her head. "No. Nothing like that. You said SoHo?"

"That's right. Do you have any idea why he would have parked there to begin with? It's such a long way from the hotel."

"I don't have a clue." She bit her lip, trying to focus. "Maybe he didn't want to drive through Midtown on Friday morning, so he took the Holland Tunnel into the city instead of the Lincoln and parked downtown. Then took the subway to the hotel. But that's just a guess."

Lennox tapped his lips a couple of times with his index

finger before speaking again. "Is it possible your husband went back downtown to purchase drugs?"

She quickly shook her head. "No, definitely not. He didn't do drugs."

"Can you think of any reason someone might want to harm him? Someone in his personal life or even someone he knew professionally?"

"God, no reason at all. Wait, I thought you said this was a robbery. Do you think someone he knew—?"

"We're not certain at this point," Lennox said. "Shooting someone during a mugging is very extreme."

The detective seemed to be holding something back. Emma's trembling resumed, and beneath it she felt a mounting wave of nausea. She bent at the waist, sucking in air.

"Is there anyone who can be with you at this time, Ms. Hawke?" Martinez asked her softly. "A friend or family member?"

Her parents were in the UK, where they'd moved a decade ago, and at the moment her brother was there, too, researching a book. Her best friend, Bekah, was an hour away in Manhattan, and though normally she wouldn't hesitate to call her, Bekah had suffered a miscarriage the week before and Emma couldn't imagine imposing.

"Yes," she lied. She didn't know how she'd get through the night, but she knew she wanted them out of her house as soon as possible.

"Why don't we leave you now, then?" Lennox said. "We're so sorry to have to ask you to do this, but we'd like for you to come to the morgue at nine tomorrow to make an identification. Is that possible?"

"All right . . . ," she said, then something else occurred to her. "Could you please contact my husband's brother and let him know? I don't have the strength to break the news to him."

There was no way she was talking to Kyle, not tonight anyway.

"Of course. Is he local? Would you prefer to have him make the identification?"

"He lives north of the city in Westchester County, but I'll handle the ID. If you could just let him know what's happened."

She'd set her cell phone on the coffee table, and after pulling Kyle's contact info from it, she scribbled the details messily on a piece of paper and offered that to Lennox. He thanked her, rose, and drew a card from his wallet.

"Here's the address for the medical examiner's office," he said as he handed it to her. "We'll meet you there. And it's fine to have someone accompany you."

Barely present, Emma led Lennox, Martinez, and the patrolman to the door and lingered briefly by the window as the two cars drove away. In the house across the street, a light blinked on upstairs. Was her neighbor, a snoopy middle-aged woman, peering out the window now, attempting to figure out what was happening?

Emma reset the security alarm, her fingers jerking across the pad. The nausea seemed to have spread through her entire torso, and the back of her mouth now burned with the taste of bile. She wondered if eating something plain would help, but she couldn't summon the energy to even drop a piece of bread in the toaster. She should lie down, she decided.

She didn't return to their bedroom, though. The thought of being in that space tonight seemed unbearable. In fact, she couldn't envision ever doing it again. Instead, she drifted upstairs to the guest room she'd scurried into earlier, which hadn't been used even once in the year or so they'd lived in the house. She flicked off the light and lowered herself onto the bed, lying flat on her back and trying to breathe.

There was no way she was going to fall back to sleep, she was sure of that. As frayed and ragged as she felt, she was also too wound up. So she simply lay there quietly, staring into the darkness above her and trying to picture what the next few days would entail—beyond the trip to the morgue.

In a few hours, she'd have to break the news to her parents and brother. Touch base with Derrick's boss. Begin to make funeral arrangements. Field phone calls from friends, neighbors, Derrick's coworkers, her own coworkers, and Kyle, of course. Emma realized suddenly that there also might be inquiries from reporters on various crime beats. Wasn't this the kind of story the *New York Post* ate up? "Exec Slain in Downtown Alley."

And what about the following days, and the weeks beyond those?

Did she dare imagine what it would be like to come home night after night to an empty house, never to see her husband's face or hear his low, husky voice again?

And more than that. Did she dare imagine how good it would be to finally feel happy again?

2

Twenty-seven months later

By THE TIME EMMA STIRS, THE MORNING SUN IS SNEAKING into the room from around the edges of the curtains. She opens her eyes and lets her gaze drift easily around the bedroom. *Today's going to be good*, she tells herself. There are blueberries in the fridge for her morning smoothie, work should be busy but not insane, she's having a drink at six with a new friend, and Tom will be home from Chicago later tonight.

Tom, whom she's missing so much after only two days apart.

Of course, there aren't any *guarantees* about how the day will turn out. She forecasts the future for a living, but as she's learned all too well, sometimes predictions, even the ones you're very certain of, can be dead wrong.

She idles between the sheets for a few extra minutes, unable to get enough of this room, with its pretty, pistachio-colored walls and the soft breeze wafting through the open window, and the knowledge that it belongs to her. This is her life now, it really is, and there isn't a day she isn't grateful for it.

By the time she's downstairs, showered and dressed, Emma's running slightly behind and briefly considers skipping the smoothie, but then fires up the blender. These past months have been about embracing pleasures both small and big, accepting that she has a right to them, and not letting her own desires be sidelined or denied.

Besides, Brittany's already left for work, and it's a relief to have the kitchen to herself.

With smoothie in hand, she exits the house through the back door and strides along the path to the restored studio on their property, which sits about fifty yards from the rear of the house. Her walk to work is only two minutes, but Emma savors the experience this morning. It's a perfect mid-June day, warm but not humid and with only a few clouds scuttling across the bright blue sky.

Emma runs a tiny boutique research business, Hawke and Company. They've received acclaim for their trend forecasting—and that's the reason Emma occasionally ends up as a talking head on networks like MSNBC and Bloomberg—but their revenue mainly comes from doing generational research for clients, most of whom are in the restaurant and hotel business. They help them understand why, for instance, millennials are often game for off-the-beaten-track destinations and try to act like locals when they travel, whereas Gen Xers want to simply kick off their shoes for ten days, drinking Bahama Mamas and relishing the chance to stare at the ocean instead of endless spreadsheets.

At the moment, Hawke and Company is just Emma, a

senior strategist named Eric Schneider, and her twenty-four-year-old assistant, Dario. They're both already on-site when she arrives and greet her warmly. The space, with its open seating plan, still has the feel of an artist's studio, and the rough-cut-pine walls give off a pleasant woodsy scent.

After she's settled at her desk, the perennially sunny Dario rolls his chair next to hers so they can review the day's to-do list, and then Eric wanders over and they set a time to rehearse the research presentation they'll be doing next week for a new client, a small hotel chain.

Eric's been with Emma for more than four years. He's smart, funny, incredibly dependable, and a whiz at analyzing research. Today he's wearing a midnight-blue long-sleeved shirt, open at the collar, paired with dark slacks, a look that not only flatters his tall, slim shape and but also manages to telegraph "professional" and "creative" at the same time.

"After we rehearse, why don't we go through the influencer surveys that came in this week," she tells him. "I'd love to get an early read."

"Sure. I actually snuck a peek yesterday and there's some interesting stuff popping up."

"Great. And then," Emma adds on the spur of the moment, "why don't the three of us finish at two today? It's so gorgeous out and this way we can all get a jump start on the weekend."

"Fantastic," he tells her. "But only if you swear you're going to call it quits then, too."

"I swear. I've got a new novel I'm dying to read, and I actually have plans later. Remember Addison Stark, the sociology professor I was on that panel with?"

"That really outspoken blonde who teaches at Fairfield?"

"That's the one. I thought it'd be nice to get to know her a little, so I asked her over for a drink."

A thought suddenly occurs to Emma. Though Eric hides it well, she knows he's still down in the dumps about a recent breakup with his boyfriend of close to a year.

"Hey, want to join us? She's coming by at six. You could swing back later."

"Thanks, Em, but I think I'll use the time to shop. Summer's upon us and the elastic's shot on every bathing suit I own. I don't want any scandalous mishaps on Compo Beach this summer."

Smiling, she tells him she understands, and though Eric's always a great addition, she doesn't mind having Addison to herself. Emma suspects the professor's outspokenness reflects a bold, unflinching interior, and she appreciates that. Plus, she's sensed some potential for friendship with Addison, and she could use a friend here in Westport, Connecticut, a town that's part well-heeled suburb, part old New England village. How nice it would be to have someone in her life who isn't simply a friend of Tom's or an employee of hers—or a person whose view of her isn't colored by all the baggage of the past.

The workday morning flies by until it's time for her and Eric to review the completed influencer questionnaires, highlights of which will be incorporated into the next *Hawke Report*, their quarterly bulletin on emerging trends that's sent to paying subscribers.

When she started college, Emma would never have been

able to imagine herself in this field. She was a communications major who hoped to work one day at a website or TV network, but after doing a research project for an elective sociology class, she was shocked to discover that research actually lit something in her. She loved digging for information, sorting through data, and experiencing the aha moment that occurred when you teased out a pattern that had been unseen until now or discovered the amazing "why" of something. She stuck with communications but after graduation, she talked her way into the research department of a Manhattan-based ad agency and moved up the ladder there before leaving seven years ago to start her own small company.

At two o'clock Emma shoos Eric and Dario out of the studio and waves goodbye as they stroll to their cars, which are parked in a small driveway separate from the house. Locking the studio door behind her, she heads home and sets her tote bag on the kitchen counter, where she spots a note from Brittany that she must have missed earlier.

> *Just FYI, I'm going to have dinner with a new friend from work and spend the night at her place. It's just easier that way.*

The news makes Emma slightly giddy, which triggers a twinge of guilt. Brittany is Tom's twenty-year-old step-daughter from his first marriage. He was only married to her mother, Diana, for four years before she passed away far too young from cancer, and though Tom never felt particularly close to Brittany during the time the three of them lived in nearby Weston, he cares about her and always tries to be supportive. He not only has stayed in touch with her, but he's also visited her intermittently at her father's home in Maine.

Late last year, Brittany caught him off guard by asking to be a summer intern at his company here in Westport, as well as to stay with Tom and Emma for the seven-week stint. A huge request, but Tom told Emma he didn't see how he could possibly say no, and a week and a half ago, her father dropped her off at the house with two enormous suitcases. Brittany's mostly kept to herself since she's been staying with them, and yet her presence in their home in the early phase of their marriage has felt intrusive—exactly as Emma feared it would.

At least she and Tom will have the house to themselves tonight.

Emma ends up carrying both her laptop and iPad out to the flagstone patio along with an iced tea. Her intention is to skim the Tuesday presentation one more time before turning to her novel, but before long she's gotten sucked into also answering business-related emails that have come in this afternoon—which she should have known might happen. She's always been a maniac when it comes to work, just as she was in school when she was young.

Her brother thinks they both developed into overachieving perfectionists because their parents were so faint with praise. Show their father an essay on blue whales that earned an A and his first comment was bound to be *Whales are fascinating, but there's been so much written about them. Why not tackle a sea creature we hear less about?* Their upbringing has left Griffin slightly bitter, but Emma's chosen not to dwell on the letdowns that came from her parents' backhanded compliments and benign neglect. Over time she's managed (mostly) to burn off the need to please—her parents and others—and since college, she's developed a nice rapport with both her mother and father. *What possibly can be gained*, she's always asked herself, *from holding a grudge?*

Besides, if her parents had been more forthcoming with compliments or engaged in the minutiae of her life, she might never have become such a voracious reader or bike rider, or taken up ice skating as a hobby, something she still adores doing in the winter months. She gravitated to activities that could be done solo with little supervision or need for parental feedback.

At a quarter to six, Emma finally puts her laptop aside and heads to the kitchen, where she quickly arranges a platter with cheeses and pâté she bought yesterday and drops a cold bottle of rosé into a wine cooler. She's excited, and even a little nervous, for the drinks date, by the prospect of having a friend of her own here in town.

The front doorbell rings exactly at six and Emma swings the door open, smiling. Addison Stark's shoulder-length hair is down today, showing off the blond balayage highlights mixed with her natural light brown color. She's wearing dark, flowy pants and a sleeveless lavender turtleneck, a striking outfit on her tall, shapely frame.

"This is so nice of you, Emma," Addison says warmly once they've greeted each other. "I've been looking forward to it."

"Me, too." She beckons Addison into the house. "Are you okay with sitting outside on the patio? I've got bug spray and citronella candles."

"Absolutely. I've been spending *way* too much time indoors this month."

"Sorry to hear that. Work?"

"Yes, and I've also been terrible about making plans. . . . Since you're here tonight, I take it you and your husband aren't one of those couples with a second home they always abandon town for on weekends?"

"Tom bought a small vacation cottage on Block Island a few years ago, but we've been renting it out this summer. We only moved into this house nine months ago—right after we got married—and we want to settle in and enjoy it as much as possible."

"I can see why," Addison says, taking in the interiors. "It's gorgeous—and such an amazing blend of styles."

Addison's nailed what Emma adores most about the decor. Though the house is modern with white walls throughout, she and Tom had the oak floors stained the color of espresso and have mixed contemporary furniture with old textiles and a smattering of rustic pieces.

"Thanks so much—though we still have a few items on the to-do list."

"Well, you're way ahead of *me*." Addison shakes her head. "I've been divorced and in my current place for three years, and I still have paintings leaning against walls."

Emma leads her through the house to the flagstone patio, where she motions for her guest to take a seat at the teak table. Once settled, Addison leans back in her chair, clearly at ease. Though her long face doesn't make her classically beautiful, she's definitely an attractive woman, Emma thinks, with great skin, expressive blue eyes, and plenty of style.

"Wine?"

"I'd love a glass, but a teeny, *tiny* one. I might grade a few papers tonight so I can go into the weekend without having them hanging over my head."

She accepts the wineglass with long slim fingers and glances across the lawn. "Wait, is that the studio you told me about?"

"Yup."

"You've clearly got the best commute in Westport."

"I know, right? The first thing I said when I saw the property was, 'I love the house, but we don't need an artist's studio.' It was my husband who suggested I turn it into office space for my company. Before we got married, I was working out of a spare bedroom in my rental apartment in town."

"Your husband's Tom Halliday, right? From Halliday Advertising?"

"Yes. Have you ever met him?"

"A couple of times at events in the area, but only in passing. I hear nothing but wonderful things about him, though."

"They're all true, I have to say." As soon as the words are out of her mouth, Emma worries that she's sounding gross or braggy. Sometimes it's hard for her to tamp down the sheer pleasure she feels about Tom. "I was just very lucky to cross paths with him," she adds, spreading cheese and pâté on a couple of crackers.

"Did you work at Halliday, too?"

"Only as a freelance consultant for a short while. Once

Tom and I became romantically involved, I bowed out for obvious reasons. The agency still subscribes to my quarterly trend report, and I do presentations there on each report—in fact, I'm doing one Monday—but that's the extent of it now."

"Sounds smart to create some distance. And where were you before Westport?"

"Um, here and there," Emma says, not eager to share anything more yet. "But tell me about *you*, Addison. You mentioned you're divorced. Are you seeing anyone these days?"

"Just a boy toy now and then when I'm in the mood." She chuckles and takes a sip of wine. "I'm forty-four, he's thirty-three, and though he can be fun, there are times when he works my last nerve."

"Ahh, a millennial. I bet he's always staring at his smartphone."

"Yes, *constantly*. Texting, checking Instagram, whatever. I tried telling him one day that Wi-Fi signals lower sperm count, but he seemed unfazed. I don't take it personally, though."

"Ha! That's the right attitude. It's totally generational."

Addison nodded. "You must be a millennial, too, but you certainly don't seem obsessed with social media. I noticed your Instagram feed has some work-related posts, but never anything personal."

"Yeah, I guess I'm an odd duck that way," Emma says.

Or, unlike so many of her contemporaries, she doesn't want the world keeping tabs on her personal life.

"Well, it might be for the best," Addison says, letting her eyes wander the property. "If you *did* post all this, people might be insanely jealous and start to hate you."

The doorbell rings suddenly, the tinny ding-dong carrying all the way from the front of the house.

"Hmm," Emma says, surprised. "Excuse me for a sec, will you?"

Addison nods. "Of course."

It's probably FedEx, Emma thinks as she strides through the house, but she still feels a pinch of concern. In their neighborhood, the houses are fairly far apart and set back from the road, and it can feel deserted at this time of day.

As soon as she's in the front hall, she gazes through the peephole in the door. The caller is a woman, probably in her late forties, Black, with hair cropped very close to her head and wearing a maroon-colored suit jacket. The look on her face triggers a swell of unease in Emma, almost like a muscle memory. She's seen that type of sober, unsmiling look before—on the faces of law enforcement.

"Yes?" she asks after opening the door a crack with the chain on.

"Emma Hawke?"

"Who is it, please?"

"I'm Detective Lisa Webster from the New York City police."

Emma's breath catches, and she watches motionless as Webster slips a photo ID from her purse, flips it open, and raises it to eye level. "Could you tell me what this is about?"

"May I come in?"

No, you can't, Emma thinks, but says, "Um, all right."

She unhooks the chain and eases open the door, allowing Webster to step into the front hall. The detective is a couple of inches taller than she is, about five foot eight or nine, slim but muscular beneath the jacket. Somewhere behind her, Emma detects footsteps, probably Addison checking to be sure things are okay, but she doesn't look back.

"What can I do for you?" she says, trying her best to keep her voice even.

"Do you have some time to talk right now, Ms. Hawke?" Webster asks. "I'm here about your husband's murder."

3

THE WORDS ARE BARELY OUT OF THE DETECTIVE'S MOUTH
when Emma hears the sound of glass shattering behind her.
She spins around to see Addison at the far end of the hall, her
mouth open in shock and splinters of glass scattered on the
tile around her feet.

"She doesn't mean Tom," Emma calls out, realizing what
Addison must be thinking. "He's in Chicago. This—It's about
the man I was married to before."

Addison nods slowly, clearly trying to process: *former
husband dead; murdered; police investigating*. "I'm so sorry
about the glass," she says. "I—"

"Don't worry, I'm sure it was a shock." Emma's doing
her best to sound calm, but her heart's drumming inside her
chest. She glances back at Webster, who's studying the scene,
and then once more at her guest. "But I need to speak to Detective, um, Webster. Can we take a rain check on our visit?"

"Of course, as soon as I clean this up."

"No, no, please leave it, Addison, seriously," Emma says. "I'm sorry to ask this, but do you mind seeing yourself out through the back?"

"Yes, of course. I'll call you tomorrow to check in."

Emma trains all her attention on the detective now, certain she wouldn't have come calling without a good reason. "I apologize for the chaos. Is there a new development?"

The detective shakes her head. "Not a break in the case, but I do have an update for you."

An update, Emma thinks. *What the hell does* that *mean?*

"Why don't we sit in the den," she says, gesturing to a doorway at the far end of the living room.

"Wherever's most comfortable for you," Webster says. She's courteous, friendly even. Or at least that's what she wants Emma to think.

As soon as they step into the cozy room, Emma motions for Webster to have a seat on the butterscotch leather couch, an attractive leftover from the single-guy town house where Tom was living when they met. Emma perches on an armchair across from her.

"First, let me apologize for alarming your friend," Webster says, crossing one of her long legs over the other. Her face is striking, with strong, well-defined features, including distinctive cheekbones.

Emma shakes her head. "It's okay. I'm sure she understands now."

"I hope I didn't alarm you as well."

"No, I knew what you meant," Emma says, which isn't true. For a split second she *did* think the detective meant Tom, and it felt like a tsunami was crashing over her head and about to suck her into the depths of the sea. But she figured it out quickly.

"As I said, I'm looking into Mr. Rand's murder and wanted to touch base with you about it." Her voice is smooth and deep like a late-night radio deejay's, and Emma warns herself not to be lulled into complacency.

"Thank you. So there's some kind of news?" she asks as evenly as she can.

"Not about the crime per se. But I wanted to let you know we're going to be reopening the case. Sometimes we do this because of new evidence—like a DNA match—but at other times, we're simply taking advantage of a temporary ease in workload to reexamine an investigation that hit a wall along the way. This is one of those times."

"So is it almost like you're starting from scratch?" Emma asks, then immediately regrets it. If there's one thing she learned from Peter Dunne, the lawyer she hired after Derrick's murder, it's that when you talk to the police, you should speak only when spoken to.

"Somewhat, yes. We're retracing our steps, reviewing the evidence. A fresh pair of eyes can sometimes make a difference."

Emma nods. "Well, that's very good to hear."

Webster withdraws a notebook and pen from her purse. "Ms. Hawke—"

"Please call me Emma."

"Thank you. Emma, I'd like to start by having you tell me a little about your late husband."

The question strikes Emma as odd—wouldn't the detective have read the file before driving out here from the city?—but she nods and begins. "Okay. Well, he was head of financial planning for a fintech start-up called Alta."

"Fintech?"

"Sorry, it's short for financial technology. He'd been there a little over two years, after getting his MBA at Columbia. And before that he'd worked in the packaged food industry."

Webster's narrowed eyes seem to hint that Emma's missed the point. "I was hoping actually for a glimpse of Derrick's personality," she says. "I find that getting to know a victim—his character, his habits, even his shortcomings—can be beneficial in trying to understand what transpired."

"Right, I see." Though she doesn't completely. "He was smart, focused, superconscientious about his work. Passionate about certain sports—squash, tennis, snowboarding—and he was pretty competitive at them."

"A risk-taker?"

"I guess you could say that."

"If someone demanded his wallet, would he have resisted?"

"I've actually gone over that question in my mind many times. He wasn't reckless exactly, but he might have thought he could outsmart a mugger. Like a lot of men might, I guess."

"How did he get along with other people in general?"

So Webster's shifting gears from the possibility of death at a stranger's hands, a mugging gone wrong, and wondering whether someone Derrick knew wanted him out of the picture for good.

Emma clears her throat as she feels her stomach tighten. "Overall, pretty well. But as I mentioned during one of the interviews with the police back then, at times he could be demanding with people working for him, and I think it rankled a few of them."

"Can you elaborate a bit on that?"

"There were a couple of incidents, but nothing that seemed relevant to the case. A guy he supervised at Alta, someone the company had been fast-tracking, left unexpectedly and apparently bad-mouthed him badly in the exit interview. And a few months before he died, Derrick refused to pay a contractor in full for redoing a bathroom at our house in New Jersey because the work was sloppy. The man cursed at him, told him to quote 'go to fucking hell.' I believe the police looked into both men at the time of the investigation and found they had solid alibis."

Webster nods. "Any issues in his personal relationships? A friendship gone sour, for instance?"

She doesn't mean just friendships, of course. She means family, too, and that includes *her*. Emma sees now that this is more than the promised "update" and that she should never have allowed Webster to talk to her without Dunne in the room. Her ridiculous need to please has reared its head and put her on the spot yet again. . . . But if she asks Webster to leave now, it might make things worse.

"You know, work kept him pretty busy, so when he saw a friend, it was generally only for squash at his club in the city, or to catch a basketball game, or occasionally to grab a beer. As far as I know, there was never any drama with his friends."

"Any drama at the party you had at your home a week before Mr. Rand's death?"

Webster *had* read the file then, and pretty carefully.

"No, it was a simple cocktail party, our first in the new house. I actually gave the police a list of people who attended and also the names of his friends. Would you like me to see if I can find it for you?" Emma offers an ingratiating smile and then worries it hits the wrong note.

"No, I have that information," Webster says. "And what about family? I understand that Mr. Rand had siblings. What can you tell me about his relationship with them?"

"Well, his sister, Heather, has been in Melbourne for probably a dozen years—she's married to an Australian guy—and the only time she'd been back to the States in years was when she came for our wedding. Though they did stay in sporadic touch on email and WhatsApp."

"And his brother?"

"Kyle?" she says, though there's only one. "He lives in Bronxville with his wife. He and Derrick played tennis together a couple of Saturdays a month—at a club halfway between our two places. They weren't superclose, but they got along."

And as Webster surely knows, Kyle was at home with his wife, Jackie, the entire night of the murder.

The detective takes a minute to thumb through her notebook and then leans forward a little at the waist, in a vaguely conspiratorial way.

"Emma, I'd like to ask you a few questions now that relate specifically to the night Derrick died," she says. "I'm sure it's very painful to revisit that time, but it's important for the investigation."

"Of course," Emma says and slowly slides her hands along her linen pant legs, trying to wipe away the film of sweat on her palms without Webster noticing. She'd like to kick herself hard for having opened the front door today.

"There's one big puzzle that was never solved—why your husband chose that particular parking lot when he arrived in the city Friday morning. Have you had any new thoughts on that in the past couple of years?"

Webster's right, that was something that had confused everyone: Why had Derrick parked in SoHo when the conference was being held at a Midtown hotel?

Emma shakes her head. "At the time my only guess was that he'd decided it was simply easier to park there than near the hotel. No other reason has come to mind since."

"Okay, but then why would he return to the garage that night?"

That was an even bigger question. He'd definitely been at the conference dinner earlier—along with forty or so other company staffers, a number of whom remembered speaking to him. Security camera footage showed him exiting the building at around nine thirty and waiting outside for his Uber ride with body language that seemed typically impatient, though it was hard to tell on the grainy recording. Twenty-six minutes later the car dropped him off at the corner of Greene and Houston Streets, just north of the garage. His body was noticed inside the small alley around 10:40 by two horrified passersby.

Emma shrugs, indicating she doesn't have a clue. Does Webster really expect her to announce she's had some bombshell epiphany in the past twenty-seven months but failed to share it with the police?

Webster says nothing, just crosses her arms and appears

to wait, her body language suggesting that if Emma only thinks a bit harder, something will come to her.

"The only thing I wondered since," Emma adds, caving into the pressure, "is that maybe he'd forgotten something in the car and went down there to retrieve it. The police did find Derrick's camera in the glove compartment, but there didn't seem to be any reason he would have gone all the way downtown for it. He could have used his phone to take pictures at the conference."

"Right," Webster says, still looking dissatisfied. "How long had you and Derrick been married?"

"Two years—and we'd dated for almost two years prior to that."

"So you were"—she glances down—"about twenty-nine when you met?"

Emma nods. "Right."

"Was it a happy marriage?"

Has the detective decided to dispense with social niceties? Emma's stomach clutches again, and though her first instinct is to look away, she manages to wrestle it down.

"I thought so." She decides to get something on the table right then and there, especially since it would be in the file anyway. "The police asked me at one point if I thought he'd been having an affair and had headed downtown to meet someone, but I never had any reason to suspect he'd been unfaithful."

Another lie—of sorts. He'd had a colleague named Zoe who he'd grown increasingly flirty with, at least according to the texts Emma had stolen a glance at (i.e., Him: You had every guy in the room eating out of the palm of your hand; Her: Is that right? Are you including yourself in that group?; Him: I'm going to plead the Fifth on that one. Her: Hmmm.). Though Emma didn't think they'd crossed the line, she'd assumed a fling might be in the cards.

She realizes that Webster must be aware of the texts, too, but she doesn't mention them, and Emma's hardly going to volunteer the information. It wouldn't be smart to come across as a woman who snooped on her husband—especially one who had reason to be boiling mad at him.

Emma waits as Webster thumbs through her notes again. The detective hasn't brought up Emma and Derrick's financial situation, but that's not surprising because there was never any there there. Their net worth as a couple consisted mainly of a house with a fairly large mortgage, two small 401(k)s, and a very modest, pretty young investment portfolio. They also hadn't gotten around to buying life insurance, all of which meant Emma lacked a big financial reason to kill her husband.

There was one detail that must have piqued the cops' interest, at least initially: At the age of forty, Derrick was due to come into a decent-sized trust fund set up by his late parents, who had died in a single-engine plane crash a few years before Emma and Derrick met. But their will decreed that if Derrick married and predeceased his wife, the money would go to several charities the parents had supported.

There was also the matter of the paintings: the Rands had left each of their three children two very expensive pieces from their collection. Derrick inherited an oil-on-paper work by Mark Rothko and a painting by Helen Frankenthaler. That had actually been part of the reason he'd wanted to host a party—the house was finally decorated and the paintings hung.

When Derrick's estate was sorted out, according to the terms of the Rands' will, the Frankenthaler went to his sister, and the Rothko to Kyle. His brother immediately willed his to a museum, getting a very nice tax write-off but no money in his pocket.

Webster's voice snaps her back to attention. "Just one more question, and then I think we're done for now."

Thank god, Emma thinks. She can't bear another second of this.

"Your husband left on Friday morning for the conference, and the first time you spoke to him was when he called you Saturday evening. Is there a reason the two of you weren't in touch before then?"

A faint siren sounds in Emma's head, like a car alarm she's hearing from a block away. She'd been questioned at the time about the Saturday night phone call, but the cops had focused on what Derrick had said during it, whether his words revealed any clue to why his life was about to be snuffed out. None of them had seemed troubled by the frequency of their contact as a couple that weekend.

"No particular reason. We'd talked Friday morning before he left and then, um, I guess we both got busy."

"And there was no time to even send a text?" Webster smiles, her expression pleasant this time. "It's just that most couples I know don't seem to go a full day without texting."

The urge to look away is too strong this time, and in spite of herself Emma glances toward the window, then forces her gaze back at the detective

"I don't remember not texting, but if that's what the records show, they must be right."

Webster shifts slightly, uncrossing her legs. "Here's something I'd love your thoughts on," she says finally. "An idea
I've been toying with a bit since I took over the case. Let's say
your husband actually did park downtown for the reason you
suggested—to avoid Midtown traffic. What if he went back
down there that night to pick up his car and drive home,
back to New Jersey?"

"*Home?*" Emma asks. She has no idea where Webster's going with this. "But the conference still had a half day to go."

"I'm wondering whether after speaking to you on the
phone, he felt a sudden desire to come home. Maybe he realized he missed you and wanted to surprise you. Or perhaps you two had had some kind of slight misunderstanding
during the call, and he wanted to address it in person?"

"Uh, no, there was nothing like that," Emma says, trying
not to sound flustered, though she can feel blood pooling in
her cheeks. "He told me he was enjoying himself, that the
speakers were good. He didn't mention anything about coming home."

Webster nods, but less like she's agreeing with Emma,
and more like she's weighing her words on a scale, then stuffs
her notebook back into her bag. "All right, it was only a theory. Thank you very much for your help. I'll let you get back
to your evening."

Get back to her evening, *right*. What kind of evening is
she supposed to have after this conversation?

As Emma leads Webster from the den to the living room
and toward the front hall, the detective's whole manner seems

to soften a bit. "Your home is amazing," she says, stopping midroom and sweeping her gaze around the space.

Emma ekes out a smile. "Thank you."

"You seem to have landed on your feet. I'm sure these past couple of years haven't been easy."

"They've been very hard, yes. I'm not sure you ever get over something like this."

"How did you and your current husband meet? Dating can be so difficult these days."

Emma tries to take a deep breath without making it obvious. "Through work, actually. Tom—my husband—runs an ad agency here in Westport. I do research and trend forecasting, and the agency hired me two summers ago to consult on some of the brands they handle."

"It's always nice meeting someone at work," the detective says. "You get such a better sense of who they are compared to someone you meet online or at a bar." She starts moving toward the door again, and once they reach the hall, Emma notices that Addison swept away the broken glass, after all.

"Thanks again for your time," Webster says.

"Thank *you*. I mean, I appreciate that you're opening the investigation again."

"I can't make any guarantees," she says, holding Emma's gaze, "but we'll do our best to finally get the person who did this."

After Emma closes the door behind the detective, she waits for the muffled sound of a car engine firing, but hears only silence. *Is Webster making a call?* she wonders. *Reviewing her notes?*

Finally, the car starts and she sinks against the door, exhaling. Webster appeared polite enough, even empathetic at moments, but Emma knows it was a charade, as it was with the first detectives on the case. The whole time Webster was here, she was clearly assessing Emma, wondering whether there was something she'd stood to gain from Derrick Rand's death.

Wondering whether Emma was actually the one who'd set the murder in motion.

4

Then

THE TRIP TO THE MORGUE WAS AS TERRIBLE AS EMMA HAD
imagined, but at the same time surreal. Not wanting to drive,
she'd taken an Uber and found herself trembling as she entered the stark, white brick building on First Avenue and
Twenty-Sixth Street. Perhaps from watching endless reruns
of *Law and Order* and other crime shows, she'd imagined
standing in the morgue while a weary-looking, middle-
aged pathologist folded back a blue cloth to reveal Derrick's
corpse, only inches away from her face. Instead, when she
arrived, she was led to what Detective Lennox called the *family* room, a space as bland and lifeless as a dentist's reception
area, lined with a gray sofa and chairs framed in cheap, blond
wood. Unlike with a waiting room, though, Emma and the
detective were the only people in it.

There was also a desk with a computer along a far wall,
and after a few moments a young woman who said she was

from the identification unit arrived and took a seat at it. She tapped a couple of keys and turned the computer screen so that Emma could have a full view.

She'd gasped at the sight: a picture of Derrick's face, a blue cloth tucked under his chin and a slight pinch between his closed eyes, as if he was only sleeping and having an irritating dream. Bile rose in her throat, and she pressed a hand tightly to her mouth.

"Yes, that's him," she said, her words nearly strangled. She'd sensed Lennox on alert in the seat next to her, watching her but trying not to be obvious.

"We're going to find who did this," he told her a few minutes later, when he'd walked her out of the building and onto the street.

Emma shivered in the cold. "Thank you."

"I know how hard this must be, but it would be beneficial for the investigation if we could spend more time with you, ask you more about Derrick."

"*Now?*"

"If you're able."

"I'm sorry, but it will have to be tomorrow. I didn't sleep at all after you left and I can barely stand up."

"All right, let's speak later today and confirm a time to meet."

Back home, Emma nearly threw herself into the shower, her second of the day. Though she'd never stepped into the actual morgue, she swore she could smell the stench of formaldehyde on her skin as she scrubbed away at it.

So far, she'd only spoken to one person she knew about Derrick's death, her brother, Griffin, who promised to snag a flight from the UK that day. He also said he'd keep trying her parents, whose phones had been going straight to voice mail. She'd seen an incoming call from Derrick's brother, Kyle, a few hours earlier, but she hadn't picked up, instead sending a text saying she would talk to him as soon as she could.

After stepping out of the shower and toweling off, Emma forced herself to consume a piece of toast, eating it listlessly as snow began to fall outside her window. Then she found herself wandering the house, a mug of tea in hand, covering the same ground again and again. As she passed through the rooms, they now felt only vaguely familiar to her, as if she'd dropped by to house-sit for friends and would never be able to find where they kept things like light bulbs or salad tongs.

She hadn't liked the idea of fleeing Manhattan for New Jersey, but Derrick had grown up in the suburbs and saw himself in this kind of environment. They'd narrowed their search to Madison because it was both charming and also had a direct train line to Penn Station, which was near enough to his office in the Twenties. Emma talked herself into the change, willing to try something new. But she'd liked it even less once they were settled in.

They'd pooled their savings for a down payment on a nice house—a three-bedroom with four well-proportioned rooms downstairs—and thanks to Derrick's generous salary, they qualified for a mortgage to cover the rest. What made things a little better for her: there was a small apartment above the garage that she'd begun using immediately as office space.

As she drifted through the rooms, she let her gaze roam. Derrick had insisted that they hire a decorator, and every piece of furniture they ended up with seemed to have flared, doweled legs. She often wondered if visitors found the effect as cold as she did. The two things she really cared about were the stunning pieces of modern art Derrick had inherited— the Rothko and Frankenthaler—and she took a minute to study each of them right now. He could have sold them for a fortune, but he liked the status they conferred on him, and besides, he knew he'd have plenty of money from the trust he'd be entitled to when he turned forty.

Finally, Emma stopped. She was in the family room, which was really an extension of the kitchen, standing in front of the built-in bookcase. Interspersed with the books were several small objects, including a wooden box they'd bought on their honeymoon in Thailand and a photograph from those two weeks, the two of them standing in front of a red-and-gold temple with a spire that gleamed in the sun.

That had been their second day there. Later, over dinner, she'd made a comment that, for some reason, had annoyed Derrick to death, and he hadn't spoken to her for the next three days, despite her apologies, despite how much she'd implored him not to let their trip be spoiled.

Emma forced her gaze away from the bookcase. It hurt to even look at that photo. But then almost every spot in the house was a reminder of moments she longed to forget.

I'm going to sell this place as soon as possible, she told herself.

From what she knew of the market, the timing wasn't great, but she didn't care about taking a loss, she just wanted to be out of here, back in the city and far away from this house.

Of course, that was the least of her problems at the moment. Within the next twenty-four hours, she needed to plan a funeral, assembling Derrick's friends and relatives, and, she'd have to show up there, presenting herself to everyone her husband knew as the grieving widow.

And it would all be a lie.

5

WHEN TOM CALLS FROM THE AIRPORT AT A QUARTER TO eight, Emma's in the den, staring at the screen of her Kindle and trying to quell her blistering unease.

She hasn't been able to get Webster out of her mind—the woman's self-confident aura, her unsettling pet theory about why Derrick was headed to the parking garage, the way she lingered in her car for a while before taking off. Maybe she was calling her partner to report back. *You won't believe the damn house*, Emma imagines her saying. *She's done well for herself. Very*, very *well.*

It would have helped so much to talk to her brother this evening, but he's off the grid right now, doing research in Greenland for a book he's writing on climate change.

"What's trending, beautiful?" Tom asks after she answers, a catchphrase she's heard many times from him.

"Me missing you."

"Good to know. I'm not interrupting your get-together with your new pal, am I?"

"No, Addison and I ended up having to reschedule." She'll wait to fill Tom in until he's home. Emma is still feeling guilty about Addison, whom she called a few minutes after Webster departed but didn't reach. "How was your meeting?"

"Excellent. I'll tell you more when I see you, which should be right after nine if the stars align in my favor."

"Great. Brittany's spending the night with a new friend, by the way."

"Yes, she texted me to tell me, hence the spring you hear in my step. I hope she's not driving you nuts."

"No, not at all. And besides, it's only five more weeks and three days."

Tom chuckles. "I hear you, Em, and I appreciate you being such a good sport. . . . Should I wolf down the pretzels I grabbed on the plane or is there anything in the fridge?"

"Why don't I put out a few things and we can eat together?"

"Oh, sweetheart, don't feel you have to wait."

"No, I'd love to. Though I might be naughty and graze a little beforehand."

"Well, if you have any naughty instincts, save a few of them for later."

"Of course. Love you."

"Love you more."

Though it was comforting to hear Tom's voice, Emma's heart is racing again as soon as she hangs up. The second she sets the phone down, it pings with a voice-mail notification from Addison, which must have come in while she was on the other line.

"Emma, I'm so sorry I missed your call and I hope you're okay," Addison says in the message. "But somehow I overlooked the warning signs of a migraine, and it's nearly leveled me now. I've taken medication and I'm crawling into bed so I should be fine by morning. I'll call you then."

Oof, Emma thinks, *maybe today's visit is what triggered the migraine.* The woman was invited to a new friend's home for wine and cheese and sent packing almost immediately when a homicide detective arrived on the scene. Addison strikes Emma as more than capable of rolling with the punches, but it must have been incredibly awkward for her.

Before getting to work on dinner, Emma heads upstairs to freshen up. As she's brushing out her hair, she realizes that both temples are throbbing in pain. Unlike Addison, she's not subject to migraines, but now she has a splitting headache herself.

Tom arrives home about ninety minutes later, as Emma's putting the finishing touches on their late supper. There's a total confidence to the sound of his car pulling into the garage—not what you'd call aggressive but at the same time lacking any hesitation.

That's Tom, of course, Emma thinks. Assured, superbly capable. She suspected that about him from the moment she'd been hired to consult for Halliday Advertising the June after Derrick had died. She'd unloaded the New Jersey house by then—it had happened as quickly as she'd prayed—and had rented a one-bedroom in Manhattan. When Scott Munroe, an account executive at Halliday, had reached out about the gig, he'd told her she could consult remotely, but she sometimes took the train to Westport and worked out of a vacant office at the firm. She found that being on-site not only provided her easy access to the data and material she needed, but also that she loved spending time in such a vibrant space.

Though it would be several weeks before she was introduced to Tom, she'd caught glimpses of the stylishly dressed founder and CEO through the glass-walled meeting rooms. He wasn't supertall—only five ten, she later learned—but he brimmed with energy, and his personality seemed infectious, clearly dazzling whoever he was talking to at the time.

And she heard buzz about him as well: staffers referencing his comments or ideas, mentioning his rise from junior advertising copywriter at a big Manhattan firm to owner of his own highly respected, award-winning agency. By all accounts, he gave his direct reports plenty of autonomy, but they also seemed to like channeling his wisdom. A phrase she heard on more than one occasion was "WWTD"—short for "What would Tom do?"

It soon became clear that Tom had a reputation not only for having impressive leadership skills but also personal ones: even-keeled and considerate of others. Emma reserved judgment on that front, however. She knew all about men whose initial charm hid an oversize ego, a short temper, or an out-and-out mean streak.

One day in mid-July, Scott mentioned that Tom had been hearing good things about her work and wanted to meet her. Tom's assistant followed up on email and set up a time, and less than a week later she was seated at the round table in his office. Yes, a round table, because Tom never wanted anyone to have to sit across from him at an imposing desk.

"So," he'd said, smiling. "I'm finally meeting the Oracle of Delphi."

"Oh, please, you're setting the bar ridiculously high," she'd replied, the ice immediately broken.

Within minutes she sensed he was all people had described—strong but not overbearing, charismatic, but also thoughtful and considerate. It was hard not to fall under his spell.

What especially impressed Emma was Tom's curiosity. Unlike so many powerful men she'd encountered over the years, who only loved to talk about themselves, he asked smart questions and wanted to know about *her*, how she'd ended up in this field, how she balanced gut instinct with the results of research.

And there was something else, something that nearly knocked her backward. Toward the end of the thirty or so minutes they spent together, she realized that she was *attracted* to him. It wasn't just his charm and sense of humor, but she was drawn to him physically—his prematurely silvery gray hair with matching scruff, blue-gray eyes, the two front teeth that overlapped ever so slightly. *Whoa, hold on*, she had told herself. *This is crazy.* Tom was single, she'd heard, a forty-three-year-old widower whose wife had passed a few years earlier, but Emma wasn't ready for anything sexual, romantic, or even lightly flirtatious. Not then or anytime soon.

As they'd wrapped up the meeting, Tom had offered her a retainer and contract, which would entail her working not only with Scott for the next year but also several other account executives. She left his office elated about the arrangement and determined to ignore the attraction she'd felt toward the man sitting next to her.

But it wasn't long before all that changed.

"Ah, what a sight for sore eyes," Tom says, entering the kitchen from the passageway to the garage. Emma strides toward him, and as they kiss each other hungrily, not only does her body relax, but the lingering traces of her headache recede almost instantaneously.

Once they've peeled themselves away, Tom's gaze finds its way to the table in the corner, where Emma's lit candles and set out a green salad, a baguette, and the pâté and cheeses from her aborted get-together with Addison.

"That looks fabulous," he says. "Thanks so much for waiting, sweetheart."

"My pleasure."

And it is. His thoughtfulness toward her seems to know no bounds, and she's always eager for a chance to repay it.

"Is red wine okay with you?" she asks. "I picked out a nice bottle from the cellar to welcome you back."

"Perfect. Just let me wash my hands first. And by the way, if you're trying to seduce me with expensive wine and pâté, it's totally unnecessary."

"Ah, good to know for future reference."

She smiles playfully or at least tries to—because her unease about Webster is advancing again.

Once they're settled at the table, Tom tells her he's pretty sure that Halliday won the business he was pitching in Chicago, though it might involve making one more trip to the Midwest to finalize details.

"So the presentation you showed me was a home run?" she asks.

He grits his teeth, feigning nervous tension. "Not exactly. As soon as I was in the room with their team and saw them interacting, I had a sense we'd taken their requests way too literally. I ended up shifting gears midstream and diverging from the PowerPoint. It was risky but in hindsight I know it was the right move."

"Wow, I would've loved to have been a fly on the wall. Was Justine able to roll with the punches?" Tom's former head of client services was promoted a while back to the number-two position and has had some trouble nailing it.

He laughs. "I tried to shoot her a warning look that I was about to go rogue, but she had this deer-in-the-headlights expression, and it took her a while to get up to speed."

"Hmm. I didn't interact with Justine all that much during my consulting days, but she always seemed so on the ball," Emma says. "And yet every time you've mentioned her lately, it's been in the context of her being out of sync or distracted. What do you think is going on?"

"I'm not sure, but it's something I'm going to have to deal with. As you know, she oversaw events in her previous position and insisted on holding on to that role, which means she's probably got too much on her plate. Enough about me, though. How was your day, Em? Did you manage to squeeze in a walk on the beach?"

"Actually, since I had the house to myself, I decided to just hang here."

"I'm sure that was nice for you." He shakes his head. "I know Brittany's presence has put a damper on our summer, but I'm going to do my best to make it up to you when we go to Napa in August."

"Oh, Tom, you don't have to make up anything to me. I just wish I could find a way to connect with Brittany better."

"Don't blame yourself. She was never an easy kid, but she's been through a lot, and I imagine she's still really suffering."

"I know. Losing her mom. Leaving the home she grew up in. It must be so hard."

Tom tears off a piece of baguette, smears it with pâté, and hands it to Emma before preparing another for himself. "So . . . tell me why your drinks date fell apart with—what's her name?"

"Addison Stark. She says she's been at the same events as you a couple of times."

"The name doesn't ring a bell, but perhaps I'll recognize her if we ever officially meet. So why did she bail on you?"

"I was the one who bailed on her." Emma takes a deep breath, steeling herself. "I know you've had a long day and I hate having to drop this on you, but something a bit distressing happened this afternoon. A Manhattan homicide cop paid me a surprise visit here at the house. Asking about Derrick's murder."

He raises his eyebrows in surprise. "Have they arrested someone?"

"No, but they've decided to reopen the case."

"Wow. Because . . . ?"

"According to this Detective Webster, there's no specific

reason besides a break in their workload that's allowing them to expend resources on it."

"Huh. But no new leads?"

"There don't seem to be. At first, it sounded like she was going to give me an update, but all she did was ask questions—about whether Derrick had any issues with anyone, why I thought he parked downtown that night, that sort of thing."

He leans across the table and lays a comforting hand on one of hers. "I'm so sorry, Em. This can't be easy for you."

"It's fine," she says, hoping he can't see how unnerved she really is.

"As hard as it was when Diana died, I was fortunate in that I wasn't hounded by endless questions."

She's not surprised Tom mentions Diana. That's been a point of connection between them in Tom's eyes, the fact that they both lost spouses. But though he knows the circumstances are very different, he doesn't know *how* different.

"I just don't want it to affect your life. As far as I know, people at Halliday and our neighbors here aren't even aware of that aspect of my past."

"Well, if you're worried for my sake, don't be. I couldn't care less what people think."

She knows it's the truth, and yet she can't help but push a bit. "You say that now, but what if we end up on an episode of *Dateline Investigates*?"

"Not very likely. And even if this detective really goes to town, most of her digging is bound to be in New York and Madison, not here in little old Wepo anyway."

"Well, Addison knows about it now since she was actually here when the detective came."

He makes a face. "Was that awkward for you?"

"Kind of. She was great though. And we're going to talk tomorrow."

"Sweetheart, I can tell from those gorgeous hazel eyes of yours that this is eating at you, but you can't let it. There's no reason to worry."

When she doesn't respond, he cocks an eyebrow. "What? Was there something else about the interview?"

"Not anything significant." She's decided not to share any more of Webster's questions with him because saying them out loud will only add to her stress. "But in hindsight I wish that I'd told her to come back when my lawyer could join us."

"Yeah, I hear you. But to play devil's advocate, it might have looked like you had something to hide. Though you probably want to loop him in as soon as possible."

"Yes, I'm going to give him a call first thing Monday morning."

Tom rises from the table to grab a fresh bottle of sparkling water from the fridge, and when he slides back onto the banquette and looks at Emma, his eyes read more gray than blue in the candlelight.

"Where'd you go?" he asks.

"I'm thinking about how much I missed you while you were away."

"Come on, talk to me."

"Okay, I'm still freaking out a little, but I promise to put it behind me."

He grasps her hand again.

"You'll get through this, Emma. You don't have any reason to be concerned."

"I know, it's just . . . well, innocent people get accused of crimes all the time."

"The police had to take a look at you back then—you were Derrick's wife—but it doesn't sound like they ever gave any credence to you as a suspect."

"Right." She offers a wan smile, but inside Emma feels her earlier gloom enveloping her again, seeping through every cell in her body. She loves her new life, loves Tom passionately, and suddenly, it all feels threatened.

Will she get through it? she wonders. Or is this the moment when her lies from the past finally come calling?

6

AFTER THEY SLIP INTO BED AN HOUR LATER, TOM PRESSES his body against Emma's and runs his fingers through her hair, indicating that despite how fatigued he must be from his trip, he's open to sex tonight. She knows he wouldn't be offended if she begged off, but she doesn't. Maybe, she thinks, this is exactly what she needs to finally chase the main event of the day from her mind.

And it works. Tom's not only a skillful, generous lover, but her physical attraction to him is fierce, something she first sensed at the meeting in his office but knew for certain when he took hold of her hand a few weeks later, sending a rush of desire through every inch of her. Tonight, she's able to lose herself in pleasure, banishing her unease to parts unknown, and afterward, she drifts off to sleep easily in his arms.

But dread sneaks back during the night like a jackal, and Emma wakes around five thirty with a pit in her stomach and a dull thickness in her limbs. Maybe, she muses, Webster's visit was strictly routine, a necessary step in the reopening of the case, and this will be the last she hears from her. Yet her gut tells her not to be a fool, that she's bound to be back.

And she's even more convinced now that it had been a big, fat mistake to allow Webster into the house without Peter Dunne present or, at the very least, to not summon the nerve to call things off the second she realized the visit wasn't a simple "update." She doesn't think she said anything stupid, but with the police you can never be sure. Had Webster seen the sweat blooming on her hands or noticed how stilted some of her answers were, especially the ones about her marriage to Derrick?

She tries for a while to drift back to sleep, but eventually surrenders, knowing it's hopeless. With Tom snoring lightly beside her, Emma slips out of bed and pads downstairs to the kitchen. After opening her laptop on the island, she types "Tobias, Hershfield, and Dunne" into the search bar. She's wasted enough time kicking herself. Though she had planned to wait until Monday to reach out to Dunne, she decides for her peace of mind to do it today.

As she tossed and turned this morning, it had occurred to her that her fiftysomething lawyer might no longer be available. During one of their last consultations, he'd mentioned in passing that he'd hoped to retire early and split his time between Palm Beach and a house in Ireland—probably a castle, if what he charges is any indication. She'd exchanged a few emails with him since then, alerting him to her upcoming marriage to Tom and then her new address, but the last was close to a year ago.

She's in luck though. A quick perusal of the firm's website confirms that, thankfully, Dunne is still practicing.

Emma had known Peter Dunne was the right choice the instant she took a seat on the other side of his sleek wooden desk. He was smart and self-possessed, and though he exuded a preternatural calm, she suspected he could turn ferocious when necessary. He listened calmly as she described her predicament, and there was no doubt in her mind that he was paying strict attention—carefully assessing her, taking measure. And surely, she assumed, trying to decide if she might actually be responsible for her husband's death.

She opens her email and types: Hello Mr. Dunne, Emma Hawke here. They've reopened the murder case and I need to speak to you as soon as possible. Could you call me first thing Monday at the number below?

"Hey, sweetheart, what are you doing up so early?"

Emma turns her head to find Tom in the doorway, already dressed in jeans and a heather-colored Henley.

"I must have had one too many iced teas yesterday and I didn't sleep well. I always make that mistake at the beginning of summer."

He comes up behind her and gives her shoulders a few squeezes. That's one of the things Emma loves about Tom— how physically affectionate he is, and especially when he senses she's in need of his touch.

"Still tense, huh? I hope you're not letting this detective business eat at you."

"No, but I did just shoot an email to Peter Dunne. I already feel better."

"Good. I'm sure he'll tell you have nothing to worry about."

He crosses the room and fills the coffee machine with water. "Hey, I've got an idea. It's not supposed to rain after all—want to take the bikes out for a ride and then grab lunch in town?"

"I'd love to," she says. Surely, a ride will distract her. Tom probably suggested it since he knows how much she loves to be on her bike, shooting along a path with her legs pumping hard and her hair blowing back, then taking it slow on certain stretches and savoring whatever nature wants to show off that day.

"Does ten work?" Tom asks. "I want to head over to the car wash first."

"Perfect."

She closes her laptop and fixes them each a buttered bagel as Tom pours two mugs of coffee. Once they're finished, Tom helps clear and then grabs his car keys from a basket. Emma promises to have the bikes out by the time he returns.

"Oh wait, what about Brittany?" she asks, suddenly remembering. "This will leave her on her own all day."

"She's actually not due back until around three."

"You heard from her?"

"Yeah, she texted me before I came downstairs this morning."

This is Brittany's M.O., Emma reflects. Tom is looped in at all times, and she's solely on a need-to-know basis. But maybe that's for the best. "Gotcha. Well, I'm glad she's made a friend at work."

"Yes, me, too. As you know, she can seem a bit standoffish. . . . Okay, I'd better get a move on."

As Tom disappears into the garage, Emma considers how much she admires his attitude about his stepdaughter. He's not blind to her flaws, but he's also incredibly sympathetic to how much change she's gone through in her young life and the grief she still feels over Diana, who was not only a very successful eye doctor but by all accounts a loving parent. He's committed to staying in his stepdaughter's life and trying to make Emma a part of it, too.

When he and Emma got engaged, Brittany was in her first year at the University of New Hampshire, and they booked a weekend getaway at a nearby inn so they could all meet for lunch.

It had been an awkward two hours but at least not a disaster. Tall, statuesque Brittany, with deep brown eyes and brown hair worn in a flapperlike bob, had shaken Emma's hand limply and offered a polite, "How do you do? . . . And oh, congratulations" before diverting all her attention to Tom. She told him she'd recently decided to major in marketing, a decision obviously influenced by her admiration for him, and over the meal she asked for his advice on a couple of courses she was planning to take, hanging on his every word.

"Thank you so much for today," Tom had told Emma back at the inn.

"I didn't mind at all, and I respect you so much for keeping the relationship going."

"The funny thing is we were never very close during the

four years I was married to her mom, but since Diana died, Brittany's been so eager to stay in touch."

"Maybe when she was younger she didn't feel comfortable expressing how much she cared about you."

"Possibly. I also think beneath that cool exterior, there's more neediness than you'd guess, and I know she misses Diana tremendously. She's probably convinced herself that I'm one way she can stay connected to her mother's memory."

Emma could see that, too, so it wasn't much of a surprise when Brittany reached out later about a summer internship. She told herself to grin and bear it, that Brittany's stay would be a tiny hiccup in a life that was otherwise far happier than what she could have imagined for herself only a couple of years ago.

The ring of her cell phone tugs Emma's attention away, and she spots Addison's name on the screen, triggering a ripple of relief. This will be her chance not only to smooth things over, making sure there's no awkwardness with a new friend, but also do damage control. Addison doesn't seem like the type who would go blabbing to everyone about what she saw yesterday, but Emma wants reassurance.

"How's your head?" Emma asks after they greet each other.

"Much better. What about *you*, though? I was so worried, but instead of being helpful, I shattered one of your lovely wineglasses and then fell off the grid for the rest of the day."

"Don't worry about it. And you were so thoughtful to clean up."

"I'd no idea that you'd lost a husband. That—"

"It's not common knowledge around here. Tom knows,

of course, and so does my colleague Eric, because he worked with me back then. But needless to say, I never share it with people right away. I don't want to make them uncomfortable."

"I won't say a word, but please know it didn't make *me* uncomfortable, Emma. It was just a bit of a shock. Is everything okay, by the way? I mean . . ."

"Yes, the detective was simply checking in. It's still an open investigation."

Though she attempts to sound nonchalant, Emma knows there's an edge in her voice.

"I'm sorry you had to deal with that on your own yesterday," Addison says. "So it happened in New York City?"

Emma has no interest in rehashing the experience, but so as not to come across as overly secretive, she offers a very quick summary—downtown Manhattan alleyway; possible robbery gone wrong; the killer never apprehended—but doesn't mention when the crime happened.

"Oh, Emma, gosh, how tough it must have been," Addison says when she finishes. "To lose a husband so young and in such a horrible way."

"Yes, very tough."

Because what could she say instead? *To tell you the truth, not so tough. I married a smart, ambitious man who seemed fairly easygoing and fun when he was in business school, but the minute he found himself in a high-pressure job became sullen, critical, and downright nasty. At least to me.*

"But then you met the fabulous Tom," Addison says warmly, interrupting her train of thought. "I'm really glad this story has a happy ending."

"Thanks, me, too. I'd love to reschedule if you're willing to chance another visit." She forces a chuckle. "I'll try to keep the cops away this time."

"Of course. I know this is short notice, but are you free tomorrow? And you could come to my place this time since you have so much on your plate."

"Oh, that's sweet of you. Actually, I could stop by at around nine thirty if that works for you. Tom's playing golf tomorrow and he won't even miss me."

"Perfect. I'll text you my address."

Okay, good, she thinks as she signs off. Not only is Addison not wigged out about yesterday, but Emma's pretty sure her new friend will be discreet.

By the time Tom returns, she's dressed for the ride, brought their bikes and helmets into the driveway, and gathered snacks and water bottles. They do a quick confab and agree on a picturesque route they've done several times before.

It's also the route they took on their very first date—or their first date if she doesn't count the awkward midday meal at a Westport restaurant.

About three weeks after they'd met in his office, Tom had asked Emma to lunch—to pick her brain about the idea for a possible ad campaign, he'd said, but she knew it went beyond that. She felt sure he'd experienced the same spark that she had in his office. Emma was still unready to even think about exploring the attraction, and yet she'd been unable to bring herself to turn him down.

At the restaurant, she'd discovered that the spark was still there, more, actually, like an electric current this time, but she'd felt suddenly tongue-tied and ill at ease. Toward the end of the meal, she knocked over her water glass and watched in horror as half the contents splashed into Tom's lap. He laughed it off good-naturedly, but she'd been mortified.

When Emma returned home that night to her Manhattan studio, she'd told herself that maybe it was all for the best, that her nervousness was proof that it *was* too soon, that it might be ages until she felt less emotionally stunted. And yet as the hours passed, she found herself resenting that conclusion. Her marriage had been joyless, nothing to grieve over, so how long was she really supposed to wait?

A few days later, she sent Tom an email: If I promise to bring a plastic tarp for your lap, can we try another lunch? My treat this time.

He'd suggested a Saturday afternoon bike ride instead, and other little excursions followed after that, including several walks on Compo Beach along the Long Island Sound. It was during one of the first outings that Emma told him about the murder. Tom listened sympathetically, and she could tell he now understood her tentativeness and respected her need to let things between them evolve slowly.

When they made love for the first time, they'd been seeing each other for more than two months. She was crazy about him by then, in an intense, ecstatic way she'd never felt with anyone else, and she already knew so much about him—his essentially happy childhood, the crazy years of getting the agency off the ground, the grief over losing Diana that had taken longer than expected to ebb.

And he knew almost everything about Emma, too. Except how deeply troubled her marriage had been and the fact that she had faked her tears over Derrick's death. She hadn't dared to tell him.

"Hey, I've got a thought," Tom calls out from just ahead of her on the path. They've been biking for close to two hours now and are headed back toward Westport. "There's one of those little hot dog stands near here with outdoor picnic tables. Want to eat there instead of in town?"

"Sure, why not?" she says. "It's too nice to be indoors."

They end up ordering tuna melts instead of hot dogs, along with huge plastic cups of Coke, and devour their meals at a table outdoors, with the sun pleasantly in their eyes.

"Man, this is good," Tom says, grinning.

"I know, I feel twelve years old again—in a good way."

These are the kind of easygoing moments Emma relishes with Tom, even more than their date nights at fancy restaurants, dinner parties at the homes of his impressive friends, or the long weekend trips they've taken to places like Nashville, Montreal, and Savannah. In the first months of their marriage, she'd waited for the other shoe to drop, for a sharp retort or out-of-the-blue insult, but Tom turned out to be the Tom who's sitting across from her now, exactly who she thought he was.

As she wipes grease from her hands, she notices Tom's staring at their bikes, leaning up against the clapboard building.

"I've never asked you this," he says. "Who taught you to ride a bike?"

Emma smiles. "My grandfather on my mother's side.

Griff and I used to stay with him and my grandmother when my parents took off for Europe in the summers. It was always heavenly. How about you?"

"My mom did, actually. Though overall she was a really good mother, she could be a little distant at times, so when she volunteered for the job, I was thrilled."

He starts to ask another question, but his phone rings, a shrill tone disrupting the tranquil moment. "Ugh, work," he says, glancing at the screen.

"Taylor?" If Taylor Hunt, his chief of staff, is calling him on a weekend, there must be a fire to put out.

"No, it's Justine." He taps the phone and asks her what's up.

As Tom listens patiently to his number two's explanation, which seems complicated, Emma studies his face, appreciating not only how attractive her husband is but also how open and amiable he looks in neutral. Over the years, Derrick's default expression became an ugly scowl.

Eventually Tom interrupts, asking, "Where are you, Justine?" Emma can see some consternation in his eyes now, but he doesn't let it leak into his voice. He nods. "All right, I'll swing by in about an hour and we'll get it straightened out."

He shakes his head in frustration as he disconnects from the call.

"Is it about the Chicago pitch?" Emma asks.

"No, there's a problem with one we're doing later this week. Apparently, part of the data is flawed, and it invalidates some of our proposals."

"Ugh, I'm sorry. Justine's in the office?"

"Yeah, and I could probably figure this out remotely, but

it means I'd be back and forth with her for the rest of the day. So I need to drop by. I'm sorry."

"Don't worry about it, Tom," Emma says sincerely. He never makes her feel like she takes a back seat to his work. "I've got plenty to do this afternoon."

They ride back to the house, and after Tom helps Emma mount the bikes in the garage, he quickly changes into jeans and a polo shirt.

"I'll be back as soon as I can," he says and kisses her tenderly on the mouth. He starts for his car, and then turns back. "You feeling a little better now, sweetheart? I sense being out on the bike did you good."

"Yes, much better."

Which isn't really the truth. All during their ride Emma had tried to focus on the fresh, bright green foliage and the hypnotic sound of their bike wheels kicking up stones along the path, anything but Webster, but she hasn't been able to drive the detective from her thoughts.

Is Webster making calls right now? she wonders. Probing around, digging through her past, flicking through paperwork? It is a Saturday, but don't some cops work on weekends?

Whatever the case, Emma feels the need to take more control of the situation. As soon as she's back inside, she shoots Dunne another email:

> If it's at all possible, can you call me this
> weekend instead of Monday? I really need
> to talk to you.

~

After changing her clothes, Emma makes a quick run to FedEx to mail a gift for her friend Bekah's daughter, who's about to turn one. She's only been home a few minutes when she hears a vehicle slow in the street outside the house and guesses that Tom must have handled the work crisis faster than anticipated. But the car never pulls into the driveway, so she makes her way to the front of the house and peers out the window. To her shock, Kyle Rand, her former brother-in-law, is striding across the lawn toward her front door, in that imposing way that reminds her so much of Derrick's stick-straight posture and decisive gait.

What the hell is *he* doing here?

7

Then

THE FIRST PEOPLE SHE SET EYES ON AFTER RETURNING from the morgue were Kyle and his wife, Jackie. Emma had wanted to avoid seeing them for a while, at least until her brother, Griffin, arrived, but she sensed that the longer she put them off, the bigger an issue it would be. So, finally, she'd called Kyle back and said they should come to the house as soon they were up for it.

They arrived around two o'clock, tall and slim Jackie teetering in heels and toting a cloth bag from a gourmet food store, and Kyle following behind her, looking shell-shocked. In her mind, he'd always been a bit of a bulldozer, a "let me talk to the manager" kind of guy, and she'd expected that after the initial shock of the news wore off, he'd go on a tear about police incompetence or New York City going to hell. That was part of the reason she hadn't wanted to break the news to him herself.

But she heard nothing like that as he sat in her living room. Though she'd always suspected that he and Derrick spent time together mainly out of a WASP-y sense of duty rather than a deep love for each other, Kyle seemed truly broken by his brother's death, subdued that afternoon into long stretches of silence.

"I feel so fucking guilty," he finally managed to say. His pale brown eyes, the exact color Derrick's had been, found hers for the first time that day, and she did her best not to look away. "I was sitting in our den last night, eating a pizza and drinking a Heineken, congratulating myself on how sweet my life was, and some maniac was killing my brother."

"Kyle, you can't possibly blame yourself in any way," Emma said.

He ran his hands through his hair for the umpteenth time. "Have you heard anything else?"

"No, though I'm supposed to talk to the police again tomorrow."

"Christ, I should have listened to my gut. As I told them, Derrick sounded off when I spoke to him on Friday morning. Did he say anything to you? Anything at all?"

He *had* seemed grouchy to her that morning, guzzling an espresso before grunting a goodbye, but by then, what else was new? And she certainly wasn't going to tell anyone about it.

"No, nothing."

Later, once the three of them had picked at the poached salmon and salad Jackie had laid out, Kyle seemed a bit more collected, and Emma broached the subject of the funeral. She'd known from Derrick that Kyle, the oldest, had been the one who'd orchestrated family events when his mother and father were alive, took care of the parents' property during their frequent travels abroad, and arranged *their* funeral service and burial, and though she generally bristled at his need to take charge, she was hoping for that now. He told her he'd be glad to set everything in motion with the funeral home he'd dealt with before.

"We want to help as much as possible," Jackie said, without a hint of her usual arrogance. "Just tell us what you need."

She'd never been close to Jackie, who still called herself a stay-at-home mom though her son, Ben, was now fifteen. And Emma didn't get the marriage. In her own case, she'd allowed herself to be blind to Derrick's flaws, but she sensed Jackie had always seen Kyle for who he was, and she accepted it all in exchange for a big house, a luxurious lifestyle, and plenty of designer clothes.

"Thank you, Jackie, I will," Emma said, though she couldn't imagine anything more she would ask of them.

"And I'm sorry I made it all about me earlier," Kyle said. "We know how devastating this must be for you."

Emma had wept before they arrived, spent from stress, and she was relieved that she must look distraught to them.

"Yes, I—I still can't believe Derrick's really not here anymore. That he's never coming home."

"Sorry if this is too painful a question, Emma, but I don't think I ever knew, how did you two meet?" Jackie asked, her mouth turned down.

Emma shook her head. "I'm fine talking about it. We met at a party."

It was a holiday gathering on the Upper West Side of

Manhattan, given by a business school pal of Derrick's who she knew from her ad agency days. Derrick had seemed as instantly enamored of her as she was with him, and she wasn't surprised when he wasted no time calling her. He was smart, attractive in a kind of straight-arrow way—short brown hair, cleanshaven—and though he could act uptight in public, their time alone together was for the most part pleasantly laid-back.

For her birthday a few months later, he gave her a stunning bracelet from David Yurman, the first of several over the next months. It seemed to be a sign that he was viewing things fairly seriously, more seriously than she'd realized. She knew that on paper he was the kind of man her parents would have envisioned for her and that she'd even envisioned at times for herself, but was there anything wrong with that? She liked him, loved him really, sensed that they could have a fulfilling life together, and she couldn't help but be moved by what he'd gone through, losing both parents several years before they met. When he proposed, it seemed like the right next step.

There were tiny red flags, though, even then. Emma's work never seemed to hold much interest for him, and his questions about her weekday life were perfunctory, but she told herself that data could make the best people's eyes glaze over if they didn't have an instinctive love for it as she did.

Derrick also tended to get sulky, and he snapped at her occasionally, what she might have once defined as biting her head off, but she chalked up those conflicts as the kind of rough spots all couples experienced. And she knew that her tendency to get a little manic or fretful at times—about her fledgling company, about life in general—worked on his nerves, and it was something she wanted to tame.

It wasn't until a few months after Derrick finished his MBA, and shortly before their wedding, that his behavior turned ugly at times. He'd gone to work at Alta by then and though he'd been so eager for the job, the pace was apparently much faster than what he'd experienced in the packaged food industry and the demands greater, which left him in a constant state of agitation. His boss, he ranted to Emma, was both gutless and overbearing, and some of his colleagues were untrustworthy. From what she could tell, he kept up a good front at work and handled office politics adroitly, but he began to bring his stress home every night and dump it at her feet as if she was somehow to blame. He barked at her more and more and seemed to find endless things to be annoyed about.

She felt like a traveler who starts off to explore a foreign city, game for adventure and a look at the unknown, and accidentally ends up in a forbidding neighborhood, one ripe with a sense of imminent danger.

A couple of times Emma considered calling off the wedding, but her parents had already dropped a bundle on the reception and booked their flights from London, and Derrick's sister was flying in from Melbourne with her husband and young children. So she convinced herself that things would get better once he felt more secure at work and they weren't caught up in planning a big reception and honeymoon.

And Emma did what she could to improve the dynamic,

expressing to Derrick how upsetting his behavior could be. For a while at least, he'd make a point of apologizing, and life would return to normal.

But after the wedding, he seemed to find endless things to criticize—her choice of outfit, the way she used her hands when she told a story, and, once, the fact that she'd managed to catch a cold the week he had an important meeting—and he would sometimes go for days without speaking to her because of some infraction on her part that he'd be unable to fully explain.

By the end of the first year of marriage, the truth was like a black, gaping hole that couldn't be ignored: she'd made a colossal mistake and there was no way of fixing the relationship. Yet the idea of extricating herself was daunting. For starters, she loathed the idea of failing, of looking—especially to her parents—like some Hollywood type whose marriage had the shelf life of a Bic pen.

And then there was her company, which had just begun to really take off. She had a full-time assistant by then, and Eric had come onboard, too. To pay their salaries she'd scaled hers back, relying on Derrick's paycheck for living expenses. If she blew up her marriage, she'd have to fire Eric. Her rent-free office above the garage would have to go, too.

But finally, Emma stopped worrying about any of that. She knew she had to save herself before his behavior escalated into something even scarier and/or before it eroded any more of who she was. She kept her head down at home and worked like crazy, signing up as many new clients as possible so that she could survive on her own. She told no one what was going on—not her parents, not her brother, not even

Bekah, her closest friend since college—but she was laying the groundwork to succeed on her own.

"Who'd like coffee?" Jackie asked, dragging Emma back to the present.

"None for me, thanks," she said. "And to tell you the truth, I think I need to go upstairs and collapse."

Of course, they'd both said, and within minutes they were mercifully gone.

Rather than trudge upstairs, Emma flopped on the couch in the small family room off the kitchen so that she'd hear her brother's knock when he arrived from the airport in Newark. Though her parents hadn't managed to snag a flight that day, her brother would be there soon.

She let her eyelids droop closed. Her nausea had returned with a vengeance. Was it from stress, she wondered, or the salmon, or sheer disgust from faking it so much with Kyle and Jackie?

Emma didn't regret faking it, though. There'd really been no choice. The only regret she had was the fact that someone like her, who as a respected trend forecaster was supposed to read tea leaves so brilliantly and glimpse what the future held, hadn't envisioned how her life would unspool this way.

She could never let that happen again.

8

Emma steps back from the window and pins herself against the wall, not wanting Kyle to see her. *Can I pretend no one's home?* she wonders. But then she realizes the likely reason for the visit. He's obviously been contacted by Webster, too, and wants to talk to her about it. And if that's the case, she absolutely has to hear him out.

"Hello, Emma," he says when she opens the door. He's dressed in crisp chinos and a blue-and-white-striped dress shirt, and a navy sweater draped around his neck. Kyle, she's always noted to herself, is the kind of guy who likes you to know he went to boarding school, either by dropping that fact into conversation five minutes after he's met someone or telegraphing it through a preppy look that went out of style a couple of decades ago.

"Hi, Kyle."

"You've gone blonder," he says, his tone making it sound closer to a vague taunt than a compliment.

"Right. What can I do for you?"

"I wanted to chat for a minute. Would you mind if I came in?"

She *would* mind. Not only does she dislike Kyle now more than ever, but his presence never fails to conjure up Derrick. She has to make nice, though, and more importantly, she needs to be looped in about Webster.

"Um, okay. But unfortunately, it can't be for long, I'm afraid. We have plans."

"Don't worry, I've got places to be myself."

Of course he does. When she was married to Derrick, she was aware that Kyle and Jackie had a very active social life, centered largely around other members of their Bronxville country club, some of whom were also clients of his hedge fund. She'd known, too, that Kyle had come close to floundering when he first launched the firm in his twenties, but he eventually pulled things together and the business seemed to thrive after that.

She and Derrick had rarely socialized with him and Jackie, but Kyle always managed to fill them in on their life with braggy asides about everything from their friends to the landscaper to the current speed of his tennis serve. And his business triumphs, too.

This is actually the second time he's showed up here at the house uninvited and without warning. The first was nine months ago, right after she and Tom moved in, with a box of some paperwork he claimed she might need but definitely didn't. He'd met Tom that day, which Emma knew was the real motivation behind his visit. Kyle clearly wanted to get a good look at her new husband, her new home, and the brand-new world she'd forged for herself.

Today, he follows her into the living room, where she pauses smack in the center to indicate that she won't be offering him a seat. With hands stuffed inside his pants pockets, Kyle swings his gaze around the space and nods appreciatively, though there's the trace of a snarl on his lips.

"Wow, you've really gone to town since I was last here," he says. "Very impressive."

Go along. Keep making nice, Emma warns herself.

"Thank you, Kyle."

"Of course, if anyone knows what the hot trends in decor are, it's you, Emma. . . . Where's Tom?"

"Running an errand."

"I'm glad you're here, though, because I took a chance coming on a summer weekend. I thought you mentioned Tom had a beach house somewhere."

The existence of Tom's Block Island house isn't anything she would have ever volunteered to Kyle, but he'd managed to worm it out of her on his previous visit.

"So what's up?" she says, steadying herself.

"You can't guess why I'm here?"

"I assume it has to do with the case being reopened?"

"Bingo. Did Webster call or show up in person?"

"She came by the house yesterday. I take it she spoke to you as well?"

"Yup. So what did you think?"

"Uh, she seems smart, capable. Willing to roll up her sleeves."

"I don't mean her personally. How did you like what she said about the investigation?"

Emma shifts from one foot to the other, hating his presence in a space that belongs to her and Tom. "Well, I'm certainly glad they're taking another look, but from what she indicated, it's a routine thing. There's no new evidence, unfortunately."

Kyle crosses his arms over his chest, and a citrusy cologne wafts off his body, too intense to be pleasant. "Hmmm," he says, and he lets the response hang there for a few ominous beats. "I don't think she was being a hundred percent straight with you."

Emma's heart skitters a little. "Oh, really?"

"Yeah. As we were talking, she kind of let slip that she was working from a recent tip."

This time her heart lurches, as if it's been rammed from behind. Where could a tip have come from? And why hadn't Webster disclosed it to *her*?

"Interesting. I mean, after all these months." She's trying to keep her tone casual, but she can hear the hint of alarm in her voice. "What do you think it could be?"

Kyle shrugs, but his eyes are leveled at hers. "No clue. She clammed up after that."

Emma wonders if he knows more than he's letting on, but she'd be a fool to reveal how desperate she is to hear. She shrugs, too. "Well, at least they seem invested."

"I just wish I'd had more to tell her. I passed along what I'd told the cops two years ago—that Derrick seemed edgy to me when we talked that Friday morning, like something was bugging him. But it wasn't something *you* noticed, right?"

Emma shakes her head. "Derrick seemed fine then, though we only had a quick coffee. The conference didn't start until noon that day, but he wanted to be on-site early."

"Well, let's hope this tip pays off and they nail someone this time." Kyle locks eyes with her again and grabs his chin between his thumb and forefinger, stroking it a few times. "Are you still in touch with that lawyer friend you used? What was his name—Peter Dunne?"

"He wasn't actually a friend, so there wouldn't be any reason for me to stay in touch with him." She's hardly going to confess to Kyle that she's been practically stalking Dunne since the detective left.

"Huh. Since this is heating up again, it might be good to circle back to him."

It feels like he's toying with her now, *implying* something. She can't take another minute of it.

"I'm afraid I really have to get moving, Kyle. Thanks for stopping by, and please give my best to Jackie."

"And you give my best to Tom, okay?"

She practically herds him from the room and out onto the stoop. "Will do. Bye" is all she says as she shoves the door closed after him.

Turning the lock, she exhales loudly. And then, behind her, she hears the faint, receding sound of footsteps. She spins around, but there's no one there. Surely it's not Tom, because he would have announced his presence.

Cautiously, Emma moves down the hall, past the stairs and the dining room, but the house appears empty. She also checks the screened room that opens onto the patio and finds no one there, either. Is she so on edge that her imagination is playing tricks on her?

Finally, she makes her way into the kitchen and jerks back in surprise when she finds Brittany standing by the island and holding a plum from the bowl on top of it. She looks as though she's been in the room for a while, but Emma realizes it must have been her footsteps in the hall, which means Brittany probably overheard at least part of the conversation with Kyle. Though she's never spoken to Brittany about the murder, she's aware that Tom has shared the broad strokes of the story with her, and Emma assumes the girl has done a Google search, reading through the three days' worth of news coverage. What she doesn't want is Brittany knowing anything beyond that and certainly not that the police have dropped by the house.

"Oh, hi," Brittany says in what Emma is sure must be feigned surprise.

"When did you get back?" she asks, a little more sharply than she intends.

"Around one. I ended up coming home earlier than planned, and I've been upstairs in my room."

So she must have been here when Emma and Tom returned from the bike ride but never made her presence known.

"My former brother-in-law stopped by a minute ago," Emma says. "If I'd known you were here, I would have introduced you."

"I heard a car leave, but I came down the back stairs, so I didn't see who was here."

Brittany's expression gives nothing away, but Emma's almost sure she's lying.

"No worries. How was the evening with your friend?" Emma asks, strolling toward the island and sliding onto one of the bar chairs. Brittany's wearing a vintagey short-sleeved white shirt with a Peter Pan collar, and though not the same period as her 1920s bob, they somehow work together, giving her a kind of old-fashioned but cool aspiring career-girl look.

"Good. She made a big chef's salad for us."

"She lives right in town?"

"Uh-huh. Her parents got her an apartment here."

"How nice you've made friends with another intern. Maybe the two of you could come by the studio one day and sit in on one of the brainstorming sessions Eric and I do. It would be a chance to see another side of marketing."

Emma is treated to a tight smile, like she's a tricky customer bothering a busy receptionist. "That's nice of you, but we aren't supposed to cut out during the day."

"Right." As if Brittany couldn't ask her stepdad for a hall pass to explore something new. But Emma wants to make a connection and moves on to plan B. "Then how about having your friend join us here for dinner one night?"

This time Brittany wrinkles her small, pert nose. "I don't know if that would be a good idea. I mean, she's in awe of Tom like everyone else there, and I'm sure she'd love to see this incredible house of his, but there's already a little bit of weirdness over me having access to him that nobody else does, and it wouldn't seem fair to give a friend special access, too."

There's an implied dig in there, about the house being *Tom*'s, but Emma lets it go and nods. "Got it."

"Where is Tom, anyway?"

"He had to run by the office for a bit, and then later, for dinner, we'll probably grab a pizza in town. Would you like to join us?"

"I appreciate the offer, but I think I'll stay in and watch a show I've been wanting to see."

She hasn't, Emma notices, taken a bite from the plum yet.

"There are plenty of those premade meals we order in the freezer, and stuff for a salad, too. Just help yourself."

"Thank you. . . . I was going to make myself a cup of tea. Would you like one?"

Okay, that's nice enough, Emma thinks, but she declines graciously, saying she has something she needs to do upstairs. Not only has she had enough of Brittany for the moment, but she's too rattled from seeing Kyle to engage in any more small talk.

On the second floor, Emma slips out onto the balcony outside their bedroom and collapses onto one of the lounge chairs. She can blow off the exchange with Brittany, especially knowing she'll be gone in a matter of weeks, but the one with Kyle is another story. *Is he full of it?* she wonders. *Has there really been a tip, and if so, what could it possibly be? Something about her?*

Webster knows she didn't shoot her husband. Everything the cops went through twenty-seven months ago, including her cell-phone and E-ZPass records, validated the fact that she was home in New Jersey the entire night of the murder. And they never found any evidence suggesting she'd paid someone to lure Derrick to that alley and do the deed for her, either.

What Webster is certainly wondering, however—just as the detectives assigned in the past must have wondered—is whether Emma really *had* paid someone to pull the trigger and had just been clever enough not to leave a single clue behind.

9

Then

IT WAS EMMA'S BROTHER WHO FIRST SAID IT OUT LOUD, BUT the idea had wormed its way into her mind hours earlier, as she stood shivering on First Avenue with Detective Lennox and he announced that the police were eager to speak to her again.

"Em, you need a lawyer," Griffin told her, and though his voice was low and weary from jet lag, she could see the conviction in his hazel eyes. It was ten at night and they were sitting in the little family room off the kitchen, Emma curled up in an armchair, and her brother on the couch, with his two long legs splayed across the coffee table.

She nodded. "You're right. But I don't even know where to start."

"I took the liberty of calling a friend of mine from college, a guy in the federal prosecutor's office in New York, and he recommended a defense lawyer named Peter Dunne. Said he's brilliant."

"I'll get in touch tomorrow, though I'm sure it's too late for my next meeting with the cops." Lennox had wasted no time—he'd called her right before Kyle and Jackie arrived and arranged for her to come to the station the next day.

"Can't you postpone?" Griffin asked.

She shook her head. "My gut tells me it would look bad to put it off."

When Emma showed up the next day for the interview, the small, sterile interview room she was led to made her heart start to race, but Lennox was cordial at first, like he'd been previously. After a while, however, the mood slowly began to shift, like a fog that rolls in from the water almost imperceptibly but eventually envelops you. He announced they were leaning away from the idea of a robbery gone wrong. There were no signs of a struggle or of Derrick resisting, so why would a mugger have shot him? And there'd been no similar crimes in the area.

"Can you think of anyone at all who might have wanted to hurt your husband?" Lennox asked. She heard something crisper in his tone than when he'd voiced the same question at the house, and to her dismay, she'd felt her face reddening and her breaths quickening.

And that's when she knew: he thought she might be behind the whole thing. Not as the shooter—they probably already had evidence she'd never left the house—but as someone who'd *paid* the shooter. At one point she caught a look between Lennox and the other detective, nothing more than a micro-expression, but she'd learned to pay attention to soft data like that and this one translated as *Are you picking up what I am?*

Emma felt gripped by fear, and it was a struggle to get through the rest of the interview. She hired Dunne later that day.

To Emma's shock she became a person of interest in Kyle's mind as well. Not right away. In the days immediately following the murder, he continued to be supportive and they sat side by side with his sister at the funeral service. After Emma's parents and brother flew back to the UK, Kyle started stopping by the house every few days—sometimes with Jackie, sometimes alone—to check on her.

No, the moment things shifted was when Kyle learned she was selling the house.

"Wow, why the hurry?" he asked with a furrowed brow.

"It's painful being here alone," Emma fudged, but he looked at her differently after that, always with a hint of suspicion in his eyes, and the next few times he dropped by, he tried baiting her with his comments.

"Any theories?" he asked her one day as she sorted through a hall closet, choosing items to keep or give away.

"Theories?" she said, confused.

"About who could have done it?"

"Nothing beyond what I told the police. About the contractor. And the former colleague who left the company."

"You really think your contractor might have staked out Derrick and shot him because he insulted the guy's grouting skills?"

"No, I don't believe either of them was responsible, and I told the police that. But they asked me to relate anything suspicious no matter how insignificant it seemed."

"Make a guess then. Who do you think did it?"

"Kyle, I have no idea. The whole thing is a horrible mystery."

And then a few days later:

"We need to talk about the paintings," he'd said.

"Okay."

"You know you don't get them, right?"

"Of course, Kyle. I know they go to you and your sister. Derrick always made that clear."

Was he wondering if she was trying to figure out a way to claim the paintings for herself?

And the last time she saw Kyle before moving he simply asked, "How are you *doing*, Emma?" with his head cocked, waiting, she thought, for any hint of insincerity in her response.

He also thinks I ordered a hit man, she thought, her stomach churning.

By then, the police had requested a third interview, simply to pick her brain, they told her, and this time Dunne accompanied her. The questions were more of the same, asked in slightly different ways though, and she sensed they believed that if they made her cover the same ground again and again, she'd begin to falter.

It felt as if a net was dropping on top of her, pinning her facedown. Afterward Dunne warned her that the police might try to obtain a warrant for her laptop and he needed to be sure she'd gone through her emails as he'd suggested and made certain there was nothing the police would find suspicious.

"Yes, I've checked, and it's all fine," she told him.

"What about your internet search history?" he asked.

"There's nothing incriminating there, either."

That wasn't a hundred percent true, however. Early that year she'd hunted online for divorce attorneys, planning to call one when she was ready, but even in her crazed, stressed state, she'd been smart enough to do the search in a public library three towns away. There was surely no way the cops would connect that search to her.

She didn't share her actions with Dunne, though. She told him only what he needed to know and nothing more.

10

ADDISON'S PLACE TURNS OUT TO BE A SLEEK-LOOKING town house in a development that's lushly landscaped, backing up onto a wooded area. As Emma waits for her to come to the door, she takes a deep breath and savors the scent of freshly cut grass. This is just what she needs right now, she thinks. Coffee, a new friend, and conversation to distract her wheels from turning.

Over pizza in town last night, Tom had urged her not to let Kyle's visit—and his revelation about the tip—rattle her, that it might be Kyle yanking her chain, but she's had a hard time letting go of it.

"Come in," Addison says, opening the door with a beaming smile.

Emma follows her from the small foyer into the living/dining room. Though the layout of the space is pleasing, with big windows facing onto a thicket of evergreens, the furniture is sparse, and the room lacks any accent pieces or hints of personality. As Addison mentioned the other day, some of the artwork is on the floor, resting against walls.

"What an enchanting view you have," Emma says, focusing on the positive.

"It *is* nice, isn't it?" Addison says. "I just hope that you'll come another time and be able to say, 'And I *love* the way you've decorated it.' . . . Coffee? I've got a pot brewed but there's tea, too, if you prefer."

"Coffee would be great."

Before retreating to the kitchen, Addison motions for Emma to take a seat, and so she chooses the midnight-blue couch. On the coffee table in front of her are a bowl of grapes and clementines and a basket of tiny bright yellow corn muffins with a stack of small plates next to it.

"Have you lived in Westport for a while?" Emma asks when Addison returns carrying two white mugs with steam ribboning from the top.

"About three years. I'd lived in Stamford when I was married, which I hated, so after my divorce, I thought I'd try Manhattan on for size. I rented in Midtown and commuted by train to campus a few days a week but eventually decided to move back to the area."

"Did the commute wear you down?"

"No, I missed the damn sky too much," Addison says, setting down the mugs and taking a seat in the armchair across from her.

"Well, there's plenty of that here," Emma says, smiling. "I love the city myself, but I've totally succumbed to Westport's charms."

"But Friday couldn't have been any fun for you. You must still be reeling."

Emma figured Addison might want to follow up about the detective's visit, but it's a topic she has no intention of lingering on. "I'm actually fine, thanks. But I appreciate you asking."

"So what kind of steps are they going to be taking next?"

"Oh, gee, I don't really know," Emma tells her. "They haven't shared the specifics."

Addison's large blue eyes shift from curious to perplexed. "You aren't being kept abreast of what they're doing? I would think that would be a top priority for them."

"I'm sure I'll hear if there's any kind of breakthrough, but they don't take family members step-by-step as they go."

Addison shakes her head, looking dismayed. "It's got to be so frustrating. I focused a bit on crime victims in one of the advanced sociology classes I taught last year and this sort of thing frustrates families to no end. They can't get answers."

Still intent on moving off the subject, Emma plucks a corn muffin from the basket, sets it on a plate, and lets her gaze wander to a large abstract painting resting on the floor.

"You know, there's something fun about the way some of the art looks against the wall. Maybe you can start a trend and then you'll never have to hang them."

"Wouldn't *that* be nice, which reminds me of something I've wanted to ask you. How do you actually spot a trend in the making? Are you just a great observer?"

Finally, a safe topic, Emma thinks. "In most cases, it's a little more scientific than that. We use software with our influencer surveys that picks up repetitions and patterns, and from there we can see what might be brewing. But sometimes I manage to spot something simply by paying attention to soft data, stuff I see and hear. I live by 'the rule of three.' If you come across something once, it's simply chance, twice it's a coincidence or a curiosity, but three times it's a pattern or trend."

"Ahh, the rule of three." Addison sighs. "I wonder if there's some version of it I could use when it comes to meeting men."

"Is it tough finding good ones around here?"

"Sure, but I think it's tough *anywhere*. How did you meet men before Tom? Blind dates? Online?"

Emma shakes her head. "Uh, neither of those. I wasn't looking yet, to tell you the truth."

"Oh, of course. Dating must have seemed so daunting after you lost your husband, considering all you were dealing with."

Emma lets the comment hang and tastes the corn muffin, even though she's not hungry. "Delicious," she says, her mouth half full.

"So glad you like them. I might not be much of a cook, but I'm an excellent shopper." Addison tosses her hair back, takes a sip from her coffee, and sets down the mug down with a clunk, then leans back and levels her gaze at Emma with a smile. "I'm really glad we were able to reschedule again so quickly. I just have to say how much I admire you, Emma."

"Thank you for that. The feeling is totally mutual. I guess we've both worked hard and have good careers to show for it."

"True, but what I mean is how well you've handled what

you've been through. That kind of trauma would level some-one else."

God, Emma thinks, *will she please let go of this?*

She shakes her head. "Thank you, but there's really noth-ing to admire. People go through all sorts of awful things," she says, still unsure how to disengage. There are only so many muffins she can stuff in her mouth as a diversion.

"But losing a loved one to murder has got to be brutal."

"Well, it all depends on your circumstances at the time. What's going on in your life. In my case . . ." She hesitates, not certain where the hell she's headed with this, and when she glances up again, she sees that Addison's eyes have wid-ened.

"Wait," Addison says, even more animated, "are you try-ing to tell me that the loss wasn't really all that hard for you?"

Emma jerks in her seat, taken aback. "Oh my god, no—um, that wasn't my point," she says, practically sput-tering. "It was *very* hard. What I meant about these things being different for different people is that the way you cope depends a lot on the support system you have. I was very lucky in that department. I mean, my friends and family ral-lied around."

She tells herself to shut up and move on, that someone could have explained quantum physics in less time.

Addison straightens her back and clasps a French mani-cured hand to her chest. "Emma, I'm terribly sorry. That was stupid of me—to put words in your mouth. I can't believe I did that."

"Don't worry about it," she says, waving her hand for em-phasis. But inside, she's horrified. Regardless of what Addison is admitting to, the woman has somehow managed to suss out the truth and wrench it out into the open.

And it's the last thing Emma needs bouncing around the universe right now, not with the case reopening.

"No, it's completely my fault," Addison says. "I have this terrible habit of filling in the blanks when other people are talking, trying to show I'm really listening."

"Really, it's not a problem," Emma says, stealing a look at her watch. "But, um, you know what? You've made me see I really *am* still reeling from Friday. I should probably head home." She rises from the couch and picks up her purse from the floor, even though she's been there less than twenty minutes.

Now Addison is the one who seems flustered, scrunching her mouth in embarrassment. A few awkward moments ensue as her host attempts to apologize again, and Emma forces a smile, saying she'll call to reschedule.

After hurrying to her car, Emma flings herself into the front seat and then sits there catching her breath. She wonders if she made things worse by taking off, but at the same time she couldn't have stayed. Addison seemed unable to leave the subject alone. Maybe she's a gossip, Emma thinks, or one of those women who likes hoarding sad or salacious details about others, guaranteeing themselves a sense of smug satisfaction over not fucking up their own lives as badly.

Could I be partly to blame? Emma asks herself. Maybe she's more transparent than she realizes, letting her true feelings about Derrick leak into the air like a toxic gas, noticeable to someone with a nose for that sort of thing. If that's true, Webster might have picked up on those feelings, too.

⁓

What she needs, Emma decides, is a little time in nature to clear her head. She'll take a walk by the water, one of the things she loves to do most in Westport. After driving the short distance to Compo Beach, she exchanges her flats for a pair of sandals she stores in the trunk and joins the dozen or so people walking along the shoreline, some with their dogs. Though it's overcast today, the sun has begun to seep through the clouds in places, making the sky look like a piece of parchment paper lit from behind.

As Emma walks the beach, seagulls mew and swoop above her. There's a faint fishy smell to the air that she doesn't mind. This is the Long Island Sound, not the ocean, so the waves tend to be on the small side, and she lets the water fizz over her sandals a little.

I should never have bolted, Emma decides. Yes, Addison's probing had been distressing, but it would have been far better to change the subject firmly and hang for a while longer. Her hasty departure might have only confirmed to Addison that she has something to hide.

Get a grip, she tells herself. She's going to make matters worse if she allows any uncomfortable conversations to throw her into a tailspin.

Emma's phone rings just as she's turned around to head back to the car. She digs it from the back pocket of her jeans, expecting Tom will be on the other end, calling to let her know his ETA, but to her surprise the screen says Jessica Hawke—her mother's name.

"Hi, Mom, is everything okay?" Emma says in lieu of

hello. Because of their busy work schedules and the five-hour time difference, they usually plan their calls in advance, and there's rarely a random one.

"Yes, fine, Em, and sorry to phone out of the blue like this."

"Well, it's a lovely surprise. I hope the weather is as mild in London today as it is in Connecticut."

"I'm actually in DC at the moment—on a consulting job."

"*DC?*" Emma says, feeling a twinge of something that she can't identify. "As in Washington?"

"Yes, I had an emergency weekend meeting with a client who's based here."

Now Emma realizes what the twinge is trying to tell her. DC is only a three-hour Acela train ride away from Penn Station, and they could have met for a day in New York if her mother had been willing to come north. Or her mother could have stayed on till Stamford and visited Emma at her new home, which she hasn't seen yet. But she can't let moments like this sadden or frustrate her. As her brother and she accepted years ago, their parents *do* love them, simply not in the way their children would like to be loved and not nearly as much as their mother and father love each other.

"I was only able to get away from London for a day and a half," her mother adds, filling the silence and perhaps suspecting Emma's disappointment. "I'm actually at Dulles now, waiting in the lounge for my flight."

"Well, at least we're getting to speak while we're in the same time zone," Emma says, still walking and keeping her tone as cheery as possible. There's nothing to be gained with her mother by acting wounded.

"Yes, that *is* nice. So tell me—is everything all right?"

The question, delivered with such a deliberate tone, throws her. The jury's still out on whether Addison is a mind reader, but her mother definitely isn't, at least not as far as her daughter's life is concerned.

"Yes, Mom. By and large. Why do you ask?"

There's a pause while her mother takes a sip of something, probably an ice-cold chardonnay. Emma pictures her leaning back in her chair, probably dressed more elegantly than any other woman in the first-class lounge, her light brown hair in a French twist.

"Well, because I got a very odd call today from Kyle Rand."

Emma stops in her tracks. Why in the world would he be calling her mother? They'd had a small amount of one-on-one contact early in her marriage to Derrick. Kyle was intrigued with her mother's expertise in certain areas of finance and how it related to his burgeoning hedge fund, and once, when her parents were visiting from London, he even invited Jessica out for a drink so he could pick her brain. But that was ages ago, and it's hard to believe he even still has her number.

She tries not to betray her alarm. "Odd how?"

"He wanted to run something by me, an idea for an expansion within his own firm, and since I had a couple of minutes to spare, I offered to listen, though it turned out to be completely out of my wheelhouse. Then he brought up Derrick, saying they've reopened the investigation into his death. Is that true?"

"Yes, it's true. I was going to mention it when we spoke

on the phone next. They claimed it's a routine reopening of a cold case, and not based on any new evidence, so I'm afraid it'll be a dead end like the last time."

"Ah, I see. Well, we'll hope for the best."

"Back to Kyle for a second. It seems incredibly strange that he'd call you out of the blue, Mom."

"My sentiments exactly. And then he started asking questions about Tom."

"*Tom?*" Emma says, feeling her blood begin to boil. "What about him?"

"Not much, because I didn't allow Kyle to get too far. He wanted to know if I'd met him, and I said of course, and then he wanted to know what kind of guy I thought he was. I told him—as diplomatically as I could—that I didn't feel it was appropriate for us to be discussing your new husband. You were devastated by Derrick's death, but you had to move on with your life."

"That's a good answer, Mom," Emma says, glad that her mother shut Kyle down fast, which isn't really a surprise. Her mother might not be super loving and affectionate, but she's always been fiercely protective of Emma and her brother. "What was his response?"

"He apologized, and said it was only meant to be a friendly call, but his tone cooled considerably."

He's clearly up to something and Emma needs to figure out what it is. But first she has to get her mother off the phone, an unfamiliar move. Usually, it's her mother who's "afraid she has to dash."

"Mom, unfortunately I have to sign off now myself."

"No problem, I should be heading to the gate anyway."

"Have a good flight."

"And you're certain everything's all right?"

"Yes, sure, Mom. Take care."

"You, too, Emma."

The call over, she quickly hurries back to the parking lot, and once she's in the car, takes a minute to decide how to handle Kyle before tapping his number on her phone.

"Surprise, surprise," he says, though there's an alertness in his voice, as if he's been waiting to hear from her. "We're getting to chat twice in one weekend."

"My mother told me you called her. What was that about?"

"Huh, she didn't explain? I wanted to pick her brain about work."

"She said that, but she seemed to think you had more on your mind."

She lets it hang there, waiting to see how he'll fill the silence.

"Really? I think she's being overly sensitive."

Since he barely knows her mother, he has no idea how funny that comment really is.

"She said you started asking her about Tom."

"I merely wanted her impressions of the guy. Needless to say, I'm curious."

"Needless to say? Why would you have any interest in my marriage?"

Emma hears Kyle sigh and senses him weighing his words.

"Not your marriage per se," he says finally. "I'm curious about Tom himself. I mean, my brother was barely in the ground before you started dating him."

11

Kʏʟᴇ's ᴄᴏᴍᴍᴇɴᴛ ɪs ʟɪᴋᴇ ᴀ ɴɪᴄᴋ ꜰʀᴏᴍ ᴀ ᴋɴɪꜰᴇ. sʜᴇ ɴᴇᴇᴅs to end the call before things get any uglier.

"Goodbye, Kyle," she says. "Don't contact my mother again. And don't contact me again, either."

Emma disconnects before he has a chance to respond and then inhales deeply. *My brother was barely in the ground*, he'd said, an accusation crouching crocodile-like beneath the surface of those words.

She probably should have seen this coming. From the moment Kyle showed at the house with that box of papers, she sensed he was stewing over her marriage, that to him she might as well have been sipping Veuve Clicquot on Derrick's grave.

All by itself, his anger doesn't scare her. She faced it before and she can face it again. But what he intends to do with that anger is a different matter. Is he going to use it to try to make trouble for her?

Emma thinks suddenly of what he dropped about the

police receiving a tip. Tom had wondered whether Kyle was simply trying to get a rise out of her, but what if there *had* been a tip, one called in by Kyle himself?

Did you know my brother's widow got married again in a hot minute? she imagines him saying to one of the detectives. *You should take another look at her.*

Up until Friday, Emma had managed to go for days at a time without letting her thoughts drift to the period surrounding Derrick's death. Now, in the space of a few days, with Webster's visit, Addison's comments, and Kyle's fresh insinuations, everything is geysering all around her again.

She feels even more desperate to speak to Peter Dunne, to have him remind her that the cops didn't conclude she was a viable suspect during the first investigation and that nothing could have happened to make them change their minds. Unfortunately, she'll probably have to wait until tomorrow since Dunne might not respond to emails on weekends.

But no sooner has she driven home and let herself back into the house when her phone rings with Dunne's name on the screen. The urgent second email clearly did the trick.

"Emma, dear, how are you?" he starts. His voice is deep with what she's always considered a calm, soothing quality, but hearing it now—after she'd convinced herself that chapter of her life was closed—is like pressing on an old bruise and finding it still hurts.

"Oh, thanks so much for calling on the weekend," she tells him. Since she has no idea where Brittany might be lurking, she quickly slips out onto the patio. "I've been good in general, but as I said in the email, they're reopening the case."

"Tell me everything you've heard so far."

Though it's been two years since they were face-to-face, she pictures him easily: short brown hair, thinning a little on top, a strong nose, a full mouth with a tiny cleft in his lower lip. Nothing out of the ordinary, but his features come together in an attractive way, probably in part because of his extreme self-possession.

She runs through the highlights of Webster's unannounced visit as well as Kyle's claim about a tip. When she's done, a long sigh escapes her lips. "I know, I know," she adds. "It was a mistake to speak to the police without you present, but this detective caught me completely off guard."

Dunne chuckles dryly. "The reason the police show up out of the blue rather than making an appointment is that they *want* to catch you off guard."

"Do you think I created a problem for myself?"

"I can't say, Emma, since I wasn't in the room with you. I do know the police investigated you thoroughly in the past and apparently found nothing suspicious, but any time you talk to the police, you are in a danger zone—and that goes at least double when you talk without an attorney present. The police don't like it when a lawyer comes into the picture because it limits them in how hard they can push you. But that's the point. You need a lawyer there to keep things in line and to make a record of what you are being asked and what you are saying."

"She really just went over the same ground those other detectives covered two years ago, asking almost identical questions."

"The police will always ask many of the same questions that they asked previously, pushing you to confirm what they have from you in the prior police report and to provide more detail. Out of nervousness or an unwillingness to sign on to whatever they might think or claim that you said last time around, you could end up saying something that they view as inconsistent—and the police don't like inconsistencies. They start focusing on them."

Her stomach drops. Had she been inconsistent with Webster in some way she can't remember? "I feel like such an idiot," she says.

"Don't," Dunne assures her. "What I'd like is for you to reconstruct as much of the conversation with Detective Webster as you can, get it all down in a Word document, and email it to me today."

"I'll do that as soon as we're off the phone."

"Also shoot me Webster's contact info when you can. I'll call her and explain that you're happy the case has been re-opened, but she should deal directly with me going forward."

Emma exhales, feeling a swell of relief. It will cost her a pretty penny, but Dunne is on top of it. "Thank you, Peter."

"I'll also see if she says anything about this so-called tip. It's more than possible the police *do* have a lead, but she doesn't want to show her hand to you."

Why not? Emma wonders, her anxiety spiking again. Is it because the tip was about *her*?

"One last question before we hang up," Dunne adds. "What did Webster seem to know about Tom?"

"Uh, not very much. She did ask how the two of us met."

"That was her being coy—because I'm sure she already knows the answer. By now she's done a thorough background check on Tom."

"A *background* check?"

"Yes, determining if there have been any complaints against him, restraining orders, that type of thing. I should warn you that she'll also probably attempt to talk to him, too."

"Like show up at his office?"

"Showing up at his office is harassment, and there's no reason for it, but she might pay him a visit at home. Keeping things all very polite. But it's key for him to say he wants to have the conversation with a lawyer present—and it needs to be the right kind."

"I don't believe this. It's totally unfair to Tom and to me as well."

"I agree, but it's to be expected, Emma."

"What do you mean?"

"When cops take on an old case and there's no active trail to pick up again, they look for something new. And Tom is brand-new."

"Of course, he's new. Almost everything in my life since Derrick's murder is new."

"That's not what I mean exactly. You remarried—what?—only seventeen, eighteen months after the murder, and though I'm certainly not passing any judgment, it's the kind of detail that makes the police sit up and take notice."

With her heart taking off at a gallop, Emma finally realizes what Dunne is getting at. The cops aren't just eyeing *her* about the murder, they're eyeing her new husband, too. They're wondering whether she and Tom plotted Derrick's death together and paid someone to pull it off.

12

"BUT, PETER," EMMA SAYS, UNABLE TO DISGUISE THE NOTE of pleading in her voice, "I didn't even meet Tom until four months after Derrick died, and we didn't really start dating until a couple of months after that. Why would that be something to take *notice* of? Aren't I entitled to a life?"

"Of course you are, and let's not get ahead of things. Send me the email with your recollections from the interview and I'll check in with Detective Webster first thing tomorrow. Sound good?"

She doesn't want to let him go. Part of her believes that if he'd only allow her more time to explain, Dunne would see that there's nothing about Tom that should be a concern to either him or the police, but this is Sunday and he clearly has better things to do, maybe a golf game of his own. And then there's his $1,000 an hour fee to consider.

Emma says goodbye and shakes her head as she disconnects the call. She'd been secretly hoping that Dunne would say she had absolutely nothing to worry about, but the fact that he's not taking this lightly has her even more rattled than she was before the call.

Happy to have a task, she grabs her laptop from the kitchen and returns to the patio table, where she starts the document for Dunne, racking her brain for every possible thing she can remember from the conversation with Webster. Her anger flares several times as she considers what Dunne revealed, that Webster must have already checked out Tom, as well as their history as a couple. The detective's chatty inquiries about him were clearly pure bullshit.

Finally, Emma does a last read-through, attaches the file to an email and hits send, then sinks against the back of the teak chair. It's turned muggy out, and the air feels oppressive, adding to her sense that something she can't quite identify is closing in on her. She decides to seek refuge in the air-conditioned house.

As she steps into the kitchen, she's surprised to find Brittany there, dressed in a white terry cloth robe and peering intently into the fridge. She'd nearly forgotten Brittany was around.

"Morning," Emma says, though it's nearly midday.

Brittany swings her head around. "Oh, hi," she says sleepily. "I thought you might be off golfing with Tom."

"No, not my sport. But Tom should be back in an hour or so."

The girl resumes her search in the fridge, plucks out a small container of yogurt, and pushes the door closed with her hip.

"Would you like to have lunch with us?" Emma asks.

"Thanks, but I'm going to take the extra bike into town,

check out some of the new shops. But Tom texted me that he's going to make pasta tonight so I can catch up with guys then."

"Great, so glad you can join us." Emma wishes she meant it, wishes she liked Brittany better than she does, and that her stay here didn't feel like such a horrible imposition.

Shortly after Brittany departs for town, Tom arrives home with several containers of sushi and they sit down for a late lunch in the kitchen. He offers a few highlights from his golf game, but says he's more eager to hear about her morning. "Did Addison seem to take Friday's events in stride?" he asks.

"I guess, but it wasn't the best coffee date. I have the sense she might be a little, I don't know, gossipy, so I cut the visit short."

That's all she dares to share. She also decides not to burden Tom with details about the call she made to Kyle and the ugly reference he made to Tom.

"That seems smart, Em. I know there are some major gossips in this town, and talking about other people never leads anywhere good. Did you find something else to do with your morning?"

"I had a brief talk with Brittany, who's looking forward to your pasta tonight. And I heard from Peter Dunne."

"Oh, that's good."

"I don't know how good it was, actually. For starters, he made it very clear I shouldn't have spoken to Detective Webster on my own. He doesn't think I shot myself in the foot, but he warned me not to do it again."

"Okay, lesson learned."

"But here's the worst part. He thinks Webster will want to talk to you, too—and you'll need to have an attorney present, one with the right expertise."

"The police want to talk to *me*?" He laughs, setting down his chopsticks. "What could they think—that you might have blurted out something incriminating in your sleep, and they expect me to throw you under the bus?"

"Ha, no. Dunne just said when police do cold case investigations, they're always looking for something new to latch on to, and a new spouse falls into that category."

"You were hardly supposed to put your life on hold."

"I know, and I said the same thing to Peter, who agreed. But it's about perception—and also the timing. He said something about how soon afterward . . ."

She trails off, wondering whether Tom will grab the thread in his mind and begin to unspool it. Could the police really be thinking that the two of them have known each other far longer than they've let on, that she hired a hit man so she could be with him, that the two of them even cooked up the murder together? She's certainly not going to give this absurd theory any airtime by putting it into words, though.

Tom reaches across the table and cups one side of her face in his hand. "Em, trust me, I'm not afraid of this Webster woman, and you shouldn't be, either. And to hell with the timing. Scarlett O'Hara didn't wait to remarry, so why should you have?"

Emma chuckles at his comment, and she suddenly feels better. Maybe she's simply overreacting, jarred by her interactions with Kyle and Addison and by Dunne's sober tone.

The rest of the day goes better for her. She and Tom read in the den, sometimes sharing bits and pieces, and later she reviews the quarterly presentation she'll be doing at Halliday the next morning. Dinner, unfortunately, proves a bit challenging. Tom serves a delicious pasta feast as promised, but Brittany, up to her usual tricks, focuses almost totally on him. The only time she speaks to Emma is when she asks her to pass the bottle of sparkling water.

"Is there blue cheese in this?" Brittany quizzes Tom at one point.

"That's right. It's really a basic alfredo sauce but with some gorgonzola added."

"If you weren't busy running a company, you could host a cooking class from your kitchen," Brittany gushes. "I love the way you designed it, by the way." Once again she manages to imply that it's Tom's house, not both Emma's and his.

But Emma lets it roll off her back because she's trying to hold on to the good feeling of the afternoon. Tom has managed to tamp down her fears and help her see that it's silly to worry. No one's actually given her a reason to—at least not yet.

The next morning Tom and Brittany leave together for Halliday, but Emma's talk isn't scheduled until ten thirty, so she stops by the studio first to review her schedule quickly with Dario. His typically cheerful demeanor adds to her good mood. On her way to downtown Westport, she picks up a box of croissants for the attendees, having learned that almost all presentations are improved by the addition of free food.

By ten fifteen she's in the Halliday glass-walled conference room, pulling up the PowerPoint on her laptop, when she hears Tom's voice from somewhere down the hall. He mostly skips her talks because he senses his staff feels more free to ask questions when he's not in the room, so she knows she won't see him in the audience today.

Out of the corner of her eye she catches a flash of red and turns to see that Justine Carr, Tom's number two, has stuck her head in.

"Morning, Emma," Justine says, smiling in that slightly enigmatic way of hers. Justine's an attractive, arresting-looking woman, with flame-colored hair, green eyes, and creamy skin. And though she's always cordial, Emma's never quite sure of what she's thinking.

"Oh, hey, Justine. I'm so glad you can make it today."

"Actually, I only popped in to say hello. I'm slammed this week and won't be able to attend."

Makes sense, Emma thinks. She's probably still sorting out the problem from Saturday, though Tom hasn't brought up the subject again.

"Totally understand," she says. "If you get a chance to read the report and have any questions, just shoot me an email."

Justine places her hands on her hips. "Will do." She's wearing a sleeveless, moss-colored dress that shows off her perfectly toned arms, and she comes across today as confident and gutsy, the version of the woman Emma's most familiar with. There's no sign of the "deer-in-the headlights" expression Tom described after the Chicago trip. *Why the discrepancy?* Emma wonders. Maybe there's some problem in her personal life that rears its head once in a while. "And I wanted to say sorry for stealing Tom away on Saturday."

Emma smiles. "Don't worry about it. I had plenty to do on my own."

No sooner has Justine departed when other people begin to file in, thirty or so employees from both the creative and account sides of the business, as well as Taylor Hunt, Tom's chief of staff. Unlike many professional people with that title, Taylor's not particularly ambitious career-wise, but she's superefficient and goal-oriented. She previously assisted a colleague of his, and when she approached Tom after the job opened up several years ago, he figured it could work if he rethought the role. She monitors his schedule in a more global way than his assistant, Janice, does, keeps tabs on interdepartmental communication flow, and makes certain everything in the Halliday office is humming along.

The presentation goes well. Emma elaborates on the findings in the most recent *Hawke Report* and then opens it up for discussion. The attendees pepper her with thoughtful questions right up until eleven thirty. After she wraps up, they thank her enthusiastically, some grabbing croissants before they disperse.

As Emma's unhooking her laptop from the large-screen monitor, Taylor strolls to the front of room. She's a thirty-something Westport native with stick-straight blond hair cropped at her chin, dark blue eyes, a small, delicate mouth, and a preppy style, including pleated skirts, collared shirts, silk designer scarves for every season—some even by Burberry and Ferragamo—and suede headbands.

"Terrific job," she tells Emma in her clipped, precise way.

"Thanks, Taylor. I appreciate you showing up." There's no real reason for her to come to these talks, but Emma assumes she does so to stay in the loop.

"Well, I always learn something new. And it's the only time I see you anymore. By the way, I heard about your trip to Napa Valley in August. It sounds fantastic."

"Yes, we can't wait. What about you? Any special plans this summer?"

"My parents have a house in Maine, and I'm going there for ten days, but other than that, it doesn't look very exciting." She sighs. "It's hard to be single."

"Well, maybe you'll meet someone this summer."

Taylor rolls her eyes. "Dubious. Every guy my age in Westport seems to be taken."

"What about trying a dating app like Tinder or Bumble?"

"Ugh. Didn't you just tell the group that people are getting tired of swiping and want to meet romantic partners in real life?"

"From what we're seeing, yes, but I can't knock dating apps, either. A decent percentage of married couples meet that way."

Taylor tucks a piece of hair behind an ear. "Right, but I really want the real-life thing."

"Does it seem more romantic that way?"

"Just more natural, organic, I guess. Like you and Tom."

It's fairly typical of Taylor to act a little too familiar, and per usual, Emma shrugs it off. Taylor plays a key role for Tom, and Emma wants to stay on good terms with her. She offers a smile. "Well, yes, it's nice when it can happen that way."

"I mean, you two must have felt an instant connection at dinner. You don't get that from swiping."

Emma cocks her head. "Tom and I did meet pretty organically, but it was here at Halliday, not at a dinner."

Taylor shrugs. "Oh, I always assumed it was in Miami."

"*Miami?*" Emma is even more perplexed now.

"Yes, at that dinner you spoke at a couple of years ago. I remember it was about how young women's interest in sustainability was affecting what they purchased."

Okay, she *did* speak at a dinner in Miami to about forty or fifty people on that very subject. Avignon, the handbag company hosting the event, had wanted a short talk—no slides, just interesting revelations to engage their senior staff and guests toward the end of the meal. But she has no idea how Taylor knows about it.

"I'm not following," Emma says. "What's your connection to that dinner?"

"Avignon's a client of ours. I was there that night along with some people from Halliday."

"Small world," Emma says. "But I don't see what that has to do with me and Tom."

"He was with us. I assumed that's where the two of you met."

Emma's brow furrows as she tries to make sense of what she's hearing. Taylor can't possibly be right. If Tom had been there, he would have mentioned it to her at some point. The event had been in January, she remembers, about five months before she started at Halliday.

And, she thinks, with ballooning unease, *two months before Derrick's murder.*

13

Taylor, i think you're remembering wrong," emma says, trying not to sound anxious. "I mean, about that last part. Tom and I didn't meet until I started consulting here two summers ago through Scott Munroe."

You're protesting too much, she tells herself, but the last thing she needs right now is someone spreading the erroneous notion that she and Tom were an item before the murder, or even the possible fact that they'd been in the same room together. She can only imagine what Detective Webster would make of that tidbit.

Taylor shrugs. "Sorry, my mistake." Her expression still reads skeptical, but Emma decides the smartest response is to just shut up and beat a hasty retreat.

"Don't worry about it. . . . Have a nice day, Taylor." She offers a cheerful wave as she leaves the meeting room, but the conversation increasingly gnaws at her on the drive home. Once she's pulled into the garage, she racks her memory for as many details as possible about the Miami dinner.

It had actually been part of a large, three-day convention of small, boutique-style retailers. Emma had been recruited to give a keynote breakfast address on the major differences between Gen X, Gen Y, and Gen Z, but since she was already attending the convention, Avignon, one of the sponsors, hired her to also speak at their dinner Friday night. Eric had accompanied her to Miami, assisting with the tech part of her keynote and, like her, keeping eyes and ears open for any intriguing trends that might be in the air that weekend.

Beyond that, Emma doesn't recall much about the trip. Though miraculously her work hadn't taken a nosedive during those last terrible months of her marriage, she was in a near-constant state of turmoil, and when she wasn't dealing directly with clients or giving a talk, she was hopelessly wrapped up in her inner angst. If Tom *had* attended that dinner, she probably wouldn't have even noticed the gorgeous, silver-haired man in the crowd.

But it's a moot point, anyway, because Tom wasn't there.

After mulling it over, Emma realizes how Taylor may have become confused. Since a group from Halliday was at the convention, they probably attended several luncheons and dinners together over the three days, and Taylor obviously merged two events—the Avignon one, and another that Tom actually did go to—into a single one in her mind.

She's tempted to call Taylor and tell her she thinks this is the case, but quickly nixes the idea. Taylor's one of those people who has to be right, and she might end up asking others from Halliday to back her up and inadvertently perpetuating the idea that Tom was there.

Emma tries to put the situation out of her mind, but it

won't let go, and around one she gives Tom a call at the office to ask him to clarify things. When his assistant, Janice, picks up, she explains that he's already left for a business lunch that will be followed by back-to-back off-site client meetings. Emma knows Tom wouldn't mind if she called his cell, but she's not going to interrupt him over what is clearly a simple misunderstanding. They can sort this out tonight at home.

But late in the afternoon, she realizes she might not have to wait for an explanation. She and Eric have finished a final rehearsal for tomorrow's research presentation for their new client, and as he's stuffing things into his messenger bag to leave, she wanders over to his workstation. Dario took off a bit early for a doctor's appointment, so they have the space to themselves.

"Hey, Eric," she says, "can I grab you a second before you go?"

"Sure, what's up?"

"Remember that Miami trip?"

"The one last winter when I got so sunburned half my body turned into a giant blister and it hurt to even breathe?"

"Oh god, of course, your vacation. I felt so bad. But no, I mean the one we did for work a couple of Januarys ago."

"Oh yeah, that retailer convention. You gave a dazzling breakfast keynote."

"But I also spoke at a dinner hosted by Avignon Handbags. Do you remember much about it?"

He leans back, his gray eyes pensive. "A little. I know Avignon didn't want to cough up your full speaker's fee—claimed their budget was tight—but they subscribe to the

Hawke Report. I believe we ended up saying yes because we were hoping it would lead to other business from them."

"Aren't *we* crafty. It didn't, though, did it?"

Eric snickers good-naturedly. "No, but they still subscribe to the report at least."

"There's that, I guess. There were about forty people there that night, right?"

"About that number, yeah. Why do you ask?"

"Uh, just trying to figure out if that's where I met a woman I ran into lately. It's driving me nuts." She hates lying to Eric, but she doesn't dare mention the real reason, not even to someone she trusts as much as him.

"Why not check the digital file we have on the dinner?" he suggests. "Sometimes with smaller events, the organizer includes the guest list."

"Good idea, I'll give that a try."

Emma's eyes are drawn suddenly to Eric's desktop, and she realizes how bare it is. He's removed all the framed photos, souvenir mugs, and little knickknacks. Her heart sinks—could this be an indication he's ready to resign or at least toying with the idea?

Maybe after nearly four years with her, he's itchy for a change. When she based her company above the garage in New Jersey, he commuted out there two days a week from New York and worked remotely the rest of the time, and he did the same after she landed in Westport, though he eventually decided to relocate here himself. She's promoted him twice so far, giving him healthy raises, but unfortunately there's really no logical next step for him. He inquired discreetly a few months ago about a possible partnership role for himself, and she had to explain that though she thought the world of him, she'd decided from the beginning never to bring in a partner. It would just complicate things too much for her.

"You Marie Kondo-ed your desk," she says, not wanting to put him on the spot, but also intensely curious.

"Yeah, most of it were little tchotchkes I bought when I traveled with Dean," Eric says. "It seemed like time to get rid of them."

Okay, good. Maybe that's all it is, an attempt to ease some of the heartache.

"I don't blame you. Stuff like that can get in the way of starting fresh."

After Derrick died, Emma didn't save a single keepsake of their life together, not even photos of the wedding.

"I know you have more wonderful trips in your future, Eric," Emma adds. "Either solo or with someone new. And you can start another, even *more* fabulous tchotchke collection."

Eric laughs. "I'm going to take your word for it, Em. See you tomorrow."

As soon as he's out the door, Emma hurries back to her desk and locates the Miami folder in the electronic file she shares with Eric and Dario. It contains contracts for the breakfast keynote and the Avignon speech, her travel itinerary, and even a letter from the Avignon communications director confirming details about the event, as well as the estimated head count. But no guest list.

She's still certain there's no way Tom could've been there. And tonight she'll be able to confirm it.

What's your ETA? she texts Tom.

7. You?

Same.

Good. Btw, Brittany's seeing a movie with a friend so we're on our own.

Great, she thinks. She'll have Tom to herself over dinner.

Emma reviews the client presentation one more time for good measure, and when she finishes up, she notices it's already a few minutes after seven. As she dashes up the path, she spots Tom setting the patio table. He's already changed into jeans and a navy T-shirt, which emphasizes what good shape he's in.

"Sorry I'm late," she calls out. "Traffic was a bitch tonight."

"Ha! I popped two of the premade meals in the oven and they should be ready any second."

They embrace when she reaches him. "Let me throw on a pair of jeans, too, and I'll be right back," she tells him.

By the time Emma returns downstairs, Tom's already plated the food and set it on the table along with a bottle of sparkling water. As they settle into chairs opposite each other, she notices he picked up a bit of a tan on the golf course and looks even more handsome than usual.

"How nice to have the night unexpectedly to ourselves," he says, pouring them each a glass of water. "Just a reminder—

I have that client dinner Thursday night, and you and Eric are off to the author event on Wednesday, right?"

"Right." She and Eric are planning to hear a talk by the author of a book on lying because one chapter touches on why people sometimes fail to tell the truth on the type of research surveys Hawke and Company does. "You and Brittany should go ahead and eat without me that night."

"Will do. She seems to understand that Friday night is generally date night for us, so we'll have that to ourselves, too. . . . So, tell me about your day, sweetheart. I heard your talk at Halliday was a smashing success."

"They seemed to like it, and they asked terrific questions. Was it Taylor who mentioned it?"

"Not her, but several others."

Emma laughs. "They're brownnosers, but I'll take the praise. By the way, Taylor said something kind of weird that I wanted to ask you about."

Tom's about to slice off a piece of shrimp and he pauses now, his knife and fork hovering above his plate. "Something weird about the agency?" he asks.

"No, not about Halliday. She seemed to think you and I were at a dinner together before we officially met."

"A dinner here in Westport?"

"No, in Miami. Back in January a couple of years ago."

"Miami? Oh right, during that crazy boutique retailer convention. There was a dinner thrown by a client of ours that you presented at."

Her jaw nearly hits the flagstone.

"Wait, Tom, you were actually *at* the dinner that night? And heard me give my talk?"

"Unfortunately, I didn't hear anything past the opening sentences. I'd gotten a toothache that morning, and by the time you were introduced, it was raging. I snuck out a couple of minutes after you started so I could track down my dentist and beg him to call in a painkiller prescription to the local pharmacy."

They were in the same room, after all, just as Taylor claimed, in a group of only forty or so people and perhaps only feet away at moments.

Her stomach twists. "Tom, why wouldn't you have ever mentioned to me that you were there that night?"

"I was sure I did."

"When?"

"At our first meeting. As soon as I saw you up close, I realized you seemed familiar, but it took me a couple of minutes to place you."

"No, it never came up."

"Sweetheart, I'm sorry—I really thought I had." He flashes a mischievous smile. "And if I'd known then what I know now about you, I would've stayed and fought through the pain, even if it meant stifling my moans with a napkin."

"It's not that I mind your missing my talk," she says. "What I don't like is that we were in such close proximity that night. You might not have stayed for the dinner, but you must have been at the cocktail hour."

"And yet we didn't spot each other across a crowded room?" He turns the ends of his mouth down, clearly in jest. "I hope you don't think this means we aren't soul mates after all."

"No, Tom, please." Emma can't dance around her fears any longer or keep them to herself. "I'm talking about something else entirely. I told you what Peter Dunne said—that the cops are clearly checking you out, and I'm sure they've been looking at our timeline, trying to figure out exactly when we met. What if they find out we were in the same room in Miami back then?"

Tom leans back in his chair, cradling the back of his head with his hands, a position he takes when he's pondering a topic he doesn't yet have a handle on.

"In other words, you think that detective will wonder if we started sleeping together before Derrick was murdered," he finally says.

"Exactly."

He shakes his head. "But we both know the answer to that."

"It won't stop her from wondering."

"The chances of her stumbling upon this are next to nil," he says, smiling calmly. "Even if she does, we can explain we never crossed paths that night. And it's not like anyone could claim to have seen us interreacting there."

But someone might be confused. Emma knows from consumer research she's done that people sometimes recall the details of events incorrectly—in the wrong order or even with the wrong participants involved.

"Honey, please don't let this get to you." Tom flashes another grin. "If necessary, my dentist can verify that I called him that night, begging to be put out of my misery."

Somehow, she manages a chuckle.

But she's going to have to let Peter Dunne know about this latest speed bump. Not really a speed bump, of course. It feels more like a buckle in the road from a minor earthquake. And she's pretty sure *he* won't find it as amusing as Tom does.

14

Then

WITHIN SIX WEEKS OF THE MURDER, AS SPRING FLOWERS were beginning to bloom, Emma moved into the small one-bedroom rental on the Upper East Side of Manhattan. The sale of the New Jersey house wasn't set to close for another five weeks, but since she had access to her and Derrick's joint bank accounts, she was able to handle most expenses, and her parents surprised her with a cash gift to not only cover attorney fees but also to help her move. As detached as her parents could be, they were clearly distraught on her behalf and mistakenly assumed it was too hard for her to live in the house without Derrick there.

Faster than she thought, she'd managed to sell off most of the furniture from the house and went on to purchase some new basic pieces from affordable places like West Elm. At moments it seemed like she'd regressed a dozen years at least, living like she had when she first moved to the city after college, and yet she hadn't cared. The silence—free of criticism, scoffing, nasty comments, or freeze-outs—was pure bliss.

Dunne wasn't happy about the relocation. His advice to Emma had been "No sudden moves."

"There's a chance they'll be watching you," he'd warned when she made it clear she couldn't stay in the house.

"There'll be nothing to see," she'd told him.

For a while she did sense she was being observed in the city, and her heart raced every time she stepped out of her building. But within a few weeks that feeling passed. The third interview with the police turned out to be the last, though she called Lennox twice after it to see if there were any updates. A short time later Kyle backed off, too, perhaps deciding that if the police weren't taking her seriously as a suspect, he shouldn't bother to, either.

By then Emma was consulting for Halliday, taking the train to Westport a couple of times a week. Though her life still felt unsettled and fraught at times, there were other moments when she was at peace, excited for a new beginning.

Dunne called her in late June, just to check in. "You doing okay, Emma?" he'd asked.

"Yes, I have my ups and downs, but overall I'm okay."

A long pause followed. *He's still not a hundred percent sure about me*, she thought. Though she'd stressed to him on several occasions that she was innocent, and the police had clearly found no evidence implicating her, Emma sensed Dunne had his doubts, that some small part of him suspected that any day a secret lover would step from the shadows and shack up with her in Manhattan.

He hears guilt in my voice, she told herself. He'd heard it from the beginning.

But what Dunne didn't realize—and she guessed the cops didn't, either—was that her guilt sprang from an entirely separate source: her indifference that Derrick was no longer part of her life. Yes, she felt sad that someone she once loved had died young and in horrible circumstances, that his life had been cruelly snatched away from him. But she didn't *miss* him.

It bothered her that Dunne might think the worst of her, and it had scared her when the cops thought that, too. But the truth was she hadn't killed her husband. Nor had she paid someone to do it for her.

That's not the kind of woman she was.

15

Emma takes a long, warm bath after dinner, hoping to subdue the disquiet she feels over Tom's bombshell. Part of what's so unsettling to her is the idea that something significant like that had happened in her life without her even being slightly aware of it, like she'd clipped a jogger with the side mirror of her car, gravely injuring him, and only learned about it now.

And what if—despite Tom's assurances—Detective Webster *does* find out? Won't it look suspicious that, just a couple of months before her husband's murder, Emma was in a room with a man she became publicly involved with by the time fall rolled around?

Dunne will know what to do, she prays. Before climbing into the bath, she'd sent him an email: There's a new development. Can we please discuss as soon as possible?

Pressing her feet against the end of the tub, Emma leans back and stretches so that her head is just above the water and the lavender scent of the bath salts fills her nostrils. She has to find a way to stop this from eating at her. She's done nothing wrong, nothing at all, and she shouldn't be so fearful.

But as she stressed to Dunne the other day, the police arrest innocent people all the time, and even if those people manage to disentangle themselves with the help of a shrewd, staggeringly expensive attorney, there's bound to be damage to their reputations, both personal and professional.

Emma finally hauls herself out of the tub and sits on the edge wrapped in a towel. So much for the healing power of lavender—she feels as tense as she did before. For the first time, it occurs to her that some of her angst may be related to the fact that she's never been honest with Tom about her feelings around Derrick's death; craving his love so badly she let him think what he wanted. Eventually, it didn't matter anyway, because the murder was far behind her. But all this business with Webster has stirred up the past, reminding her every day how much she's kept secret.

When Emma emerges from the bathroom, she picks up the murmur of voices below, so she throws on a pair of yoga pants and a T-shirt and follows the sounds down the back stairs to the kitchen. Tom and Brittany are sitting at the table, sharing some shortbread cookies. Though Brittany clearly got dressed up for her evening out, her makeup is faded now, her red lipstick just a faint stain and her mascara smudged.

"Hey there, how was the movie?" Emma asks.

Brittany drags her attention away from Tom and offers her a disarmingly warm smile. "Nothing worth recommending, but we had fun hanging out."

"Well, I'm glad you found the silver lining," Emma says. She notices Tom observing them, his face softening in pleasure at the exchange. "Would you like something else to eat? Some actual dinner?"

"Thanks, but I grabbed food before the show. . . . Oh, by the way, I got you two a little something, just to show my appreciation." She rifles through her slouchy bright red purse and pulls out two gift certificates to the movie theater, which she proudly hands to them.

"Brit, that's so nice of you," Tom says, and Emma concurs, touching her shoulder.

"It's the least I could do," Brittany replies. "Both of you have been so welcoming."

Hmm, that's a surprise. Maybe they're making a little progress at last. But Emma doesn't have time to analyze it, not tonight anyway. She's got too much else to focus on.

Emma doesn't hear from Dunne the next morning, which annoys her. He hasn't acknowledged her email from the prior evening, and certainly he should have talked to Webster by now and called her with an update on that front.

When it's finally time to leave for her client presentation, she throws on a carefully selected hot-pink summer blazer, relieved to focus all her attention on work. It's scheduled for 2:00 p.m. at the company headquarters just outside of Westport. Since she's not sure how long the meeting will go, Emma suggests to Eric that they drive to the location separately so that if things run late, he can head home from there.

They end up pulling into the parking lot right behind each other, and shortly after they sign in with the receptionist, Scott Munroe strides off the elevator to greet them. Scott left Halliday a year ago for a new opportunity with the small hotel chain, and a couple of months ago he recruited Emma to do this particular research project, with the potential for additional work in the future. He's a handsome guy, tall and lanky with dark brown skin, brown eyes, and fairly short hair worn in twists. He's dressed today in perfect-fitting jeans and a blue-and-white-checked shirt, the sleeves rolled to his elbows. After ushering them to a fourth-floor conference room, he promises to return shortly with the CEO—whom Emma met at the start of the project—and about ten other staffers.

By two o'clock all the attendees, including the forty-year-old CEO, are seated, introductions are made, and Emma strides to the head of the table. She'll start the presentation today, and then, before she wraps up and takes questions, Eric will jump in to highlight certain findings. It's her way of giving him a chance to have more practice in front of groups. At this point in her career, she not only feels comfortable speaking in public but actually thrives on it, savoring the rush that comes from enlightening people with knowledge and watching their eyes widen as the dots are connected.

She's only a couple of minutes into her portion when she notices one of the attendees, a youngish brunette, sneaking peeks at her phone. Though Emma finds that type of behavior rude, it's rarely a distraction, but this time it succeeds in throwing her. She ends up flubbing a word and briefly loses her train of thought. A few minutes later she stumbles over a set of stats.

And to make matters worse, she feels herself flush. *Great,* she thinks, *my face is going to match my blazer if I don't get a handle on this.*

Despite her less-than-stellar performance, the attendees seem riveted by the research findings. As soon as she and Eric finish up, there's a slew of questions, including a couple of really smart ones from the CEO, and Emma manages to regain her composure. When the CEO nods vigorously as Emma extrapolates on some of the findings about generationally different travel goals, she sees Scott flash her a discreet thumbs-up from the back of the room.

Once people begin to file out, Scott strides toward her and asks Emma if he can have a minute. She nods and tells Eric to go ahead without her. Since it's only three thirty, Eric says he'll see her back at the studio.

"Wow, Emma, that was a ten out of ten," Scott tells her when they have the room to themselves. He's donned his black-framed Clark Kent glasses for the presentation but now pushes them up on top of his head.

Fortunately, her clunky moments must have been less noticeable than she thought, or maybe the neon effect of her blazer helped distract the audience.

"I'm so glad you're happy, Scott," she says. "How's the job going, by the way?"

He leans back against the table, grasping the edge with both hands. "Very well. I was a little nervous about making such a big switch, but it's been a good fit for me here."

"I'm sure they miss you like crazy at Halliday."

"Oh, I don't know about that."

"What do you mean? You were revered over there."

He tugs his mouth to one side. "I'm pretty sure I got on Tom's nerves at times."

"Really?" The comment totally surprises Emma. "Well, I've heard nothing but praise from him."

"Aw, thanks. Send him my regards, will you?"

"Will do."

Scott accompanies her to the lobby, where they say a warm goodbye. Striding across the parking lot, she's relieved by Scott's reaction and fairly confident that she'll be asked to do a second round of research.

And yet she's also miffed about getting flustered during the presentation, allowing herself to be rattled by a twenty-something who was probably checking to see if her Saturday night hookup had finally texted her. She's let this business with Derrick's case affect not only her state of mind but her performance on the job.

Emma has just reached her car when her phone rings, and she sees that Dunne is calling. *Finally*, she thinks, at the same time her heart skips. After quickly unlocking the door, she slides into the front seat to pick up.

"Sorry for the delay, but I've been in court until now," he says.

"Well, thanks for making the time. First, have you had a chance to connect with Detective Webster?"

"She left me a voice mail last night saying she's off today but will try me tomorrow."

"Huh. Could that be a good sign—that she doesn't seem anxious to talk?"

"Could be, but I wouldn't waste any time trying to interpret it. . . . So what's this new development?"

Emma takes a deep breath, steadying herself. "Um, it's the weirdest little thing actually. I found out yesterday that Tom and I attended the same event in Miami two years ago this past January, a dinner I was hired to speak at. We were never introduced, though, and Tom didn't even get to hear my talk because he had a toothache and left early."

An ominous silence follows.

"Not good," Dunne says finally.

Her stomach clutches. But what was she expecting? That Dunne would tell her she had the plot for a charming rom-com on her hands?

"But you have to understand," Emma tells him, and cringes at the pleading in her tone, "it's all a crazy coincidence."

"Unfortunately, the police don't like coincidences any more than they like inconsistencies. The fact that you and Tom met before your husband's death is going to be a red flag for them."

"But we *didn't* meet until July of that year."

Dunne clears his throat. "Correction. That you were in the same room together."

This is becoming . . . Kafkaesque: she and Tom having to defend themselves when all they've done wrong is attend the same event as total strangers.

"Okay. So what do I do about it?"

"There are two possible approaches. One is to try to 'battleship' it through—you remember the kids' game? In other words, wait and see if they ask the question and if they do, answer truthfully. If they don't, keep mum. The other is to get it on the table ourselves. In this instance, I would recommend the latter approach."

"You mean I call up Webster and share this with her."

God, won't *that* be a fun conversation.

"No, no. But—um, I'm thinking that Tom could weave it in when Detective Webster makes contact with him. As in, 'I was introduced to Emma on such and such day, but funnily enough, we recently discovered we came close to meeting a few months before then, though it never happened.'"

"Okay."

"I trust you've told Tom he needs to have an attorney present and it can't be his company attorney. It has to be someone who specializes in criminal law."

Emma's breath catches at the word *criminal.*

"Yes, I've told him."

"There's something else he needs to do now. Remember how I had you investigate yourself when we first met—so we'd be aware in advance of exactly what the police would turn up in their own investigation?"

Of course she remembers. It had been a mind-numbing job, but at least she knew for sure going into her third interview with detectives that everything from her phone records to her E-ZPass account would confirm that she was home that Saturday night and hadn't been calling a burner phone belonging to a hit man or otherwise orchestrating the murder from home.

"Yes," she says.

"Tom needs to do that, too. He should look through his search history, phone logs, texts, emails, calendar, as well as his credit card statements. He should cover the time between this conference you both attended and when the world knows you met. Then all the information is fresh if Webster asks specific questions."

She can't believe Tom is going to be stuck with this task, particularly at such a crazed time for him. And there's something so morbid about it—gathering all these bits and pieces of your life to prove you're not a cold-blooded killer.

"Okay," she says, wearied by the conversation. "I'll explain to Tom what to do."

They exchange goodbyes, and before she can toss her phone in her bag, it rings again. Tom is on the other end.

"Hey, sweetheart," he says. "The presentation go well?"

"Overall. I can tell you more at dinner."

"That's part of the reason I'm calling. I planned to be home to eat with you, but there's an issue I need to deal with and I'm going to be at the office till at least nine."

Emma feels a twinge of frustration, though not at Tom. She never doubts she's his biggest priority, but she was hoping to fill him in as soon as possible on the homework Dunne gave him. And beyond that, she was counting on the comfort of his company after such a stressful day.

"Not a problem. Is it the situation you've been working on with Justine?"

"No, something else. There's a bit of confusion about the second-quarter numbers, and I need to go over them with Dan." He's referring to the long-standing chief financial officer at Halliday.

"Got it. Shall I make a plate for you and stick it in the fridge?"

"Actually, if I'm going to have to stare at spreadsheets for a few hours, I'd love to eat first. What if we meet at the Whelk around six and we can grab a quick bite together? I'm sure Brittany will be fine on her own."

"That sounds like a perfect plan B," she says, pleased with his suggestion. "See you there at six."

Emma hangs up and is just about to start the engine when her gaze catches on a piece of white paper tucked under the windshield wiper and quivering in the afternoon breeze. *Did Eric leave it?* she wonders. But wouldn't he have texted her rather than opt for a written note that might blow away?

She exits the car, plucks the paper out, and quickly unfolds it. There are only six words, written with pen in block letters.

You'd better watch what you're doing.

16

THE WORDS STARTLE HER. EMMA SWINGS AROUND, SCAN-ning the parking lot, but there's nothing to see besides rows of empty cars, hunkered down in the afternoon sunshine.

Why would someone leave this note for her?

And then it hits her: the note must be from another driver. Did she unwittingly cut someone off when she pulled into the lot, or steal another person's spot? Well, it's an immature, peevish gesture, and she can't let it add to her stress level. It's high enough as it is.

After stopping by the house to swap her three-inch stilettos for flats, Emma heads to the studio and then retreats with Eric to the conference room. Their normal routine after every major presentation is to do a postmortem, reviewing what worked and what they might have done better.

Plopping down at the table, Emma opens a bottle of water she's brought with her while Eric makes an espresso using the machine on the counter.

"So I'd say that was a slam dunk, wouldn't you?" he says as he joins her at the table.

"They did seem to love the findings—and based on Scott's response, I think they'll probably hire us for more research."

"That's great. In hindsight, I wish our survey covered more on securing repeat customer business. There were quite a few questions on that."

"True." It's the kind of insight she's usually the one to offer, but she appreciates the way Eric's been more proactive in recent months. "We can include plenty of questions on that next time. . . . By the way, I'm sorry that I wasn't at the top of my game today. Was it obvious I lost my train of thought in the middle?"

"I noticed, but only because I knew what was coming. I don't think anyone else picked up on it. Was it because of that girl texting?"

"Yeah, I let her distract me," Emma says, though of course it's not the full story.

"She did it while I was talking, too." Eric rolls his eyes. "What a brat."

"Speaking of people behaving badly, did you notice me cutting anyone off as we pulled into the parking lot?"

"No, why?"

"Someone left a pissy note on my windshield. Said I needed to watch what I was doing."

"Oops, maybe they meant to put the note on *my* car. There was someone right behind me, and I think I took the last place in the row."

Emma sighs. "Well, hopefully they're over it by now."

Eric drains the espresso and plunks down the cup. "If that's all, I think I'll take off. . . . Oh, I almost forgot. Are you still trying to decide if that woman you ran into was someone you met in Miami?"

"No, I actually remembered," she says quickly. "It was from someplace else entirely."

"Glad you figured it out. That kind of stuff drives me nuts, too. . . . But hey, you know who I think *was* at the Avignon dinner? *Tom.*"

Her breath catches. "What makes you say that?"

"It occurred to me on my drive back here that I took a bunch of pictures during the convention in case we needed them for social media. I pulled up the file when I got back and as I glanced through them, I saw a guy in one shot who I swear is Tom."

She flashes a smile that she hopes doesn't look as fake as it feels.

"Yeah, it's funny—Tom *was* there," she tells him. "But we only recently made the connection because we were never introduced then."

"That's actually pretty cool. It's like the universe kept doing its best to nudge the two of you together."

"Ahh, right."

"Anyway, I emailed the pictures to you in case you want to take a look."

"Aw, thanks."

The second Eric's out the door, Emma makes her way to her desk and scans through the photos. Though she knows for a fact that Tom was at the dinner, she wants to see it how Eric had. When she finally locates the photo he's in, her heart skips.

It was taken during the cocktail hour and captures Tom, in three-quarters profile, speaking to someone she doesn't recognize, probably an Avignon executive. He's wearing a sports jacket she's never seen before, and his hair is a little shorter and slightly less silver than it is now. What Emma notes most of all is the discomfort in his expression. Not that she doubted Tom, but she's glad to see proof of the toothache.

And yet he was *there*, and she wishes he hadn't been.

Just please, for god's sake, she thinks, *don't let Eric mention the coincidence to anyone.* She shouldn't have even raised the topic of Miami with him.

Checking the time, Emma sees that it's already twenty to six, which means that no matter how much she hustles, she's going to be a little late for dinner. Fortunately, traffic turns out to be light, and she finds a parking spot easily.

Tom's already inside the Whelk, sitting at a shiny wooden table and reading something on his phone. Since it's early, the restaurant's only a quarter full, and he has an area to himself. The small candles on all the tables have already been lit and flames seem to twinkle everywhere.

"Hey, you," she says, sliding into the seat across from him. "So sorry to be late—I lost track of the time."

"Don't worry about it. I'm just glad you were up for this."

"So what's going on at work? Is it anything serious?"

"Things aren't lining up the way they should, but fortunately it seems to be an accounting error. Dan's in the office now, crunching numbers, and he says he should have a better idea by the time I get back."

"That's a relief," she says. "But I'm sorry you have to deal with the aggravation."

"Well, seeing you is already putting me in the right frame of mind." He cocks his chin toward the menu on the table. "You want the usual tonight, sweetheart?"

"Sounds good."

Tom signals for the waitress and requests several of the restaurant's signature appetizers, including deviled eggs and a dozen raw oysters.

"So tell me more about your presentation," he says, filling her glass from the bottle of sparkling water on the table. "I'm so glad it went well."

"Yeah, they seemed very pleased with the research." Emma shares a few of the more interesting findings she and Eric presented but doesn't bring up her flubs—because mentioning those will only draw attention to how agitated the Webster situation is still making her feel. Before the meal is over, however, she'll have to tell Tom about all the crap Dunne expects him to do.

"Scott did a really nice job of running the meeting," she adds. "He sends his regards."

"He's a smart guy, a real dynamo."

"He said something that surprised me, though—that he thinks he used to get on your nerves when he was at the agency."

Tom nods lightly and cups the small glass jar used as a candleholder on the table.

"He's not totally wrong. You worked at the agency long enough to know I hate 'yes people.' I'm eager to hear opinions other than my own, *plus* give those opinions consideration. But at a certain point I decide what I want and there's no need for further discussion. Scott never quite seemed to get that."

Just then, their food arrives and they each slide items onto to their plates.

"Huh. Would he keep pressing?" Emma asks, curious.

"Yup. I'm sure he never meant to be obnoxious. He'd just sometimes have trouble letting go, even when it should have been clear I'd made up my mind."

"Please promise to let me know if I'm ever guilty of that, will you?" she says.

Tom reaches across the table and lays his hand over hers. "I will. But you intuit me better than anyone I've known, Emma."

She smiles and takes a breath. "Well, I'm glad I have those points in the plus column, because you're not going to be happy when you hear the latest from Dunne."

Tom's eyes narrow. "Has there been a new development?"

"No, I'd asked him to call me so I could fill him in on the Miami business." She leans in, lowering her voice. "I was praying he'd tell me it was no big deal, but he's concerned about it."

"I don't see the problem. We didn't meet that night, we didn't speak, and no one would claim otherwise."

"Dunne says it's one of those coincidences cops don't like. Since Webster is probably going to contact you, he's recommending that you do the same thing he had me do two years ago." She explains the task and all the steps it entails.

"So I'll be searching for what exactly?" Tom asks, looking less than thrilled.

"Mainly you want to refamiliarize yourself with the time period. But you'll also want to note anything that the police might stupidly misinterpret, so that you and your lawyer are prepared."

Now his expression darkens. "You mean like a restaurant receipt indicating I was in SoHo that night in March," he says grimly.

Emma can't stop herself from wincing. "We know there's nothing like that, Tom. But if Webster asks you where you were on a given day and you've already refreshed your memory, you're less likely to give her an answer that you might have to correct later on. Like I said, Dunne had me do the same thing back then."

He withdraws his hand from hers and, with elbows on the table, brings a fist to his mouth. Emma can see he's struggling with the request, but she can't read what aspect of it is bothering him the most. Is it all the work involved or the fact that the cops might view him as a suspect—or both?

"Okay, I guess I can handle that," he says finally.

"But unfortunately there's still a bit more for you to do." She explains that when Webster finally speaks to him, as Dunne has predicted is in the cards, he needs to slip in the detail about the two of them being at the same Miami event, which will be better than having the police stumble upon the information themselves.

"Tom, I'm so sorry about this," Emma adds at the end. Her stomach is knotted by now, and she feels that the pall she's cast over the table must be visible to other diners. "This is not only a huge pain for you, but I know how crazy things are for you right now."

He lowers his hands and to her surprise, he suddenly smiles, one of his irresistible life-couldn't-be-better-could-it? Tom Halliday smiles.

"Don't worry about it, Em," he says. "Yeah, it's a pain, but we've got nothing to hide, and who knows, maybe when I go through my records, I'll finally find contact info for that fantastic massage therapist I went to once."

Checking his watch, Tom says he has time for a quick coffee if she's game and she tells him absolutely, eager to have the dinner end on a better note. He's no sooner ordered when Emma sees Taylor Hunt entering the restaurant and making a beeline for their table.

"Everything okay?" Tom asks as soon as she reaches them. She's still in office attire—navy pants, a crisp white cotton shirt, and a designer scarf knotted around her neck.

"I'm sure it is, but Dan's eager to talk to you and couldn't reach you on your cell. I told him that since I had to go by the restaurant on my way home, I'd stop in and let you know."

"Um, okay, let me call and see if he needs me to leave immediately."

Tom rises and steps away from the table, fishing his phone from his pocket as he goes.

Taylor's gaze trails him for a couple of seconds and then finds its way back to Emma. "So sorry to disturb your dinner."

"No problem—and we're almost done anyway."

"By the way, did you ever clear up the confusion about that dinner that you and I were talking about?"

Emma groans inwardly, alarmed and frustrated. What if Webster talks to people at Halliday and learns about Miami before Tom can tell her?

"I did, thanks. And you were right, Tom was there, but we never met. Sadly, he had to leave before it was my turn to speak."

Taylor wrinkles her nose, looking perplexed. "Oh . . . really? Well, that's a shame, but I know he loves to hear you give speeches. He says you're brilliant in front of a crowd."

Emma's quarterly talks at Halliday don't exactly qualify as speeches, and she would hardly tag them as brilliant, but she lets it go, and looks away, scanning the restaurant. Tom's outside, just beyond the door and still on the phone, his expression pensive.

Taylor seems to take the hint. "Sorry again about interrupting. Can you tell Tom I'll see him tomorrow?"

"Will do. Have a nice night."

When Tom returns, he explains that Taylor misinterpreted Dan's comment. The CFO isn't quite ready for him, so there's no reason to skip coffee. She and Tom squeeze in a few more minutes together, as Emma does her best to stay upbeat. As soon as they finish their drinks, she urges him to leave, saying she'll pay the bill and see him later. He kisses her goodbye and hurries off.

Though Tom's composure quelled some of her unease, Emma feels agitated again by the time she gets into her car. It doesn't help that when she arrives home, eager to collapse in the den in front of anything with subtitles that will keep her mind occupied, she finds Brittany in there, stretched out on the sofa in sweats and watching one of the *Real Housewives* shows.

"I'll tell you how I'm doing," one of the women on-screen sneers at the other. "Not well, bitch."

"Hi, how was your evening?" Emma asks.

Brittany takes a second to shift her attention away from the screen, as if she can't bear to miss a second of the riveting repartee.

"Oh, hi," she says at last. "I didn't hear you guys come in."

"It's only me. Tom had to run back to the office. Did you have a nice night?"

"Thanks, yes. I made a salad with some stuff from the drawer in the fridge."

"Good, I hope that was okay. Do you need anything before I head upstairs?"

"I'm all set, thanks. . . . Oh, did you want to use the den yourself?"

Well, it's nice that she thought to ask, Emma thinks.

"No, I'm fine. I'm going to read upstairs. Good night."

"Night. Oh, one thing before you go. I was mulling over what you said about observing one of your brainstorming sessions. I think once I hit the midpoint in my internship, I'd feel comfortable asking for an afternoon off."

"Oh, that's terrific," Emma says. "We'll find a good time." *It's looking like the next five weeks will definitely be smoother than the last two.*

After dressing for bed upstairs, Emma plops into the armchair with her iPad. Though she manages to lose herself at moments in the novel she's reading, it's not long before she's spiraling again. She needs to channel Tom, she decides. They *didn't* meet in Miami, and there's nothing for Webster to uncover there, no matter how hard she digs.

At one point she looks up, thinking she's heard the tread of Tom's footsteps outside their room, but the sound is followed by the soft thud of a door closing, meaning it was only Brittany turning in. Another fifteen minutes pass. Then another fifteen more, and the clock on the bedside table reads ten thirty. Emma's never known Tom to work this late, and she feels a prick of concern.

She's just about to call Tom when the bedroom door pushes quietly open and he slips into the room. His blazer's draped awkwardly over his arm, and the sleeves of his cobalt blue dress shirt are wrinkled and rolled to his elbows, a rumpled look that's unusual for him.

"Hey," he says. "Sorry to be so late."

"Is everything okay, honey?"

"Yeah, I'm just tired."

"You and Dan figure out the problem?"

"Uh, pretty much. It was just tedious going over all those numbers, which has never been my favorite part of the job." He stabs a hanger into the arms of his blazer and starts to unbutton his shirt, letting his gaze bounce around the room instead of looking at her.

"You want to vent with me for a bit?"

"I would, but like I said, I'm bushed. I need to wash up and hit the hay."

As he disappears into the bathroom, Emma crawls between the sheets. Though the windows are open, there's not a sound coming from outside, and the house is silent, too, except for the faint splash of water from the bathroom. *Something's funny*, she thinks, but she isn't sure what.

Tom emerges a few minutes later, and as he's peeling off the rest of his clothes, Emma captures what feels so odd. It's not simply that Tom looks fatigued and disheveled. His unworried demeanor has dropped out of sight, and he seems distracted, distant even. Though he gives her a peck on the lips after sliding into bed, he then rolls over on his side, his back to her, and hoists the summer duvet up to his chin.

At the restaurant he'd managed to convince her that he wasn't going to let the reopening of the investigation get to him, but clearly that's not the case. And why *wouldn't* it get to him? Tom's built a hugely successful business and from what she's seen, he's incredibly respected. How's it going to sit with people in their tony town if word gets out that his new wife is a possible suspect in the murder of her first husband?

And even worse, what if rumors start to spread that Tom might have been in cahoots with her?

Emma never believed she could completely bury her past. God, no. If anyone googled her former husband's name, the first thing that would come up would be a news story about him being shot dead in an alley. But she thought she could at least leave it in the shallow grave she'd dug in her mind, mostly out of sight. Now, in the space of a few days, everything's been churned up again, and poor Tom has been dragged into it, too.

Her past is not only threatening to take her down, but it's after Tom now as well.

17

THROUGHOUT THE NEXT DAY, EMMA CHECKS HER PHONE repeatedly, making sure she hasn't missed a call or email from Peter Dunne when she's been brainstorming with Eric, paying bills with Dario, or being interviewed for a podcast later in the afternoon.

But no such call comes in. Maybe, she tells herself, her gut was right, that it's a good sign the police have been incommunicado. Wouldn't it be nice if the lull in work-load that allowed Detective Webster to turn her attention to the Derrick Rand case has abruptly ended, and she's been forced to focus on *this* week's big Manhattan murder, what-ever that might be? It seems heartless to want the case to re-main unsolved—there's a brutal killer at large, and beyond that, Derrick's siblings need closure, and she does, too—but Emma can't have her life with Tom become collateral damage.

He'd seemed less distracted this morning, chatting as they polished off breakfast at the kitchen table, but once or twice she'd caught him looking into the middle distance, his mind elsewhere.

"What time do you expect to be back from the library tonight?" he'd asked as he slipped on his blazer to leave.

"Eight thirty or so, I'd say."

"Great. Since you'll be out, I think I'll take Brittany someplace fun for dinner."

"That's a wonderful idea, Tom. I'm sure she'd love time alone with you."

Emma's preparing to leave for the library that evening when Dunne phones her at last. Since Eric and Dario have already departed, she answers at her desk.

"I finally heard from Detective Webster, but unfortunately, I don't have much to report. I explained that though you were eager to assist in the investigation, it was essential she go through me. I then delicately probed about any developments in the case, but she didn't have the slightest inclination to share."

"Is it possible there's not much to say? That she might be suddenly busy with something else?"

"Oh, she's busy—she was in a car headed somewhere—but I don't have any reason to believe she's moved on. There was a caginess to her tone, and—though this is merely a guess on my part—I think she's got something up her sleeve."

Oh, fabulous.

"Like what, do you think?"

"No idea, I'm afraid. I take it she hasn't surprised Tom with a visit?"

"No."

"Hmm. If he doesn't hear from her in the next few days, let me know and we'll revisit our strategy regarding the dinner in Boca."

"Miami."

"Miami. Of course. Have a good evening, Emma."

She's running late by the time she hangs up, but that's fine with her because the scramble to lock the studio and the dash to the garage are welcome diversions.

The library is situated in an old brick building overlooking the Saugatuck River with several modern additions, and when she pulls into the parking lot at ten of seven, Emma discovers that she's not the only one curious to hear from the author of *Liars in Our Midst*. She assumes some of the attendees have been burned by dishonest spouses, lovers, or friends and want to learn how to do a better job of separating fact from fiction.

The event room is less full than the parking lot suggested, but there's a decent-size crowd. Emma takes a seat toward the front and saves the chair next to her for Eric. Since he's superpunctual, she's surprised he's not already here, and even more surprised when the introduction starts and there's still no sign of him. She was in the middle of the podcast interview when he left for the day, which meant she hadn't had the chance to call out, "See you at the library," but Eric isn't the type who ever needs reminding. She shoots him a text asking if everything is okay, but ten minutes later, when she glances down at her phone, he hasn't written back.

Emma tells herself not to worry, that something important clearly came up and he'll explain tomorrow, and for a while, she's able to lose herself in the presentation. The bearded, fortysomething author never does touch on why people lie on surveys, and since he doesn't call on her during the Q&A, she isn't able to ask a question on the subject. She briefly considers trying to chat with him while he's signing books but decides to bag it. At this point, all she wants is to be home.

There are two texts waiting when she digs her phone out from her purse. The first from Eric:

> Omg Emma, sry!!! Fell asleep on my couch and just woke up.

> No problem. I'll fill you in tomorrow.

> Thanks, feeling a tad under the weather but I'm sure I'll be fine in the a.m.

And one from Tom:

> Something came up so wont be back frm dinner till after 9. Sry. Will explain later. xo

She tells him no problem, too, and says she's headed home.

Except for several outdoor security lights set to a timer, the house is pitch-black when Emma pulls into the driveway, and it looks forlorn against the dusky, indigo-colored sky. After coming inside through the garage, Emma turns on a few lights and then forages through the fridge, putting together a plate of leftovers. She decides to take it out to the screened room at the back of the house.

Dusk has fully dissolved by now, and it's completely dark beyond the screened windows. A breeze rustles the trees and bushes, dispatching the pleasurable scent of honeysuckle into the room, and though Emma knows she should be savoring the moment—sitting in this lovely house that she and Tom were lucky enough to find, a beautiful summer ahead of her—Webster's face is lodged in her brain again. Dunne thinks the detective has a card up her sleeve, but what could it possibly be?

She hears the muffled rumble of a car coming down the street and nearing the property. *Tom and Brittany*, Emma thinks, waiting for the sound of footsteps and voices, but the house is soon still again. It's after nine thirty, so surely they'll be home any minute now. She's about to gather her plate and glass when her attention is snagged by something odd: a light glowing through one of the windows in her studio. She's nearly positive she turned them all off when she left for the library, and she also could swear the glow wasn't there ten minutes ago.

There's no way it could be a break-in, she reassures herself, because the alarm company would have alerted her. Yet she can't imagine Dario coming by this late, and Eric is at home. So maybe she did leave the light burning. She's got a ton on her mind after all.

Returning to the kitchen, Emma grabs her keys from her purse and a flashlight from a drawer and lets herself out the back door. It might be anal, but she won't be able to relax if she doesn't check to make sure everything is okay. The lights from the house illuminate the first half of the path, but after that only the beam of flashlight guides her.

Outside the studio, she squints at its small driveway, which is separate from the one for the house. It's empty, which means Dario's not inside. Should she wait for Tom? she wonders for a moment, until her curiosity overtakes the thought.

Reaching the door, she runs the beam of the flashlight along the edges and is relieved to see no sign of a break-in. But then she freezes, hearing a noise that seems to come from the other side of the door, before deciding that it's only the tree leaves rustling behind and above her. Emma takes another breath, turns the key in the lock, and shoves the door open. The alarm is still activated and chirps steadily until she taps in the code and presses off.

The high, open space is mostly dark, except for a single desk lamp burning. With a start she realizes it's the one at her own workstation. She quickly sweeps the beam of the flashlight across the room and simultaneously fumbles for the light switch to pop on the overheads.

With the room now ablaze in light, she roams through the space, poking her head into the bathroom, the meeting room, the walk-in storage closet. Nothing appears disturbed.

Maybe she's remembered wrong. In her rush to get out the door, she must have neglected to switch off her desk lamp and then simply not noticed it at first from the house. After all, it was still dusky, not totally dark, when she was in the kitchen.

She turns the light off, along with the overheads, and locks up to head back to the house. There's no movement in any of the windows, which means that Tom and Brittany must still be out.

As Emma walks, a sound punctures the silence. Footsteps, she thinks, followed by the snap of a twig, coming from behind a row of evergreens on her right. She jerks in that direction, but the noise seems to recede, moving away toward the street. She swings the flashlight toward the trees and flicks the beam back and forth, but all it connects with are dark, featherlike branches shivering in the breeze.

This time her curiosity loses. She breaks into a jog, and after reaching the house, quickly enters through the kitchen. But after a moment's thought, she hurries to the front hall and peers out one of the windows. Though some of the neighboring homes are brightly lit, there's not a person in sight and no cars on the road. She eases open the door and steps onto the stoop, looking both right and left. Still nothing. But suddenly from the right, around a bend in the road, she hears the faint rev of a car engine.

Then comes the sound of another vehicle, but this one turns out to be Tom's Tesla. As he slows and turns into the driveway, she lifts her hand in a wave, grateful he's home. She steps back into the house, locks the door, and greets Tom as he enters from the passageway that leads to the garage.

"Hey, sweetheart," he says. "What were you doing outside?"

"Something kind of strange happened. Where's Brittany?"

"She dashed up the back stairs to call her dad. What's going on?"

Emma explains about the light in the studio, the footsteps by the trees, and the sound of a car starting.

Tom looks serious but not panicked. "Could your mind have been playing tricks on you?"

Is *that* all it was? Has stress made her imagination go rogue?

"Uh, I don't think so. I mean, I definitely heard something moving around."

"It might have been a skunk or a racoon—I've heard about some coyotes in the area, too. And I'm sure the car was just a neighbor heading out."

She shakes her head. "I still feel weird about the light being on."

Tom scrunches his mouth, thinking. "Maybe Eric or Dario was working late and left right before you arrived?"

"Nope, Eric went home and actually slept through the library event. And Dario doesn't have enough work to bring him back here at night."

"Huh. Had you set the alarm when you left for the day?"

"Yes, and it was still on, which means that if someone was there, they had an access code. Wait, I've been so rattled, I forgot I could check my ADT app to see whose code was used."

Emma grabs her phone from the screened room and checks the most recent history for the studio alarm.

"Okay, this is weird," she says as she walks back into the kitchen. "Somebody was definitely in there. It shows I deactivated the alarm around twenty-five minutes ago, but it was also deactivated around thirty minutes before *that*—and then reset a few minutes before I went in."

"So whose code was used?"

"That's the weirdest part. It was mine."

"Whoa. And you definitely didn't pop in earlier?"

"Not unless I was sleepwalking."

"How would anyone know your code? Do you have it written down somewhere?"

"No . . . but I guess Eric and Dario could have noticed it over my shoulder." She presses fingers to her lips, her mind racing. "But Eric would have told me on the phone if he was going to drop by. And why would Dario need to sneak around in there at night?"

"Do you trust him?"

"He's only been on board a year, but I don't have any reason *not* to."

Tom pours himself a glass of water from the tap, but from the look on his face she can tell he's still tossing the situation around in his mind.

"Is it possible he fell behind and snuck in to get caught up without making it obvious? And used your code so you wouldn't know he'd been there?"

Emma nods slowly, considering. "Maybe, but we have a pretty easygoing workplace, and if he did have any issues keeping up, I'm pretty sure he'd feel comfortable telling me."

"I hope so," Tom says. "Either way, better change your code first thing in the morning."

"Right, I will. Now, enough about *my* night. Let's go up and then I want to know how the dinner went."

After locking up and retreating to the bedroom, they both undress for bed.

"*So?*" Emma asks, as she slips between the covers next to Tom.

"It went really well. I feel like I've made some progress with Brittany this summer, and tonight we had a really nice, relaxed conversation."

"That's terrific, Tom. What did you guys talk about?"

"The work she's been doing, some of the agency's newest campaigns, and a fair amount about Diana. There's no doubt she's still very grief-stricken, which of course makes me feel a bit guilty. Since I've met you, I've been able to be truly happy again, but it's different for Brittany. No one's going to take the place of her mother."

Emma nods. "And I'm sure it's hard for her to see that you've moved on, that you're in such a different place emotionally than her. Why don't you try to squeeze in a few more one-on-one dinners before she leaves? I can always find something to do on my own."

"That's a good idea, thanks. It also makes me realize I haven't asked about your author event. Was the guy interesting?"

"Yes, but I'll save it for our dinner at the Spotted Horse Friday night."

She reaches over to switch off the bedside lamp by her side of the bed and Tom does the same with his.

"Oh wait," Emma says into the darkness. "You said you'd explain what came up at work today. Are you and Dan still trying to sort through the numbers?"

"Yes, but that wasn't the reason for the delay. I was going to spare you tonight, but I hate sitting on it. The infamous Detective Webster paid me a visit late this afternoon."

Emma launches forward from the waist, swivels in Tom's

direction, and then props herself up on an elbow. The detective must have been in the car on her way to Westport when Dunne spoke to her.

"Oh, Tom, I'm so sorry. I was hoping she wouldn't just show at your office."

"Well, in a literal sense she didn't. She waited in the parking lot for me to leave the building and approached me as I was unlocking my car."

"That's basically an ambush. How did she respond when you said you wanted a lawyer present?"

"Promise not to kill me, okay?" Emma's eyes have adjusted to the dark and she sees Tom's mouth form a wan smile. "I decided to take the bull by the horns and invite her out for coffee."

She gasps, stunned. "When?"

"Right then. I pushed back dinner by an hour, and Webster and I went to a café. And now it's behind us."

Emma's heart sinks. He's done the very thing Dunne warned him not to do. And she very much doubts that it's behind them.

18

"Em, look, please don't be upset," Tom says, clearly sensing her dismay. "I had to make a split-second judgment call, and I thought it might look suspicious to lawyer up after Webster told me she was just hoping for a brief chat. So I went with the flow. If things had gotten the least bit hairy, I would have found a way to hit pause."

"But the thing I learned about cops," Emma says, flopping on her back again, "is that things can get hairy without you even realizing it."

"There really didn't seem to be any obvious danger signs. She wanted to know how we'd met, and I told her the story, which gave me a chance to slip in the part about us being in the same room in Miami without knowing it. I kept it really casual. She also asked if you and I had discussed the murder, and I said that we had, of course, and that the experience had been devastating for you."

As she imagines Tom sitting across from the detective at the café, Emma's stomach knots even tighter. Her husband is a master at reading people and navigating dicey situations, but he can also be overly optimistic on occasion. The more she's reflected on her own encounter with Webster, the more she's envisioned the tricks the other woman could be up to.

Emma sighs. "But we talked about you following Peter Dunne's advice and contacting a lawyer, and I was sure you were going to do it."

"I *did* actually contact a lawyer yesterday, and I called her to fill her in about the meeting as I was driving to pick up Brittany. She slapped my wrist but thinks I managed fine. And I ended up following *some* of your guy's advice to the T."

"Which part?" she asks, still disheartened.

"The research project. I spent a chunk of this morning doing a deep dive on myself and so I was all set when Webster asked if I remembered where I was the night Derrick died."

Unintentionally, she lets out yet another gasp. "She came right out and asked you that?"

"Yeah, she said it was routine, which we both knew was a lie. But I was able to tell her, since I'd already spent a couple of hours wading through calendar entries and endless emails and texts. I even found the name of that massage therapist I'd been looking for."

"And?" she whispers into the darkness.

"*And?* You want a massage, too?"

"Tom, this isn't funny. Where did it turn out you were that night?"

"Stowe, Vermont. The agency did a three-day ski weekend up there for a client, about twenty people in all."

At that moment it feels like her body practically liquefies

with relief. Tom has a rock-solid alibi—out of state, plenty of witnesses to back it up.

"I told Webster I happened to remember because it had come up once when you and I were discussing Derrick's death," he continues. "Hey, you aren't pissed at me, are you?"

"Not pissed, no." Though not happy, for sure. "I don't love that you did the interview without a lawyer, but it sounds as if you handled it well."

"As well as can be expected, I think. I'd love to celebrate with some great sex," he says, stroking her arm, "but I'm pretty spent. Can I take a rain check?"

"Of course."

As Emma drifts off to sleep, with Tom spooning her, she can still taste her disappointment that her husband acted against advice. Yet when she stirs awake around six, she's shocked to feel a lightness she hasn't experienced in days. It's as if there's been a constant, maddening ringing sound in her ears and it finally disappeared.

Lying in the stillness of the early morning, with Tom sleeping quietly beside her, it takes her a minute to get where that lightness has sprung from. As troubled as she's been by Webster's insinuation into her life and Taylor's revelation about the dinner, her biggest concern, one barely recognizable to her, has been that Tom might be vulnerable in some way. That maybe when he searched his records he'd find that he was actually home alone that night in March, with no alibi, or even worse, that in some *other* horrible coincidence, he'd been in Manhattan that evening.

But there's no second, terrifying coincidence. Her husband was hundreds of miles away with a big group, and it will be a cinch to prove if necessary.

While she's showering, Tom comes into the bathroom and joins her in the stall. After soaping up, he washes her hair for her, and she takes pleasure in the feel of his strong fingers kneading her scalp. As they towel off together, he reminds her of his client dinner that evening but says he should be home by ten at the latest.

Through breakfast, she's carrying the feeling of contentment, but there is still one matter for her to deal with. As soon as Eric arrives at the studio, Emma beckons him into the meeting room and closes the door.

"So sorry about last night," he tells her. "I was slightly under the weather, and planned to take a short nap, but the next thing I knew it was seven thirty-five."

"It's so not a problem. But are you feeling better now?"

"Much. I think it might have been the leftover smoked salmon I had for lunch."

She shakes her head. "Yuck. I'll give you my copy of the book later so you can read the chapter I found so interesting. There's actually something else I wanted to discuss."

She tells him about the light being left on and asks if he has any reason to think that Dario might have snuck back into the studio last night.

"*What?* God, no, or at least I don't think so. As far as I know, once seven o'clock rolls around you can't tear him away from *Line of Duty* or *League of Legends*."

"Video games?"

"Right, and he takes gaming very seriously. . . . How odd *your* code was used, though. Does Dario have it?"

"Not that I'm aware, but he could have seen it over my shoulder as I punched in. I've changed it, of course."

Eric stiffens a little. "You know that it wasn't me in here last night, right?"

"Oh, Eric, I'd never think that. Not for a second."

She's glad to see his body relax again. She'd hate for him to feel she was accusing him.

"Here's a thought," he says, looking off. "One of the days the freelancers were here last month, we all left at the same time. Remember? What if one of them saw you use your code—and they came back to steal something, or snoop around, or who knows what?"

Emma *does* remember. There was a night in May when they were all bunched together by the door at the end of the day, and though the three women they've hired to help them tabulate the surveys each month have been thoroughly vetted, one of them could be a bad egg.

"But there's a hitch with that theory," she tells Eric. "None of them has a key."

"True," he says, "but you sometimes leave your key lying on the table by the front door all day. If someone wanted to get in badly enough, they could have found a way to make a copy at lunchtime."

Eric and Emma hatch a strategy in which she'll take a closer look around the studio to see if anything is missing, and he'll find an excuse to call each of the freelancers and try to take their pulse over the phone.

Please, she thinks, as they return to the main room. *Let us figure this out.*

Toward the end of the day, Emma and Eric reconvene. Nothing is off in the studio, and Dario seems his normal, easygoing self. She's feeling terrible for having even suspected him for a moment.

"I talked to all three of the freelancers," Eric reports. "I said I was confirming that with the arrival of summer, they were going to be available at the end of the month. It was clear I caught each of them a little off guard, so it was hard to tell if there was something going on. Maybe we'll know more when we see them."

Emma shakes her head in frustration. "Which of course won't be for two weeks."

"How should we proceed from here?"

"Like, I said, I have a new code now and why don't I give you one, too. And we still should keep our eyes peeled for anything that seems the least bit irregular."

"Right, will do."

The situation will continue to weigh on her, she knows, but there's nothing more to do about it now.

After wishing Eric good night, Emma walks back to the house, eager to see Tom, and doesn't remember that he's hosting a client dinner tonight until she's halfway up the path. She figures she'll cobble together something simple for herself again, and Brittany can nuke one of the prepared meals from the freezer whenever she wants.

When she enters the kitchen, though, she finds Brittany

fully occupying the room: there are bowls and utensils on the island along with a carton of eggs, heavy cream, and a log of goat cheese. She's changed from work clothes into a pair of red capris and one of her Peter Pan–collared shirts, and she's briskly whisking eggs in one of the bowls.

"Hi, there," Emma says, deciding it's probably best to let Brittany do her own thing and come back later to fix dinner for herself.

"Oh, I was about to text you," Brittany says, glancing up at her with a smile. "I'm making dinner for myself and wondered if you might want to join me since Tom is out for the night."

"That would be lovely," Emma says, trying to mask her surprise. "What's on the menu?"

"Omelets with goat cheese and chives. Is that okay?"

Though Emma knows from her research that the breakfast-for-dinner trend has exploded in a big way, she's not much of a fan of it herself, but she's so pleased by Brittany's thoughtfulness that an omelet sounds suddenly divine to her, and she offers to make a green salad to accompany it.

As Brittany turns her attention back to her task, Emma dumps Bibb lettuce into a ceramic bowl, whisks together a simple vinaigrette, dresses the salad, and sets the table. Within a few minutes, Brittany's cooked two omelets in two different pans and slides them each onto a plate.

"How delicious," Emma says after tasting her first bite. And it is.

"Well, this and penne with tomato sauce are the only things I can really make so far, but I'm determined to learn more."

"You should ask Tom to give you a few lessons or even shadow him a couple of nights. He's such a fantastic cook."

"I'd love that," Brittany says. "You don't think it would be an imposition?"

"Not at all."

"It sounds great. You guys have already been so generous just letting me stay here. And I really owe you a special thanks, Emma. Because I know it had to be your decision, too, and not only Tom's."

Wow, Emma thinks, *how mature of her to express this so thoughtfully.* "Thank *you*, Brittany. That means a lot."

Over dinner, she quizzes Brittany about her current work project and then raises a topic she'd been hoping to find a time to address. "Overall, what's it been like for you to be back in the area? Has it been nice—or too intense at times? Or both?"

"I guess I'd have to say both," Brittany says after a few beats. "I've loved being reminded of the time my mom and I spent here, but it's been really sad sometimes for that reason, too."

"I can only imagine." Emma feels a vicarious pang of sorrow. "Are any of your old friends around?"

"Not really. The two girls I hung out most with in junior high aren't in the area anymore. But last night before dinner, I asked Tom to drive me by the old house in Weston. I cried when I saw it but I'm glad I went. My mom made our life there really special."

Her eyes brim with tears and so do Emma's. She's been so preoccupied by little annoyances related to Brittany's presence and attitude that she hasn't allowed room for enough empathy until now.

"Tom's shared with me what a wonderful woman your mom was. And such an amazing doctor."

"He was her patient, you know."

"Yes, he told me. He said he never thought he could be so grateful for a scratched cornea."

Brittany takes her last bite of omelet and smiles, a catlike expression Emma hasn't seen before now.

"What?"

"That's not really how they met."

"No?" Emma doesn't mean for her brow to wrinkle in confusion, but it does it anyway.

"My mom told me that she and Tom were actually introduced at some kind of glitzy charity auction seven or eight months before he came into her office."

"Oh, I hadn't realized that."

"She'd just split up with my dad and wasn't interested in dating yet, so when Tom asked if she'd like to have dinner with him one night, she said no. And then she barely remembered Tom when he showed up as a patient."

"Well, how lucky for him that he needed an eye doctor."

Another mysterious smile.

Emma doesn't question her again. Instead, she gives Brittany the chance to say more, which is clearly her intention.

"My mom said he didn't really have a scratched cornea," she says a moment later. "He said his eye hurt and that he thought he'd rubbed too hard at it, but she couldn't detect a scratch."

"Well, then how lucky he *thought* he'd scratched it—even if he was wrong."

"Yeah. But my mom always felt sure that his eye didn't even *hurt* and that he'd made up an excuse to see her. I remember her saying then that people always thought of Tom as really spontaneous, but one of his of superpowers is patience when he really wants something. She called him the master of the long game."

19

EMMA FEELS A SWELL OF UNEASE, THOUGH SHE CAN'T EX-
actly put a finger on it.

Is it because Brittany's talking about Diana and Tom
with such reverence? Or because she's sharing charming details about their courtship, which Emma would prefer not to
have prancing around in her head?

She certainly doesn't resent Tom's love for Diana—or at
least she's pretty certain she doesn't. Yes, early on in their
relationship, when she was praying his obvious infatuation would morph into something deeper, she experienced
twinges of jealousy about the years he'd shared with his first
wife. He had clearly adored Diana, and Emma knew he must
still grieve for her at times. But those twinges subsided as she
became more certain about her and Tom's future. And the
fact that he had loved someone passionately and been totally
devoted to her during her illness only made her appreciate
him more.

Brittany's staring at her, she realizes, expecting a response, but Emma decides to shut down this line of conversation. Beyond that, she feels a sudden need to be alone.

"Well, Tom has many superpowers, doesn't he?" she says. "Uh, this has been such a nice treat, Brittany. Since you cooked, why don't I handle the cleanup?"

"I'm happy to help, Emma."

"No, no, go turn on the TV and relax. There's not much to do in here anyway. You're such a neat cook."

"All right." After Brittany fixes herself a glass of ice water, she retreats from the room without further comment. Is she miffed, Emma wonders, because their conversation was brought to a halt, or is this simply Brittany being Brittany? It's a puzzle she's not going to solve tonight.

Even with the kitchen to herself, Emma's unable to shake her disquiet. *Why?* she asks herself. *What's going on here?* And finally, she knows. There's something vaguely off-putting about Brittany's description of Tom's behavior. If her account is true, it means he might have kept thinking about Diana for months, and when he thought the moment was right, come up with a fake reason to schedule an appointment with her. Brittany made it sound romantic, but in Emma's mind it's borderline creepy.

She pushes herself out of her chair and loads the dishwasher, then takes a wet sponge to the island, wiping away a few splatters of vinaigrette and raw egg until she realizes that she's been buffing the same spot over and over again.

Wait a sec, she tells herself. She's looking at the situation through the lens Brittany provided and it's not necessarily the right one. Tom might have asked Diana out when he first met her, but then never thought of her again until he needed an ophthalmologist. And even if his cornea wasn't torn, his eye probably was bothering him, enough to get it checked out.

Sure, Tom can be patient when it's required, but one of his most impressive superpowers—since Brittany raised the subject—is decisiveness. If there's something he wants, he goes after it then and there, and if thwarted he doesn't simply bide his time ("Life is too short," Tom would say), but moves on, choosing an appealing alternative and going after *that* instead. She'd witnessed this at work with their house hunting. There'd been a home they had seen earlier, one they'd loved and bid on, but the owner had suddenly announced he needed a few more months to get his ducks in a row. He'd asked them to wait, promising to circle back to them, and though Emma had been game to hold off for a bit and remain in Tom's town house, he'd argued that they should start their search up again and find a new option, which they did. One they ended up liking even better than the first place.

And most important, Tom's not a deceptive person. He's a straight shooter, a truth teller, which is one of the many things that attracted her to him.

Either Brittany's exaggerated the story in her mind over time, or Diana was simply being fanciful when she told it to her daughter years ago—but Emma's not going to worry about it for a moment longer.

She tosses the sponge in the sink and makes her way upstairs, where she settles into the armchair in her bedroom with her iPad, returning to the same novel she attempted to read earlier this week. Miraculously she has more luck to-night.

When Emma eventually glances up from the screen, she's shocked to see it's ten thirty, but Tom's not back yet. A sense of déjà vu floods her. This isn't the first time this week she's worried about Tom's whereabouts. But before she can over-react, she hears steps on the staircase, and a minute later he pushes open the bedroom door.

"There you are," she says brightly.

"Hey, sweetheart." He sets his soft leather briefcase on the floor next to the dresser. "Sorry to be this late, but I found myself at a dinner with people who refused to leave."

"The clients?" She bounces up from the armchair and meets him in the middle of the room, where she plants a kiss on him. There's a faint taste of red wine on his lips, which surprises her a little. Tom always springs for a big-name wine at business dinners, but generally limits himself to a glass early in the evening.

"Yeah," he says. "They ordered coffee, sipped it like it was a twenty-year-old single-malt scotch, and then once I'd paid the check, they sat at the table for another twenty minutes."

"Maybe you're just too charming for your own good."

"Well, let's see if they do their next campaign with us."

"How many were in your group tonight?"

"Three of us from the agency. Four from the client. A long night but I'm hopeful it will pay off."

"Good."

He crosses to the armchair she's abandoned, lowers himself onto the seat, and slips out of his slim brown loafers, which he's worn without socks. "Tell me about *your* day, Em."

"Overall productive, though I never figured out who my mystery visitor was last night."

"Very odd. You changed your code, though?"

"Yup."

"You might want to check with the security company and see if there was a glitch on their end. . . . Anything else going on?"

"Well, I'm happy to report I made progress on the Brittany front. She even cooked me an omelet tonight."

"That *is* progress! How did it taste?"

"Delicious, actually."

As she says it, Brittany's comments worm their way inside Emma's head again, and she feels an echo of her earlier unease. But then she watches Tom toss his pants onto the chair in that easy, boylike way of his, and reassures herself once more that he doesn't have a dishonest bone in his body, that he'd never tell a lie to engage with a woman.

"That's nice to hear," he says distractedly, his attention now on his shirt buttons.

"And since she's had dinner with one of us the last two nights, surely she won't mind being excluded from date night tomorrow," Emma says as she wanders to the bed and peels back the covers.

"Are you turning in now?" he asks.

"I thought so. Aren't you?"

"In a bit, but I need to pop into my office and review a contract for another client. We want to get it to them first thing tomorrow."

"Um, okay."

He pulls on a pair of pajama bottoms and kisses her on the forehead. "See you in the morning."

Emma waits for Tom to leave the room before switching off the light on her bedside table. A light breeze slips in through the partially open window, rustling the curtains and tickling her bare arms, and as pulls up the sheet a little, she hears the click of Tom's office door shutting at the end of the hall.

Her sense of déjà vu intensifies: Tom wasn't only late again, but he seems as distracted as he did Tuesday night. Perhaps, despite how long people lingered at the dinner, the evening fell flat somehow, or maybe his meeting with Webster is continuing to reverberate, unsettling him despite his solid alibi.

Emma makes a valid effort to summon sleep, but she's still awake an hour later when the bedroom door eases open and Tom crawls in between the sheets.

"Everything look good?" she murmurs.

"What?"

"With the contract?"

"Oh, yeah, by and large," he says. "Needs some tweaking. Night, sweetheart."

"Night."

Another hour later, Emma's still awake, and she can tell from his breath patterns that Tom is, too. When she shifts onto her side and peers through the darkness with her eyelids mostly closed, she sees that he's lying on his back, his eyes wide open and fastened on the ceiling. She's tempted to ask him if he's okay, but she lets the urge pass, not wanting to nudge him at this hour.

Out of the blue, she feels a sudden longing to speak to her friend Bekah. There's no way she's going to burden her with this whole story, not when Bekah doesn't even know her true feelings about her first marriage, but she wishes she could at least be in her friend's company and feel the comfort her presence never fails to provide.

And then, the next day while at work, in one of those rare moments when the universe seems to read her thoughts, she gets a text from Bekah with a photo of her daughter, Hadley, wearing the dress Emma sent for her birthday.

> Omg, cutest outfit in the world. Thank you. Btw, got a new part-time nanny and I'm free for a while at one today. Any chance you can talk? Would LOVE to catch up.

Warmth fills Emma's chest. Up until now she's convinced herself that she's been okay with the limited contact they've had in the last year because Bekah has needed to devote most of her attention to the baby she craved so desperately. But she misses her friend, she really does. She checks her calendar and confirms that she's free at lunchtime.

One is perfect, Emma writes back. wcu. can't wait.

There's enough work all morning to keep Emma distracted, including a call from Scott Munroe saying his

company is hiring her for a second round of research. Period-
ically, though, she finds time to steal glances at Dario, trying
to assess his behavior. He seems as cheery as ever, and the
only way she's going to know for sure if he's up to anything
is to install a nanny cam in the studio, which she has no intention of doing.

At twelve thirty, Emma heads back to the house to grab a
quick bite and have a private spot to call her friend.

"Oh, Emma, it's so good to hear your voice," Bekah says
immediately.

"Ditto. But shouldn't you be using this precious free time
for a mani-pedi?"

"Don't worry, I have every intention of squeezing that in
this week as well."

"Tell me what Hadley's up to."

"She's into everything, and saying a few new words every
day."

There's a real ease to Bekah's tone, which Emma loves to
hear. It appears that the depression she struggled with after
her two miscarriages has dissipated.

"Send more pictures, will you? Trust me, I can't get
enough."

"Ha, be careful what you wish for. . . . Listen, I know
this is a really personal question, but a while ago you said you
were on the fence about trying for kids with Tom. Have you
thought about it lately?"

Emma *has* thought about it, though certainly not during
these last crazy days.

"I'm still not sure, actually," she says. "Since it's a second
marriage for both of us, I want us to focus right now on

finding our way as a couple, and then we'll figure out the rest later. I know I don't have all the time in the world, but my gut tells me first things first."

"That sounds smart. Are you still feeling good about things with Tom?"

"Definitely. I can't believe how happy I am."

"No hiccups?

That's a funny question.

"Nope. . . . Though as much as I like Westport, I really miss you—and the city. Now that we're done with the house, Tom and I want to start coming in more, so I hope we can lure you and J.D. out for dinner one night."

"Of course! And I'm sure your other friends in the city would love to see you, too. Did you hear Kelly got promoted?"

"Yeah, she texted me. And what a cool new role for her."

"I was sorry, by the way, to read about that friend of Derrick's—the one who passed away so unexpectedly."

The skin on the back of Emma's neck prickles. She has no clue what Bekah's referring to.

"Who?"

"Chris Shelbourne. I saw he died in a scuba diving accident a week or so ago. In the Caribbean, I think."

"Oh my god, I had no idea." The news is shocking and sad, but not shattering for her. Chris and Derrick had met through squash, and Derrick, dazzled by Chris's success and wealth, had arranged a couple of double dates with him and his wife, Lilly, the year before Derrick died—and yet the couples had never been close.

"So you hadn't heard?"

"No. They wrote me a note after Derrick died, but I lost

touch with them after that. How did you remember I knew him?"

"I didn't, but J.D. did," she says. "We talked to Chris and his wife at the party you gave, and J.D. was kind of in awe of what a Renaissance man the guy was. You know—megamillionaire, mountain climber, art collector, the whole nine yards."

"What terrible news, but thanks for letting me know—I'll drop his wife a note." She'd really liked Lilly, a food photographer, the few times they'd met.

They chat a little while longer, promising to make a date soon, and after they've signed off, Emma vows to do a better job of staying in touch with Bekah.

Before returning to the studio, she searches on her phone until she finds the obit for Chris Shelbourne. Dated six days ago, it offers little about the circumstances of his death, other than the fact it occurred, as Bekah had indicated, while he was scuba diving off the coast of the Caribbean island Bonaire. Emma can only imagine how horrifying the experience must have been for Lilly.

Because Emma had been tasked with sending out the paperless invitations to their cocktail party, she has Lilly's email in her address book, though not her home address, and she takes a minute now to compose a message to her, saying how truly saddened she is to hear the news.

For a few seconds, Emma finds herself back at that party, mingling with guests in the Madison house while doing her best to keep a smile plastered on her face and not give away that her life now resembled the ninth circle of hell. Though she barely recalls seeing Lilly that night, she does remember talking to Chris, who peppered her with questions about current trends or some such. It had been a welcome opportunity to take refuge in a corner of the living room and let the awful party throb on without her.

How strange, she thinks, that just two years later, he and Derrick have both died young—one at the hands of a murderer and the other in a tragic accident.

The afternoon speeds by even more quickly than the morning did. Though Emma always looks forward to her Friday night dinners out with Tom, this one matters even more to her. She wants to assess Tom's state of mind after seeing him unusually sleepless last night.

They've agreed to meet at the restaurant and as Emma changes for dinner at the house, she takes her time, giving herself a chance to relax a little. Tom has texted to say that Brittany is spending the night with her friend again, which means Emma has got the house to herself, and she relishes it. She dons a lacy bra and matching thong and then slips into a short-sleeved, fairly low-cut yellow dress she knows Tom loves.

As soon as Emma steps inside the Spotted Horse—a few minutes ahead of schedule—she's grateful they picked this spot. With its beamed ceiling, barnwood paneled walls, and dark wood tables, it always feels so inviting to her. The horseshoe-shaped bar is already fairly crowded with customers—it's Friday night, after all—but the hostess leads her to a table by the window that's removed from the fray. Emma takes a deep breath, exhales, and then breaks into a grin after noticing that the horse in one of the huge black-and-white photographs on the wall seems to be eyeing her intently. Clearly, he digs the dress, too.

Tom arrives just as Emma's being served the glass of wine she ordered. Before the waitress leaves, he requests a Dewar's on the rocks, and then kisses Emma softly on the lips.

"Man, I've so been looking forward to this," he says, taking the seat opposite and running his eyes over her. There's not a hint of his recent distractedness.

"Me, too," she exclaims. "The end of this week felt a little crazy, both of us being out."

"Agree, and much to my annoyance, it looks like I definitely have to head back to Chicago on Monday to seal the damn deal."

She feels a twinge of disappointment, but work is work. "Well, let's make the most of the weekend, then."

Tom smiles, shrugs off his blazer, and drapes it on the back of his chair. "Agree. You know, part of me wishes we hadn't decided to rent out the Block Island house this year. It's got such a lonely-bachelor vibe, but at least we'd have it to escape to on Friday nights."

"Oh, but I love being in our house here—and besides, it wouldn't be nice to ditch Brittany every weekend."

"True," he says, with a lighthearted grimace. "And while we're on the subject. . . ." He reaches behind him and digs into the pocket of his blazer to withdraw a small box wrapped in silver and tied with white satin ribbon. "This is to say thanks for being such a good sport about Brittany."

"Oh, Tom, you shouldn't have." And Emma means it. He doesn't need to give her gifts, though she appreciates that he's seen the effort she's put in to making it work with his step-daughter. "But thank you." She gives the box a playful shake. "Should I open it now?"

"Definitely. It's going to look great with that dress."

After undoing the ribbon, Emma wiggles a finger beneath the ends of wrapping paper on the back of the package until the tape breaks away. Smiling in anticipation, she eases the black box out of the paper and sees it's upside down.

"My, my," she says, "what do we have here?"

She flips it over, and her breath catches as she sees the name on the front. David Yurman. The jewelry designer whose pieces she wore during her marriage to Derrick but not in the years since.

The designer she swore she'd never wear again.

20

Then

IN LATE OCTOBER, SEVEN MONTHS AFTER DERRICK'S MURder, Emma decided to swap her New York City rental apartment for a two-bedroom in Westport. She was consulting on several big projects for Halliday Advertising by then, and so it made sense workwise, but her decision was also based on encouragement from Tom. They were spending more and more time together and the schlep back and forth from the city was a pain. She knew that if things got really serious between them—and by this point she was hoping they would—it would probably be best to relinquish her gig with his company and focus on other clients, but for now the arrangement seemed okay since she wasn't a regular employee.

Moving turned out to be simple enough. She'd been living a very pared-down existence, having gotten rid of every trace of her life with Derrick, right down to a couple of souvenirs from the trips they'd taken.

The one thing she'd hesitated about relinquishing were the five or six David Yurman bracelets and cuffs he'd given her early in the relationship. It's not that she wanted any keepsakes from their life together, but she loved the jewelry—she'd had her eye on it even before Derrick gave her the first bracelet—and she almost always wore the pieces when she was doing talks and speeches. People often complimented her on them, and she liked that she'd developed a kind of signature look for herself professionally.

But when she slipped one on several weeks after Derrick died, the sight of it had made her nauseous, and she knew those had to go, too, that she wanted nothing at all that could remind her of him. A cousin of hers who lived on the West Coast became the grateful beneficiary.

21

Tom, oh my goodness," emma exclaims, unable to come up with anything else.

She lifts the bracelet from the box and lets it dangle from her fingers. There are four strands of thick, sterling silver cables interspersed with freshwater pearls. It's a cuff as much as a bracelet, a striking piece of jewelry she might have even picked out for herself.

But not *now*. Not at this point in her life. And why would Tom think of it for her? She's never mentioned the brand to him—and beyond that, it's nothing like any piece of jewelry Tom's given her in the past.

"Do you like it, Em?"

"Yes, I do—I love it," she says, hoping he doesn't detect the hesitation in her voice.

Tom inserts his fingers beneath the bracelet, tugs it gently from her fingers, and undoes the clasp. He's obviously expecting her to put it on now.

She stretches out her right arm in his direction, and smiling, Tom fastens the bracelet around her bare wrist.

"It seemed very *you* to me," he says. "Bold, but with a lovely tender side, too."

"What gave you the idea?"

"I saw a photo of it in a magazine and thought you might really like it."

And she does. But it doesn't change the fact that she associates this type of jewelry with the ugly life she left behind.

"Well, thank you so much, honey," she says. "It's going to look great with everything, even jeans."

The waitress returns with Tom's drink and takes their dinner orders. Over the next hour they catch up and discuss plans for the following day. Tom's playing nine holes of golf in the morning while Emma intends to do a little shopping and then, if the weather holds, they hope to head to the beach. A couple of times, she notices the bracelet shifting on her wrist as she gestures, making soft clicking sounds, and her discomfort resurfaces. It's only a piece of jewelry, she tells herself, one from *Tom*, not Derrick, and she's going to have to find a way to let go of her association and appreciate his gift.

They're home by nine thirty and decide to watch an episode of a spy thriller series on Netflix before turning in. A couple of times when Emma glances over, she notices that Tom's eyes have drifted off the TV screen and he's staring into the distance.

"Had your fill of ruthless arms dealers?" she asks.

"What?"

"Your mind seems to be elsewhere, honey."

"It's just been a long week at work, I guess. Putting out fires, dealing with Dan about the numbers, finding out I have to go back to Chicago first thing Monday."

"Not to mention the buzzkill of an NYPD detective showing up in the Halliday parking lot."

Bringing up the elephant in the room certainly qualifies as buzzkill, too, and yet Emma had made a split-second decision to stop ignoring it. If that's what's bothering Tom, she needs him to share that with her.

He shrugs. "Well, hopefully, she's out of our hair, and we'll only hear from her again if she makes an arrest. You haven't learned any more on that front, have you?"

Emma shakes her head. "Peter Dunne said he'd call if he knew anything. . . . Tom, are you sure this isn't eating at you?"

He smiles ruefully. "It could if I let it. But why borrow trouble?"

She wishes she could be more like him.

Tom's tee time the next morning is at nine, so breakfast is a bit rushed, but after he leaves, Emma indulges in a second cup of coffee before heading to the farmers' market. It's held in a parking lot, but the peaked white tarps over each of the tables give it the feel of a medieval fair, and she almost expects to see jousters on horseback.

After parking and grabbing her cloth shopping bags, Emma wanders down each aisle at least once, checking out the produce and enjoying the scent of homemade bread and muffins wafting from the bakery stands. Finally, she circles back to a couple different tables to pick out a head of lettuce, fresh peas, and a pint of bright red strawberries.

She's rounding one of the stands, ready to leave, when she nearly collides with a tall, redheaded woman, then realizes she knows her.

"Justine, hi," she exclaims. "Excuse me for nearly mowing you down."

"Oh, no, it's totally my fault," Justine Carr says in her typically silky voice. "I wasn't paying attention." She's dressed in a cropped black tee and pink workout pants, probably both from Lululemon. Her long hair is pulled back today in a ponytail and her skin is bare of makeup. Justine apparently engages in everything from boxing to CrossFit to SoulCycle, and Emma assumes she's come from some kind of workout.

"But what a nice surprise," Emma says.

"Yes, it is." Justine shoots a glance at the bags in Emma's hands. "It looks like you two are going to be eating very well this week."

"I hope so. If it doesn't work out, I can hardly blame the ingredients. What about you? What are you picking up?"

Justine's cloth bag appears to be empty. By this point she's moved a little closer to Emma, who can't help but notice the fatigue in her eyes. She wonders if Tom's number two is still scrambling to fix the problem that emerged last weekend.

"Not sure yet. Is Tom with you?"

"No, he's playing golf this morning."

"Glad to hear it. He . . . he's had so much on his plate lately."

Justine fastens her olive-green eyes on Emma's, her expression slightly inquisitive. Surely Tom hasn't told her about what's going on with the reopening of the case. No, he wouldn't have. She must be referring to the items Tom mentioned last night—putting out fires, trying to resolve the numbers with Dan, and so on.

"Well, you know Tom, he'll figure it all out," Emma says.

"Oh, I'm sure, but even *he* must need a break at times. I hate to see him pushing himself so hard."

This conversation is starting to feel weird. Justine's never been this forthcoming with her, and beyond that, Emma feels uncomfortable discussing Tom behind his back.

She shrugs. "He's had crazy periods before. I don't think we need to worry about him."

She hopes that's enough to move them off the topic, but Justine purses her lightly freckled lips, obviously eager to continue.

"I just want him to be aware that he can dump as much as he wants in my lap."

"I'm sure he knows that." But even as Emma says it, she recalls Tom's point about Justine not being on top of her game lately, which could be the reason he isn't delegating much.

"Sometimes I worry he's afraid he's imposing. Like the other night after the client dinner, I hated that as we were piling into our cars to go home, Tom had to head back to the office. Whatever the issue was, it would have been fine if he'd asked me to handle it."

This is the first Emma's hearing about him returning to Halliday. It seems odd he didn't mention it, but they didn't speak for very long that night before he popped into his home office.

"Justine, I think it would be best for you talk to Tom directly and tell him your concerns."

She nods. "You're right, and I will. But . . . did he seem okay when he got home? There's not some issue at the agency, is there?"

"Not that I'm privy to, and as you know, even if I was aware of anything, it wouldn't be appropriate for me to mention it."

"Of course. Like you said, it's best for me to speak to Tom directly."

Emma extricates herself, wishing Justine a good day. After retrieving her car, she makes a quick run to the dry cleaner and then stops at Winfield Street Coffee, where she orders a cup of herbal tea and sits at one of the slatted wooden tables on the sunny patio out front. She's briefly tempted to pull out her phone but instead leans back and lets her gaze go to a soft focus. This is the first time in ages that she's given herself permission to do absolutely nothing for a few minutes, and it isn't long before she feels some of the tension in her shoulders begin to melt a little.

She knows it would be smart to allow herself regular downtime, to be more of a laid-back kind of girl, but she's come to accept that she's an anxious person, partly by nature, and partly, she guesses, from having grown up with hard-to-please parents. She also knows that in her case, things like deep cleansing breaths and showers with myrrh-scented body wash don't help very much. Even if there's not an immediate issue on her radar, she seems to have an internal tracking system that searches until it finds *something* to latch on to, like a phone call she's made that hasn't been returned yet.

And this anxious tendency has probably been compounded, she knows, by her professional training. As a trend forecaster, she's always looking for signs and patterns, trying to guess their meaning and what impact they'll have on the future.

And that's exactly what she's been doing lately: *projecting*, convincing herself that the detective's visits mean that Derrick's death is somehow going to come back to haunt her. To steal a phrase from Tom, she's been borrowing trouble.

She has to stop, she realizes. Stop brooding and stewing and expecting the worst. Though it's disruptive to have Webster snooping around, she and Tom are innocent and there's no reason to think that the other shoe is about to drop.

After slowly finishing her tea, Emma pays her bill and returns to the parking lot. She's halfway to the car when she halts in surprise to spot another a slip of white paper pinned beneath her windshield wiper.

She looks around and sees that the only other adult in the parking lot is a thirtysomething woman holding the hand of a young girl and walking toward a nearby SUV.

Emma leans across the hood and snatches the paper from where it's fluttering. The note is written in the same block letters as the last one, and the message is just as cryptic.

You're not as smart as you think you are.

The words make her heart skip. She quickly scans the area again but finds nothing suspicious. It seems unlikely now that the first note was written by an irate driver. Someone is keeping tabs on her whereabouts and trying to put her in her place.

But why? And *who*? *Who would do something like this?*

Kyle's face pops into her mind immediately. Based on his recent behavior, it's not a stretch to picture him drumming up ways to rattle her, but sneaking around parking lots doesn't fit with his direct, confrontational style.

No, someone else has left them and it's unsettling. So much for a relaxing cup of tea.

She's about to take off when Tom calls.

"You done shopping, sweetheart?"

"All done and about to head home," she says. "How about you?"

"The course is pretty crowded today, but I'm expecting we'll finish up on schedule and I'll be back a little after noon. Should we take a picnic lunch to the beach today?"

"Yeah, I like that idea."

"Is everything okay?"

Tom might be preoccupied lately, but it hasn't dampened his intuitive skills. Though she's barely spoken to him yet, he can sense the distress in her tone.

"Uh, not quite. Something kind of odd just happened."

Emma explains about the note, and the earlier one as well, which she hadn't even bothered to mention to him.

"Jeez, how creepy. Do you want me to drive over there?"

"No, no, it's not necessary."

"But why don't you go home now, okay?"

"Yes, I'm about to. Oh, by the way, I ran into Justine at the farmers' market, and she cornered me, telling me she was worried about how much work you have and wished you'd delegate to her more. And how she couldn't believe you went back to the office after dinner the other night."

"Why in the world would she say all this to you?"

"I know, it seemed odd, like she was fishing for intel or wanted me to reassure her that she was in good standing."

"That was totally inappropriate of her. Sorry to put you in the middle."

"It was weird, but it wasn't a big deal. . . . Did you really go by the office?"

"What? Oh, after dinner? Yeah, to pick up something related to the contract I had to review," he says, sounding distracted again. "See you in a couple of hours, okay?"

After signing off, Emma tucks the note into her purse. She'd tossed the other one but thinks it might be smart to hold on to this one, as much as she hates having it on her person. If not Kyle, who could possibly have left them? Most of the people she knows in Westport are casual friends she's met through work or Tom, and she's not aware of having pissed any of them off.

When Emma enters the house a short time later, she discovers that the alarm is still on, meaning Brittany has yet to return. She's unpacking the produce when her phone rings. To her surprise, it's Taylor Hunt.

"Hey, Emma," the chief of staff says. "Is Tom standing right there?"

"No, he's playing golf. Have you been trying to reach him?"

"Actually, you're the one who I wanted to talk to. I hope I'm not bothering you on a Saturday."

"Not at all. Is everything all right?" Justine's comments

echo in her mind. Is Taylor also going tell her that Tom has too much on his plate?

"Everything's fine, and sorry to alarm you. I just wanted to ask—did you like the bracelet?"

The question takes Emma aback for a moment, before she realizes Tom might have consulted Taylor about the gift.

"I love it, yes. . . . Did you have a hand in picking it out?"

"No, it was all Tom's doing, but he showed me a picture and asked my opinion. I wanted to be sure I hadn't endorsed something that you secretly hate."

"No, it's beautiful."

"Tom was pretty certain you would. He said you're a big David Yurman fan."

Her heart skips a beat before she answers. "*Fan?*"

"That you really love his pieces."

This time her heart seems to lurch forward, ramming into her rib cage. "Tom said that?"

"Oops, did he have it wrong?"

"No, no, I *do* like them. But I didn't know he was aware of it."

"Well, you know Tom. He doesn't miss a thing."

"Right . . . oh, sorry, I need to take care of something now. Thanks for checking in."

Without giving Taylor time to respond, Emma ends the call. For a second she stays stock-still in the middle of the kitchen, her mind racing, and then upends her purse onto the island, shaking out the contents. She grabs her keys from the pile and races over to the studio.

After booting up her desktop computer, she opens the

file of Miami photos Eric emailed her and hurriedly scrolls through again to the ones from the Avignon dinner. She's in a number of the images, wearing orange silk capris and a matching tunic—and on her right wrist, a gold-and-silver David Yurman cuff. It would have been hidden at times beneath the bell-shaped sleeve of the tunic, but not when she raised her hand to gesture, something she must have done at least a few times during her talk.

Next, she pulls up the shots from her Saturday breakfast keynote, and exactly as she remembered, she'd worn a hot-pink, sleeveless dress with a braided silver cuff—another Yurman piece.

Is it possible, she wonders, that Tom stayed longer at the dinner than he let on, long enough to get a good look at what she was wearing? Could he have also attended her breakfast keynote, sitting close enough to the front to see the cuff? Because, otherwise, how would he know she liked this kind of jewelry?

Only minutes ago she'd told herself to stop spiraling, to stop imagining the worst, but it's looking like her husband hasn't been straight with her. A warning noise has begun to sound in Emma's brain, shrill and insistent.

What if he'd had his eye on her ever since Miami? She thinks again of Brittany's comment from the other night, the one she'd told herself not to stew about—that Tom was the "master of the long game."

Had he somehow played a long game with *her*—without her ever knowing it?

22

Two seconds later, Emma realizes she's overreacting again. Tom probably told Taylor she *would* love the designer, not that she already did, and Taylor misheard. The fact that he bought her the same kind of designer bracelet Derrick used to give her is simply a coincidence. Surely plenty of women in the tristate area owned jewelry by the popular brand at any given time.

And it's not as if Tom ever had the opportunity to play much of a long game with her. Yes, they crossed paths in Miami, but it was nothing more than chance that put them in the same room together six months later. *Right?*

Emma struggles up from her desk chair, grabs a bottle of water from the minifridge, and gulps down half the contents, hoping the hydration might help defuzz her brain. Bottle in hand, she circles the large, quiet room. When she worked in advertising research, a wonderful female mentor used to say that if the information you've gathered to help solve a problem doesn't immediately make the next steps clear, the solution isn't necessarily to keep studying the data. What you need is even *more* information.

That's what she needs to do: gather additional data. One thing that would really reassure her would be confirmation of the reason she was recruited at Halliday: because Scott Munroe read about her work in an article and thought it would be great to bring her aboard. Meaning, Tom wasn't in the picture at all.

After locking up, Emma hurries back to the house, giving Scott a call on the way.

"Oh, hey," he says, clearly surprised to hear from her on the weekend.

"Sorry for interrupting your Saturday, but I have a small favor to ask. Since I have a block of free time this weekend, I'd love to sketch out preliminary thoughts about our next project, and I wondered if I could pick your brain? It shouldn't take more than ten minutes on the phone."

"Yes, of course. You mean today?"

"If that works. Or tomorrow if it's better."

"I'm shopping for potted herbs at Terrain right now, but I should be done in ten minutes and—hey, do you just want to drive over and meet me at the café here?"

Emma glances at her watch. She has just enough time to squeeze in the trip before Tom gets back.

"Perfect," she says, and less than fifteen minutes later Emma rushes into the café at the garden center to find Scott sliding into one of the apple green-cushioned chairs. Though he's dressed casually—cream-colored pants and a dark purple T-shirt—he looks as spiffy as usual.

"My pleasure," he says after she thanks him for giving up time on a Saturday. "You've spared me a trip to buy car mats, so I should be thanking *you*."

The waiter stops by almost immediately, and after ordering cappuccinos, they spend a couple of minutes discussing the herbs Scott purchased and the recipes he'll use them in. The café abuts the garden center, and the air is redolent with the smell of clean dirt and mulch.

With the small talk out of the way and the cappuccinos in front of them, Emma runs through several questions regarding the goal of the next research project, questions she'd drummed up on the drive over and which Scott answers thoughtfully. Though they're a pretext for what she really needs to know, his feedback will actually be beneficial to her.

"I think that does it," she says, having kept her queries to about ten minutes. "I'm so grateful, Scott."

"Glad I could help. It's great to be teaming up with you again."

As she hoped, he's given her an entry point.

"How long ago was it, anyway, that we first started working together? Around two years, right?"

"Yeah, around there. You were still living in New York at that point."

Emma takes a final sip of her coffee and sets the cup into the saucer with a clink. "Remind me, too, will you?" she says lightly. "What first gave you the idea to reach out? I think you said once that you saw me quoted in an article."

"Yeah, that's right—and I was really impressed by your predictions about the travel industry, which, by the way, are proving completely accurate."

Instinctively she breaks into a grin as relief gushes through her that the story is as simple and innocent as she thought.

"What's so funny?" he asks, grinning himself.

"Oh, nothing really. It just amuses me how some connections happen."

Scott nods, but as he presses the rim of his cup to his lips, he lifts his eyebrows. *Something's coming*, she thinks, feeling a ripple of worry.

"I'm sure you know, though," he says, lowering the cup, "that I can't take all the credit."

Oh, no, she thinks. *Please, no.*

"It was Tom who got the ball rolling," he continues. "He read the piece first and passed it along."

"He told you to call me?" she says, tensing inside.

Scott chuckles. "Well, he didn't come right out and *order* me to. Though when your boss forwards a link to an article with a note that says, 'This woman really seems to know her stuff,' you don't blow it off. Especially when that boss is Tom."

She stares at him again, unable to even fake a smile.

"Don't get me wrong, I would have called you even if I'd come across the article myself," Scott says, misjudging the reason for the distress she can't wipe from her face. "It was clear from your comments that the agency could really use someone like you."

"Thanks, Scott," she manages. "And there's no issue. I just hadn't been aware that Tom had read the article, too."

"And he'd heard you, too, of course."

"Heard me?"

"At a talk you gave. Someone at the agency once mentioned that she and Tom had gone to it together."

"You mean in Miami?"

Scott frowns and taps a finger to his lips, trying to summon a memory. "Not Miami. In New York City, and I think it was Stacey Manning who brought it up. You know—the former number two who Justine replaced?"

Before the murder, Emma *had* given talks in the city, and also participated in panel discussions—at places like the Ninety-Second Street Y and the Harvard Club—but Tom certainly hadn't attended one of those events.

"It doesn't matter," she says. She's sure Scott must be wondering why the conversation has taken such a weird turn.

"Well, if there's any confusion, at least we know how to clear it up," he says, flashing a smile. "Just ask your husband."

"Ha, exactly. And speaking of Tom, I should see if he's done with golf and also let you get back to your day."

Scott insists on paying for their coffees and they exchange goodbyes in the parking lot. Emma doesn't leave right away, though. She sits stunned in the front seat of her car, trying to make sense of what she's heard.

There was a chance Taylor was confused, but Scott surely isn't. Contrary to what Tom has led her to believe for the past two years, it was *him* who initiated her involvement with the agency. And yet he's never admitted he put things in motion.

And what's this business about a speech in New York? When Stacey spoke to Scott, she surely must have been referring to the Miami dinner since it's likely she was there, too. But it suggests Tom might have heard more of that talk than he told her. No wonder he's aware of the jewelry she was wearing.

All this is making Emma feel like Tom *has* played some kind of long game, attracted to her from the beginning and then surreptitiously drawing her into his orbit. The whole thing feels manipulative . . . even slightly stalkerish.

And what would Dunne think if he found out? Or worse, Webster?

Emma sinks back into the seat, massaging her temples. Is she getting ahead of herself yet again, *projecting*? Part of Tom's success at work comes from regularly passing along interesting items to staffers as a way of seeding ideas, counting on employees to take it from there—and often deflecting credit for the role he initially played. Perhaps when he read the article and passed it to Scott, he didn't even remember her from the Miami program.

Still, she would like to be sure that Tom hasn't had some creepy obsession with her.

The alarm's off when Emma enters the house, indicating that Tom or Brittany's there, though a second later she remembers that in her rush to leave for Terrain, she never punched in the code. She calls out both names but there's no reply.

She feels grungy from running around in the warm weather this morning and also from her endless worrying, and she decides to change into a fresh top. Upstairs, the long hallway is utterly quiet. She picks up the lingering scent of the cypress candle she sometimes lights when she and Tom make love.

There are four rooms on this level: their bedroom, the guest room that Brittany's using, a backup guest room, which one day—depending on what they decide and whether fortune smiles on them—might become a nursery, and finally, at the very end, a home office for Tom.

Emma touches the doorknob to their bedroom, but then, barely conscious of what she's doing, drops her arm and stares down the length of the hall. The next thing she knows, she's making her way toward Tom's office. She feels a little like a sleepwalker who's woken with a jolt in some distant part of the house, but she knows exactly what her intention is. She wants to glance around. Not for anything specific, just something to confirm that her husband is exactly the person she thinks he is, and their relationship began as organically as she's always assumed.

She's reaching for the handle when the creak of a door behind her makes her nearly jump out of her skin. Spinning around, she discovers Brittany emerging from the guest bedroom.

"You're here?" Emma asks, realizing how lame that sounds.

"I got back about twenty minutes ago. Sorry, I didn't mean to scare you."

"Oh, I called your name."

"I must have been in the shower."

There's another sound now, on the stairs, and they turn in unison to find Tom reaching the top step. His gaze quickly bounces from Brittany to Emma, who's still standing inches from his office door.

"What are you doing?" he asks, not sharply but with a tiny hint of vexation in his tone.

"I needed a pencil," Emma says, flustered. The room is hardly off-limits to her, and yet they both know she's never had a reason to go in there since it was first set up. "I thought you might have one."

Though she's looking at Tom as she speaks, she can see Brittany in the corner of her eye, and Emma notices her glance up with a look that says, *Oops, someone's done something she shouldn't have.*

"I don't think I have any in my office, but there's some in a drawer in the kitchen," Tom says.

"Great, I'll grab one there." Emma makes her way back down the hall, taking a deep breath and forcing a smile. "How was golf?"

"Not bad." He glances at Brittany, who's still frozen on the threshold of the guest room. "Hey, Brit, how was your night out?"

"Really nice, Tom," she says, breaking into a smile that, unlike Emma's, looks genuine. "Thanks for asking."

"I was glad to get your text a little while ago, but that's the first we heard from you since last night. Going forward, you need to be better at updating us, okay?"

The gentle scolding clearly catches Brittany off guard, and her smile fades fast, but she quickly recomposes her face. "All right" is all she says.

"I'm not trying to play warden, honey, but I gave your dad my word I'd take good care of you, and it's good for us to have a rough idea of where you are."

"Of course." Within seconds she's back in the guest room, closing the door with a gentle thud. She's pissed and Emma knows it's because Tom expressed his concern more like a dorm RA or camp director than a person central to his life. And Brittany wants to be central.

"So tell me about these notes?" he asks, turning back to Emma. "Any more thoughts about who could have left them?" If he was actually bothered by the sight of her outside his office, he's not showing it.

"None, but it's pretty clear I've made an enemy in town."

"Hard to believe, and yet it does seem someone has a bone to pick with you. My first instinct is to alert the police, but I'm sure they'd say that leaving someone mean notes isn't criminal, and there's nothing they can do."

"Agree." Besides, the last thing she wants is any more police involvement in their lives.

"Just promise me you'll be careful and keep your eyes open."

"Will do."

"Okay, give me a minute to change and then we can head to the beach," Tom says, turning back to Emma.

"I'll go make some sandwiches we can take with us."

The time alone in the kitchen gives Emma a chance to order her thoughts. Maybe it's for the best that her attempt to snoop was aborted—because it would have been wrong to trespass there, to rifle through Tom's things. Really, the best way to settle her mind is to come right out and address her concerns with him, and she shouldn't be afraid to that.

"Ah, look what's trending," he says when he bounds into the kitchen ten minutes later. "Tuna salad on whole wheat. My absolute favorite."

"You want an iced tea, too?"

"Perfect."

"Hey, before we leave, I have a question for you."

"Shoot," Tom says, spearing a pickle from the open jar on the counter and helping himself to a bite.

She takes a breath. "I ended up having a spur-of-the-moment coffee with Scott this morning to talk about our next project. And I'm confused about something he said."

"Related to your research?"

"No, something else. He said it was you who first came up with the idea of me working with Halliday. I'd always thought it was Scott himself."

Tom swallows and she can't tell if his expression is due to her question or the tartness of the pickle.

"He said *I* told him to call you?" he says finally.

"Not that you told him, but that you sent him a link to an article about me, the implicit message being that he *should* call."

"If that's his memory of how things went, I'm not going to question it."

"But if you sent the link about me, why didn't you mention it after we started dating? Or now, especially with this weird Miami coincidence."

He shrugs. "I must have skimmed the article, not realized you were the same person on the program at that dinner, and forgot sending him the link when you came to work with us. Which is a shame because I could have given myself a pat on the back for shaping my own destiny so successfully."

Instinctively, she steeples her hands and presses them against her lips.

"What?" he asks, studying her.

"So you didn't actually hear my speech and decide you wanted to have me consult for you?"

"Sweetheart, we've been over this ground before. I staggered out of that dinner before you even opened your mouth, in desperate search of painkillers."

He steps closer and envelops her in his arms, and her body softens against the counter. *This has got to be the end of all the crazy worrying and projecting*, she tells herself.

Maybe some of her anxiety relates back to her first marriage, the experience of seeing the darker side of someone emerge without any real warning, like a person stepping out of the shadows in a slasher flick. That's not going to happen with Tom, though. There have never been any red flags, no hints of anything other than his boundless kindness and trustworthiness.

"*I* know what's going on," Tom says, his lips against her hair. "This investigation is still getting to you. But you can't let it, okay? As I've said before, we don't have a thing in the world to worry about."

"You're right," she says. *And thankfully*, Emma tells herself, *the NYPD is unlikely to talk to Scott.*

From there, the weekend manages to feel normal, even easy at moments, with their picnic at the beach, an impromptu dinner with friends of Tom's on Saturday night, and a movie the next day.

On Sunday night, while Tom's packing for Chicago, Emma makes a chicken dish and a salad with lettuce from the farmers' market, and they eat with Brittany, who seems cheery enough. If she was annoyed with Tom from the day before, she's let it go.

Later, despite how tired Emma is, she finds herself lying wide-eyed in the dark in bed again, unable to let herself drift off and replaying Tom's assurances. As genuine and logical as they sounded, something continues to gnaw at her. She turns his words over and over in her mind, then reminds herself that there's nothing to see.

But then she *does* see something. A hairline crack. Yesterday he told her that he never heard a word of her speech in Miami, but a week ago he'd said he'd managed to catch the first few minutes.

Has she been stupid to believe him? Has she ignored the rule of three—and four, and five? There's no way she's getting back to sleep now.

Patting her bedside table, she locates her phone and then slips nearly silently from bed. After easing the door open, she tiptoes down the long hall and finds herself outside Tom's office once again.

After a furtive glance back toward their bedroom, she eases the handle downward, pushes the door open, and quickly steps inside. Her nerves are on fire, like she's just drilled her way into a bank vault in the middle of the night, and yet she can't bring herself to turn back.

Emma decides to leave the door open so she can hear if Tom steps into the hall, but it means she'll have to rely on the flashlight in her phone. She activates the beam and trains it ahead of her. They worked on the room together, and it's nicely furnished, with a wall of bookcases on one side, a comfortable armchair and ottoman at the opposite end, and, directly in front of her, a sleek and elegant wood desk set between two windows. At the same time there's a slightly unfinished feeling to the space because Tom uses it so rarely.

Inching forward, Emma reaches the desk. There's nothing on top of it other than the printout of a creative concept for an ad campaign, and when she tugs open the solitary drawer, she sees only a few stray pens and paper clips, a pad of blank Post-it notes, and a roll of stamps.

From there she turns right to the bookcase. It's barely a quarter full, with a small selection of business books, as well several framed photos and a few knickknacks from the several trips they've done as a couple. They tell her nothing about Tom that she doesn't already know.

This is ridiculous, Emma thinks. *What could I possibly hope to find?*

As she turns back around, her eyes fall on the filing cabinets in the built-in credenza to the left of the door. She'd forgotten about those. She'll take a quick look and leave, she tells herself, before she feels any worse about sneaking in here.

One of the drawers is entirely empty except for a dozen hanging folders waiting to be assigned their jobs, and another is filled with hard copies of financial records, but the bottom one seems to contain personal files. Her breath quickens as she flicks quickly through the tabs, spotting titles like "Medical records," "Travel ideas," and "Condolence cards, Diana."

And then her fingers freeze. Because one tab has just two letters: E. H. *For Emma Hawke?* she asks herself.

After a glance back at the door, she slides the file from the drawer and opens it on the top of the credenza.

There are a dozen clippings related to her—a short profile

in a business trade magazine as well as printouts of online magazine articles she's been quoted in. The one on top is from about a year ago—no surprise there, she keeps track of Tom's press, too—but as she sorts through the pile, she sees others from farther back. Her stomach knots at the sight. It's like he's prepared a dossier on her.

There's something at the bottom of the file that's not a clipping, but a program. Within a couple of seconds she recognizes the crimson crest of the Harvard Club. The date on the front is February 24, just over two years ago.

Her eyes skim the page and she quickly processes what she's holding—the program for an event she participated in. Not a speech, but a panel discussion on emerging trends that calendar year, and her name's right there along with the other panelists. She'd been recruited by a professional contact who'd gone to Harvard.

It was one month after the Miami dinner and one month before Derrick died.

With her heart racing, she peers more closely. In the margins are notes in pencil, and as she reads each one, there's a prick of recognition. She's almost positive they're snippets of remarks she made that night. And the handwriting looks just like Tom's.

23

THERE'S A SPLIT SECOND IN THE MORNING WHEN EMMA surfaces from a dream and the only thought in her head is how cool the sheets feel against her skin.

And then, a moment later, images from the night before explode in her mind like a firecracker. Her furtive walk down the hall in the dark. The folder full of clippings about her. And worst of all, the program. If that's really Tom's handwriting in the margins, it means he was at the event that night, that he *did* come to hear her speak in New York, that he's been completely dishonest about not being more than vaguely aware of her before she arrived at Halliday.

It's early and barely light out, but Tom is up. She hears him padding around the room, dressing in preparation of his trip, though he's obviously doing his best to be quiet. She breathes deeply and rhythmically with eyes closed, praying he'll think she's still sound asleep.

His getting-ready process seems to go on forever, but finally she hears him take a few steps across the room, probably toward the door. He stops abruptly, however, mere inches away, and she practically feels the heat coming off his body. Is he hoping that her eyes will flutter open and she'll wish him a sleepy goodbye?

Or is he simply studying her? Did he awaken last night to find her side of the bed empty and wonder where she disappeared to?

But she doesn't open her eyes. She doesn't move a muscle.

It isn't until Emma hears the purr of the car backing out of the driveway that she throws the sheet off and slips out of bed. The clock on the bedside table says 6:02, which means she has roughly two hours before Brittany emerges from her bedroom.

Downstairs in the kitchen, she reads a note from Tom saying goodbye and that he'll see her Tuesday night, then brews coffee on automatic pilot and takes it to the table. A loud sigh escapes her lips. She's done what she set out to, gathered even more information than she had initially, but rather than helping her, it's chilled her to the bone. Tom clearly developed some kind of fascination with her after Miami, an obsession even. He kept a file of her media clippings, went into Manhattan to see her speak, and then subtly manipulated an employee into bringing her on board at Halliday: a "long game" that came to a head when he finally asked for a meeting with her in his office. He orchestrated their love affair, and ultimately, their marriage.

And how convenient for Tom, she thinks, that she was newly widowed by the time she arrived at Halliday. What would have come of his little infatuation if she'd still been with Derrick? Would he have made a play for her regardless, turning on his charm at full wattage to seduce her into stepping out on her husband?

So what does she do now that she knows all this? She feels like the dog that caught the car.

Listlessly, Emma brings the mug to her mouth but then sets it back down, her stomach too queasy to face the caffeine. She needs to take some kind of action, but right now she can't imagine what that could be. Things might actually be worse than she can see at the moment; there might be more Tom has misled her about. *Is* there? Is there even more?

A thought breaks through her mind, like an axe hacking through a door, and her lips part in shock. What if her first husband's death hadn't been simply *convenient* for Tom? What if he'd become so obsessed with her that he'd actually killed Derrick so he could have her all to himself? He wouldn't have turned up on the police radar then because, like in the classic Hitchcock movie *Strangers on a Train*, he'd never met Derrick, never had contact with him, not even exchanged a single phone call.

Stop, Emma tells herself. She's started down another crazy rabbit hole, and she can't let herself go there. Maybe there's some other explanation for the Harvard program and the handwriting isn't Tom's. And even if he *was* keeping tabs on her, he's not a murderer. Despite her failures at judging people, she knows that. Plus, he has an ironclad alibi, one that he's shared with Detective Webster.

Just for her own satisfaction, though, she picks up the phone from its spot on the table and googles "How long does it take to drive from Stowe Vermont to New York City?"

The answer: "5 hr 24 min." Which means if Tom had

snuck away from the client weekend to kill Derrick, he would have been missing in action for well over a dozen hours, which though possible seems highly improbable. Of course, he could have paid someone to do the killing for him.

No, the whole idea is absurd, outrageous. But then so is the idea of Tom tracking her over months and manipulating her recruitment to his agency, and yet she now has proof that he did those things.

Emma holds out her hands and lets her head sink into them. She's loved Tom fiercely, finally been so happy in her life, and it's shattering to think he's not who she believed he was, that he might be responsible for something truly horrible.

But she can't let her distress either undo her or immobilize her, the way it did for far too long during her first marriage. Instead, she needs to keep digging, to find out the key pieces of information that will put her mind at ease once and for all.

The first step that occurs to her off the top of her head is a LinkedIn search for Stacey Manning, the former number two at Halliday, who left shortly before Emma started there. If she can connect with Stacey, she might be able to tease out whether, as Scott suggested, the woman attended the panel discussion with Tom.

Emma finds her on LinkedIn and discovers to her dismay that she's a Harvard grad, which suggests things are exactly as she thought. But—longshot idea—maybe Stacey went to the panel discussion on her own and later passed on the program to Tom. She's going to have to talk to her.

Seeing that there's no current job listed in the bio jogs Emma's memory—she'd heard that Stacey had decided to step off the treadmill for a while. She drags the cursor to the message icon on LinkedIn and writes her a quick note saying that she's Tom's wife, has heard a lot about her, and wonders if she's open to being interviewed about switching gears for some research she's doing.

Unfortunately, if Stacey has stepped off the treadmill, she's hardly going to be checking her LinkedIn messages every day, and it might be a while before she hears back.

Emma's running late by this point and after a shower, she slips into a simple summer dress and sandals and grabs a container of yogurt from the fridge. She's preparing to leave when Brittany comes down the back stairs. She offers Emma a pleasant smile.

"Morning," Emma says, happy that overall things still seem to be in tune with the two of them. "Would you like me to order an Uber for you before I go?"

Brittany had mentioned at dinner that she'd be using Uber for work the next two days since she wouldn't be able to hitch a ride with Tom.

"No thanks, I already scheduled one, and Tom was nice enough to say he'd reimburse me. I'm just going to have a little breakfast first."

"Have a good day then."

"You, too, Emma."

When she arrives at the studio, Emma discovers her two co-workers are already at their desks. As she reviews the day ahead with Dario, she senses him on alert, probably noticing how tense she is, and she takes a few deep breaths, trying to force herself to stay present. For the next couple of hours she manages to draft some questions for the next influencer survey with Eric and tackle a mass of emails. She's halfway through them when she finds a message from Lilly Shelbourne responding to her condolences.

Thanks so much for reaching out, Lilly's note says. I'm doing okay, putting photography on hold for a while. If you have any time, I'd love to meet you for coffee or a drink. There's something I want to ask you, woman to woman.

Emma's brow wrinkles. She can't imagine what kind of question Lilly could have for her since they've only met a few times. Does she want Emma to share any wisdom she's gleaned for dealing with the sudden loss of a husband? She's the last person who would have anything worthwhile to contribute on that front.

But it would be cruel to rebuff the request. She writes back saying that she hasn't any plans to be in the city in the near future, but she would love to speak by phone or FaceTime, and gives Lilly her cell number.

Emma tries after that to refocus her attention on work, but her thoughts are constantly dragged back to Tom and all she's learned about him. She's desperate for reassurance. There's no other way she can think of to confirm whether Tom was at the Harvard Club panel discussion, but, she realizes, she *can* at least suss out more information about the Stowe weekend and make sure he was fully present. Justine would be the best source because she would have organized the event, but considering their weird exchange this past weekend, she doesn't want to get into anything with her. So she'll reach out to Taylor. Maybe by asking the right questions, she can feel confident that Tom was in Vermont for the entire weekend, and therefore not anywhere near New York. Grabbing her phone, she shoots Taylor a text message.

> Do you have a couple of minutes to spare this morning? I'd love to drop by and ask your advice about something. Won't take long.

The reply comes almost immediately.

> Sure. Now? I'm free for a while.

> Great, should only take me fifteen minutes to get there.

> Want to give me a hint so I can prep?

> Thanks, but no need to prep.

Emma leaves immediately, telling Dario she has an errand to run.

At Halliday, Emma enters the building through a side door and approaches Taylor's cubicle from the rear, where she finds the chief of staff typing on a PC whose monitor is festooned with a dozen multicolored Post-it notes.

"Morning," Emma says quietly.

"Oh, hi," Taylor replies, spinning around. "Come with me. I thought we could talk in one of the conference rooms."

Snatching her phone with one hand, Taylor motions with the other for Emma to follow her down a hall. She's looking preppy as always in a white cotton top, a hot-pink and white Lilly Pulitzer–style skirt with a starfish pattern, and black flats with gold buckles. Dressy compared to the rest of the crowd at Halliday, but that's her style.

As soon as they enter the small conference room, Emma grabs a seat with her back to the door. She's not worried about Justine seeing her because she must be in Chicago with Tom, but she's trying to avoid being spotted by his executive assistant, Janice. There's a chance she'd mention it to Tom, and Emma then will have to concoct a lie to explain her presence.

"So what kind of advice are you looking for?" Taylor asks in her typically crisp manner.

"I want to plan a surprise ski trip for Tom during the Christmas holidays, and I was hoping to enlist your help."

Taylor straightens in her chair. "Gosh, I'd love to be of assistance, Emma, but I haven't skied in a couple of years."

"That doesn't matter. What I'd like is to find out a little about a client event in Stowe, Vermont, a while back. He raved about it, and I thought I'd see if the hotel that was used had availability. Do you remember where everybody stayed?"

Taylor frowns. "I can usually pull anything recent about Tom's schedule off the top of my head, but that goes back at least, what, two years? I'm pretty sure they stayed at the Cedar Pine Inn—though I'll have to double-check. Justine actually put the whole thing together with the event planner she uses."

"Thank you, but it's not important enough to bother Justine about."

"Okay, I can probably find all I need in the event file."

"That would be terrific. I know the holidays seem far off, but I heard these resorts book up really early."

"Makes sense to act now, then."

Emma pushes on. "Could you also see if there are any notations about the restaurants the group ate at? There was one that Tom absolutely loved—I think it was where they went Saturday night."

She feels a spasm of shame as she speaks. What a cheap trick for trying to determine whether the man she adores could be a cold-blooded killer. And she doesn't even know what she'll do with the information once Taylor provides it—call the restaurant and ask the manager if they remember whether a group that dined there years ago included a dazzling, silver-haired man in his forties? But she's hard-pressed to think of another way to produce the results she needs.

She's glanced off for a moment, and when she looks back, Taylor's expression is bemused.

"What's so funny?" Emma asks, more sharply than she intended. She doesn't have the patience today for coyness.

"Oh, sorry," Taylor says. "I was thinking how sweet it was of you to go to so much trouble."

"I doubt it will be much trouble," Emma says, softening her tone. "And the trip will be fun for me, too."

Taylor cocks her head, which waggles her gold hoop earrings. "Can I make a tiny suggestion, though?"

"By all means."

"I remember that before Tom met you and was doing a lot of skiing, he always went to Killington. I think he preferred the trails there, though it's a longer drive."

"Hmm. Well, why don't I start with Stowe and then look into Killington as well?"

"Sure. I mean, you know Tom best of all."

Emma thanks Taylor for her help and says she'd love the information in the next day or two if that's possible. "And remember, mum's the word," she adds. "I don't want to spoil the surprise."

As soon as she departs, Emma lets the fake smile evaporate from her face. The only thing she can do now is wait for Taylor to get back to her.

For the rest of the day, Emma does her best to lose herself again in her work, though she dreads dinnertime when she'll have to fake cheeriness with Brittany. But at around five Brittany texts her to say she's spending the night again with her new pal.

Sorry for late notice, she adds. But my friend got concert tix at the last minute. I'll stop by in the a.m. to change.

It seems Brittany's taken Tom's feedback to heart, being less vague about her overnight plans. Emma texts back, Have fun and tx for letting me know.

At about five, Eric and Dario start packing up, and Eric reminds her that they're headed out to see the latest Marvel release on the big screen. Dario is a superfan, but Eric merely likes to keep up with blockbuster movie trends for work. She smiles and wishes them a good night.

The studio is totally silent now, except for the faint groan of the minifridge at the far end of the room. *Better to be home*, Emma thinks, where she can eat in front of the TV, the sound drowning out her thoughts.

After answering a long email from a client, she slips her tote bag over her shoulder, switches off her desk lamp, trudges wearily to the door, and swings it open. A small movement startles her. It takes her a second to realize that a piece of paper has fallen to the ground, alighting on the wooden threshold.

It's a note. One that must have been wedged between the door and the outer frame. With a start she spots the block letters in pen, the exact same style as the two notes left on her car.

Dropping to her knees, she plucks the paper from the ground.

Are you really too stupid to see the truth?

Her heart's thudding now. This time the person's ventured onto her property—while she was sitting alone in the studio, no less. As she raises her eyes to scan the grounds, the doorway suddenly darkens, and then to her shock, a figure appears only a few feet away.

Emma leaps to her feet, so fast that her bag slips off her shoulder and lands on the floor with a thud.

The figure advances and Emma finally sees who it is. Detective Lisa Webster.

24

FOR A FEW TERRIFYING SECONDS, EMMA WONDERS IF WEBster has come to arrest her—or Tom.

"Good evening, Emma," the detective says, smiling wanly.

No, that's not about to happen, Emma decides, wanting to cry in gratitude. Webster wouldn't be on her own and addressing her this congenially if she was about to snap on a pair of cuffs and haul her off in a squad car. *But what the hell is she doing here?*

"Hello," she manages to respond. She takes a single step across the threshold, preventing Webster from entering the studio. "What can I do for you?"

"Is everything all right?" the detective asks in lieu of a reply. Her eyes have dropped to the floor behind Emma, where her bag is lying in a heap with files poking out. Webster clearly saw her stooping over and might have even spotted her reading the note.

"Everything's fine," Emma says, slowly squashing the paper in her hand. "Can I help you with something?"

What she'd really like to do is ask why Webster's on pri-vate property without permission, but she knows she has to play it cool right now.

"There was no answer at the house, so I decided to try your office. I was in the area, and I wanted to follow up on one point from our original conversation."

Why in the world is she in the area—or is that a lie, a cover for simply trying to catch Emma off guard again? And is Webster thinking she'll invite her in or suggest they head into town for cappuccinos like Tom did? That's not going to happen.

"I'm glad to hear you're still working on the case, but as I believe Peter Dunne told you, he's going to be addressing questions on my behalf going forward."

Webster frowns, creating a furrow across her wide, smooth forehead. "That's a shame. All I wanted was the an-swer to a single query—just to help me straighten something out in my own mind."

"Mr. Dunne will be happy to be of assistance with what-ever it is."

Another frown, as if Emma's hired some 1-800 lawyer and the detective is concerned on her behalf. "You can't take one minute, Emma, to tell me yourself? It'd save me valuable time."

A prick of anger pierces Emma's unease. Webster has no right to pressure her this way. She takes a breath, trying to summon the words that will get the detective out of her hair without seriously pissing her off.

"According to the notes from our interview," Webster con-tinues, as if Emma's momentary silence means she's willing to answer the question, "you and your husband met while you were working at his ad agency, but when he and I spoke, he mentioned that you'd first crossed paths in Miami. Would you mind clearing up that discrepancy?"

A wave of panic rolls through her. Tom said he'd managed to drop that detail in casually during his interview, but Webster has obviously fixated on it. As much as Emma wants to enlighten her, tell her that they *didn't* actually meet, she knows she has to resist the temptation to explain.

"Why don't I have Mr. Dunne call you and clarify everything? And if you don't mind, I really need to lock up now and get back to the house."

The detective allows the words to hang in the air for a couple of moments, then finally nods, keeping her dark eyes fastened on Emma's. "As you wish."

Webster pivots slowly and retraces her steps along the path, her head swiveling like she's a prospective buyer taking in the grounds with her eyes. Finally, nearing the house, she steps off the path, veers left, and crosses the side lawn in long strides toward the street, where she's obviously parked her car.

Once Webster's out of sight, Emma gathers her things again, locks up, and returns to the house, her heart still thrumming. The police must be digging around the edges of the theory that she and Tom actually met in Miami and hit it off. And it must mean that Webster will be looking into the client weekend in Stowe, if she hasn't already.

As soon as she's dumped her bag on the counter, Emma calls Dunne, and to her relief, he answers the phone himself. She blurts out what transpired just now.

"I'm going to have another chat with Detective Webster,"

he says after she's finished. "But unfortunately, this Miami detail definitely seems to have piqued her interest."

"I'm sure Tom never would have used the phrase 'crossed paths' because it implies we spoke or even made eye contact and we didn't. So why would she say that?"

"To goad you into responding. To trick you into giving something away that you don't want her to know," he says, then pauses briefly. "Emma, I think it's important that the two of us talk in person. Would you be able to come into Manhattan and meet me in my office tomorrow?"

Her anxiety spikes even higher. Is he thinking that the police have tapped her phone?

"Uh, of course, but why in person?"

"I feel this is the kind of conversation that's best had face-to-face. Let me see . . . is eleven o'clock possible for you?"

She tells him yes without hesitating since she knows tomorrow is a light day for her—but even if it wasn't, this is feeling scarily urgent. After signing off, Emma pours herself a glass of white wine and sinks into one of the bar chairs at the island.

For the first time she's aware that what she's experiencing is no longer simply the worry or agitation that have dogged her since Webster first rang her doorbell. Instead, it's a low-grade terror, not unlike the kind she lived with when the police were eying her as a possible suspect twenty-seven months ago. Now they're not only circling *her*, but they're doing the same with Tom. And maybe they have good reason to be looking into him.

As Emma takes a sip of wine to calm herself, her gaze falls on the crumpled note, which she'd dropped on the island when she came in. She has *that* to contend with, too. The idea of touching it again creeps her out, so she grabs a banana from the fruit bowl and uses the stem to smooth out the paper.

Are you really too stupid to see the truth?

This one isn't simply dismissive like the others were; the tone here is downright contemptuous, possibly even menacing.

Who in Westport not only dislikes her enough to leave these notes, but has the incredible nerve to risk being caught on her property? A thought strikes her out of the blue. What if the notes are somehow related to the person sneaking into the studio the other night? She still doesn't think it could be Dario, and besides, her two employees are together at the moment. But just to be sure she taps out a text to Eric: Just curious. Dario's been with you the whole time, right?

Grabbing her glass, Emma slides off the bar chair and paces the kitchen, ruminating. In terms of the police inquiry, meeting with Dunne tomorrow feels like a decisive move, the right step, but the notes are a whole different matter, and she has no clue how to proceed.

Her phone rings and when she snatches it from the counter, she's surprised by the sight of Justine's name on the screen.

"I hope I'm not catching you at a bad moment," Justine says.

"No—is everything okay?"

"Yes, fine." Her voice, however, sounds tense. "But I've been unable to reach Tom with a quick update, and I thought you might know where he is."

"He's in Chicago. Aren't you there with him?"

"Not this time. . . . Tom said he wanted to keep this trip pretty streamlined."

"Um, it's possible his meeting ran late, or if they signed the deal, perhaps they've gone out for drinks to celebrate. When he calls later, I can tell him you're eager to speak to him."

"Or I'll just wait and fill him in tomorrow," Justine says. Her voice has reclaimed its usual silkiness. "Have a nice evening, Emma."

Odd, Emma thinks after ending the call. Was this simply another instance of Justine trying to insinuate herself or is there something else going on?

In other words, is there even *more* for her to stress about? She feels suddenly desperate for something, *anything* to tamp down her anxiety. On the spur of the moment, she snatches her phone from the counter and texts Bekah.

> Hey, I have to be in NY unexpectedly to-
> morrow. Any chance I could stop by in the
> afternoon + say hi, see the baby?

It's only a minute before a response appears on her phone.

> Omg, I'd love that. Would 6 be too late? J.D.
> has a business dinner, but Hadley and I will
> be footloose and fancy-free and she'll have
> had her nap and dinner by then and won't
> be fussy.

Six is a little later than Emma would like, but, understanding that when you're a parent your schedule isn't your

own, she texts back saying she'll be there with bells on. She
certainly can't tell Bekah everything, not now anyway, but at
least she'll have the comfort of her friend's company.

After changing into sweatpants and a T-shirt, Emma
wanders back to the kitchen. She's got zero appetite, but she
nukes one of the premade chicken dinners from the freezer
and forces herself to take a few bites. The note's still on the
island and her eyes are drawn to it again.

Are you really too stupid to see the truth?

She wishes she'd held on to the first note but at least she's
got the second tucked in a drawer upstairs. And the words
from both are seared in her memory.

You'd better watch what you're doing.

You're not as smart as you think you are.

Could there be more to the messages than a show of dis-
dain and contempt? For the first time she sees that there's a
warning implied in each one, an admonishment to watch her
back, wise up, and pay better attention.

Is someone trying to warn her about *Tom*?

The room suddenly darkens. Glancing out the kitchen
window, Emma sees that the early evening sky is now
bunched with thick, dark clouds that seem to have come out
of nowhere. *How fitting*, she thinks, for the state her mind is
in tonight.

Emma struggles up from the table. As she's dumping the
remains of her half-eaten meal in the trash, her phone rings.
Tom. Somehow she'll have to manage to sound normal.

"Ah, there you are," he says, and it's only then that she
notices a missed call from a bit earlier, probably from when
she was upstairs.

"Oh, sorry, I didn't hear the phone before."

"Everything okay?"

"Yes, I was just upstairs changing clothes. How did the meeting go?" she asks, deflecting attention away from herself.

"A home run. They're definitely bringing us on board."

"That's great, congratulations. . . . Oh, Justine called a little while ago, trying to reach you. I take it you didn't invite her along."

"No, she seemed so unfocused last time that I thought it would be better without her."

"Any idea what's going on with her?"

"Not yet. . . . Oh, one other piece of good news. Since we got the deal done today, they canceled the follow-up meeting that had been planned for tomorrow afternoon. I have a breakfast meeting with another other potential client, but I can fly home right afterward."

"Great, but, um, I won't be here till later, probably around nine or ten. I'm going to be visiting Bekah in the city."

"Bekah? I haven't heard her name in a while. You're going in just to see her and the baby?"

"Well, not exactly. Peter Dunne asked me to come in for a catchup, so that's the main reason for my trip."

"A catchup? Has there been a new development?"

She's already decided not to tell him about Webster's visit until he returns. It was about the Miami dinner, after all, and if she brings that up to Tom, she'll have a hard time camouflaging the distress related to him in her voice.

"He thinks it would be good to do a face-to-face and review where we stand."

She's aware there's a slight shakiness to her voice.

"Is everything all right, Em?"

"Yes, fine."

"You sure? If there are kidnappers in the room with you, say something like, uh, 'How about salmon for Wednesday night?' and I'll call 911."

Emma chuckles in spite of herself. This is *Tom* after all. The man who can make her laugh no matter what. She hates engaging in this awful charade, but what choice does she have? Until she has more information, she has to proceed as if everything is normal.

"I'm a little tired, that's all. I might even crash early."

"Well, sleep tight, sweetheart. And have a nice visit with Bekah and Hadley."

"Will do."

"Love you."

"Love you, too."

Setting the phone down, her attention is drawn to the sudden rustle of tree leaves outside the kitchen window, and moments later, drops of rain start to spatter on the flagstone patio out back. Usually, she finds the sound of rain relaxing, but tonight the fast tattoo of the drops echoes her jittery nerves. She decides to retreat to the cocoon of the bedroom.

After doing a sweep through the house, making sure windows and doors are locked, Emma leaves a couple of lamps burning, sets the alarm, and wearily mounts the stairs. Her attempt to read in bed proves futile, so she turns on the TV, but all the shows she comes across—thrillers, true crime documentaries, dystopian dramas—seem guaranteed to agitate her even more. Sleep seems to be the best option.

Knowing it won't come easily, Emma fishes through the

medicine cabinet for the Ativan prescribed for her after Derrick's murder, by a doctor, who, like everyone else, mistook her anxiety for grief. The three remaining pills have expired, but she pops one anyway, praying it's still potent enough to work.

From experience she knows she has to give it twenty to thirty minutes to take effect, so after crawling into bed, she lies on her back, waiting for the pill to make her eyelids heavy and dissolve her muddled thoughts. Finally, she drifts off.

A noise wakes her, though, and as her eyes flutter open, Emma senses she hasn't been asleep for long. She groans and pushes the pillow away. What she's hearing, she realizes groggily, is a chirping sound coming from the ground floor.

She struggles to sit up in bed, trying to interpret the noise. Could it be the smoke detector warning that the battery is low? No, not that. With a start she realizes it's the sound the security system makes when one of the doors is first opened.

There's someone else in the house.

25

EMMA JERKS HER HEAD TOWARD THE DIGITAL CLOCK. *11:23. Could it be Tom,* she wonders, *somehow able to catch a flight home tonight?* But he would have called to alert her.

Patting frantically for her phone on the stand next to her, her fingers find nothing but the wood surface. She reaches out, fumbles for the bedside lamp, and snaps it on. Except for the clock, the top of the nightstand is bare.

And then, distraught, she sees in her mind's eye, the phone resting on the kitchen island.

The house has gone deadly silent. No more chirping. In a second, the alarm should begin to shriek and the police will be notified. But the shriek doesn't come. Whoever has entered has clearly used the code to deactivate the system.

Emma kicks the duvet off the bed and swings her legs around to drop both feet to the floor. She stares at the open doorway of the bedroom and the darkness of the hall beyond it, her heart beating crazily. She and Tom dismissed the idea of landlines when they bought the house, so there's no way to call 911 from this floor.

A sound punctures the silence. A footstep on the stairs. And then another. *Lock the bedroom door*, Emma thinks. *Lock it now.* She propels herself from the bed, but as she starts for the door, her leg is snagged by the duvet and she pitches forward. It takes a frenzied couple of seconds to right herself, and by the time she's across the room and near the door, the footsteps are already in the hall.

She shoots out her arm for the door, desperate to slam it shut and turn the lock.

"Emma?" someone calls from down the hall. A female voice.

Brittany.

A second later, the girl appears in the doorway, dressed in jeans and a cotton sweater, her wet hair flattened against her scalp.

"What the hell?" Emma snaps.

"Oh gosh, I hope I didn't scare you," Brittany says.

"Didn't *scare* me?" She pauses to catch a breath. "You terrified me. What in god's name is going on?"

"The concert got rained out, so there was no reason for me to stay at my friend's." Brittany bites her lower lip for a second. "You didn't get my text?"

"No. No, I didn't. When—when I didn't respond, you should have called me, told me what was happening." Though would she have even heard the call with her phone parked in the kitchen?

"I figured you were asleep and that I'd just come in quietly and try not to wake you."

Emma doesn't have the psychic energy to discuss this one more second. She needs to crawl back beneath the covers and slow down her breathing.

"You should dry off and get to bed," she tells Brittany curtly. "Good night."

Brittany lifts her shoulders and dark brown eyebrows simultaneously. "Again, I'm so sorry." But there's a shadow of a smile on her face.

As the young woman disappears down the hall, Emma considers going to the kitchen to retrieve her phone, but instead shuts the door with a thud. She staggers toward the bed, yanks the duvet from the floor, and collapses onto the mattress.

She doesn't like me, Emma thinks. She'd convinced herself she was making progress with the girl, slowly winning her over, but that's not the case at all.

As she stares through the darkness at the ceiling, a thought wiggles up through her mind: Could Brittany dislike her enough to put it in writing?

It isn't until she's on the train for New York the next day, dressed in a short-sleeved white silk blouse, black pencil skirt, and low heels, that Emma finally feels some of the tension melt from her body. She's never been a fan of Metro-North trains, the cramped beige-and-red faux-leather seats and overly bright interiors, but the 9:14 isn't all that crowded today, and she's able to spread out a little. Before long, she begins to lose herself in the chug and rattle of the car along the track.

Of course, she's aware her unagitated state is only temporary. The meeting with Peter Dunne is bound to be tense, and though her get-together with Bekah should be a peaceful interlude, she'll be back in Westport tonight, lying in bed beside a man who's misled her from the moment they met. *Then* what? She doesn't have an answer.

As the train crosses the river into the city, about to descend into the underground tunnel, a text pops up from Eric:

> Sry, just seeing this. Yes, we were at the movie till 9. We did drive there separately, though. Everything okay?

Separate cars means that Dario could have circled back to the studio five minutes after they left and slipped the note into the crack between the door and frame. It doesn't seem like something he'd do—but she's realizing every day that she's done a dreadful job of reading some of the people around her.

> Nothing urgent. Will fill you in.

The train jerks to a stop at the end of the tunnel and Emma joins the stream of passengers making their way into Grand Central Terminal and then out onto the street. Dunne's office is a fairly short walk away on Park Avenue and Fifty-Fifth. As she heads up the wide street, grateful that last night's rain clouds have cleared, she realizes it's been ages since she strolled through Manhattan like this. She and Tom have been so busy with the wedding and the house during the last year that they've only come into the city together for a couple of plays and concerts. And when she's done TV appearances here, she's left right afterward, often jumping into a town car that's been arranged by the show's producer.

Arriving at Dunne's office on the fifteenth floor of a black granite and glass building, she gives her name to the receptionist and to her surprise it's the attorney himself who comes out to greet her.

"Emma, good to see you," he says, clasping her hand. He's dressed in a navy suit and an expensive-looking patterned silk tie. "My office is overrun with documents, so I thought we could duck into one of the conference rooms."

"That's fine," she says as he leads the way.

Dunne's only about five nine or ten but he has a taut, powerful presence. At moments he can seem preternaturally calm, but she senses he's always watching and listening intently, noticing others' subtle cues of body language.

When they reach a sleek conference room at the end of the corridor, the lawyer motions her in, and once inside, taps a button that fogs the outer glass wall. He gestures to a tray on the table with a carafe, asking if she'd like coffee, and she greedily accepts. Dunne declines her offer to pour him a cup and takes a spot on the other side of the table where a folder, yellow legal pad, and Montblanc pen have been placed. With her coffee in hand, Emma settles in the chair directly across from him.

"I'm glad we could meet in person, Emma," he says, both hands resting quietly on the table.

"Me, too. Did you have a chance speak to Detective Webster yet?"

He shakes his head. "I left a message for her this morning but haven't heard back."

"I can't believe she just showed up that way, like she was trying to catch me off guard."

"That will be addressed when I connect with her. . . . So, let's talk about Miami, Emma."

She takes a breath. "Right. Well, as I mentioned the other day, I was there to speak at a convention. For retail—"

"I got that. What I want to focus on is the dinner," Dunne interrupts, pinning her with his gaze. "Could anyone there have seen you and Tom interacting that night?"

"No, of course not," she says, slightly taken aback.

"You're certain of that? Because I've been wondering if the tip Webster's supposedly received had to do with the dinner. And you and Tom."

So she'd been right the other day when she guessed that Dunne might have been contemplating whether she and Tom met that night, embarked on an affair, and then plotted to remove Derrick from the picture—being careful and clever enough not to leave a single clue.

"No one could have seen us speaking there because as I stressed to you before, we *didn't*." She leans in, pressing her forearms against the table. "Peter, I know that over the years plenty of guilty clients must have claimed innocence to you, but I swear I'm telling the truth."

He offers a small but warm smile, one that seems to re-affirm his steadfast support, but offers no indication whether he believes her. "Emma, I hope you see that I'm only doing my job, making sure there aren't any potential land mines. Because if I'm oblivious to them, I can't protect you properly."

"Yes, of course."

"And a land mine would be not only you and Tom meeting that night but the two of you having contact in the weeks immediately afterward."

Panic spikes through Emma. She has to come clean with him—at least about some of it—or else she *will* be pushing him on a path toward a land mine.

"Peter, you have my word that I had no direct contact with Tom during the Miami trip or in the weeks immediately following. But, um . . . there's another weird wrinkle. It turns out that Scott Munroe, who first hired me as a consultant at Halliday, learned about my work from an article that Tom gave him. Tom often forwards articles from the business press to his staff, and he didn't realize when he sent Scott the link that I'd been the speaker in Miami. Like I said before, he had to leave early because of a toothache."

For a few moments, Dunne is silent, his lips pursed the tiniest bit. Behind her, through the fogged glass wall, she hears the muffled drone of voices, people in conversation as they move along the corridor.

"And this person, Scott Munroe," he says finally, "he works at Halliday?"

"Not anymore. But I'm doing a consulting project with him, and it came up the other day when we were chatting."

"What are your thoughts on this, Emma?"

Part of her wants to unburden herself completely, confess what she's learned about Tom's behavior, even her fear that he might be behind Derrick's death, but another part resists throwing Tom under the bus. He's her husband, the man she loves, and, beyond that, she still doesn't have all the facts. Maybe that isn't his handwriting on the Harvard Club program and he never actually attended the panel discussion. Maybe Tom's assistant got hold of the program when she was putting together the press file. Maybe, maybe, maybe.

"I . . . I know it's another awkward detail, but I give you my word I never met Tom until the summer."

"All right," he says again, "then there's nothing for Webster to turn up."

Emma nods. But of course, things aren't "all right." There might actually *be* something for Webster to discover.

Out on the street a few minutes later, Emma feels deflated. There had been a moment when she could have spilled everything to Dunne, giving herself a sense of control, but she'd lost her nerve.

She trudges south along Park Avenue, unsure where she's going next. When she'd agreed on a six o'clock get-together with Bekah, she'd vaguely assumed she'd roam the East Side beforehand and have a late lunch alone in a little bistro. And yet she finds herself slightly overwhelmed by the city today—the blaring horns, the cloying smell of toasted pretzels from a sidewalk vendor, the constant feeling of people hurrying by her. If only there was someone she could invite for coffee or a quick lunch, but her old friends from the city must be at work, and it's not likely any one of them could duck out on such short notice.

Lilly Shelbourne's name suddenly springs to mind. She'd wanted to meet in person, and since Lilly had said she was taking a break from her work, she might be available.

Emma veers off the sidewalk, and after stepping onto the gray granite plaza of the Seagram's Building, she sends a text to Lilly.

> Ended up in NY today on spur of moment. Any chance you're free for coffee in the next hour or two?

It takes Lilly only a couple of seconds to respond.

> Would love that. Where are you?

> Nr Grand Central—but let me go to your area. u have so much going on.

> How about my apt? Come now if you want.

After Emma texts a thumbs-up, Lilly gives her an address on Lispenard Street in Tribeca. She's just stepping off the escalator into Grand Central to hop on the subway downtown when her phone rings and she sees Taylor's name on the screen. Before answering, she darts out of the crowd and sidles up to one of the terminal's walls.

"Emma, hi," Taylor says briskly. "Have you got a minute?"

"Yes, of course." Emma's pulse quickens, realizing that Taylor must be calling with information.

"As promised, I did a little digging about the Stowe weekend, but unfortunately I don't think I have the answer you're looking for."

"Well, I'd love to hear whatever you have," Emma says, doing her best to keep her tone breezy.

"According to the itinerary I found, Halliday hosted three dinners in Stowe. The first, on Friday night, was at a little tavern across from the inn. I checked it out online and it's cute, but it's hard to believe that's the place Tom raved about."

"What about the restaurant Saturday night? I think that must be the one Tom liked so much."

"Are you sure? Because it looks like the dinners on Saturday and Sunday were held at a private dining room at the inn, which doesn't really qualify as a restaurant."

Damn, Emma thinks. *It's going to be tough to track down any additional information unless she speaks with Justine.*

"Hmm . . . I guess I assumed it was at a restaurant in town. Oh well. But thanks so much for looking into it for me."

"Of course, and just FYI, it couldn't have been Saturday anyway."

"Pardon me?"

"I found out Tom wasn't at the dinner Saturday night. He had some kind of emergency."

Emma's knees go weak. Tom was never at the dinner. So where was he?

"Uh, okay. Thanks."

"Maybe he ended up eating someplace else later and that's the place he raved about. Would you like me to double-check with the event planner Justine used? Or try to sneak the information out of Tom?"

"No, no, don't bother because I must have had it all wrong. Look, I have to run, but thanks for your help, Taylor."

Shaken, but not wanting to be late, Emma hurries to the nearest staircase, descends to the lower level, and wedges herself into a crowded car of the number 6 train moments before it departs. She's never been a big crier in a crisis, but right now she feels an urge to sob, to curse fate right here in the subway car. Her whole goal in talking to Taylor had been to confirm Tom's alibi, but he doesn't fucking have one. *How can this be happening?* How can her life have unspooled so badly for a second time?

There's nothing she can do right now, but once she's back in Westport, she has to come up with a discreet way to pump Justine about that Saturday night and find out if Tom was at least somewhere in the vicinity of Stowe.

When Emma ascends out onto Canal Street fifteen minutes later, it resembles an overturned beehive with countless vendors swarming the sidewalk and pedestrians darting by. She hurries west, eyes straight ahead, past grungy storefronts and sidewalk racks displaying endless stuffed animals, cheap toys, fake Gucci and Louis Vuitton purses, straw hats, and tacky NYC souvenirs.

A half block later, she pauses to get her bearings. According to Google Maps, Lispenard is one block farther south, running parallel to Canal, and she needs to take a left a little farther ahead on Church. She starts walking again, forcing herself to think of nothing but reaching her destination.

She's only gone a short distance, however, when her eyes are drawn to a street sign on her right, and she freezes in her tracks. *Greene Street.* It dead-ends here at Canal, she realizes.

She swivels slowly in place and with her heart clenching, glances at the buildings to the north. She can't see the parking garage from where she's standing, but she knows it's there, a block or so away with its ugly red-and-black lettering and oil-stained entranceway.

And next to it is the alley where Derrick was shot and left for dead.

26

Then

Around four months after the murder, Emma finally visited the site where it happened. She'd originally intended to go in the days immediately following, as she thought seeing the location firsthand would help quiet her fraught imagination and make it stop creating endless, horrible snapshots of the scene in her mind.

And she'd hoped, too, that being there in person might jog something in her memory. Perhaps a street number would ring a bell, or she'd notice an establishment Derrick had referenced in the past, and finally his presence in SoHo that night would be explained. And finally, too, there'd be a lead for Detective Lennox to run with.

Though she might not be prostrate with grief, she certainly wanted the killer caught.

But she changed her mind about going as soon as she

realized the police were suspicious of her. Maybe it was a cliché that criminals frequently return to the scene of the crime, but if the NYPD were indeed keeping tabs on her, she didn't need to be observed anywhere near the garage or alleyway.

In July, though, things seemed to shift. The police had seemingly lost interest in her, and the sense she'd had of being followed passed. So Emma headed there one hot afternoon from her uptown apartment, taking a couple of different trains just in case.

She walked slowly along Houston then turned onto Greene Street, her dress sticky with perspiration and her heart thrumming between her ears. Nothing she saw triggered even a sliver of a memory, though. She still had no idea what would have brought Derrick there, particularly that late in the evening.

This meant she still couldn't hazard a guess about who could have killed him or why. If it was someone he knew, then based on everything she'd read about homicides, the motive must have been vengeance or lust or greed, but she couldn't imagine how one of those compulsions had played out in a disastrous way for him. There were people who'd disliked Derrick, but not enough, it seemed, to kill him; he might have been fantasizing about an affair, but it apparently hadn't blossomed into anything; and his wealth at the time had been tied up in two paintings he had no intention of selling.

At last Emma reached the parking garage and then a little farther ahead, the small alleyway where he'd been found.

She stared down the short length of it, the brick walls caked with grime and soot.

To her surprise, she'd broken down and cried, thinking of him lying on the ground as his life slipped away. Because despite all the ugliness in their relationship, she'd once loved him, married him, and hoped for the best with him.

27

BARELY PAYING ATTENTION, EMMA BOLTS ACROSS CANAL Street, darting between cars until she's safely on the other side. *How totally stupid of me*, she thinks. It never crossed her mind that she'd be so close today to the alley where the murder happened. Lilly's apartment is in Tribeca, not SoHo, but of course, Canal is the dividing line of the two neighborhoods.

She takes a left on Church and then a right onto Lispenard, where she's so flustered that she overshoots Lilly's address and has to backtrack several yards. By the time she presses the bell, she's out of breath, and her face feels damp with perspiration. She uses the elevator ride to the ninth floor to wipe it dry with a tissue and compose herself.

"Oh, Emma, it's really great of you to come," Lilly proclaims when Emma steps off the elevator, which opens directly into the apartment.

"I'm so happy we could do this, Lilly—and, gosh, I'm incredibly sorry for your loss." Though they've only met three or four times, Emma feels comfortable offering her a warm hug.

"Thank you." Lilly accepts the embrace gratefully, but her voice is tinged with sadness. "Come in, I made us some coffee."

As Emma follows her across the length of the enormous room, her attention is torn between her hostess and the space. Lilly's extraordinarily pretty, lithe, and graceful with long chestnut-colored hair, slate-blue eyes, and full lips with a dimple at each end. And then there's the apartment—a loft-style space with high white walls, featuring a stunning north-facing view of Manhattan and a curving, sculpturelike staircase leading to an upper level.

Not to mention the art. There are at least a dozen large, abstract paintings on the walls, including two Rothkos, as well as a portrait of a woman with an elongated neck that Emma thinks might be by George Condo. It's an art collection worth many millions of dollars.

They reach a long metal dining table with eight oddly shaped, white-cushioned chairs and Lilly motions for Emma to take a seat at the end, then slips into one across from her. Porcelain cups and saucers and pretty cloth napkins have been set at each of their places, and in the middle of the table is a tray with a French press, milk, sugar, and artificial sweetener, as well as a platter of little finger sandwiches.

"I hope you don't mind sitting here," Lilly says. "There's really not a comfortable spot in the entire apartment, but at least at the table we don't have to balance our cups on our laps."

Her comment takes Emma by surprise. "To me this place

is breathtaking, but it must be terribly hard to be here on your own right now."

"It *is*—especially since I've never actually liked it. People keep telling me that after a spouse dies you shouldn't make any rash decisions like changing where you live, but I'm about to put it on the market. You left Madison pretty soon after Derrick died, didn't you?"

"Yes, in a matter of weeks. I never regretted it, but still, I think it's all about doing what's best for *you*. Are you going to look for something smaller?"

Lilly sighs heavily and pours them each a cup of coffee, revealing that the nails on her elegant fingers have been bitten to the quick. "Ha, yes—small, womblike. I want to tuck into a place that feels warm and safe."

"Oh, Lilly, I know you must be reeling. Do you mind me asking what happened?"

"From what they could determine, Chris developed gas bubbles in an artery while he was diving, maybe from ascending from his last dive too quickly, and that might have led to a stroke. It's also possible he had an undiagnosed medical condition that played a role."

"Did you have anybody in Bonaire to help you through it all?"

She shakes her head. "I wasn't even there. Diving was Chris's thing and he said he wanted to squeeze a trip in while he had a break in his work schedule. I only went down to collect the body."

Emma's heart squeezes as she imagines everything her host had to manage on her own.

"I feel so terrible for you, Lilly, I really do," she says. "Is there any way at all I can be of help?"

"Actually yes. As I said in my email, there's a question I wanted to ask you."

"Of course, anything."

"First, please understand that I won't judge you, Emma, no matter how you answer." An awkward pause follows. "What I need to know is whether my husband ever hit on you."

Emma's just taken her first sip of coffee and nearly chokes.

"Omigod, Lilly, no, never. Did something make you think that?"

"Nothing on *your* part." Lilly touches a hand to her collarbone, and Emma notices how pronounced it is. Lilly's black V-neck tunic seems to be hanging off her, and she looks at least ten pounds thinner than when they were last together. "But I saw the way he looked at you during those few dinners we had—and he seemed to corner you at your party."

"Uh, we did speak for a while at the party, but I think he was just asking me about my work, about generational trends."

But even as Emma answers she's raking through her memory. She doesn't recall anything that qualified as flirtation from him, but maybe she was such an emotional wreck that she was incapable of detecting the signals.

"Thank you, Emma," Lilly says softly. "And thanks for letting me go there."

"Of course, I don't mind at all. Can I ask you—are you concerned Chris might have been unfaithful?"

It's a horribly blunt question for a woman who's recently

lost her husband, but Emma suddenly senses that it's not only grief that's tearing Lilly up inside.

Lilly scoffs. "*Might* have been? By the beginning of this year, I'd figured out he was a total womanizer, and since he died, I've been learning the full extent of it. Though it seems totally masochistic, knowing more is helping me feel like less of a fool. Turns out there was even a woman in Bonaire with him when he died."

"Oh god, how awful."

"I know, and it makes the situation so . . . so complicated right now. People assume I'm nearly prostrate with grief, but it's something else entirely—a whole mixed bag of anger and sadness and disappointment. And then all the guilt I feel for not mourning him twenty-four seven."

Emma can't believe what she's hearing. It's like an echo from her own mind.

"Had you thought about leaving him?"

"More than thought. Before Chris took off for Bonaire, I told him I was filing for divorce in the next few weeks. So now I have that to contend with, too—that I somehow woke up the karma gods and set his death in motion."

"You can't think that way, Lilly. And isn't karma supposed to be about *balance*, anyway? If it was really at work here, Chris would have come home alive and well to find you in bed with Ryan Gosling."

Lilly chuckles. "Thank you for that, Emma. I'm sorry to be dumping all this on you. But I needed you to know why I asked such a batshit crazy question."

"I'm glad you *did* dump it on me. Because . . . because I've gone through something similar." She takes a breath and

exhales loudly. Finally, after all this time, she's about to utter the truth. "Derrick was a real prick to me, and though
I'm sorry he lost his life so young and so brutally, I've never
missed him, even for a second. I had to fake my grief, too."

It takes her a couple of seconds to realize that tears of
relief are running down her cheeks. Lilly lays a hand on top
of Emma's.

"I really appreciate you sharing that with me. Maybe we
could start a support group—the Unwailing Widows."

Emma smiles softly. "Count me in."

"How long has it been? About two years, right?"

"Yeah, two years ago this past March. Strangely enough,
on my way here just now, I was a stone's throw from the alley
where he died, which I'd visited only once. It's a couple of
blocks north, next to a parking garage on Greene Street."

Lilly bites her lip and swivels slightly in her chair to gaze
out of one of the oversized windows. "I knew the murder
happened downtown," she says finally, "but I wasn't aware it
was that close to our apartment."

And then, in an instant, Lilly's expression morphs from
pensive to stricken, and Emma feels the skin on the back of
her neck prickle.

"Is everything okay?" she asks gently.

"It's probably nothing, but Chris was supposed to get together with Derrick here the day before he died."

Emma hears the words, but they're sliding across her mind
like a car on ice, failing to gain traction. "I'm sorry, *what*?"

"They had a plan to have coffee here at the apartment on
Friday morning. The reason I remember it so specifically is

because we heard about Derrick's death just a couple of days later."

The revelation almost knocks the wind out of her, but Emma manages another question. "And did they?" she says. "Meet?"

"No, Chris canceled on him at the last minute, supposedly because of a work emergency, which was so typical of him. But I think Derrick might have already been in the neighborhood when he got the call."

"Oh my god." One question has finally been answered after more than two long years. "Well, that solves a part of the mystery."

"What do you mean?"

"Derrick was attending a conference in Midtown that weekend and no one's ever understood why he parked so far away from the hotel where it was being held. I bet he picked a garage near here because of his meeting with Chris. After Chris canceled, Derrick must have jumped on the subway rather than bothering to drive the car uptown."

Lilly groans. "I feel terrible. Chris had a piece of the puzzle all this time."

It is *a piece of the puzzle*, Emma thinks, one she'd never imagined despite how much she racked her brain. It's not like Derrick and Chris had been close, after all, and she certainly hadn't considered him making a stop before the conference. She'll have to inform Webster, though Emma doubts a canceled appointment could shed much light on a murder that happened over thirty hours later.

"You can't blame yourself, Lilly," Emma says. "And

besides, it still doesn't explain another key mystery—why he came back down to the garage the next night."

"He wasn't picking up his car to go home?"

"No. He obviously had plans to drive somewhere, but the conference wasn't over yet. Did the police ever contact Chris, do you know?"

Lilly sighs dispiritedly. "They did. They said they saw from phone records that Chris had called Derrick midweek, which must have been when they set up the meeting—and then again on Friday, when Chris canceled."

"Huh. So that means the cops knew why he'd parked down here, but never mentioned it to me for some reason."

Lilly shakes her head. "They *didn't* know—because Chris lied and said he'd been chatting with Derrick about the stock market or something. He told me that since he'd canceled the meeting, there was no point in complicating things by bringing it up. I see now that I should have pressured him to volunteer more, but at the time I didn't think there could be any connection between Derrick being shot and an aborted meeting the morning before."

"Don't worry, I'm sure there *isn't* a connection. For some reason I'm probably never going to know, Derrick returned to the garage that night and just got really unlucky."

But . . . what if these things could be linked? Emma thinks even as she says there isn't a connection. Does the murder have something to do with Chris Shelbourne—who's now also died tragically and far too young?

"Lilly," Emma continues, her voice almost a whisper. "Where was Chris that Saturday night? Do you remember?"

Please, she thinks, *as crazy as it sounds, let Chris be the killer.* Let him have murdered Derrick for some reason she can't possibly imagine. Anything that means *Tom* didn't do it.

"He was at home with me," Lilly says, meeting her gaze. "You have my word. He'd twisted his ankle running and he wanted to hole up in the apartment to recuperate. We didn't hear the news until the next night when we were having dinner."

"Okay, thanks for being straight with me. And thanks for telling me about the meeting. It at least ties up one of the things that's been plaguing me."

Emma ends up staying for a little while longer, nibbling on a couple of the smoked salmon and egg salad sandwiches and feeling a new connection to Lilly, but at around two o'clock she finally rises, saying she'd better make her way back uptown.

"Are you okay?" Lilly asks as they traverse the length of the great room. "This all must be such a shock."

"It's a shock for sure, but it's good to have something finally answered. I'll have to tell the police, Lilly, and I'm sure they'll call you."

"Understood."

They're halfway to the door now when Emma stops in her tracks.

"Did Chris ever volunteer the reason they were supposed to get together that morning?" she asks. "I'm finding it hard to understand why Derrick made time for coffee with him on the opening day of a big conference."

Lilly's gaze shoots to a row of paintings, all riveting abstract pieces.

"From what I remember, they were going to talk about

art. I assumed he was coming here so Chris could show him our collection."

"Hmm. Do you think Chris wanted to buy one of the paintings Derrick inherited?" Which would be a surprise since her husband had sworn he never wanted to sell the two pieces unless he was destitute.

Lilly shrugs apologetically. "Maybe. But Chris usually worked with a specific dealer for any pieces he bought."

"Another mystery," Emma says, smiling wanly. They hug goodbye and promise to talk again soon.

After taking the 6 train back uptown, Emma wanders the Upper East Side for a while, checks in with both Eric and Dario by phone, and still hungry after two tiny sandwiches at Lilly's, orders a smoothie at a small café. She's still processing what she's now learned about Derrick's movements that fateful weekend, trying to determine if there's a clue hidden in there somewhere, but eventually she pushes those thoughts aside and forces herself to confront what she heard from Taylor earlier. She can't ignore it any longer.

Tom wasn't at the dinner in Stowe on Saturday night, which is extremely odd. Besides the fact that it means he might not have an alibi, it's unlike him, and also inappropriate for the head of a company not to show at one of the main events of a client weekend.

So where was he, if not at the dinner? Certainly, Webster will want the answer to that question, as well. According to what Google revealed, the driving time between Stowe, Vermont, and New York City is about five and a half hours. If

Tom left there in the late afternoon, he could have made it to the city in time to park near the garage, lie in wait, and shoot Derrick. Then he could have hightailed it back to Stowe and reached the ski resort by early morning. It would have meant missing the dinner Saturday night, but he would have been around to ski with clients on Sunday, even if exhausted.

No, it can't be, Emma tells herself. There has to be some other explanation. Besides, how would Tom have known where Derrick was that evening?

Of course, it's possible he was stalking him, too, keeping tabs on his comings and goings. It would have been relatively easy to learn about the conference, but that doesn't explain how he'd know that Derrick would hop into an Uber and barrel down to SoHo Saturday night. Unless . . . unless he had lured him down there somehow. Tom had lived downtown back in his twenties, when he worked in advertising in the city, and would be familiar with the general area.

A horrible image muscles its way into Emma's mind: her first husband and her second husband crossing paths in an unlit downtown alleyway, one of them holding a gun.

If the police close in on Tom, they might assume he did it all at her urging.

And as she's sitting there in the café, Tom actually texts her. His plane has landed, he says, and he's going to skip the office and work from home for the rest of the afternoon. She can't bring herself to respond.

By the time Emma reaches Bekah's building in the East Seventies, her brain seems ready to explode, but the feel of

Bekah's arms around her in a warm hug has a momentary calming effect. It's also great to see her friend looking deliriously happy.

"I can't believe we're finally doing this," Bekah exclaims.

"I know. And, trust me, I'm never going to let so much time pass between visits again."

Hadley, who she hasn't seen in months, is adorable—strawberry-blond and green-eyed like her mom. She toddles along with them to the dining area, where Bekah has laid out an antipasto spread to be enjoyed as they talk.

But they've barely sat down when the baby begins fussing, and soon she's crying at full volume.

"I'm so sorry, but she seems to be teething today," Bekah says with a grimace.

From that moment on, their conversation and eating happen in endless fits and starts, which is a blessing, Emma realizes. The usually inquisitive Bekah isn't focused enough to notice her distress. And there's no way she could unload all this on her friend, not now anyway. How would that even go? *Hadley, sweetie, shhh for a sec, okay? I need to tell your mommy that I might have married a cold-blooded murderer.*

They have a few minutes of quiet after Bekah puts Hadley to bed, but by then it's nearly 7:30, and Emma wants to catch the 8:20 train back to Westport.

"Oh god, I'm sorry this was so chaotic," Bekah says as Emma rises to leave. "I've barely asked you a single question."

"Please don't worry for a second. It was fantastic to see both of you."

As they embrace in a goodbye, Emma feels a sharp pang of sadness. She *did* love being here, seeing her friend so fulfilled at last, but the gulf between them suddenly seems enormous.

Emma is hoping the train home will calm her like the morning's ride did, but she ends up in a crowded and noisy car, and by the time it pulls into Westport, she feels a weird combination of twitchy and spent. And she's dreading the idea of walking into the house. Tom won't have a teething toddler to distract him from noticing how disturbed she is.

Maybe the smartest thing to do is talk it through with him again, to come right out and ask him about the Harvard Club, about Stowe, about everything. But the idea of such a conversation scares her. If Tom's really behind Derrick's death, he's hardly going to confess it to her, and she could be putting herself in danger by letting him know she's on to him. And if he isn't responsible—well, then, she could be putting her *marriage* in danger with her insinuations. How would they come back from her accusing him of murder?

When her phone pings with a text a few minutes later, as she's sliding into her car in the station parking lot, she assumes it's from Tom, wondering why he hasn't heard back from her. But it's actually Addison Stark's name on the screen. After their very awkward breakfast date last weekend, Emma's surprised to hear from her.

Is everything okay?

Reading the message, Emma groans. Is Addison still trolling for gossip about the investigation—or her state of mind? Yes, fine, she writes back. How about with you?

All good on my end. I just wanted to check in because I saw all the police cars near your husband's office.

28

EMMA'S HEART JERKS TO A STOP. COULD THE NYPD HAVE come to Tom's office to arrest him? Has Webster investigated the Stowe weekend, too, and discovered he was missing for a whole night?

Frantic, she returns the call. "The police?" she says as soon as Addison picks up. "They're at Halliday?"

"Well, at least they were ten minutes ago when I drove by," Addison tells her, sounding worried. "There were several vehicles near the back side of the building and a whole bunch of people in uniform. I hope Tom's okay."

"I'm sure he is," Emma says, recalling his text. "He was in Chicago on business today and coming straight home from the airport. But I so appreciate you alerting me."

"I was just concerned. After—"

"Thank you, Addison, but I really should go."

Emma chucks the phone back into her purse. After firing up the engine, she tears out of the parking lot, crosses the Saugatuck River, and heads up Imperial Avenue into the main part of Westport. Halliday Advertising isn't far now, but two blocks away, she catches a red light, one of the interminably long ones that tonight makes her want to lean on her horn and let the sound blare into the night.

As she gets near enough to see the back of the building in which Halliday leases two floors, her panic mushrooms. The entire parking lot has been cordoned off with yellow caution tape, and there are at least seven or eight official-looking vehicles parked haphazardly along the curb, as if their drivers sprang out with the motors still running. Among them is a Winnebago-like vehicle and five or six police cruisers.

This can't be about Tom, though, she tells herself. Not only did he say he was going to work from home, but the only police vehicles she sees are either the local cruisers that she recognizes from Westport or Connecticut state police cars. It seems unlikely that the job of arresting a suspect in a Manhattan murder would be delegated to local police.

Emma slows the car and flicks her eyes back and forth between the street ahead and the chaotic scene on her right. There are twenty or thirty people standing outside the tape in small groups, perhaps a mix of rubberneckers and local media, and inside the artificially lit cordoned-off area, at least a dozen cops and emergency workers milling around like patrons on the deck outside a bar, though they don't look like they're having any fun.

And—oh god—an ambulance on the other side of the tape, too.

Behind her a driver toots his horn, and Emma has to speed up. Farther up the block, she spots the outdoor furniture store where she and Tom bought their patio table, parks behind it, and practically rockets from her car. Maybe this isn't about Tom, but something has clearly gone wrong right outside his building and she has to know what it is.

She takes off at a jog, with her purse banging against her hip and her shoes chafing against the heels of her feet. It's possible, she realizes, that there's been a collision in the street at the rear of the building and one of the cars jumped the curb into the parking lot, causing an injury and even some property damage.

By the time she's reached the building, she's out of breath and has a stitch in her side. She slows to a fast walk and makes her way toward a bunch of stylishly dressed people around her age talking to a thirtysomething patrol cop.

"Can't you tell us what's going on?" a young woman presses the officer.

"You can read about it tomorrow on Twitter, okay?" he tells her.

"Please, we live around here, and we need to know. Is someone really dead?"

Dead?

"I'm not at liberty to say," the cop replies. "Why don't you move along and let the police do their job."

Begrudgingly, they do as he asks. As soon as they've departed and the cop turns his back, Emma inches forward to get a decent view of the scene. Besides the patrol cops, there are what seem to be police in plain clothes, as well as at least three people in white Tyvek suits and silver booties over their shoes.

Her first instinct, that someone's come to arrest Tom, is definitely wrong. Thank god for that. But sadly, it seems someone from the town might have lost his or her life, possibly an employee at Halliday or one of the other firms in the building. *Has Tom been called at home and alerted to what's going on?* she wonders. What if he decided to go into the office after all, and something's happened to *him*? She has to find out.

As Emma fishes through her purse for her phone to call Tom, she continues to move, searching with her eyes and straining to overhear snippets of conversation from the huddles of police. Her eyes are suddenly drawn to the back of a man on her side of the caution tape, his silver hair gleaming in the artificial light. As if sensing her gaze, he spins around.

"Tom!" she exclaims in total surprise. For a split second she's flooded with relief that he's okay.

"Emma. What are you doing here?" he says, advancing and pulling her into a tight embrace, then releasing her but holding on to one arm. He's dressed super casually in jeans and a cotton Henley, indicating he's probably rushed over from the house.

"Someone alerted me as I was coming from the station. What's going on?"

"I'm not sure yet. I was at home and Dan called to say he'd heard there was a ton of police activity and that I should get down here. I've told a patrol cop my company leases half the building and I need to speak to one of the detectives, but that was five minutes ago, and I haven't seen her since."

Still grasping her arm, Tom pivots to scan the parking lot, and instinctively Emma trails his gaze. Within the cordoned-off area, the police in one of the clusters shift slightly, like pieces of a kaleidoscope, and before they can rearrange themselves, Emma catches a flash of white on the ground. Her stomach clenches. She's seen enough procedural TV shows to know that it's the kind of cloth they drape over a dead body. Tom's hold on her arm tightens a little and she knows he's seen it, too.

"Where's Brittany?" she asks, her voice choked.

"Home, upstairs in her room."

"Thank goodness."

As they stand there at a loss for further words, a female patrol officer approaches the tape from the other side and signals for Tom to step closer, which he does.

"Mr. Halliday, I have a detective who'd like to speak to you," she announces. "Please come with me."

Tom agrees turns back to Emma. "Sweetheart, please go home, okay?"

She nods. In the heat of the moment, her fears about Tom had been nudged aside, but they barge back in now as she watches him duck beneath the yellow police tape. Within seconds he's swallowed into the throng and is out of sight.

Despite what she indicated to him, Emma doesn't go home. Instead, she moves farther along the perimeter of the tape, snaking through the crowd and hoping for clues to what has happened. But there's no telltale evidence, like shattered glass, to suggest an accident, for instance. She does a quick search on Twitter for any news about a fatality in Westport but finds nothing yet.

Finally, she reaches the edge of the crowd, just past the end of the parking lot, and one of the guys in khaki pants and a dark, short-sleeved shirt, maybe part of the crime scene unit, wanders past her on the other side of the tape, absorbed in a phone call.

"Another couple of hours," she overhears him say, and then two more words: "paired wounds."

Paired wounds? What in the world does that mean?

A second later he looks up and, after locking eyes with Emma, turns his back to her.

There doesn't seem to be any more to learn here. Besides, she's exhausted and frayed around the edges, and all she wants now is to be home. Tom must still be talking to the police because he's nowhere in sight.

She troops back up the street toward her car. Though there's still a sizable crowd near the Halliday building, the main street is deserted, so she stays alert. She's seen no sign that the police think there's a threat to public safety, but she's glad when she's finally inside the car with the doors locked.

After arriving home a short time later, Emma pops her head into the front hallway and picks up the muted sound of movement in the guest room upstairs. She decides to stick to the main floor—there's no reason she can think of to fill Brittany in and cause her to panic until they have more information.

She peels off the cotton sweater she'd worn on the train and tosses it in a heap on the banquette. She's trying to pull her thoughts together, but her mind, already flooded with anxiety and endless questions, has finally stalled.

After settling at the island, she checks Twitter again, but turns up nothing about a death. Maybe Tom will be able to infer certain details from the questions the cops ask him and can tell her more when he comes home. The words *when he comes home* echo in her head. How can she possibly be alone with him and pretend everything is normal at this point? Tom didn't seem to pick up on her distress when they were by the parking lot, but he'll surely guess something's wrong when it's just the two of them.

Her phone rings, and Emma nearly flings herself across the island to grab it, thinking it's someone calling to tell her what on earth is going on. To her surprise, Lilly Shelbourne is on the other end of the line.

"I just wanted to be sure you made it home, and that you're okay," Lilly tells her.

"That's so sweet of you. Yes, all set." There's no point in sharing the Westport news with her when she has so little idea yet about what's happening.

"I still feel terrible that I never put two and two together about Derrick coming downtown that morning and then being killed in SoHo the next night. Those events never seemed connected at the time."

"Don't worry, Lilly. As I said before, it's pretty clear they're *not* connected. The real question is why he went back to the parking garage Saturday night, and we might never know the answer."

A few seconds of silence follow, heavy as wet sand.

"Oh god, I actually think I know," Lilly says.

Emma's heart skips. "What do you mean?"

"Derrick was actually planning to see Chris that Saturday night. They'd rescheduled from Friday morning."

"What? Why didn't you tell me this afternoon?"

"I had no idea then. But after you left, I was feeling awful about the whole thing, so I decided to check Chris's old email to see if it might shed any light. He never shared his password with me, but after he died, I managed to access his account, and I found out that Derrick was supposed to come back to our place the night he died."

"Huh, weird." That makes no sense to Emma. "The cops reviewed Derrick's emails and texts, but they never said a word about him planning to see Chris that night."

"The exchange I found actually wasn't between Derrick and Chris—it was Chris and Jacob Whaley, this gallery owner he used to buy art from. And, in fact, it affects *you*, Emma, because it's about one of the paintings you have. I hate telling you this—and bear in mind, it might not be true—but it looks like Chris thought it was a forgery."

The breath freezes in Emma's chest.

"Here, I'll forward the email," Lilly says. "Let me know when you get it."

It takes a couple of seconds to arrive.

Jacob, I need your take on something. A guy I know socially has what he assumes is a Rothko oil on paper that I think might be a fake. I almost kept my mouth shut but then decided I'd better let him know. Naturally he's freaking out. I told him it might help to look at my paintings for comparison, so he's gonna try to drop by tomorrow night if he can get away from some work thing. Would you be willing to talk to him next week?

※

For a moment Emma's too stunned to speak. The painting, supposedly worth millions, might not be *real*?

"Emma?"

"Yes, still here. Wow, this is a lot to process. But wait, you didn't find anything between Chris and Derrick confirming Saturday night? What about a text?"

"I haven't been able to get into his phone."

And it probably wouldn't reveal anything, Emma decides. Because again, if there'd been an exchange between Chris and Derrick, the police would have known about it.

"Here's what I think happened," Lilly continues. "When . . . when Chris canceled the original meeting, they probably worked out that Derrick would come here on Saturday night. And when he never showed, Chris must have assumed he couldn't get away from that conference."

"And Chris wouldn't have minded someone dropping by your place after nine on Saturday night? You two wouldn't have had plans?"

"Nope, because of his ankle we were vegging out in the apartment for the entire weekend," Lilly reminds her.

"Right." Emma keeps turning Lilly's revelation over her in her mind, trying to see if it will lead to others. "There's one thing that doesn't quite make sense, though," she says, thinking out loud. "Derrick had an Uber driver leave him at the corner north of the garage near where he was killed. If he was coming to see Chris, why wouldn't he get dropped off right in front of your building?"

"Maybe he was going to the garage first for some reason."

"Possibly. Oh, wait, I'm just remembering that the police found his camera in the glove compartment. I wonder if that was related."

"It could be that he wanted to use the best camera possible to photograph the Rothkos here."

"That makes sense. It still doesn't explain why someone murdered him, but it's really good information for the police to have. I can't thank you enough, Lilly."

Lilly sighs. "I just wish Chris had come clean about it at the time."

"Well, at least we know now."

Maybe this new kernel of information will actually get Detective Webster off her back, Emma thinks. Or then again, maybe it won't. It's not hard to imagine Webster thinking: *Derrick Rand called Emma Hawke from the dinner that night and told her exactly where he was headed—and then she told the killer where to find him.*

She'll have to call Dunne, of course, before saying even a word to Webster.

"Oh, and I'm so sorry to be the bearer of bad news about the painting. It must be devastating to hear it might be fake."

"Don't give it another thought. It isn't mine—it went to Derrick's brother when he died. I'll let him know as well. He's willed the painting to a museum, but that will change if it's worthless."

"Okay. And I'll email you Jacob Whaley's details in case you want speak to him directly."

They sign off, with Emma promising to be in touch once she's spoken to the police. A second later she notices that Lilly has already forwarded the dealer's info, and she enters it into her contacts.

Emma rests back against the bar chair, her mind racing. If the Rothko is fake, could that mean the Helen Frankenthaler painting is, too? And what about the paintings that went to Kyle and Derrick's sister, Heather? A chilling thought follows: What if, in a way she can't imagine at the moment, Derrick's death is connected to the forgeries? If Derrick had contacted the dealer or gallery his parents used and voiced his suspicions, might that person have arranged to have him killed? Maybe she's suddenly holding a key to everything, and it has nothing at all to do with Tom.

Though it's urgent she speak to Dunne, Webster, and Kyle, none of these conversations is going to happen tonight. Her priority is figuring out what went on outside Halliday Advertising.

She's wondering where Tom is when she hears the hum of the garage door rising and the purr of his car. She jumps up in anticipation.

"What happened?" Emma exclaims as he steps into the kitchen. His hair's mussed and standing on end in places, as if he's been raking his hands through it, and his mouth is set in a grim line.

"The body we saw in the parking lot?" he says, his voice hoarse. "It's Taylor Hunt."

29

No, IT CAN'T BE, EMMA THINKS. THE NEWS NEARLY KNOCKS her off her feet.

"The police told you it was her?" she says.

"They actually had me identify her," Tom replies, his voice cracking. He moves toward one of the bar chairs and sinks into it, resting his chin in his hands. "Apparently she had her work ID in her purse and once they were convinced I ran the company, they asked me to take a look."

"Oh my god, how awful." Her eyes brim with tears.

"I know. It was dreadful to see her like that,"

"I'm just sorry you had to be the one to do it."

Tom shakes his head. "Thank you, Em. It's still so hard to grasp."

"Who's going to tell her poor parents?"

"The police are taking care of that, and I'll follow up with her family tomorrow."

Emma breathes deeply, trying to force her brain into sync with what's unfolding in real time. For the past week and a half, she's been totally focused on the drama created by the reopening of the case—but now this horrifying news is coming at her out of nowhere, like an animal bolting across the highway in front of a car.

"Do they know what happened to her?"

Tom shakes his head again, with it still resting in his hand.

"The detective didn't share anything with me, just asked a few questions, like what I knew about her schedule today. From the quick look I got, I didn't notice any bruises on her face or head, but there was blood seeping through the sheet—from what seemed to be the torso area. So I guess it's possible she was struck by a car in the parking lot."

Emma trudges to the far end of the kitchen, and grabs the electric kettle. It's always her instinct in a crisis to make tea, not that it actually helps.

After filling the kettle with water, she wanders back to the island but only leans against it.

"As I was leaving, I heard one of the men inside the tape say the words 'paired wound.' Is that really the kind of injury you'd sustain if you were hit by a car?"

Tom raises his head and finally meets her gaze. "What are you saying?"

"I'm not sure. I mean, it sounds more like she was struck with some kind of object—or even stabbed."

"Jeez."

"If that's the case, who could have done that to her?"

"She certainly didn't seem to have an enemy in the world. Maybe someone tried to rob her—or, god, even rape her."

Emma shudders. "But when? If she was attacked leaving

work, it would have been light out and surely someone would have seen what was going on—or at least noticed her body right afterward. You've got security cameras in the parking lot, right?"

He nods grimly. "We do, but there are a couple of blind spots. The cops are going to look at the footage."

Only local police seem to be involved at the moment, but Emma suddenly realizes that Webster will eventually find out about Taylor's death. Maybe she's asked the Westport police to let her know if there's any news related to her and Tom, or perhaps police databases are set up to offer convenient prompts, like Amazon alerts, to detectives across jurisdictions: "Because you expressed an interest in Emma Hawke and Tom Halliday, you might like to know . . ."

Either way, it's not a good thing to have more drama swirling around them.

Tom rises from the island, grabs a glass from one of the cabinets, and adds a fistful of ice, followed by a couple of splashes of scotch from a bottle stored in the kitchen.

"Do you think Brittany's aware of what's going on?" he asks, turning back around.

Emma shakes her head. "She's been quiet as a mouse upstairs, so I don't think so."

"We should call her down and let her know. I don't want her finding out from someone else."

After parking his glass on the counter, Tom mounts the back stairs and Emma hears him knock softly on the door of the guest bedroom. A murmuring of voices follows. A minute later, Brittany descends behind him into the kitchen, dressed in leggings and a long white shirt, and looking apprehensive.

After asking his stepdaughter to take a seat at the island, Tom relates solemnly that Taylor has been killed and that her death might be a homicide.

Emma had no doubt that Brittany would be disturbed by the news. After all, she must have seen Taylor around the office, even chatted with her, and it's bound to be an awful blow. But she's taken aback by the degree of the girl's reaction. A look of sheer terror passes over Brittany's face, as if she's been cornered in a room by the killer herself.

Tom clearly picks up on it, too. He lays a hand over one of Brittany's.

"I know this is terribly shocking," he tells her. "But we're going to do everything in our power to help the staff get through it, okay?"

"But who would *do* that to her?" Brittany demands, her words nearly strangled.

"Honey, we don't have any idea. There's still a chance it was an accident of some kind."

Brittany doesn't respond, just stares at Tom with her mouth open in shock.

"The police will be coming to the office tomorrow and speaking with everyone," he says, "but there's no reason for alarm. If it does turn out to be a homicide, they'll probably ask if you noticed anyone suspicious around the building, questions like that. What time did you get home tonight, anyway?"

"Five thirty." Brittany's begun crying now, and breathing in short little bursts.

"Okay, then I doubt there's anything for you to contribute because this must have happened later, probably after dark."

"Brit, you know who Taylor was, right?" Emma says.

She nods, her gaze resting on the island surface. "She introduced herself the day the summer interns started, and she invited us all to lunch once. In the cafeteria."

"That was so nice of her. And I'm sure that makes the news even worse—the fact you knew her a bit."

"Are the police even any *good* here?" Brittany asks plaintively. "Are they going to figure it out?"

"I'm sure they will." It suddenly occurs to Emma that Brittany must be scared as well as upset, and why wouldn't she be? Someone's killed a young woman right there in the company parking lot. "And we don't want you to be worried about your own safety. Tom will continue to take you to work each day, and if he has to stay later than you, I'll come pick you up. And for the time being, I think it might be good to scale back your social life and, you know, not do any overnights."

Emma wonders if the girl is about to shoot her a withering look and announce she has no intention of curtailing her fun summer plans, but she nods. "All right."

"Would you like to hang down here with us for a while, have a snack or some tea?" Tom asks.

"No, I want to go back upstairs." Brittany's expression has gone back to the blank look she so often favors, but Emma senses she's roiling inside.

"If you change your mind, we'll be up for a while," Emma tells her. "And just know that we'll be looking out for you."

Brittany nods almost listlessly and slides off the bar chair.

"Why don't you sleep in?" Tom suggests. "The police told me they'll need to continue to process the scene tomorrow morning, and I can't open the office until I get word from them."

Another dull nod, then they watch her disappear into the back stairwell. Tom shakes his head, obviously perplexed.

"I'm glad we told her tonight, but she's much more upset than I expected," he says.

"I know—she must feel so vulnerable." Emma runs her gaze around the kitchen, as if she might find something, anything, that will tamp down her own distress. But she comes up empty. "So what's next?"

"I made some quick calls from the car, but there are a few more people I want to get through to. We need to be sure we handle this as sensitively as possible as a company, probably bring in a psychologist. And I also want to see what I can find out about Taylor's timeline this afternoon and tonight."

He crosses the room to the fridge, scoops up a few more ice cubes from the freezer, and refreshes the drink he's left on the counter.

"You must have checked in with her after your flight, right?" Emma says.

"I actually saw her—at about five," he replies, his back to her. "I ended up swinging by the office for a few minutes to check in with her and Janice."

Emma feels a tiny pulse of unease.

"Did everything seem okay with her?"

"Yes, fine, though we didn't speak for long."

He takes one sip of his drink and slides his phone out of his pants pocket. "I think I'll make the calls from the screened room—I could use the air."

Emma's own phone pings as soon as he leaves the room,

and she checks it nervously, wondering if it has something to do with Taylor's death. But it's only Addison, following up.

Is everything okay, Emma?

She's so not in the mood to engage but wants to seem polite.

Thanks for asking. Tom's fine but someone was actually killed tonight in the parking lot. We don't know much at this point.

Goodness. Glad he's all right, but that must be quite a shock. Would you like to grab coffee this week and talk?

Maybe this weekend. I'll have to let you know.

For a minute or two Emma stands in the room, unsure of what to do next. Finally she boils the water in the kettle, drops a chamomile teabag in a mug, and carries it along with her to the den, where she collapses on the sofa. In the silence of the room, she finally absorbs how shaken she is by Taylor's death. Though she didn't know her intimately, she respected how loyal she was to Tom and how tenacious she was on his behalf. Wincing, she remembers what Taylor shared a week or so ago, her hope to meet a guy "in real life" this summer, and not from a dating app.

A *dating app*. Taylor seemed put off by them, which suggests she'd tried at least one in the past. Had she met someone dangerous who came after her tonight? If she *has* been murdered, the police will surely be able to find and interview everyone she's been in phone contact with in recent days and weeks.

With a start she realizes this means the police will want to talk to *her*. In general, the only time she and Taylor engaged was when Emma gave her quarterly talks at Halliday, but lately there'd been a burst of contact—the call today, of course, and the one on Saturday, in addition to their meeting yesterday.

She can be honest about Taylor's inquiry regarding the bracelet, but what can she say about today's conversation, just hours before Taylor's murder? She'll have to come up with a lie. Maybe something about her presentation.

The room suddenly seems strangely cool for a summer night, and she grabs the light throw on the arm of the couch and pulls it up to her waist. It feels as if the world is turning faster than she can bear, and yet she has to keep up, and most of all, she can't take her eye off the ball: learning more about Tom's whereabouts the night of Derrick's murder, even if it means the end of her marriage.

There's a sudden movement by the entrance to the room, and Emma looks up to find Tom standing on the threshold. She realizes she's been sitting in here alone for at least a half an hour.

"How are you doing, Em?" he asks.

"Hanging in there." As awful as the thought is, at least

Taylor's death is providing her with an excuse for acting anxious and aloof. "Did you hear anything else?"

Tom nods solemnly. "It's been confirmed it's a homicide, though as of yet, the police haven't given any details or issued a warning to the community."

Emma swallows hard, absorbing the news.

"I'm sure the cops don't want me doing their job for them," Tom adds, "but I talked to Janice—who's devastated, needless to say—and according to her, Taylor left work at around six. Like you said earlier, it's hard to believe she could have died before dark without someone noticing the body, so I'm thinking she returned to the office later. Maybe she forgot something and was headed back to get it."

"Or maybe she left her car there while she had a drink or dinner in town, and then came back for it."

"Right, that would also make sense. . . . You ready to go up?"

She's about to nod, but her body feels frozen in place. "Um, not quite yet."

"Oh?" he says, clearly surprised.

"I'm just so wound up," she explains. "I want to try to sit here for a little while longer and see if I can calm down before trying to sleep."

"Okay, see you in a bit then."

But he won't, Emma decides, as she hears him ascend the front stairs. She doesn't want to go up there. The idea of being next to Tom tonight frankly scares her. What if he really did murder Derrick, or paid someone to do his dirty work?

Regardless of whether or not he's caught and sent to

prison, it would mean the life she's loved so much, her life with a man she adored, will be over. The thought is crushing.

For a couple of minutes, she attempts to read on her iPad, but her eyes refuse to latch on to the words. So she flicks off the standing lamp at the end of the couch, tugs the throw up to her chin, and finds a spot for her head on one of the decorative pillows.

It couldn't be quieter in the house, though every so often the silence is broken by the faint sound of a car driving along their street.

And then there's another sound—footsteps in the front hall? Holding her breath, she waits, but the sound doesn't come again.

Her thoughts drift back to Taylor, and what the poor girl's parents must be going through at this exact moment. How awful it must be for them, knowing that they'll never see their daughter again and that she'd exited the world so violently.

Could the killer be someone Taylor knew? Or was she murdered by a predator, as Tom wondered? Against her will, Emma imagines the horrible scene in the parking lot—Taylor struggling for her life as someone viciously attacked her.

Emma's eyes suddenly spring open. She's been reminded again of the expression she heard the man behind the caution tape use: "paired wounds." After fumbling across the coffee table for her phone, she googles the phrase and quickly finds an explanation: "Paired wounds are made with scissors," it reads, "with varying distances between the pairs."

Scissors. Not a weapon you tend to associate with predators. But they're in abundance in office buildings, and there's probably a pair in every desk drawer at Halliday. Is it possible Taylor was killed by someone who worked in the building, maybe even a coworker?

Emma closes her eyes again. She can't believe there's another murder in her life, another nightmare playing out in front of her. A thought grips her, like a python trying to squeeze all the air from her lungs. What if it's all connected? What if somehow everything leads back to Tom?

30

EMMA WAKES IN THE MORNING WITH HER HEART IN HER throat. She has no clue where she is or why there's an awful crick in her neck. But when her brain defogs, she realizes she's in the den, that she really did spend the entire night here.

And then everything rushes back—Taylor's death, Lilly's revelation, her lack of any new information that would clear Tom—and she groans, hit by a fresh wave of sadness and dread.

From the light coming in the window, it seems to be around seven thirty or eight already. As she props herself up on her elbows, trying to organize her thoughts, Tom appears in the doorway.

"Emma," he says, his voice tinged with alarm. "Is everything all right?"

"Um, yeah."

"I checked on you earlier but didn't want to disturb you. What's going on, why did you sleep down here?"

"I . . . I dozed off reading," she lies, "and . . . I guess I never woke up." She kicks off the throw and slides up into a sitting position. Her neck feels like it's being pinched hard and her eyes are crusty with the mascara she never got around to removing. "Have you found out anything more? About Taylor?"

"Only from what's in the local news this morning. She was definitely stabbed, though there's no mention of the term you heard. According to one report, it probably happened between nine and nine thirty."

"So it was long after she left the office."

"Yup. I had someone from HR check her key card, and it turns out she never reentered the building after leaving at six, but it still seems like she must have been on her way back there. To pick something up, maybe."

Or to meet someone, Emma thinks. *A colleague?*

And yet if the person she met is the person who killed her, Emma can't begin to fathom what the motive might be. Taylor could be tenacious, "a dog with a bone" as Tom once described her, but how could that have led to her murder?

Tom takes a few steps over the threshold, and she notices he's already in slim gray pants and one of his crisp, cobalt-blue shirts, his hair still damp from the shower. He's dressed to take on the day, and yet even with his early summer tan, his face is pale, and his eyelids are hooded from fatigue.

"Any idea when they're allowing you back in the building?" she asks.

"Around eleven thirty, as soon as they've finished processing the parking lot and examining Taylor's workstation and her computer. They're going to start interviewing the staff once we all come in."

"By the way, the police are probably going to want to speak to me," she says. She has to get that on the table.

"You? How come?"

"Uh, Taylor and I had a quick meeting on Monday morning when you were in Chicago. It was nothing important, I just wanted her thoughts on my last presentation, but I assume the cops will inquire about it."

"Okay," he says, eyes narrowed, as if the explanation falls a little flat for him.

"Will you try to work from home for a while?" she asks, quickly changing the subject.

"I'm actually going to meet with some of my team this morning so we can get all our ducks in a row."

"Here?"

"Dan offered his place since it's more conveniently located. I left a note under Brittany's door, saying I'll be back for her at around eleven fifteen."

Emma nods. "I'd better jump in the shower myself," she says. As she rises and starts to gather her things from the coffee table, Tom hesitates, and she wonders if he's expecting her to offer him a comforting hug, even a kiss. But she can't fake it *that* much. Because though Tom desperately needs her now, she's unable to let go of what she's learned about him. Beyond that, there's still a pit in her stomach asking her whether Taylor's death is intertwined with everything else.

"I'll let you get out of here," she says, sidestepping him on her way out of the den and heading upstairs.

The shower gets rid of Emma's grungy feeling and soothes her aching neck a little, but it does nothing to dispel her dread. Afterward, drying off, she glances around her pretty bedroom and wonders if soon she won't be sleeping here any longer. Even if Tom had nothing to do with Derrick's death, it's possible her marriage was based on a series of lies and she'll have no choice but to move on.

Somewhere, somehow, she *has* to figure out the truth about Tom. Yesterday she'd decided that since Justine was in Stowe for the client weekend, talking to her might be a way to learn Tom's whereabouts Saturday night, but it would be crass to do that in light of the latest development. So she's stuck in a horrible holding pattern for now.

Emma's pulling on a summer dress when the sound of quiet footsteps carries into the room from the upstairs corridor. She's left the door slightly ajar to be able to hear if Brittany emerges from her bedroom in need of help or comfort, but when she steps toward the door and peeks outside, she sees Tom instead. His back is to her as he makes his way down the hall to his office, now wearing a navy blazer and with a small green shopping bag tucked under one arm, visible enough that Emma can see the logo of Terrain, the plant nursery, café, and gift shop where she'd met Scott Munroe for coffee.

Something about the sight of Tom makes her heart skip. She thought he was heading straight out of the house, but he's still here, practically walking on tiptoe. She quickly slides on a pair of sandals and hovers a foot away from the threshold of the door to give herself a view into the hall. He must have gone into his office.

A minute or so later, she hears the faint thud of a door closing, followed by footfalls on the carpet, soft ones again.

Tom's shadow passes in front of the small crack she'd left and then is gone, as fleeting as a thought.

Emma inches closer to the door, quietly opens it a bit farther, and peers out. Tom is about to descend the stairs. He still has the bag but he's carrying it by the handles now, as if something's been added.

Paperwork for the meeting with his colleagues? she wonders. But surely he'd put that in his briefcase instead. Her unease swells.

After giving it a few more seconds, she creeps down the back stairs and quietly approaches the kitchen, which she finds empty. A second later, the sound of the garage door being raised penetrates the room, followed by the firing of the car engine, and finally the hum of the Tesla backing out into the street.

Without stopping to think about it, Emma grabs her purse and her car keys from a basket on the counter, quickly sets the alarm for Brittany, and makes a dash for the garage. She backs out her car and points it toward the center of town.

She can't believe it, but she's actually attempting to tail her husband. She feels like the protagonist of some TV movie about a woman coming unhinged after she's learned her husband's been cheating on her. Tom might not be cheating, but something's wrong, she knows it. She thinks of his overly quiet footsteps upstairs and the bag gripped in his hands.

It turns out she's guessed right about the turn he took out of the driveway. In no time she spots Tom's car, just two ahead of hers. Emma slows slightly, praying he won't see her, though her bigger problem is going to be keeping him in her sights. She's a far less experienced driver than he is.

But somehow she manages to do it. Tom's car is a shiny deep blue, so it pops out in traffic. And since hers is one of a zillion medium-sized white cars on the road these days, she doesn't think he'll notice her if she stays far enough back.

After a mile or so, and a turn onto Main Street and then another onto Weston, Tom takes the Merritt Parkway going north, in the direction of New Haven. Her stomach tightens. From what she recalls, Dan lives within Westport, so Tom can't be driving to his house.

Which means he lied to her.

Maybe, she quickly tells herself, the meeting location was changed to avoid press, and one of his HR directors or a publicist is hosting it instead. But ten long minutes later, Tom exits onto Route 25, a road that will take them to Bridgeport, a city at least a dozen miles east of them. Even if the meeting had to be moved from Dan's, this location would surely be inconvenient for everyone else. The only answer is that there *is* no meeting.

As they approach Bridgeport, she watches as Tom suddenly takes one of the city exits. Emma just has time to signal and follow suit. She slows as much as possible, so she won't have to pull up right behind him at the stop sign.

He makes a left at the end of the exit ramp, with an authority that suggests either he knows where he's going or his GPS does. Emma signals a left-hand turn as well, but before she can take it, several cars coming from the right cut her off and muscle in behind Tom's car.

Dammit, she swears under her breath. She's lost him.

They're now on a busy four-lane local road lined with office buildings and stuccoed one-story retail stores, and though she's pretty sure his car is still in the pack ahead of her, there's no sign of it. She stretches her neck, straining for a glimpse but without any luck.

And then, several cars ahead, there's a sudden flash of blue, gleaming in the sun. It's his Tesla. He shifts lanes, fast as a bee changing course, and turns into one of the lots on the road. To her utter surprise the building sign says Goodwill.

With barely any time to think, Emma manages to change lanes herself and turn right into the front parking lot of the building next door, a dental clinic. She quickly finds a parking spot, kills the engine, and twists in her seat for a view of the Goodwill building. Tom's car isn't in sight, but she's almost positive it's over there.

Perhaps he's lost, she thinks, and only pulled into the lot to turn around. It would make a lot more sense than him suddenly deciding this was the day to donate some household item. But then she spots him, moving across the parking lot on foot and swinging open the door of the building—with the green bag by his side.

It feels as if she's having one of those awful dreams in which ordinary snippets from daily life patch themselves together in an illogical but terrifying sequence of events.

Only a minute or two passes before Tom emerges, empty-handed, and ducks back into his car. She gives him time to pull from the lot, turning in the direction of home, before she makes the short drive over to Goodwill herself.

Emma shivers as she steps inside, and she can't tell if it's from fear or the air-conditioning or both. The interior is mammoth, with endless aluminum racks of clothes and free-standing shelving units holding toys, dishes, glassware, knickknacks, and even Christmas decorations.

"May I help you?"

Emma turns. The question has come from a middle-aged woman in a blue Goodwill apron behind a glass display case, which also seems to function as a checkout counter.

"Uh, I guess I'm just going to poke around for a minute or two," Emma tells her. There's no way she can ask, *What did that man just bring in here?* without arousing suspicion.

"Of course," the woman says kindly. "Let me know if you need help finding your way around."

"I will, thank you. I—" And then she sees the Terrain bag, resting on the counter to the right of the cash register. The saleswoman's eyes trail her gaze and rest in the same spot.

Emma's mind races. She only has one chance, and she can't blow it.

"Ah, someone loves to shop at Terrain just like I do," she says, smiling.

"I'm not actually familiar with the store. A person used the bag to drop off an item."

"Was it something from there, do you know?"

"I'm not sure. I haven't gotten a good look yet."

"Maybe that's what I should buy today," Emma says, forcing her smile even wider. "Whatever's in that bag."

The woman cocks her head a little, her expression the slightest bit wary now. Emma sees she's rushed it, started to look a little desperate.

"I haven't even had a chance to catalog it."

Emma takes a breath, forces her shoulders down. "Could I just take a peek, though? I know it sounds a little crazy, but I got some sad news this week and I promised myself a little treat to help cheer me up."

The woman's face softens again. "Why not?"

With her heart racing, Emma watches as the woman reaches for the bag, slides it down the glass countertop, and tugs it open.

"Oh, wow, it's actually quite lovely," the woman says, looking inside.

A moment later, she pulls out the contents: a large silk scarf covered with birds and colorful wildflowers and the name Salvatore Ferragamo in script along the edge.

Exactly the type of scarf Taylor used to wear.

31

A FEW MINUTES LATER EMMA'S BACK ON THE ROAD, BARELY aware of her exit from the store. She'd muttered some kind of a response, like, "No, actually, no, thank you."

Her heart's beating so hard, she can feel it in her fingertips as she grips the steering wheel, but she wills herself to calm down and try to think clearly. Tom had a scarf that might have belonged to a dead woman and he's taken strange, deceptive measures to get rid of it. Does that mean he *killed* her?

No, it's not possible, she thinks. What could the motive be? He seemed to like Taylor, to be satisfied with her work, even if she occasionally got on his nerves.

A horrible scenario worms its way into her mind: What if Taylor, in that tenacious style of hers—and as she'd suggested earlier—tried to extract details about the Stowe weekend from Tom, wanting to be helpful without telling him she was acting on Emma's behalf? She might have said someone on staff heard him rave about a restaurant and was she trying to track down where he ended up eating Saturday night, and inquired why he hadn't been at the group event. He would have felt cornered, worried that she'd share the information with the wrong person.

He'd admitted to Emma he'd seen Taylor when he dropped by the office around five yesterday, but he could have also arranged to meet her later, claiming he had a crucial matter to discuss. She'd do whatever her boss asked, after all. As for the scarf? Maybe he'd touched it in the course of stabbing her and decided to take it with him, fearing he'd left traces of his DNA. He might have decided the safest strategy was to unload it at a Goodwill outside of town rather than dropping it in a dumpster or trying to burn it.

So what the hell does she do now? Go to the police and announce that her husband might have not only killed Taylor but Derrick, too? That he might be some kind of sociopath, wearing a dazzling mask of sanity?

No, she can't. She still has no proof that Tom left Stowe that weekend and thus would have a reason to silence Taylor. In a day or two, she'll have to find a way to speak with Justine about Tom's whereabouts, even if there's a danger of Justine relaying the conversation to him. For now, she has to tamp down her fear and stay in control, and at the moment that means driving home without ramming her car into the rear of another vehicle. She forces her mind back on the road.

When Emma finally pulls into the garage twenty-five minutes later, Tom's car isn't there. He's probably at Dan's, just later than he told her he'd be. She texts Brittany, telling her she's heading to work but to call if she needs anything before Tom picks her up.

Prior to entering the studio, Emma does her best to steel herself and wipe the distress from her face. She has to appear as normal as possible to her two colleagues and mentally prepare for the inevitable conversation with the police about her recent contact with Taylor, a call that might very well come today.

And that's not all. She can't forget about the paintings. Though Lilly emailed her Jacob Whaley's contact info, her gut tells her to check in with Kyle first and alert him to what's going on. Once that's accomplished, she'll ask Dunne to fill Webster in on the latest development.

Dario and Eric are both on calls when she enters, which gives her a chance to get her bearings. She waves hello and heads to the meeting room to make an espresso, and as she's waiting for the cup to fill, Eric enters, shutting the door quietly behind him.

"I heard the news about the girl from Halliday," he says, looking stricken. "How awful."

Emma shakes her head. "I know, it's devastating. Um, you met her a few times, right? When we presented there together?"

"Yup, and eerily enough I spoke to her just yesterday."

She pivots back in Eric's direction. "How come?"

"She called here looking for you at around noon or so. Dario was away from his desk, so I picked up your phone."

Taylor must have tried her office line before calling her cell.

"Did she say what she wanted?" Emma asks, doing her

best to keep it light. Surely, she tells herself, Taylor wouldn't have taken the time to spell out the reason to Eric.

"No, just that she had some information you were looking for."

"Right, she did catch up with me later. . . . It's all so sad."

"Well, let me know if there's anything I can do, will you?"

"Thanks, Eric," she says, touched by his concern. "I so appreciate that."

After he returns to his workstation, Emma uses the privacy of the meeting room to call Kyle. She dreads talking to him, especially after she warned him never to contact her again, but it can't be avoided. She's a bit relieved when the call goes straight to voice mail.

"There's something important I need to discuss with you," she says. "Can you get back to me as soon as possible?"

She hasn't even left the room before he returns her call.

"What's up," he says, more a demand than a question. It's clear from his tone that she's caught him off guard.

"Like I said, there's something fairly urgent I need talk to you about."

"Shoot."

Has the irony of his word choice escaped him?

"You know, it would actually be best to do it in person. Would tomorrow morning work?" Though she hadn't realized this before hearing his voice—and she hates the idea of sitting across from him—it seems only fair to drop this bomb face-to-face.

"What's this about, Emma?"

"I'd really prefer not to do it over the phone."

"Sounds very cloak-and-dagger. Are you expecting me to drive to Westport?"

Kyle sounds annoyed at the idea, but funny, he didn't seem to mind coming here when his goal was to rattle her.

"I was thinking we could meet halfway—maybe White Plains? There's a coffee shop I've been to called Caffè Ammi. How would ten thirty or eleven be for you?"

"Neither of those work. But I could meet at eight."

The commuter traffic will be brutal at that hour, but better to get it over with.

"Okay."

"You're not even going to give me a hint of what's going on?"

"I'd rather not, but trust me, it's important. I'll text you the address of the café so you have it."

As soon as she finishes, Emma sends an email to Jacob Whaley, explaining who she is, how she acquired his address, and why she'd like a few minutes on the phone with him. He might have had a follow-up call with Chris, she realizes, discussing the Rothko, and it will be good to learn what she can from him before she talks to Kyle.

For the rest of the morning, Emma tries desperately to concentrate on her work, making a few calls and meeting with Eric to brainstorm about the second round of research for Scott's company. But it feels like there's a brush fire racing through her veins, and she's unable to push the image of the scarf from her mind. The cops have spent the last hours interviewing Taylor's colleagues, and if she was wearing the scarf yesterday, someone might have mentioned it. Are they already searching for it by now? Is there a chance they would look at the Goodwill in Bridgeport?

Around three, after she's picked at a midday salad back at the house, a number with a local area code pops up on Emma's cell. A female police officer is on the other line, saying that they would like to speak to her as part of their investigation into the death of Taylor Hunt, and asking if she's available today.

"Yes, today's fine," she tells her. At least she doesn't have to wait and wonder any longer. "I could actually come to the station now if that works."

"Good. Just give your name at the front desk."

Emma decided last night that she wasn't going to ask Dunne to accompany her. Bringing a lawyer to help you explain a couple of phone calls to one of your husband's staff would surely send the wrong message.

The police station is about ten minutes away in an old brick building Emma's passed dozens of times but never paid much mind to. Based on how packed the parking lot is, she's not surprised to find the interior of the station throbbing with activity. In addition to uniformed Westport cops, she notices plainclothes detectives with badges on their belts and men and women in state police uniforms. She assumes the throng has to do with Taylor's death.

After a short, nerve-racking wait on a bench at the front of the station, Emma's led into a large, crowded bullpen and to the metal desk of a detective named Tim Hartwick. He's in his late forties, she guesses, with receding dark hair and a thick, bristly mustache. He greets her courteously and asks her to have a seat in the chair next to the desk.

After taking down some basic information, Hartwick tells her that phone records show that she and Ms. Hunt spoke twice on the phone over the past couple of days. Though it's not a question, he lets the comment hang there, presumably to see how she reacts.

"Yes, we spoke—and we actually met in person Monday morning at Halliday," she tells him. It seems prudent to get that on the table because the police are bound to learn about the meeting at some point.

"What was the nature of those conversations?"

She's already rehearsed an answer several times in her head.

"The call on Saturday was her checking to see if I liked a bracelet she helped my husband pick out for me. The meeting and the other call were about the most recent presentation I did at Halliday," she adds, amazed by how easily the lie rolls off her tongue. "Taylor had attended it and I asked her to give me some feedback."

Hartwick nods, appearing to accept her comment at face value. "How did she seem to you when you met in person?"

"Our meeting was pretty brief, but she seemed fine to me. Her usual self."

While Hartwick takes a minute to thumb through his notebook, Emma attempts to overhear the conversation several cops are engaged in halfway across the room, but their voices are too low. She realizes that Hartwick has looked up again and uttered Tom's name.

"I'm sorry, I didn't catch the question," she tells him.

"What kind of relationship did your husband, Tom Halliday, have with Ms. Hunt?"

"She was his chief of staff, so she did all kinds of things

for him—scheduling, keeping an eye on the operation, troubleshooting."

"I understand her role. I was wondering how they got along?"

"Uh, very well. He thought she did a great job."

Does this question mean that the police might suspect Tom? She waits on alert, fearing what might come next.

"Okay, thanks for coming in" is all Hartwick says.

As Emma hurries from the station, she can feel that the back of her dress is wet from nervous sweat. And for good reason. She's not only lied to the police, but if the scarf Tom took to Goodwill *did* belong to Taylor, Emma's withholding information that could help solve the murder.

The garage is still empty when she pulls into it ten minutes later, which means Tom must still be at work. She decides to change her dress inside the house before returning to the studio.

But someone is home. Emma discovers that the alarm has been deactivated, which must mean Brittany came back before Tom. She should at least check on the girl, make sure she's okay.

Emma steps from the small passageway into the kitchen and jerks back in surprise. Tom is sitting on the banquette in the kitchen with a can of Diet Coke in front of him.

He glances up, and locks eyes with her, his face unsmiling. She's not sure at first why he's sitting there like that, but then she realizes: He's been waiting for her.

32

O<small>H, YOU'RE HOME,"</small> <small>EMMA SAYS, HER HEART STARTING TO</small> drum.

Tom offers a tight smile, not an expression she's ever seen from him. She notices he's shed the morning's navy blazer and laid it on the banquette next to him.

"The police finished interviewing people at around four, though they'll probably be back tomorrow," he says. "Once they left, I sent everyone home and then decided to get out of there myself."

"But where's your car?"

"I let Brittany take it into town. She wanted to shop, and I figured the distraction would be good for her. What about you?"

"Me?"

He nods. "Where were you coming from?"

"Uh, I was at the police station. I was right about them wanting to speak to me, but they seemed to understand my meeting with Taylor was inconsequential."

"I suppose they didn't drop any hints about the investigation."

"They didn't, no. Have you heard anything?"

"Not a word."

But something's up. That's why he's been waiting here.

Emma sets her purse down on the counter, drifts over to the sink, and washes her hands. As soon as she turns off the faucet, the room goes totally silent again. She swivels around slowly to see Tom's still at the table, his arms resting in front of him, and his eyes glued on her.

"What is it, Tom?"

"I need to talk to you. Can you sit down for a minute?"

There's a weird flatness to his tone, as unfamiliar as the tight smile from a minute ago. Has he sensed her suspicions? Did he spot her following him today?

"Sure." Emma forces a tiny smile and moves toward the table, where she clumsily pulls out a chair. *How can this be happening?* she wonders. Two weeks ago they sat in this same place together, happily catching up over cheese and pâté.

"I know how upsetting Taylor's death must be for you," he says after she's seated, "but there's clearly something else troubling you."

She inhales roughly, desperately weighing what to say. She's certainly not going to admit her fear that he might be a murderer.

"Uh . . ." She's struggling for words when Tom juts out a hand, palm forward.

"Actually, why don't I begin, because I'm pretty sure I know what's at the root of it. For starters, I've been extremely distracted lately—at a time when you've really needed me."

She stares at him, confused. He thinks her mood relates to him not paying enough attention to her?

"But there's been a reason for my distractedness," he continues, "and I need to be honest with you about it."

Her heart makes a dead stop in her chest. Is he about to confess to her?

She nods slowly. "Okay."

"For starters, there's a pretty serious situation going on at work, one I didn't want to burden you with until I knew more. But I can tell you now that someone's been embezzling from Halliday."

Her mouth drops open in shock. This was the last thing she expected to hear.

"*Taylor?*"

"No, no," he says, shaking his head. "Not her. It's Justine. Dan and I began to figure it out last week with a forensic accountant. It looks like she might have siphoned off more than half a million dollars over a six- or seven-year period."

"That's horrible. How has she been pulling this off?"

"Oh, she's had a whole smorgasbord of tricks, but mostly it involved the events she organized, which is clearly why she wanted to hang on to that responsibility. She's apparently been in cahoots with the event planner she was using, and they'd been getting kickbacks from some of the vendors. She also regularly padded the charges that were submitted."

Emma presses her lips together, thinking. This explains why Justine was distracted at work and probing so much lately about Tom, eager to know where he was and with whom. She must have surmised that the jig might be up.

"Wait," Emma says, as a thought practically explodes in her head. "Do you think there's any way Taylor's death could be connected to the embezzlement?"

Tom blows out a gust of air and leans back wearily on the banquette, his head resting in his hands.

"Based on what we've determined, it doesn't appear anyone but Justine and the event planner were involved—and since Taylor didn't have anything to do with company finances, it would have been nearly impossible for her to help Justine funnel off money or play some kind of role. Regardless, I need to fill in the police."

"You must feel really overwhelmed right now."

"Yes, especially by my own failure to spot it earlier—and because I know it's affected things between us. Please know how sorry I am, Em."

"I appreciate you telling me." Because what else does she say? She has no reason to doubt this information about Justine, but it doesn't alter the bigger picture or do anything to quiet her fears.

"There's something else," Tom says, sweeping a hand through his hair. "Over the last few days, I've realized what a mistake it was to have Brittany stay here during the first summer in our new home. I should have offered to get her an apartment in town or simply told her the timing wasn't right."

At the moment, Brittany is the least of their problems, Emma thinks and manages a small smile. "Tom, you did the right thing, and I don't fault you for it."

He picks up the empty Diet Coke can and traces a couple

of circles on the table with it. "But in some way, it's shoved Diana in your face, and I know that troubled you."

"*What?*" Emma shakes her head. "No, Diana's not an issue for me. She never has been."

"Really?" he says, looking dubious.

"I swear. I've never minded—"

"I know you were in my office the other night."

Emma flinches. So he had heard her in there, pulling drawers open to see what evidence she might find.

"Tom . . ."

"You don't have to say anything, Emma. I assume you came across a few of the things that I'd squirreled away in there—mementos from my life with Diana. I'm sorry. I just hadn't been able to part with them."

She's too dumbfounded to speak. He's wrong again, completely misunderstanding her motive.

"There are things I'd like to keep," Tom continues, and his eyes brim with tears. "Photos for instance, a few cards and letters. But today I gave away something that belonged to Diana—a scarf that I suspect you saw in the office. I realize it was almost morbid to have held on to it, to have something so personal of hers here in the house with you."

Relief sluices through Emma. The scarf belonged to *Diana*, not Taylor. Tom wasn't trying to get rid of evidence from a murder scene, but rather removing a keepsake from his life with his first wife, just to make Emma feel more comfortable in their home.

But there are still other questions she doesn't have answers to.

Her hands are in her lap, and she squeezes them together. Considering what's going on with Justine, she's not going to be able to question her about the Stowe weekend. The man she married is sitting across from her, and she needs to hear the truth from him, or at least his version of it, and then judge for herself.

"Tom, that wasn't why I was in your office. I actually went in there to try to get a better sense of who *you* are. Because lately I've felt I don't know you at all."

"Who *I* am?" he says, clearly flabbergasted by the comment. "You don't think you know me, Emma?"

"My conversation with Scott really threw me. It sounded like you'd been keeping tabs on me in some weird way, that you orchestrated my involvement with Halliday."

"But I already told you that wasn't the case."

"You have a whole *file* on me, Tom—one that goes back several years."

He narrows his eyes, as if he has no clue what she's talking about, but a second later he nods.

"Right, I do have a file on you, though I'm not sure how it ended up here instead of the office. I asked my PR department to put it together once we got engaged, partly out of pride but also so I'd sound halfway decent if I was asked in interviews about your work."

Fair enough, she thinks, but the file is merely the tip of the iceberg. "Not just that, Tom. Scott said you heard me speak in New York, and there's a program in there for a panel I was on a month after Miami. Your handwriting is in the margins."

"What? No, that can't be mine."

"So it just dropped out of the sky and into a file with my initials on it?"

He throws up his hands, looking baffled. "Can you show me so that maybe I can make some sense of it?"

The two of them mount the back stairs and enter his office together, something they haven't done since she was helping him set up the space. Tom watches as Emma tugs open the correct drawer and withdraws the file with her initials on the tab. As she does so, she feels a sudden swell of embarrassment. After a few seconds, she locates the program and passes it to Tom.

"Thanks," he mutters. His eyes race down the page until eventually he raises his head so his eyes meet hers.

"It does look like my handwriting, but it's not, Emma," he says. "I didn't attend this event."

"Okay, so what's it doing in the file?"

He tosses the program onto the top of the cabinet and rakes a hand through his hair again. "Let me talk to the PR folks and see where they found this. Someone on staff might have gone, saved the program for some reason, and passed it along for the file."

Could it have been Halliday's former number two, Stacey Manning? Maybe, as Emma had hoped, Stacey had attended *without* Tom. Emma wants so desperately to believe him, to have her life back. But even if she accepts what he's telling her about the program, there's another big unanswered question.

"Where were you the night of Derrick's murder, Tom?"

"Where *was* I?" He narrows his eyes, confused. "In Stowe, like I told you."

"Are you sure?"

"Wait," he says, reeling back. "Are you asking if I *murdered* Derrick?"

"Did you?"

"My *god*, Emma, how can you possibly think that?"

"I know you were MIA that night, Tom. You weren't at the client dinner with everyone else."

He studies her for a second, then flicks his gaze away.

"You're right," he says, looking back. "I wasn't."

Fear ripples through her. Is she in danger, she wonders—in danger from her own husband?

He seems ready to speak but lets out a long sigh instead and slides his phone from the pocket of his slacks. His fingers move quickly, tapping at first and then scrolling, before he thrusts the phone toward her. When she takes it from him, she sees an email from an address that's unfamiliar to her, and she draws in a breath as she spots the date: the Sunday after Derrick's murder.

> Tom, Debra and I want to thank you from the bottom of our hearts for everything you did for Jack. He's going to be okay—except for a nasty concussion and shattered femur—but how awful if he'd been on his own, trying to navigate the hospital when he couldn't even think straight. Your kindness means the world to us.

For a few seconds she doesn't even breathe.

"Who's Jack?" she manages to ask.

"A seventeen-year-old snowboarder who hit a tree up ahead of me during my last run of the day. I alerted ski patrol and stayed with him till they got there. He was completely out of it, and since his friends were just kids, too, I decided to meet the ambulance at the hospital and I stayed there until his parents arrived around midnight from Upstate New York."

After all this worry, here's the proof that he couldn't have driven into Manhattan that night.

"Tom, I'm so sorry," Emma says, pressing her hands to her temples. "I've just had all these crazy thoughts ricocheting around my head. I—"

"Emma, don't worry," he says, stepping forward and wrapping an arm around her. "*Everything* is crazy right now. But I want things between us to be okay again."

"Me, too."

As she stands there, Emma feels the tension melt from her body. Tom didn't kill Taylor. And he didn't kill Derrick. And from what she can tell, he's not going to let the suspicions she's had undo their marriage. Maybe things really will be okay.

They have dinner together at the kitchen table, just the two of them, because when Brittany arrives home right after six, she says she ate in town. Tom presses her to sit with them for a minute, but she insists on going straight upstairs. To Emma, she still looks shell-shocked.

There's a pall over their meal because of Taylor's death, and yet she feels an incredible sense of relief, knowing that at least things with Tom have returned to normal. Though he has to take a quick call from Dan and another from his PR director, he's mostly engaged in their conversation and focused on her. As they're loading the dishwasher after dinner, he pulls her into his arms and presses his lips against her forehead. It is *okay*, she thinks, it really is.

But as she's lying in bed later, after they've made love for the first time in almost a week, Emma senses her fears edging back, trying to gain a stronghold. There are still questions she has no answers to. Who left her the notes on her car and in the studio, and had that person been trying to warn her about Tom? What about the bracelet Tom had given her, by a designer she'd worn in another life? When she and Tom hashed things out earlier, she'd forgotten to bring that up. And if it's not Tom's handwriting on the program, which she's willing to accept, whose is it and why did the file end up in the house?

There are still loose ends, and each time she stuffs one in a box, another springs out, refusing to be contained. It's as if the universe is trying to warn her about something, and she's not paying attention at all.

33

Emma's on the road before seven the next morning, headed to White Plains to meet Kyle. Traffic is as bad as she'd anticipated, bumper-to-bumper in spots, but she manages to reach the café at eight on the dot.

Kyle is already inside when Emma enters, and though several two-tops are free, he's parked himself at a table for four. *Of course*, she thinks, plopping down across from him. He's always hijacking the biggest table possible, getting as much of the pie in life as he can lay his hands on.

"So are you finally going to tell me what got your knickers in a twist?" he asks.

She ignores the ugly wording and breaks the news without any preamble—that according to an old email she's suddenly become privy to, the Rothko painting that passed to him after Derrick's death and has since been willed to a museum might be a forgery. She purposely leaves Lilly out of it, as well as the art dealer, who hasn't yet gotten back to her.

Kyle's expression remains blank as he listens, but she can see his nostrils flare.

"Oh, I get it," he says after she finishes. And then shakes his head dismissively.

"Meaning what?"

"It's a smoke screen, isn't it, Emma? A feeble attempt to deflect suspicion from yourself and your silver fox for killing my brother?"

This is the first time Kyle's ever done more than insinuate and it stings like a fast slap on her face. She wants to pick up and leave, but fights the urge. She needs him to *get* this.

"I'm not throwing up a smoke screen, Kyle," she says evenly. "For one thing, I'm trying to help you. You and your sister need to have all the paintings appraised to see if they're the real deal or not. And we *have* to take this to the police. Even if it's an outside chance, there's a possibility that Derrick's murder is linked to it."

"What do you mean?" he asks bluntly.

"I'm just spitballing here, but think about it for a second. The timing feels significant. It might all be a coincidence, of course, but what if Derrick contacted the dealer who sold the paintings to your parents, and the call set off an alarm, making someone feel really threatened?"

A few beats of silence follow.

"My god," he says finally. His whole tone has shifted and there's concern in his voice now. As he presses a hand to his mouth, she realizes her question has triggered a memory. She waits, holding her breath.

"When Derrick and I spoke that Friday," he continues,

"he asked if I knew the name of the dealer our parents had used. I assumed he wanted to buy some art and I told him I'd locate the contact info when I had a chance. It seemed so irrelevant, I never brought it up with the cops."

"You told them he sounded stressed, though."

"Yeah, but I had no idea it was related to that. Shit."

"Kyle, what do you know about the dealer?"

"Just what I learned from my parents as their executor. He's a private dealer, last name Cohen. I can't recall his first name off the top of my head."

"He needs to be investigated. If he sold forged art intentionally, it might not be just the Rothko that's a fake. Derrick's other painting might be, too. And . . ."

He rears back in his chair. "What you're saying, of course, is that my sister and I might be fucked as well."

"Maybe."

For a brief second, she *almost* feels sorry for him.

"You're right, we need to tell the cops," he says, visibly distressed. "But I want to do a little digging myself first. Can you give me until Monday? If you're game, maybe we can even arrange to speak to that detective together, which might make her take it more seriously."

Kyle as her ally? That's certainly a new twist, but at least it's better than having him as her adversary, making all kinds of insinuations.

"Of course, good idea. But when you're digging, it's probably best not to have a conversation with the dealer yourself. He might be dangerous."

"Yeah, I'm not about to do anything stupid. What about the email you mentioned? I should probably take a look at it."

"I can tell you that it was written by someone knowledge-able who saw the painting and suspected a problem. For now, I need to protect that person's privacy."

He shrugs and gulps down the rest of his coffee, making her realize that she never took a moment to go to the counter and order one for herself. At least there's no reason to have to linger.

"I'll call you this weekend as soon as I know more," Kyle says. "You'll be around, I take it?"

"Yes, I'll be home."

He doesn't thank her for what she's shared with him, but at least the usual hostility isn't seeping from his pores as they say goodbye.

On the drive back to Westport, Emma's relieved to have the meeting done with, and yet she can't stop thinking about what might ensue from Kyle's efforts. What if she's actually stumbled onto a real lead in her first husband's death? It will not only get the police off her back, but also resolve the end-less, torturous questions about the murder, for her and for Derrick's remaining family.

Two hours later, as Emma's sitting at her desk in the stu-dio, the sound of the door opening drags Emma's attention away from her computer. Looking up, she's surprised to see Tom standing on the threshold. Dario and Eric glance over, both startled, too. Tom's never dropped by midday before.

"Hey, Em," he calls out, "can I grab you for a minute?"

He makes it sound casual, but she can pick up the strain in his voice.

"Sure," she says, jumping up. Though she kept her tone light, just like her husband tried to do, it must be obvious to Eric and Dario that something's up.

"Is there news?" she asks as soon as she and Tom have walked a few feet from the studio.

"Yeah, something weird," he says, no longer trying to hide his agitation. "But first, do you still have those notes that were left on your windshield?"

"I stupidly tossed the first one, but I've got the second upstairs in our bedroom. And there's one more that was left the other day, right here in the door of the studio. With everything that's been happening, I forgot to mention it."

"Can you get them for me?"

"Why? Tom, what's going on?"

"You're not going to believe this, but I think *Taylor* wrote them."

She stares at him. Why would Taylor have wanted to mess with her head that way? "That makes no sense."

"Let me see the notes and then I think I can explain."

She hurries with Tom to the house and into their bedroom, where she retrieves the two notes from the dresser drawer and hands them to him. He smooths them out and studies both with a knitted brow.

"So?" she asks.

"Yeah, I'm almost certain Taylor wrote these."

He gestures toward the bed, indicating they both should sit. She's close enough she can smell traces of the almond soap he uses.

"Tom, please," Emma urges. He's staring at the notes again, biting his lip. "Explain this to me."

"Sorry, I'm still trying to wrap my head around this. Okay, the police asked me to come in this morning—I had my lawyer with me, by the way—and when I got there, they explained that they'd found some things in Taylor's apartment that suggested she might have had a bizarre crush on me. They didn't offer a lot of specifics, but it sounds like she'd kept a journal filled with pages about me, saying we were meant to be together."

"Holy cow," Emma says, floored by the revelation. "She was in love with you?"

"I wouldn't call it love. More like some kind of obsession."

"Did she ever come on to you in any way?"

He shakes his head. "Definitely not, but in hindsight I realize there were some odd warning signs. As you know, she'd always been superattentive, but around six months ago, it started getting fairly extreme. She was always double-checking things with me, often in person. I talked to her a couple of times about relaxing a bit, but she didn't, and I hate to say this about someone who's so recently died, but I found it annoying. Like . . . like that night we were having dinner at the Whelk when she came in to tell me Dan really needed to see me. He hadn't been in a rush at all."

A memory flutters to the surface of Emma's mind: the way Taylor's eyes lingered on Tom that night at the restaurant. It had seemed a little strange to her, but she'd had enough going on not to dwell on it at the time.

She kicks up her chin toward the papers in Tom's hand. "And you're guessing she left me those notes to rattle me? As her rival?"

"It's more than a guess. The police showed me a note she'd drafted at her home and asked if I'd ever received anything like it. I hadn't, of course, but I realized that the wording was similar to the language in the notes you found. It said, 'You still haven't figured it out, have you?'"

"Yeah, that's very similar."

"And the lettering looks basically identical to what's on the note the cops showed me, printing rather than any handwriting I might be able to recognize."

Emma clasps her head in both hands. This is all so bizarre. It's also incredibly distressing to think Taylor had not only secretly disliked her but had also wanted to break up her marriage.

"Have you told the police about the notes I got?"

"No, I didn't want to open a can of worms until I spoke to you. I'll call my attorney later and we'll figure out the best way to circle back to them."

A terrifying thought suddenly blooms in Emma's mind.

"The police don't suspect *you* killed her, do they?"

"Thank god, it doesn't seem that way at the moment, and there'll be nothing in her emails or texts to suggest I reciprocated in any way. Plus, it seems like she was murdered right after dark, and my cell-phone records will show that I was on the phone around then with the forensic accountant we've been working with on the embezzlement."

"Good—and thank god I was on the train or they might suspect *me*."

Emma flops back on the bed, staring up at the creamy white ceiling. She wishes her mind was like it, a total blank instead of a crazy chaotic jumble of thoughts and emotions.

Taylor had been bold enough to leave the last note in the studio door when Emma was working inside. Would she have eventually escalated things, found other ways to mess with her head?

A second later Emma propels herself back into a sitting position.

"Wait," she says, looking at Tom. "It was *Taylor* who first told me that we were both at the Miami dinner."

Tom cocks his head, his expression perplexed. "Right?"

"I wonder if it was more than a casual reference. Maybe she wanted to stir something up."

"Gee, I hadn't even thought of that."

"And—" Emma's thoughts begin to crystallize. "Did you tell Taylor I was a David Yurman fan and that's why you bought me the bracelet?"

"*What?*" Tom says, clearly taken aback. "No. It . . . it was actually Taylor who first showed me the ad after I'd told her I was trying to find a gift for you. She said you'd mentioned the designer to her and directed me where to find the bracelet in town."

Emma shakes her head, shocked. "I never told her anything of the kind, but she must have remembered seeing me wear one of the bracelets in Miami. And when you gave me the gift, it was one of the reasons I worried you'd been paying attention to me longer than you'd let on."

"Ugh. It sounds like she was doing little things to make you suspicious and drive a huge wedge between us."

And that's exactly what had happened. For days Emma has mistrusted and even feared Tom, been convinced that he'd been fixated on her, might have killed Derrick or hired someone to, and all along Taylor had been the catalyst, stirring doubts and then flaming them in subtle ways.

She can't believe that she let Taylor put her marriage in jeopardy, and that she allowed herself to think the worst of Tom.

"I bet *she's* the one who stuck the Harvard Club program in the file," Emma says. "She might have been cooking up a plan to get me to find the file and look through it."

He shrugs. "There's probably a lot we don't know at this point—and might never know."

On the other hand, there's much Emma does know now. Last night she'd been running through all the unanswered questions, worried there were still so many, and yet Taylor had been behind most of her lingering doubts.

Slowly, Tom gets to his feet. "I'd better head back to the office, but I'll call the lawyer from the car and ask how we should inform the police about the notes."

As she follows him out of the bedroom, Emma's eyes drift down the corridor. She notices something she hadn't when they'd rushed upstairs: the door to Brittany's bedroom is wide open.

"What is it?" Tom asks, sensing her alertness.

"Brittany always shuts the door when she leaves. Is she home now?"

"I don't think so. . . . Brittany?" Tom calls out.

There's no response, and in unison they make their way to the guest bedroom and peer inside. Emma's mouth drops open. The dresser drawers are yanked out as far as they go and empty now, and piled on the unmade bed is a tangle of clothes hangers.

"My god, has she *left*?" Tom exclaims.

As he takes out his phone to see if there are any messages from her, Emma advances into the room. The closet door is wide open, revealing that it's empty, too, and when she checks the bathroom, she sees that all Brittany's stuff has been cleared out.

"Okay here's a text from her I missed, sent over an hour ago," he calls out and begins to read. "Tom, because of what happened, I don't feel comfortable staying in Westport any longer. My dad drove down and picked me up. Thank you for your hospitality."

He drops his hand to his side and looks at Emma in dismay.

"We knew she was upset about Taylor's death, but I had no clue it was this bad."

"Me either. . . . Oh, Tom, gosh, this must sting."

"Yeah, for sure. She couldn't even wait to say goodbye in person."

Emma reaches out to touch his arm, and when he pulls her to him, she sinks into his embrace.

"I didn't think the week could get much worse," he says.

"Me either."

When they break apart, Tom's blue-gray eyes meet hers.

"Look, here's a crazy idea," he says. "There's no one renting the Block Island house this week. What if we went there for the weekend, got totally away from it all? We don't have Brittany to worry about now."

The suggestion intrigues her, but the timing doesn't feel quite right. Plus, though Tom has a landline in his office, cell service can be spotty in certain parts of the house. "I mean,

I'd love to, but do you really think it's a good idea to take off in the middle of all this?"

"Since the police are almost done interviewing my staff, I plan to close shop early again tomorrow. I might have to talk to a couple of key people this weekend, but mostly I want to stay out of everybody else's hair."

"Let's do it then," she says, smiling.

Emma follows Tom downstairs, and after a lingering kiss goodbye, he exits through door to the garage. Instead of returning immediately to the studio, Emma ends up pulling out a chair at the kitchen table.

She wants a couple of minutes to savor her relief, to let it sink in that her lingering questions about Tom have been answered and that her marriage is on solid ground.

That doesn't mean there still isn't plenty of crap to deal with. Taylor's killer is out there. And so is Derrick's, though maybe the information about the painting will prove to be a valuable lead and Webster will shift attention from her and Tom.

But right this second in the kitchen of her wonderful home, none of that matters to Emma. Though she'd stupidly allowed the crazy, worrywart part of her brain to take hold for a while, to project and to borrow boatloads of trouble, things will be okay. Tom is exactly the man she thought he was. And her life with him is not about to be hijacked.

She's glad he suggested Block Island, a spot they've visited only once together. Tom had purchased the cottage as a summer weekend retreat after Diana died, and though he'd considered selling it once he and Emma became involved, she encouraged him to keep it, with the idea that they'd spend more time there once they were settled in together in West-port. It will be exhilarating to escape the mess all around them, if only for a few days, and more importantly, to be alone with her husband, in a quiet place far away from anyone.

34

THE NEXT DAY THEY CATCH AN AFTERNOON FERRY AT POINT Judith, across the state line in Rhode Island, for the fifty-five-minute journey to Block Island, with their car onboard below. Though the boat is crowded with weekenders, the two of them manage to find a quiet spot on the top deck, away from the fray. As soon as they settle at the end of a bench, Tom wraps his arm around her, and Emma relaxes into his shoulder.

"Wow, this feels good," he says, as swooping, squawking seagulls escort them out of the harbor. "I'm so glad you were game to come."

The morning had been especially hectic for both of them. Tom had left early for the office to connect with his team again, and after securing approval from the police, he sent most of his staff home before lunch, while Emma had crammed as much work in as possible. It wasn't an ideal day for her to take off early, but Eric agreed to handle two sched-uled client phone calls that afternoon. She'd texted Addison, saying she and Tom had decided to head to Tom's weekend house and she wouldn't be able to have coffee with her after all—something she hadn't wanted to do anyway—and she'd also sent a message to Kyle, letting him know that she'd be on Block Island with limited cell service. If he had any news to share about the paintings, she didn't want him wondering why she wasn't picking up. He'd responded with a thumbs-up.

At a couple of points, Emma had been tempted to check in with Brittany, in an effort to unravel why she'd left so abruptly, but decided that it was best for Tom to handle the situation in his own way when he came up for air.

What Tom *had* made the time to do was contact his attorney, Hollis Langley, about Emma's connection to the notes. She and Langley, a woman of about fifty with stunning, prematurely white hair, had met midmorning and then left for a scheduled appointment at the police headquarters. In a small interview room, Emma turned over the two unsigned notes to Hartwick and another detective and described the first, as well as how she'd found each of them. There'd never been a moment, she told them truthfully, when she'd thought they had any connection to Taylor Hunt. After Hartwick asked a few follow-up questions, he thanked her politely for her help and dismissed the two women.

"Okay, that's weird," Hollis said as they headed across the parking lot afterward.

"You mean the fact that neither detective seemed at all interested in what I was saying? What do you think it means?"

"Best guess?" the lawyer said. "They've got some other line of inquiry they like a whole lot better."

Thank god, Emma thought. Hopefully they were closing in on Taylor's killer and had lost interest in the young woman's obsession with Tom.

Now on the ferry, with a light breeze lifting her hair, Emma promises herself she'll do her best to chill out this weekend, banish her nonstop thoughts about these open investigations, and get fully back in sync with Tom.

"You feel like a hot coffee, sweetheart?" Tom asks, tearing her away from her thoughts. "The air's a little brisker than I'd thought."

"Yes, actually, I'd love that."

"Okay, be back in a bit," he says, zipping his cardigan. His cheeks have turned a little ruddy from the wind. "I'm also going to check in with Pierce," he says, referring to the man who looks after the property.

Though there are a few nice restaurants in New Shoreham, the tiny town not far from Tom's cottage, he had told her he'd rather hole up at home, keeping the world at bay for a couple of days, and cooking for themselves. They've brought some food in a cooler, and Pierce has stocked the kitchen with other fresh food and supplies. As Tom weaves his way to the concession stand, Emma trails him with her eyes. A day ago she'd been sure that things were over between them, that her only viable option was to walk away from him, and their life together, and the seemingly boundless happiness of the past two years. But it's worked itself out after all, and she feels yet another swell of gratitude.

A gigantic cumulus cloud suddenly muscles across the sky, blocking the sun, and at the same moment the wind picks up, whipping Emma's hair across as her face. She digs an elastic from the pocket of her jacket and ties her hair back into a low ponytail.

As she glances up, she spots Tom across the deck, coffee-less and talking on the phone—to Pierce, she assumes, but his expression is stricken. Clearly, they're not just discussing a zucchini shortage at the farmers market.

She's about to jump up when her own phone rings, and she spots Eric's name on the screen. They hadn't planned to do a catchup until six.

"Hi, everything okay?" she says in lieu of hello.

"I was just calling to see if *you're* okay," he says.

She looks back at Tom, who's still on the phone, his free hand flipped over in dismay.

"What do you mean, Eric?"

"You haven't heard?"

"Heard *what*?"

"Just got an alert on my phone that the police made an arrest in Taylor Hunt's murder. You're not going to believe who it is."

"Tell me."

"Justine Carr."

Emma shakes her head in disbelief. The revelation seems too improbable to be true.

This explains the look on Tom's face, though. He's off the phone and striding toward her now, clearly very upset.

"Thanks for letting me know, Eric. Let's still plan on talking at six, okay?"

Emma hangs up, leaps to her feet, and meets Tom half-way. "You heard?" she says above the wind.

"Yeah, that was Dan. This is unbelievable."

"I just talked to Eric. Do you know anything more?"

He takes her arm and ushers her back to the bench and away from the other passengers. "Very little," Tom says as they sit. "Just that she was apparently arrested at her house a short time ago."

"Could . . . could this be connected to the embezzlement after all?" Emma asks.

"You mean were they in it together and had a falling-out? I just don't see how Taylor could have been an asset to Justine in that regard."

"Or . . ." Emma says, her mind racing. "What if Taylor figured out what Justine was doing?"

"I suppose that's possible, but as I mentioned before, Taylor had nothing to do with T&E or any of the financial accounts, so how could she have stumbled on it?" Tom leans forward, his hands clenched. "I should call Hollis and see what she knows. And also start doing damage control."

This will definitely be horrible for the agency, Emma thinks. The chief of staff murdered by Tom's number two.

"While you do that, I'll check the ferry schedule. We'll want to grab one back as soon as we can."

Tom shakes his head. "I don't think we have to, Em. I can do as much on the phone as I could in person."

"I really don't mind turning around."

"Let's stay for the weekend, okay?"

She nods and slides over on the bench to give him extra space. As he begins his calls, Emma tries to process what she knows so far. Coming on each other's heels, it seems the murder *must* be connected to the embezzlement. She agrees with Tom, it's hard to picture Justine bringing Taylor into the fold, and besides, since Taylor seemed obsessed with Tom, why would she want to damage him and his company in an embezzlement scheme? What seems most probable is that she did find out about it somehow, confronted Justine, and was killed so that she didn't report it back to Tom or the police. As the idea takes shape in Emma's mind, a vague suspicion niggles around the fringes, but she's unable to grab hold of it.

The ferry horn jars her from her thoughts, and she sees that they're almost in port, the seven-mile-long island stretching in front of them. Tom ends a call and looks at her.

"Anything new?" she asks anxiously.

"I managed to reach Hollis. She heard through back channels that the police have physical evidence linking Justine to the crime scene, so there seems to be little doubt."

She shudders. "Tom, are you sure we shouldn't head home?"

"Let's see what tomorrow brings. I need this weekend alone with you, Emma, away from the nightmare. I really do."

"I need it, too," she concedes.

They hurry to their car, and soon Tom is driving them off the ferry ramp onto the island. The wind has chased the clouds from the sky, the temperature is hovering in the high seventies, and the late afternoon couldn't be more beautiful.

Yes, we do need this, Emma thinks, yet she finds herself fighting off an encroaching sense of dread. Her first instinct in any kind of professional crisis is to place herself in the thick of things and navigate in person, and she can't understand how Tom can feel comfortable being away, especially considering how unreliable the cell service can be at the house. At the same time, she understands that he's desperate to unwind, and to bridge the distance that's grown between them.

"Oh, before we leave town, I should pick up some bottled water," Tom says. "I forgot to put it on the list for Pierce."

"Why don't you double-park, and I'll stay with the car," she tells him.

As he heads into the small market, Emma's phone rings. She digs it out of her purse and can't believe what she sees on the screen.

Brittany.

"We've been so worried about you," Emma says as soon as she's answered. "Are you okay?"

"Not really." She recognizes Brittany's typical sullenness, but there's also a hint of anguish in her tone.

"I'm sorry to hear that," Emma tells her. "Losing Taylor so tragically has been a blow. But you really scared us by taking off."

"I'm sorry, but there's something else I need to apologize for even more. It's—it's about what I did to you."

Emma pulls in a breath. "And what was that, Brittany?"

"I tried to make you doubt Tom, make you worry something was wrong. . . . Taylor and I both did."

Her pulse quickens. She doesn't like where this is going.

"Taylor?" She's keeping her voice calm, afraid that if she betrays any anger, Brittany might clam up.

"Taylor was the friend I was always hanging out with—we got to know each other after the intern lunch. She thought you were using Tom for his money and connections and wanted to get you away from him and . . . and she talked me into helping her."

"Helping her with what?"

"Mostly screwing with your head. She thought you had some suspicions about Tom—because of something she told you about a dinner—and she wanted to make it worse."

Emma feels like she's been punched in the gut. "Make it worse how?"

"Like by saying certain things to you. And having me say things, too. So you'd wonder about him."

For a split second she's back in the kitchen, observing Brittany's catlike smile and hearing her describe Tom's love of "the long game."

"That's all? Just saying things?"

Brittany groans. "Uh, she had me stick a note in the door of the studio before we left for the concert. . . . And leave a file in Tom's office after I told her you seemed to want to sneak in there. And—I'm *really* sorry—she made me give her a key and the security code to the studio so she could get a look around in there."

Emma sighs. She has so many answers now. But at what cost? She knew Brittany didn't like her, but she can't believe she would be part of such a concerted campaign to hurt her. And Tom.

"But *why*? Why did you go along with Taylor?"

"I thought you were wrong for Tom, too, that you just liked the money. And then when I could see that you actually loved him, I tried to pull away from Taylor, but she wouldn't let me. She said she'd tell him what I did."

"You have to call Tom and come clean, Brittany. You can't leave it to me to fill him in."

"I can't . . . because . . ."

"Because what?"

"That's another thing I need to tell you." She lets out another groan. "Oh god, I think he killed Taylor."

Emma's heart skips. "That's not true. He had no reason to do that. And besides—"

"He *did* a have reason," Brittany blurts out. "Taylor told me she was asking him about this ski trip he took—and where he had dinner. It was the night your husband was killed, and Tom snapped at her, told her to stay out of his business. He—"

"Brittany, stop. Justine Carr killed Taylor. She was arrested this afternoon."

"*What?* Then why did he snap at—?"

"He's been under enormous pressure—there's a lot going on that you know nothing about."

Emma realizes as she's speaking that Taylor must have suspected the real reason she was eager for details about the Stowe weekend, and Taylor brought it up to Tom even though Emma had asked her not to. After all, it was an additional opportunity to cause trouble, make Emma keep doubting her husband.

"Brittany, you *have* to call Tom," she adds. "He needs to hear this from you."

More silence.

"I will," Brittany says finally. "I promise I will—but tomorrow. I need to think through how to say it."

Emma manages a subdued goodbye, roiled by what she's heard. At least it's answered her last, lingering questions: who'd snuck into the studio that evening and how Tom's "E.H." file got into the home office.

As she watches Tom dart from the store with a case of bottled water under one arm, she considers filling him in herself and trying to soften the blow. But Brittany promised to do it and she needs to give the girl a chance to follow through.

Tom and Emma continue out of town and soon afterward Tom turns the car to the right and heads uphill. When Emma rolls down her window, she's greeted by the smell of the ocean and the scent of endless bayberry bushes.

And then, up on a rise, the house is in sight, the small one-story home Tom swore she wouldn't like, but that she finds enchanting. It's constructed of unfinished wood and features a vaulted roof and wraparound covered porch that reminds of her pictures she's seen of old Australian farmhouses. There's also a tiny outbuilding Tom uses as an office. Though the rooftops of neighboring homes are visible in the distance, the immediate area has a secluded, remote feel.

"Wow," Emma says as she unfolds herself from the car and gazes at the endless Atlantic. "I forgot just how fantastic the view is."

"It never gets old for me," Tom says, staring out. "Hey, what do you say we eat soon? I'm famished."

"Sure, I think we need an early night."

They spring into action, grabbing their bags and the cooler from the trunk and lugging them into the house.

The layout is as simple as the exterior suggests—an open kitchen, dining and living area, with a bedroom on either end. As soon as they set down their belongings, Emma notices that everything has been recently cleaned to sparkling, including the glass doors with their stunning view of the ocean.

"Why don't I cook," Tom says, starting to unpack the cooler.

"You sure?"

"Yeah. I need to make a call or two later from the landline in my office, so it'll be nice to have a diversion now. Give me thirty minutes."

"Okay. And I can use this time to check in with Eric."

After carrying their overnight bags into the larger of the two bedrooms, Emma returns to the veranda and steps down into the garden on the south side of the house. As she reaches the spot where she'd had luck with cell service on her other visit, she finds a few bars displayed on her phone and places a call to Eric. It's six on the dot, so she's surprised when she reaches his voice mail.

She turns her attention back to the garden. Since Tom's been renting out the house, he hasn't been as fastidious about it, but the overgrown patches of wildflowers and blackberry bushes only add to the lush mysteriousness of the setting. Emma lowers herself to sit on one of the boulders at the end of the garden, grateful for the emotional comfort the spot provides.

And she needs comfort. Though she's put her concerns about Tom to rest, the days of endless worry have drained her, and she can't believe how much has unfolded this week—the bombshell from Lilly, Taylor's death, Justine's arrest, and now the disturbing revelation Brittany dumped on her. Tom's going to be beside himself when he hears what his stepdaughter did.

As Emma thinks back to her conversation with Brittany, she realizes something else. Brittany spent a huge amount of time with Taylor, which means she might have an inkling of why the chief of staff ran afoul of Justine—and if so, it might be contributing to her anguish about Taylor's death. Someone is going to have to tell the police about the relationship, for Brittany's own sake.

A thought stirs in her mind, slightly out of reach, something about Taylor. She recognizes its outlines from when it started to form on the ferry ride, but she has no better luck this time grabbing hold.

Her phone rings and she assumes it's Eric, but when she pulls it from her pocket, she sees a Maine number she doesn't recognize.

"Is this Emma Hawke?"

"Yes, who's calling?" she answers, struggling to a standing position.

"This is Stacey Manning. You left a message on LinkedIn for me?"

Of course, Stacey, Tom's former number two. It feels like months ago that Emma reached out to her.

"Thanks so much for calling back."

"Sorry to track you down at the start of the weekend, but my mom's in hospice care, and these days I only have a few minutes here and there."

"Oh, gee, I'm so sorry to hear that, and we can certainly talk at another time. I wanted to pick your brain a little— about, um, stepping off the treadmill."

Emma can barely call up the lie she'd written in the LinkedIn message.

"Would you mind if we did postpone it? It's a subject I'd actually love to chat about. I left for Maine to be with my mom when she started to fail and I'm so grateful to have had these past couple of years with her."

"Absolutely. Just reach out whenever you can, Stacey."

"Will do. I hope everything's good at Halliday. I'm not very connected to the place anymore, but Tom and I spoke at one point last year, and he sounded deliriously happy to have met you."

It doesn't seem like the news about Taylor's death or Justine's arrest has reached Stacey yet, and Emma decides that this isn't the moment to burden her with it.

"Ah, good to know. And I've heard such wonderful things about *you*, Stacey. I'm sorry we never had the chance to meet."

"Same here. Though we've actually been in each other's company once."

"When I first came to Halliday?"

"No, I'd left for Maine by the time you got there. It was before that—in Manhattan."

Emma's chest compresses, a breath trapped inside.

"Really?" she says. *Please no*, she prays.

"Yes, Tom and I heard you on a panel once. At the Harvard Club."

35

THE GROUND SEEMS TO DISAPPEAR BENEATH EMMA'S FEET.

"The panel on trends?" she manages to say. She knows the answer, but she's buying time now, trying to get a grip.

"Yes, you were wonderful. I hadn't heard of you at that time, but Tom was already a fan."

"Speaking of your mother, Stacey," Emma says, needing to end the call as soon as possible. "I don't want to take you away from her any longer. I—I . . . I'm so sorry for what you're going through."

"Thank you, Emma. I look forward to speaking at another time."

After mumbling a goodbye, Emma stuffs the phone back into a pocket of her jeans, stumbles back to the boulder, and collapses onto it, covering her face with her hands.

Her husband's a liar, just as she'd thought—and worse than that. He stalked her after the Florida event and later ensured she was hired at his company, pretending it was all by chance, the stars aligning in their favor. And he sat in their kitchen two days ago denying her fears, making her think she'd let her imagination run amok. Though Taylor and Brittany tried to rattle her about Tom, make her suspect there was something unsavory about him, they didn't actually believe those things then—and yet they'd been right all along.

What else has he lied about? she wonders.

Stowe? He claims he was helping a snowboarder that night, but that might be only something he told his colleagues at the time. He could have composed the email he showed her himself—once he sensed she was checking on his whereabouts that weekend.

And then there's the incident Taylor reported to Brittany. Maybe Brittany was right, that Tom snapped at Taylor because he sensed she was digging in places where he didn't want her to be. And he might have killed her because of it. He claimed the scarf was Diana's and yet he could have made that up after he heard Emma snooping in his office or spotted her car on his tail.

According to Tom, he was on the phone with the forensic accountant during the window of time in which Taylor was killed, but perhaps he was able to slip away—and then plant evidence against Justine. How perfect to use her, the unscrupulous embezzler, as the fall guy.

So what is she supposed to do next? With her stomach twisting, Emma realizes that she might even be in physical danger. If Tom *is* a murderer and suspects she's wise to him, maybe he has nasty plans for her, too. That could be the whole reason he organized this little getaway, and now she's stuck in this fairly isolated cottage with him on an island in the Atlantic Ocean, an hour's ferry ride away from the mainland. She needs to get out of here.

Emma pulls up the ferry schedule on her phone but first has to walk around the garden to get just a few bars of service. When she finds the website, she sees that there's only one more boat tonight—at 8:20. If they eat in ten or so minutes as planned and Tom retreats to the office afterward to make calls, she can probably catch it. No, she *has* to catch it. Her fingers tremble as she reserves a seat online.

And then what? she thinks. She'll have to Uber back to Westport, grab whatever belongings she can fit in a bag, and find someplace to stay for the night.

She's scared but also heartsick. She wanted to believe her husband so badly, wanted to buy into the idea of him as the total opposite of Derrick, and she allowed him to convince her time and time again, allowed him to blind her with his fucking Tom Halliday charm.

"Ahh, I *wondered* where you were hiding."

Here he is now, changed into khaki shorts and a navy polo shirt, and standing at the other end of the garden, his face shadowed by the leaves of a raggedy apple tree.

"Hey." It's all she's able to force out of her mouth.

"Food's about ready."

"Be right there."

She takes sixty seconds to flesh out her escape plan, which will only work if Tom retreats to his office after dinner. She has to make sure that happens.

Returning to the veranda, Emma finds Tom at the grill, basting salmon fillets with his typical enthusiasm. It's all a fraud, though. He *looks* like the Tom she married, *acts* like the Tom she married, and yet—that person was never real.

"Pierce made a great selection," he says, cocking his chin toward the salmon.

"Nice."

"Everything good at the office?"

"Uh, I don't know. For some reason Eric's not picking up."

"That wasn't him?"

She looks at him, confused.

"When I first checked the garden, you were on the phone. I figured it was Eric."

He'd seen her speaking to Stacey. Could he have overheard what she was saying?

"No, that was someone else. A possible client."

He carefully flips the fillets and then turns back, locking eyes with her. A chill races down her spine.

"Is everything okay?"

He can tell something is chewing away at her insides.

"Uh, not exactly. To be honest, Taylor's death is still really getting to me."

"I know, me, too. But let's try to forget about it for a few hours. And relish being here together."

She forces herself to nod. "Yes, you're right."

"Would you mind grabbing the wine, sweetheart?"

After collecting a bottle of white from the fridge, Emma takes a seat at the nearby table, which Tom has already set. He's also lit a citronella candle to ward off mosquitoes as well as two kerosene hurricane lamps even though there's still quite a bit of light in the sky. *Please*, Emma prays to herself, *don't let this be a sign he wants to linger over the meal.*

He plates the salmon and they take turns serving themselves the rice and simple green salad he's prepared.

"That's all you're having, Em?" he says when he sees her plate.

"It all looks wonderful. I just don't have a huge appetite tonight." She sweeps her gaze around the veranda, forcing a smile. "We talked a little about Block Island when I was here last, but tell me more. What do you know about the history?"

Fortunately, he's happy to oblige, and as he shares what he's read—about the early American Indian inhabitants, the arrival of Europeans in the 1600s, the sense of comfort his property provided after he became a widower—all Emma does is nod and keep forcing smiles. The light begins to seep from the sky. She glances surreptitiously at her watch and almost gasps: she doesn't have much more than an hour.

"Look, I know you have calls to make, and you did all that cooking," she says once they've set down their utensils. "So let me clean up, okay?"

"I can at least give you a hand."

"No, no. I have nothing else to do tonight."

"Okay, thanks. PR wants to fill me in on the game plan for the next few days. We have to minimize the fallout, of course, but transparency will be key."

She wants to laugh. *Transparency. That's going to be tough for you*, she wants to say. *Because you're the master of deceit.*

And for the first time she notices another emotion lurking beneath her fear and distress: *anger.* Yes, maybe she's been a fool for believing him, but he tricked her and put her whole world at risk.

⇐

While Tom heads to his office, Emma grabs a tray and quickly piles it with plates and utensils and once inside shoves it onto the counter. Her eyes dart around the kitchen area, hoping to spot his car keys but there's no sign of them. Like usual, they must be in his pants pocket. She's going to have get a taxi to the ferry dock and try to make sure Tom doesn't spot her climbing into it.

After bolting to the bedroom, she grabs her duffel bag and purse and runs her gaze over the bedroom, making sure she hasn't missed anything important, and is halfway out the door when she decides to swap her sandals for sneakers. Her hands work jerkily, tugging the back of the sneakers up over her heels, tying the laces.

She's almost done when she hears the sound of the veranda door—and her heart stops. She tiptoes into the open doorway and peeks out. Tom's nowhere in sight. It must have been the breeze rattling the glass.

But it forces her to realize that there's no way she can simply exit from the veranda and do a mad dash down the road. It's not dark yet and Tom will be bound to notice her since his office window faces that direction. Steeling herself, Emma slips out the rear door instead, makes her way to the garden from the back of the house, and then plunges into the thick foliage that lines the road.

It turns out to be tough going. Tree branches swipe at her face, and though she's wearing jeans and a cotton sweater over her T-shirt, the thorns from the berry bushes tear at her exposed skin.

After five or six minutes of staggering through the brush, wondering what might be scurrying around in there at this hour, Emma steps closer to the road, pokes her head out, and looks back up at the house, its lights twinkling in the dusk. She's pretty sure she'll be out of sight if she emerges now. After breaking through to the road, she scurries downhill, her duffel bag bouncing against her leg, until she reaches the driveway of the first house on the left after Tom's.

Dropping her bags, she digs her phone from her back pocket and summons the number for one of the cab companies she'd programmed in when she was here last. Thankfully, after close to ten rings, the dispatcher finally answers. She tells him she needs a cab as soon as possible on Bayberry Road, at the second to the last house on the right before the top of the hill.

"Best I can do is twenty-five minutes," the guy tells her.

Her heart sinks. "Uh, never mind."

Uber isn't an option since it's not allowed on the island, so she tries the number of the other cab company, pleading with the gods.

"You're trying to catch the 8:20?" the woman says after Emma blurts out her request. "You're cutting it awfully close."

"Please, it's an emergency."

"Okay, ten minutes."

"I'll be at the end of the driveway."

Exhaling, Emma tucks herself behind a tree and peers through the dusky light back at Tom's office outbuilding. The lamp is still on and there's no sign of movement in the main house, meaning he's probably still in the office and hasn't discovered she's missing.

The wait for the taxi is hell. She'll make it, she tells herself, and then a second later, she despairs, sure she won't. Finally, two minutes later than promised, Emma hears a car roar up the hill. She steps out of the driveway and waves, her heart beating hard. Tom might be looking up, she thinks, wondering who's headed in his general direction. She wrenches open the back door and nearly hurls herself inside with her bags.

She's expecting a weather, wizened driver, but it's a blond surfer type, early thirties, his skin already the shade of a walnut and flecks of it peeling off his nose.

"The ferry, huh?" he says, turning the car around in the driveway.

"Yes, please." She twists around, making sure through the rear window that Tom hasn't stepped outside of his office, curious, but there's no sign of him anywhere.

The driver's eyes flick to the rearview mirror and take her in.

"You're supposed to be *arriving* here Friday night, not leaving."

"Right. I just have to get the ferry, okay?"

He gets a move on at least, spraying stones as they descend the hill. She checks her watch every fifteen seconds. They're on the shore road now and finally she spots the white-and-blue ferry boat up ahead, still moored at the dock and a few people bunched near the ticket window. She actually has time to spare. She pays the driver, shouts a thank-you, and bolts toward the gangplank, flashing the ticket on her phone.

Once on board, Emma finally exhales. After taking a second to untangle the straps of her purse and duffel bag that twisted together on her frantic race here, she glances around. The western sky has brushstrokes of filmy pink and lavender, lingering traces of the sunset. Below her the waves lap gently against the hull of the boat, and from somewhere she picks up the coconut-tinged scent of suntan lotion. She can't believe that only hours ago she stood on a deck just like this one, thrilled to be getting away for the weekend with Tom. Now she's fleeing from him, her life totally unraveled.

Better to sit inside this time, Emma decides. Not only will she be warmer that way, but if Tom comes into town looking for her, she won't be conspicuous. She climbs to the second deck and locates a seat in the enclosed area. There's only a small crowd onboard tonight, mostly day-trippers returning home, she guesses.

From her perch inside she scans the marina and the tiny town of New Shoreham just beyond. Things are as bustling as expected for a Friday night—people strolling around the marina and along the main street of the tiny town, some spilling out of boutiques with shopping bags or gathered with friends out in front of the bars and ice cream shops. The women are all in shorts or flirty summer dresses, the men in khaki pants or shorts and weathered T-shirts. There's absolutely no sign of Tom, she's relieved to see.

But a short distance away one man catches her eye. He's striding down a weathered dock where the private boats pull up, leading a bicycle on foot and, in sharp contrast to everyone else, wearing black jeans and a black sweatshirt with the hood up over his head. He steps off the dock and starts across the ferry parking lot.

As he pauses beneath one of the outdoor lights and leans the bike against a post, Emma realizes she's looking at something completely familiar: the man's build, his gait, the stick-straight posture.

And in one brief, terrifying moment, she puts it together. The man standing in the marina parking lot is Derrick Rand. The husband she buried twenty-seven months ago.

36

For a few brief seconds, Emma wonders if she's the victim of a bizarre, incredible hoax, that Derrick really isn't dead after all.

But she knows that can't be true. She saw the photo of the body in the morgue, she signed the papers at the funeral home. It's clearly someone with a haunting resemblance to her first husband.

The man seems to be studying something in his hand, his phone, she thinks. Leaving her duffel bag on the seat, Emma dashes outside for a better glimpse. After a couple of moments, he looks up and the movement causes the hood of the sweatshirt to shift backward a little. Emma squints, taking in his features.

No, it's definitely not Derrick. It's *Kyle*.

Or at least she's pretty sure it is. But what would he be doing on Block Island? She'd told him she was going to be here, of course, and that she might be hard to reach. What if he's learned something critical about the paintings and hasn't been able to get through to her?

Instinctively, she starts to lift her arm to flag him down but drops it just as fast. Instead she digs her phone from her purse and checks the screen. As it turned out, she'd had better reception on the property than she expected, so if Kyle had tried, he probably *would* have gotten through, but there are no missed calls or texts on her screen.

When Emma looks back onto shore, she sees that Kyle's glancing down again at what's in his hand, perhaps GPS on the screen of his phone, trying to get his bearings. What on earth is he up to? And why is he dressed like that, instead of in his usual dated preppy gear?

A voice inside tells her to duck so he won't see her, and she drops into a crouching position. Scrolling through her contacts, she locates Kyle's number and taps it. She swears she hears the faint ring of a phone from the parking lot, though it might be her imagination. But a second later the man in black lifts his hand to his ear.

"What's up?" Kyle's voice says into her phone. So it's definitely him, standing right there in plain sight.

"Hi, Kyle, I was just checking in. Have you come across anything about the paintings yet?"

"Yeah, maybe. I should know more in a day or two."

"Oh, wow, what have you found so far?"

Is he about to tell her that what he's uncovered is so big and shocking he's hightailed it all the way to Block Island to fill her in?

"I don't want to say until I dig a little deeper. We're about to sit down for dinner, but I'm going to delve into things again tomorrow—and I'll have something for you later."

Her breath quickens. He doesn't want her to know he's here.

She clears her throat. "All right, let me know."

"Anything more on your end?"

"No, just waiting to hear what you turn up."

"Did you manage to get away this weekend?"

"Yes. It's good to be here."

"Enjoy. Unfortunately, I really need to run. Remember, let's keep this between us until I know more."

"Of course."

She should never have admitted they came to Block Island, she thinks as she disconnects. Because he's on some kind of clandestine mission here that must involve her.

Is he out for vengeance, still blaming her for Derrick's murder? Seems unlikely since he's had two years to come after her for that. Then what?

Still squatting, she replays their brief exchange. For the second time he's asked her to keep it quiet for a few days about the possible forgery. Maybe he's not really looking into the situation. Maybe he's simply been buying time for himself.

The only way this makes sense to Emma is if Kyle doesn't want her to reach out to Detective Webster, that . . . that he wants to shut her up. And it must have something to do with the paintings, that he was involved in the forgery himself somehow. She cautiously raises her head and peers through the railing, wondering what he's doing now, but both Kyle and the bike have disappeared.

Something's not right and she can't simply sail away. Emma dashes back inside, grabs her duffel bag, and after returning to the deck, nearly scrambles down the stairs.

Reaching the exit, she sees a man about to remove the gangplank and tells him, please, she needs to get off.

"You can't get back on, you know?" he says in a chiding tone.

"I know, I know," she yells and rushes off.

Emma's heart is pounding hard by the time she reaches the parking lot, still trying to make it all compute.

She's got her phone in her hand still, and she scrolls through her contacts for Jacob Whaley, the art dealer she's never heard back from. It takes five rings for Whaley to answer, and when he does, his voice is accompanied by background music and the sound of people chattering nearby.

Emma blurts out her name, her connection to Chris and Lilly Shelbourne, and reminds him of the message Chris sent him over two years ago, all the while scanning the parking lot with her eyes. Kyle has definitely vanished.

"Uh, yeah, I remember, and sorry not to get back to you this week. I do want to talk, but it'll have to be tomorrow. I'm in the middle of hosting a dinner party."

"I just need one minute of your time. My husband was murdered two years ago, and I think it's because of the painting. The one Chris thought was a fake."

"I'm really sorry, and I wish I could help, but I buy and sell art. You need to talk to someone who authenticates paintings."

"Um, right. But—"

"Look, I really have to go. I could give you a call tomorr—"

"Please, this has turned into an emergency. Just tell me—how does fake art even show up in a private collection? Is it possible that a dealer sold forgeries to my parents-in-law?"

He sighs. "It wouldn't be the first time, but Chris and I also spoke on the phone about it. And according to what I recall, the painting—a Rothko, right?—had been sold by a very reputable gallery, one that thoroughly investigates a painting's provenance."

The foghorn on the ferry sounds and the engine roars to life. Emma covers one ear with her hand as the boat pulls out of the harbor.

"Then what could have happened?"

"My best guess—and then I really have to sign off—is that your in-laws might have swapped the real painting for a fake when they needed cash. Or someone else did, when they weren't paying attention."

"Okay, thank you so much for your time."

The line goes dead before she can say another word. But things are starting to come together. If Whaley is right about the gallery, the forgery must have occurred after the purchase of the real painting. Based on what she knows about Derrick's parents' very healthy financial situation, it seems unlikely they were the ones who substituted the fake.

So, that brings her back to Kyle. There had been a period early in Kyle's business when, according to what Derrick told her, his brother had struggled to keep the firm together. When things rebounded, Kyle had attributed it to an infusion of cash from new clients, but the money probably came from selling the Rothko painting—or maybe *all* of the paintings—on the black market and swapping in forgeries.

And it wouldn't have been hard for him to sneak the paintings out of the house. His parents liked to travel, sometimes for a couple of weeks at a time, and he was the one who kept an eye on the property.

Sure, there must have been moments of panic for him, especially when his parents died unexpectedly and the paintings were distributed to his siblings. But Heather's two paintings went into storage and Derrick was happy with his, thrilled to show them off to the world. Kyle could relax . . . until, that is, Chris Shelbourne came to their party and planted the first seeds of doubt.

And then, fast and furious, the truth begins to unfurl in front of her. Thanks to Chris, Derrick was about to figure out what his brother was up to.

Which means Tom didn't murder Derrick. *Kyle* did.

And his wife, Jackie, obviously covered for him, claiming he was home when he was clearly in New York, hunting down his brother.

Emma glances nervously around, wondering where Kyle has gone. Is he on the bike now, headed to the house in search of her and ready to kill her because he knows she's closing in on the full story?

Tom. He's alone at the house, maybe still in his office and unaware that she's fled the scene.

She has to warn him.

With a shaky hand she searches for the number to his office landline and taps it. The call goes straight to voice mail.

"Tom, you need to get out of the house," she says. "I'm

not there anymore. I'm down by the ferry—I can explain later—but I've just spotted Kyle in the marina. I think he killed Derrick and is on his way to the house to hurt me. Please, Tom, you have to get out of there."

She tries his cell phone next but he doesn't answer that either, and she leaves another frantic message. She has no idea where he's gone. Maybe he returned to the house, saw she wasn't there, and went looking for her out in the garden or along the road and doesn't have a signal now.

Emma gives it a minute and makes another attempt. Voice mail again. Tom's life is in danger, and she has to do something.

There's no other option, she realizes, than to call 911. Gulping a breath of air, she taps the number.

"911, what is the location of your emergency?" the female operator says.

"Uh, Block Island. The last house on Bayberry Road—at the top of the rise."

"Is that your current location?"

Maybe the operator can tell from the screen that she isn't calling from there. "No, I'm in the parking lot of the ferry, but I need the police to go to Bayberry Road. It's urgent."

"Ma'am, tell me exactly what's happened."

Emma does her best not to trip over the words, explaining that she has good reason to believe a man she spotted in the parking lot is headed on a bike to her house, intending to harm her husband. That he's wearing dark pants and a dark hooded sweatshirt—and might be armed.

"Please stay on the line while I transfer your call to the New Shoreham police," the operator says.

A male police officer answers, giving his name and rank in a blur. After the 911 operator recaps the situation, Emma is assured by the officer that local police will be dispatched to the house as soon as possible and that a police car will be sent to pick her up at the ferry.

The call over, Emma attempts to reach Tom one more time. Still nothing. She gulps air, trying to calm down. It's going to be okay, she reassures herself. The police are on the way, and the island is small. They'll get there in time.

She hurries to a spot closer to the road so the police will be able to find her, and after dropping her duffel bag to the ground with a thud, starts to pace. The sky is dark now, and the parking lot behind her is empty of people, but she can see plenty of island residents and tourists moving about the town, their laughter and shouts carried by the breeze.

Where are *they?* Emma wonders as she covers the same ground back and forth. She checks her watch. It's been more than ten minutes since she made the 911 call.

She digs her phone from her pocket and googles "North Shoreham police," clicks through to the webpage she finds, and scrolls down until she finally finds it at the bottom—a local number. She jabs the link.

This time a young-sounding woman answers, her voice bright and friendly. Emma reminds her of the 911 call and pleads for an update.

"Yes, we have the information," the woman says. "Officers are being dispatched to the house."

"*Are* being dispatched?" Emma exclaims. "They haven't left yet?"

"We've been dealing with a serious medical emergency,

but someone will be there, I assure you. And a car will be coming to your location as well."

It's clear the woman can't be any more committal than that.

"All right," Emma says, chagrined. "Just please, do what you can—my husband might be in grave danger."

Emma tries Tom yet again, but there's still no response.

Kyle must be closing in on the house by now, she realizes. He would surely have researched their location and used his GPS, and from what she recalls, he's a serious biker. Knowing it's crazy, she calls the cab company she used to get to the ferry and begs for a cab. Because she can't wait for the police.

"It's probably going to be at least fifteen minutes," the woman says, her voice nearly drowned out by background noise.

"It's an emergency, please," Emma tells her.

"We'll try, hon, but that's probably going to be the best we can do. All our cars are out."

Emma says she'll wait, but once the call is finished, she phones the other company she has a listing for. She gets only a busy signal, and then again when she tries two seconds later.

There's got to be another way to get there, Emma thinks, hoisting the duffel bag onto her shoulder again. A moped? She jogs across the parking lot, the bag banging against her leg, and then into the center of town, navigating through the clusters of people sauntering along the street. There's a moped store where she and Tom rented a pair for fun when they came to the island before, and she knows it's nearby, right at the edge of the tiny town. But before she's even reached the front of the shop, she sees that it's closed.

Nearly crazed now, Emma notices a car at the intersection, and on the spur of the moment, she darts toward it.

"Please," she calls into the driver's window. "Is there any chance you could give me a ride to Bayberry Road? I have an emergency."

She's talking to a girl barely out of her teens, raven-haired and possibly inebriated.

"Sorry," the girl says with a shrug. "This isn't my car and I need to take it back right away."

Emma steps away without saying another word. How can she blame this stranger? And what would she even do if she got there? She's no match for Kyle, with or without a gun.

Her mind racing, she scans the area, thinking she might actually be able to spot the police vehicle headed in the direction of the house and flag it down. And then, as her gaze briefly settles on the ferry parking lot, she sees the taxi she called pull up.

She breaks into a run, crazily waving her arm, afraid the driver will take off if no one is waiting. He spots her after a moment. He's the same one she had on the way here, surfer boy.

"Changed your mind?" he asks through the open window with a smile as she reaches the car.

"Look, I just need to get back, okay," she says, then yanks open the back door and jumps in. "But take me all the way to top of the hill."

"Got it."

Emma holds her breath as they eventually make the turn onto Bayberry, wondering if she'll spot Kyle on his bike, but what she sees instead, parked in front of the house, is a police SUV, white with a dark horizontal stripe. She presses her hands to her face in relief.

"You going to be okay?" the driver asks, having obviously seen the SUV as well.

"I hope so."

As she leaps from the car, thrusting a twenty-dollar bill at the driver through his open window, two male police officers step into view from around the side of the veranda, both young, brown-haired, and dressed in dark pants and short-sleeved shirts.

"I'm Emma Hawke, the woman who called 911," she shouts, not giving them time to speak first. "Is my husband okay?"

"Can we please see some identification?" one of them asks.

She fumbles through her purse for her wallet, nearly tears out her license and passes it over. As the officer who made the request takes a look, she glances anxiously around. She sees that the office is dark now, but lights are on in the house, more of them than when she left. And Tom's car is still in the driveway, on the other side of the house.

"Thank you, ma'am," he says, handing it back. "Can you please tell us what's going on?"

"Yes, but first I have to know—is my husband here, is he okay?"

"We've checked the interior of the house, but there's no one inside."

Has Kyle taken him someplace? she wonders in despair. But he couldn't have, not on a bike.

"My husband has to be here *someplace*," she insists, trying to sound calm. "That's his car. We need to check his office, too." She flings her arm in the direction of the outbuilding.

"We're going to do that, but we need you to tell us what's going on."

Emma blurts out an answer—about being on the ferry and seeing her former brother-in-law when he has no business being here, about having good reason to think he killed her first husband and was on his way to the house to hurt her and Tom.

She watches as their expressions morph the tiniest bit, as if they're finally seeing how serious the situation is. Or they're wondering if she's unhinged.

"All right," the cop says, "we're going to clear the rest of the property now. What does your husband look like?"

"He's forty-five, in good shape. Silver hair. Please, can't I go with you?"

"No, it's important for you to remain in one place," the other cop says.

It makes sense, she knows, but the idea of waiting is unbearable. She nods in acceptance and parks herself next to their vehicle, her bags at her feet. The two cops move off toward the office, their hands lightly resting on their service weapons.

She directed them there, but she doesn't actually see how Tom could be inside. Since the lamp is off, it means he must have finished his calls and returned to the house, snapped on a few more lights, and then wondered where she was. Did he decide to go out searching for her?

After barely a second inside the tiny office, the officers emerge, shaking their heads.

"I think he must be outside," she calls out and thrusts a finger to the left. "In the garden over there or in the back of the house."

The cops nod and after one activates a flashlight, they cross the veranda and descend the steps into the garden on the other side. She hears rustling as they tramp through the brush and then the sounds of them moving off toward the rear of the house. After the longest five minutes she can remember, only one of the officers returns.

"Ma'am, can you come with me?" he calls out.

Emma tears in his direction, her heart in her throat. There's light being cast from the house, and as she rounds the house right behind him, she sees the other officer crouched on the ground and cries out. To his right are a pair of crumpled legs. Kyle's shot Tom, she realizes. *Killed* him.

But as the officer shifts position, she sees that Tom is half sitting up, the cop's hand on his back.

"Tom," she screams, rushing forward and dropping down next to him and the officer.

"I'm okay, sweetheart," he says. "At least I think I am. I might have been out cold for a bit."

"We'll call an ambulance for you," the cop says.

"Please, hold off a second," Tom urges. "I really think I'm okay. I probably need to see a doctor, but I'd prefer to do it on my own steam."

He straightens into a full sitting position. In the light coming from the house, Emma sees an ugly gash on his forehead, though it doesn't seem to be bleeding now.

"Can you tell us what happened?" the cop says.

"Uh, yeah. I'd come outside looking for my wife." He

pauses, momentarily confused and looks at Emma. "Where did you go?"

"I went into town," she says quickly. "I can explain later."

"As soon as I was outside, I heard someone come up behind me. I spun around and before I knew it, this guy in a ski mask was grabbing me, punching at me. And then—we both heard a car coming and he took off, but not before whacking me hard on the side of the head a couple of times and knocking me to the ground. It might have been with the butt of a gun."

"Is there anything you can tell us about his appearance?"

"He was six feet, maybe, well-built, dark clothes. Oh wait, I took a swing at him and connected with his face. There'll probably be a bruise there eventually."

One of the officers steps away and Emma hears him talking urgently into his radio, giving the description, while the other one asks Tom if he feels up to standing yet.

"Yeah, I think I'm good." With the cop's help, he struggles to his feet. "Does anyone have any idea what's going on?"

"I do," Emma says, "but I'll tell you in the car. If you're sure you don't want an ambulance?"

"Yeah, yeah, I'm not dizzy or anything."

She exhales finally, some of the tension melting away. She's so relieved Tom's okay, that the sound of the police car coming up the road clearly drove Kyle away. And that she was wrong, so wrong, about Tom having any connection to Derrick's death.

But that doesn't erase the lies he's told her.

37

IN THE MORNING EMMA AND TOM TAKE A VERY EARLY FERRY back to the mainland, the only one on which they were able to get a reservation for the car, but that's okay. All Emma wants is to be back in Westport in her own bed. Every inch of her body aches with tension and fatigue.

The police had helped Tom to the car last night and alerted the small medical center they were on the way. During the drive, Emma explained that it was Kyle who attacked him and why. Another police officer met them in the ER and took their statements as they waited for Tom to have an MRI. The doctor diagnosed him with a minor concussion, in addition to the gash above his eye, and told him that mental and physical rest was the best way for his brain to recover.

Fat chance of him getting any rest with Kyle still at large, Emma thinks. But while they were finishing up at the hospital, they'd been alerted that her former brother-in-law had been apprehended at the marina, where he seemed to be planning to board a small, rented powerboat that was moored there, and he was now in custody—at least for the night. They had let themselves back into the cottage just after one o'clock and fell immediately into bed.

It's overcast and on the cool side today, so as soon as they're on board the boat, they leave the deck and find seats inside. They're mostly quiet during the trip, occasionally glancing at their phones. At one point Tom goes out onto the deck to take a call from his attorney, whom he'd left a message for earlier. As he exits, Emma sees several passengers take note of his appearance. He's got a big bandage over the gash on his forehead, and there's a bluish black half-moon under one eye.

Emma's already been in touch with her own lawyer this morning, and it was clear that last night's news stunned even the unflappable Peter Dunne. He assured her he'd call Webster immediately, though the police in New Shoreham had indicated they would do that as well.

Kyle's aborted ambush of Tom doesn't prove he's a killer—and if he had a gun in his possession she doubts it's the one he used to murder Derrick—but she suspects Webster will get there soon enough by following both the evidence from last night and the forgery trail, and surely she'll also spend the next few days undoing Jackie's alibi.

Emma leans her head back against the plastic seat. As fatigued as she feels, she hasn't been able to turn her mind off, even for a second. She's not only still distraught about how close Tom was to being killed, but she's having a hard time coming to grips with the horrible truth that emerged last night: that Derrick was murdered by his own brother.

Events and experiences from the past two years keep reshaping themselves in her mind, like a magician turning a rabbit into a dove. Kyle's moroseness and brooding silence after the murder, for instance, which she'd mistaken as a sign of crushing grief. It must actually have been due to the weight of his actions and his fear that he'd somehow be exposed.

And then there's the way he kept pointing the finger at her, insinuating that she was behind the murder when he was actually trying to undermine her confidence and deflect attention away from himself. She should have stepped back, analyzed the evidence in front of her, and seen what Kyle was doing, but she'd been too guilty over her own lack of remorse to see what was going on.

It's all about the data, isn't it? Emma says to herself. And right there, at that moment, the fuzzy thought that eluded her on the outbound ferry and again in the garden, finally surfaces. It's about Taylor's murder.

Her stomach twists as the revelation forms fully for her. She'll need to tell Tom about it, and the Westport police as well.

By the time Emma and Tom are off the ferry and on the highway to Westport, it's raining hard. She's driving, having refused to allow Tom behind the wheel, and because of the downpour, she has to keep all her attention on the road. Which means that at least for now, she doesn't have to think about what to do in regard to Tom.

The rain lets up right around the time they reach Westport, and as she pulls into the driveway, Tom tells her not to bother opening the garage.

"I think I'll make a fast trip to Whole Foods and pick up a few groceries for us."

"Tom, let me go," she insists.

"Em, I feel fine now, really, and I just want to do something that seems normal. I won't be long, I promise."

She nods, climbs out of the car with both of their duffel bags, and enters the house on her own. She pours a water for herself and takes it to the screened porch, where, after opening the main door, she drops wearily onto the couch.

Her feelings about her husband are in a terrible tangle. She knows without a doubt that he didn't kill Derrick. She's aware, too, that a big part of her still loves him passionately—it was hell during those minutes when she thought he might have been injured or killed. But she can't let go of the lies he told her.

The sound of water splashing tugs her away from her thoughts, and Emma looks up to see Eric dashing toward the house from the studio driveway, carrying a soggy paper bag.

"Knock, knock," he calls out through the screen door, having spotted her on the couch.

"I can't believe you're here on a Saturday. Door's open, by the way."

After entering, he pauses for a minute, letting the rain drip from his slicker onto the stone floor.

"I thought you might be home by now and could use a pick-me-up!" He carefully removes his slicker and tears open the bag to reveal a large smoothie. "Blueberry, your favorite."

"Oh, Eric, thank you. Do you have a few minutes to sit?'

"Of course," he says, handing her the drink and then dropping into a chair. "You doing better?"

She'd filled him in this morning about what happened last night, and told him that Kyle probably killed Derrick, but she hasn't shared anything about her issues with Tom.

"Yes, a bit. The word *closure* is overused, but it's such a relief to finally know who did it. I would have been wondering about it for the rest of my life."

"A relief but tragic, too, to think it was your brother-in-law. Is there anything I can do for you, Em?"

"Nothing beyond this smoothie. It's going to work wonders."

"I also wanted to apologize for forgetting about our six o'clock call yesterday. I was on the phone with Dean, of all people, and to be honest, that was also the reason I slept through the library event. I'd been up late the night before talking to him."

Emma cocks her head, a little surprised. "Are you two thinking about getting back together?"

"Not sure yet. I'm still trying to decide if his shitty behavior last spring qualifies as a go or a gone."

She looks at him quizzically.

"Oh, it's just something kind of silly an influencer said in one of our relationship surveys. A go, she said, is something someone does that you should let go of and not worry about. A gone, though, is a big deal and it should have you gone from the picture immediately."

"Ha, she probably already has a book deal. But good luck whatever you choose."

"Regardless of what I decide, I promise not to let the relationship interfere with my work again. I love my job and working with you."

"I'm so happy to hear that, Eric." She *is*, and it means she misinterpreted some of his recent behavior. But inside she's also cringing. Who knows what will happen with Hawke and Company over the coming weeks and months? Will they still be working out of the studio? Will she be living in this house with Tom? At this exact moment, Emma doesn't have a clue.

"I should let you get back to decompressing," he says, rising. "Oh, before I forget, that professor pal of yours, Addison, called the office at the end of the day yesterday. She said she'd tried your cell but wasn't able to reach you."

She *had* noticed a message from her but hadn't bother to call. Maybe Addison means well, but Emma bets she's probably nosing for gossip. She'll send her a text and tell her she's fine and then let things fade. The friends she wants in her life right now are women like Bekah and Lilly.

About a half hour after Eric departs, and just as Emma is starting to worry, Tom returns with a rotisserie chicken and several salads.

"How are you feeling?" she asks.

"It helped to be out and about for a bit, though I could see people eyeing my shiner. I was tempted to say, 'You should see the other guy.'"

They ready the lunch together, working side by side in silence, though it doesn't feel like one of those good, companiable silences. It feels portentous.

"The reason I was gone a little long," Tom says as they set the food on the table, "is that I got a call from Brittany on my way back and I decided to pull over to fully concentrate. You know the whole story, right?"

"Yes, but I felt she should tell you directly. I'm so sorry, Tom. It must have been terrible to learn what she did."

"Yes, and honestly, I'm not sure how I go about trying to fix things between us. It's such a betrayal."

"Do you want to bat around some ideas?"

He shakes his head and locks eyes with her. "At some point, yes, but what I want right now is to talk about why you left the house last night. You said on the voice-mail message that you were at the ferry terminal. Were you intending to go back to the mainland?"

Emma inhales deeply.

"Okay, I want to talk about it, too," she says, taking a seat, "but before, there's something important I need to share with you about Taylor's murder. I . . . I think I'm partially responsible."

Tom pulls back in shock and then drops into a chair on the other side of the table.

"What do you mean?"

"The day before she was killed, I asked her to dig up information for me about the client weekend at Stowe."

He narrows his eyes, and she senses he knows where this is going. "You asked *her* about Stowe."

"Yes, specifically about what restaurant you ate at Saturday night. It was before I knew about the injured snowboarder. I lied and said I was planning a ski trip for the two of us, but I really wanted to confirm your whereabouts when Derrick died." As she speaks, Emma knows how awful it must sound to Tom.

He winces, visibly pained. "Ahh, so that's why she brought the weekend up with me—which annoyed the hell out of me at the time. Stowe was one of the events Justine and her event planner had cashed in on, and I didn't want anyone drawing any attention to it until the forensic accountant was done with the investigation."

"I told her not to tell anyone I was asking about it, but you know how Taylor could be. She clearly asked you, and I'm thinking she said something to Justine, too."

Tom leans forward, listening intently. "Because Justine did the planning?"

"Right. She said she'd just look in the file, but I bet that when she called me to report you hadn't been at the dinner, it must have been because she'd ended up asking Justine about it. And now I'm thinking that Justine might have mistakenly thought Taylor had started to figure out what was going on with the embezzling."

He flops back in the chair, stunned. "Whoa, there's the motive. We need to let the police know."

"I know," she says, tearing up. "And then Justine must have come up with some way to lure Taylor back to the building that night. God, I feel terrible about it."

Tom's expression softens. "Look, sweetheart," he says after a beat, "it's possible you inadvertently triggered Justine, but *she's* the murderer. You can't feel guilty for a second."

She shrugs. "Easier said than done."

"Here's something else to consider, then. I think that part of the reason Taylor talked to Justine was that she wanted to do some digging herself. Something I learned from my conversation with Brittany is that Taylor had begun to wonder if I *did* have something to do with Derrick's death—maybe because you'd been asking about that weekend. So you had one very troubled person colliding with one very unethical one, and you're not to blame for what ensued."

"Thanks for sharing that with me."

"I'm glad you got that off your chest. But now I need to know why you took off last night."

Emma straightens in the chair and presses her palms on the table.

"When you were cooking dinner on the veranda last night, I found out you lied to me. You *did* come to hear me speak in New York and despite what you told me, it was no coincidence that I ended up at Halliday. Please don't insult me any more by trying to suggest otherwise."

For a moment Tom studies her, saying nothing.

"Yes, I lied, Emma," he says finally. "And it's been eating at me for weeks. . . . Can you allow me to at least explain?"

Though she'd no longer had any doubts, it's heartbreaking to hear him admit it.

"I'm not sure what good it would do at this point."

"Please, let me try at least. . . . I'll start with Miami. What I told you about the toothache was accurate and I really did sneak out of the room shortly after you were introduced. But we'd actually been in close proximity at the cocktail party. I was standing there, feeling miserable and wondering how soon I could split, when I suddenly heard this woman behind me say something incredibly insightful—about confirmation bias, I think. I turned around and it was you."

"Did we speak?"

"Not a word. You were busy talking to someone from

Avignon and a guy who I later realized was Eric. I took one look at you and I was enthralled. That was the first time that had happened to me since Diana died."

If she'd noticed at the time, she has no memory of it. The anguish she was experiencing over her marriage had dulled her senses.

"I googled you after that night," Tom adds, "and a month later, in February, purely by chance, Stacey suggested we go into the city one night with a couple of people to hear this panel discussion on trends, and lo and behold, I saw you were one of the participants. I said yes in a heartbeat."

"*Stacey* was the one who suggested going?"

"Yes, and you're free to ask her. To me it seemed a bit like destiny putting us together, but as soon as you started speaking, I spotted the ring on your left hand and that was the end of the road for me."

"But then you orchestrated my hiring at Halliday."

"I dropped a hint with Scott after reading an article you were quoted in, and if he hadn't taken the bait, I probably would have pressed him to bring you on board. Not, however, out of any romantic interest. As I just said, I knew you were off-limits. But I thought the company could use you."

Emma has her guard up, refusing to be duped again or let her need to please take hold, and yet his account fits with the man she thought she married—a guy who knows what he likes and goes after it, and if it doesn't work out, moves on—not the obsessive stalker type she'd allowed herself to imagine.

"But when you asked me to lunch, you were clearly interested in more than my thoughts on which hotel ads tended to be the most seductive."

"By then Scott had mentioned in passing that you'd lost your husband, and the more I saw you in the halls, the more smitten I allowed myself to become. And this time I thought I might have a chance."

Okay, so he was never playing some kind of creepy long game, but that doesn't change the fact that he wasn't straight with her.

"Why didn't you admit any of this to me in the beginning?"

"At our first meeting?" He flips over a hand. "I think telling a new consultant that you're slightly gaga over her might qualify as harassment as well as insanity. And then by the time we started hanging out, it would have been awkward to simply bring it up."

"Okay, but once Taylor told me we'd both been at that dinner together, why didn't you come clean about seeing me there and your reason for sending Scott the article? And the fact that you'd attended the talk in New York?"

He shakes his head. "I could see how distressed you were about Derrick's case reopening, and I thought that if you knew there were any other overlaps in our lives before that summer, you'd worry even more. Once you suspected I'd misrepresented things, I realized I'd made a total mistake, but I was afraid that if I confessed that late in the game, you'd think it was weird—some gray-haired guy like me carrying a torch for you."

Emma sinks back, pressing her hands to her eyes.

"I don't care about the torch, Tom—at least not in the way you explain it. What disturbs me is the lies. How am I ever supposed to trust you again?"

His eyes narrow, making him look even more stricken. "Please tell me this isn't a deal breaker, Emma."

She thinks suddenly of what Eric said today about the goes and gones. And she realizes she doesn't want to be gone from Tom. For all her doubts during the past days, certain truths about him have crystallized. He loves her passionately. He always has her back. And he's a good person, the kind of guy who wants to be there for his difficult stepdaughter, who forgoes an important night with clients to help an injured teenager, who's determined to help his staff deal with the death of a coworker. She still loves him—she knew that last night as she desperately tried to warn him, as she imagined him hurt or even dead—and she wants to try to save her marriage.

There's something else Emma realizes. If she's going to make it work, she's going to have to accept the fact that Tom, for all his superpowers, is human. After her disastrous first marriage, she went hunting for perfection, but there's no such thing.

"No, it's not a deal breaker, Tom," she says softly. "Not at this point anyway. But I need to explain why what you did was wrong, and make you understand it."

"I'm listening."

"As far as I'm concerned, there's no need for you to share every thought and moment of your life with me," she begins. "You didn't tell me initially about the embezzlement and that's okay. It was a private work situation for you, and you had to keep it under wraps. You didn't tell me you had Diana's scarf in the closet, and that's okay, too. You loved her and you're entitled to keep your grief about her private.

"I don't even mind that you didn't tell me when we first started dating that you'd had your eye on me earlier. We all hold back when we meet someone new—I mean, I certainly didn't tell you that I googled the hell out of you. But once I asked you about it, and there was so much at stake, you needed to come clean."

"I get what you're saying, I do."

"And it can't happen again. It doesn't matter if you think telling me something will unsettle or upset me. I'm not some fragile creature."

"I hear you, Emma. I really do. And you have my word I won't make a mistake like that again."

Wearily, Tom pushes back from the table, rises, and returns with two glasses and a bottle of sparkling water.

"And you're right," he says, lowering himself back in his chair. "I probably have treated you with kid gloves at times, starting from the very beginning. I could see how much you were suffering, how much Derrick's death had devastated you."

Emma's breath catches as he utters those words. *Tom's not the only one who's lied, is he?*

From the moment they met, she's allowed him to fill in the blanks about what she was going through. Though she's dropped hints to him that her marriage to Derrick wasn't working, Tom has no idea the depths of it.

It's time to finally come clean with him.

"Now there's something *I* need to confess—about my

first marriage. Something I've never had the guts to share with you before."

"Please," he says.

Emma clears her throat. It will be hard, but she's pretty sure Tom will be understanding.

And then? Will they be okay? The nearly two years they've been together have been loving, passionate, fun, and incredibly fulfilling, and Tom has never given her any reason to doubt his love or fidelity. It seems to be, overall at least, a pretty solid foundation, what a good marriage should look like.

She knows from her work that you can't really predict the future, no matter how many signs you read, but Emma thinks they have a chance.

ACKNOWLEDGMENTS

As an author I always try to be as accurate as possible in my books, and fortunately these days it's possible to do a huge amount of research online. But sometimes the only way to get the real scoop is to consult with someone in the know. I'm incredibly grateful, therefore, to people who generously took the time to speak to me for the book and help me get my facts straight: Susan Brune, Brune Law; Barbara Butcher, consultant for forensic and medicolegal investigations; Paul Paganelli, MD; Joyce Hanshaw, retired captain from the Hunterton County Prosecutor's Office; Steven Murphy; Jim White; Jack Rohan; Emma Stevens; Joel Benenson, founder and CEO of the Benenson Strategy Group; Doug Smith; Jonathan Santaflor; Natasha Lerner; Paul Woolmington; Emily Heyward; and Director J. David Smith, Rhode Island E-911.

Thank you, as well, to my fantastic editor, Emily Griffin, for another wonderful collaboration, and to the great team at Harper Perennial, including Amy Baker, VP/associate publisher; Lisa Erickson, director of marketing; Robin Bilardello,

VP/senior director of art; Stacey Fischkelta, production editorial manager; and Micaela Carr, assistant editor.

And I couldn't have done it without my *own* fantastic team: website editor Laura Nicolassy Cocivera; social media manager Imani Seymour; and website tech director and designer Bill Cunningham.

Finally, a huge thank you to my amazing readers. You are such a devoted bunch, and you really put the wind in my sails. I really appreciate it when you take the time to review my books on Goodreads, BookBub, barnesandnoble.com and Amazon.com, and I also love hearing from you via katewhite .com, Facebook, Instagram, and Twitter. Please keep sharing details about yourself and the mysteries and thrillers you love to read and listen to.

ABOUT THE AUTHOR

Kate White, former editor in chief of *Cosmopolitan* magazine, is the *New York Times* bestselling author of eight stand-alone psychological thrillers, including *The Fiancée*, *Have You Seen Me?*, and *The Secrets You Keep*, as well as eight Bailey Weggins mysteries. White is also the author of several popular career books for women, including *The Gutsy Girl Handbook* and *I Shouldn't Be Telling You This: How to Ask for the Money, Snag the Promotion, and Create the Career You Deserve*, and the editor of *The Mystery Writers of America Cookbook*. You can learn more about her at katewhite.com.